Praise for Rebecc[...]
Forbidden [...]

"From its evocative retro movie title to its densely glittery post-present detail, *Forbidden Cargo* hits the future running at full speed and never glances back. Though author Rebecca Rowe's literary persona is indisputably 21st century, her sf DNA is imbedded with classic enhancements — a sprinkle of Robert Heinlein stem cells, coils of *Neuromancer* and *The Matrix,* and a breathless plot that would do justice to the breakneck inventiveness of A. E. Van Vogt. Any debut novel that can use a virtual pickup bar populated by bats and rats, smart intelligence meta-agents, Herculean avatars, and self-assembling fish to illuminate coming of age, falling in love, interplanetary political chicanery, honorable behavior, brutal betrayal and accelerated human evolution is okay by me. Rebecca Rowe's star is rising above the horizon at the speed of light."
— Edward Bryant
Author and literary critic

"Rebecca Rowe's *Forbidden Cargo* is a gripping and moving novel that makes you think about where humanity will be a century from now. Rowe draws you into a virtual world so vividly rendered that it is both entirely believable and utterly fantastic. There, she brings you face to face with the frightening and thrilling possibilities, and the inevitable conflicts, that will arise when technology begins to radically alter the course of human evolution. This is a really enjoyable and provocative read."
— Dr. David Grinspoon
Curator of Astrobiology,
Denver Museum of Nature & Science,
author of *Lonely Planets.*

FORBIDDEN CARGO

Rebecca K. Rowe

EDGE SCIENCE FICTION AND FANTASY PUBLISHING

AN IMPRINT OF HADES PUBLICATIONS, INC.

CALGARY

Forbidden Cargo
Copyright © 2006 by Rebecca K. Rowe

Released in Canada: April, 2006
Released in the USA: August, 2006

EDGE

Edge Science Fiction and Fantasy Publishing
An Imprint of Hades Publications Inc.
P.O. Box 1714, Calgary, Alberta, T2P 2L7, Canada

Editors: Adam Volk / Matthew Hughes
Interior design: Brian Hades
Cover Illustration: David Willicome
ISBN10: 1-894063-16-3
ISBN13: 978-1-894063-16-6

EDGE Science Fiction and Fantasy Publishing and Hades Publications, Inc.
acknowledges the ongoing support of the Canada Council for the Arts and the
Alberta Foundation for the Arts for our publishing program.

The Alberta Foundation for the Arts   Alberta
COMMITTED TO THE DEVELOPMENT OF CULTURE AND THE ARTS

Library and Archives Canada Cataloguing in Publication

Rowe, Rebecca K., 1965-
   Forbidden cargo / Rebecca K. Rowe. -- 1st ed.

ISBN-13: 978-1-894063-16-6
ISBN-10: 1-894063-16-3

   I. Title.

PS3618.O965F67   2006   813'.6   C2006-901391-8

FIRST EDITION
(zk-20060310)
Printed in Canada
www.edgewebsite.com

Contents

Acknowledgments

Dedication

E. Thomas Rowe

who believes in
and inspires
our dreams

FORBIDDEN CARGO

Lightning Strike

I invoke great Juno.
Mother of Mars,
Wake power in me
Herculean ability.
Our day will come.
With your reborn son,
We claim the place of our birth
As did man on Earth.
— Imagofas mantra —

As the sun set, Sashimu waited for the power of Juno to illuminate the Martian sky. She imagined the mother of Mars prostrate across her dead son sparking life back into him, willing him reborn with the help of her people.

The first sign of Juno's power came: a tiny glow, then flare after flare lit the plains, revealing the rolling veil of a dust storm in the distance. Arcs of lightning burst from the clouds and seared the heavens.

Sashimu pressed her eyes closed to bring the lightning inside her, and its afterimage lived on for a moment.

Juno's voice called to her through the lightning, through the ice clouds and dust storms that howled over desert valleys and parched seas. Sashimu felt the weight of Juno's calling and answered with prayer.

As an Imagofas, Sashimu belonged to Mars. She watched the storm sweep toward her, all too conscious that she and her fellow Imagofas must become the guardians of their planet. They would answer Juno's call to bring her son back from the dead. It was their destiny to infuse their barren world with life.

The storm raged from Hellas Basin toward the biosphere, smothering everything beneath its vast veil of dust, even penetrating the filters to scent the evening breeze. The converters purred loudly, lapping up dust while trading carbon dioxide for oxygen-rich air.

Watching from the roof of the Hale Observatory, Sashimu felt the pulse of the biosphere as though it were an extension of herself. She drew in a ragged breath and exhaled slowly, willing her muscles to relax and her anxiety to slip away.

The Observatory Park stretched below her, its great trees, lawns and flowers all imported from Earth. From the building's curved and ivy-covered walls, meandering paths forked out in several directions, winding past memorial statues of the first pioneers from Earth — to merge again at the main entrance.

Beyond the park, out where the biosphere divided to go south toward downtown and west toward Lowell Interplanetary Port, Sashimu could see the bleak stretch of salmon-pink utilitarian housing and research facilities. The squat buildings lacked the ornate architecture of the observatory's carved stone arches and high, wide dome.

The colonies took special pride in both their park and their observatory — one an homage to their blue-green planet, the other a monument to the ancient architecture of home.

Sashimu saw in their precious trees, ivy, flowerbeds and stone arches only wasted energy and resources. When she visited the observatory it was to look beyond the biosphere, to feel closer to her gods. Here was the best place to experience the unharnessed power of dead Mars and his distraught mother. Here she could bear witness to the violence of their dust clouds and ice storms.

Sashimu valued these brief moments alone in the observatory. In two weeks, she and her friends would graduate from the Feynman Academy and would move to a new biosphere located hundreds of kilometers away at the foot of Olympus Mons. The Imagofas were the chosen ones; they would spearhead the next generation of colonists and terraform Mars under the guidance of Project Inventio. For months, they and their guardians had been planning the move. Sashimu's guardian, Zazen, had regularly taken her to visit the new facility; she had already selected and decorated her favorite living space.

Many of her classmates had resisted the move to Olympus Mons, complaining that it was too remote and cut off from the colonies. The facility's original design had caused a scandal: the living quarters were cramped, with scant space for entertainment, although the labs where they would work were enormous and lavishly equipped.

As chief scientist, Zazen tried hard to dispel fears that they would be consigned to a lifestyle even more provincial and monotonous than that offered by the colonies. On the other hand, he promised colonial support for any terraforming projects they might undertake, and even eventual self-rule. The promises won Sashimu over, and her excitement proved infectious. Now all the Imagofas looked forward to the move, especially since it meant they would be escaping the curfew recently imposed by the Order.

High security was a way of life in the colonies, but the rumor of an unplanned arrival of Interplanetary Council agents from Earth recently triggered a security crackdown on Mars. Everyone chafed under the restrictions. Sashimu accepted that the curfew was to keep her and the others safe, but its restrictions nevertheless aggravated her, no matter how many times Zazen preached its necessity.

Now she scrambled to her feet, to balance precariously on the observatory ledge. With arms outstretched and head thrown back, she whispered, "Juno, forgive me my fears and protect me. Please keep the Imagofas safe."

Preoccupied with the storm, she ignored the sunset. The park lights snapped on, blocking out her view of the storm, their humming overriding her whispered prayers. She saw shadows moving beneath the trees near the observatory. Imagofas were supposed to be home before dark but she was breaking curfew to meet her best friend, Thesni. Sashimu nervously surveyed the ground several stories below.

Where was Thesni? She was late. Sashimu was beginning to think she would not come if it meant violating the rules. Tomorrow she would offer some lame excuse. *Or maybe she has come after all*, she thought. Sashimu glimpsed movement near the base of the main stairs that wound up and around the face of the observatory. She called out, "Thesni?"

Whoever was on the stairs began taking them in twos and soon disappeared from Sashimu's view around the side of the building. From the way the figure moved, she knew it was not Thesni. She worried that it might be an Order regular intent on enforcing curfew. If Sashimu was caught, she would be in trouble.

She leapt from the observatory ledge onto a narrow maintenance ladder hidden by ivy, scaled down the side of the observatory to where the ladder ended abruptly meters above the ground. She jumped, diving into some bushes and turned to look up. Silhouetted against the lights of the observatory, standing precisely where she had stood, a tall thin man leaned out over the ledge and peered down.

Silently cursing, Sashimu froze. The man had probably spotted her from as far away as the park entrance. With the light behind him, she could not make out his face or his uniform, but he was definitely following her.

Now he was coming down the stairs. Sashimu sprinted out of the bushes and ran through the trees. Ahead, she heard a man's voice and skidded to a stop behind a large elm. She peeked out and saw a heavyset man speaking into his Companion.

"...but if she's coming my way, where is she? Wait. I've locked in on her."

Sashimu turned and dashed toward the park entrance just as the man rounded the tree. He came after her and she could hear his heavy breathing as he put on a burst of speed to close the distance, then dropped back unable to keep up.

Beside the turnstile at the park gates, two women stood in conversation, their heads bent towards each other. Relief washed over Sashimu as she saw that they were not Order regulars. She recognized their gray uniforms; they were animal handlers from one of the ships that carried supplies between Earth and Mars.

As Sashimu ducked underneath the turnstile the women looked at her in alarm.

"Watch out, there are two weirdoes in the park," the Imagofas said, then turned to run for home.

"Wait!" The larger of the two animal handlers ran after Sashimu and awkwardly seized her arm. The woman's hands felt cold and clammy against Sashimu's skin.

"Hey, let go of me!" Sashimu said. She tried to yank her arm from the handler's grasp.

The shorter woman came up behind them and stopped. She was trying to pull something from her belt.

"Would you hurry up?" the big one shouted. Her hands felt like a death grip on Sashimu's arm.

"You're hurting me! Look, I've got to get home," Sashimu said, struggling to break free.

"Yes!" The short handler said in relief, dislodging a Biosecur baton and pointing it at Sashimu.

The two men from the park leaped the turnstiles. Sashimu saw that they too wore gray uniforms.

"You've got her," the fat one said, badly winded.

Their arrival distracted the handlers and the big woman's grip momentarily loosened. Sashimu twisted free and ran, but her captor snagged her sleeve, yanking her back. Sashimu stumbled and the sleeve tore. Regaining her balance, she spun around and slammed her fist into the handler's nose. With a howl of pain, the woman fell back. Before Sashimu could escape, the smaller one got a grip on the back of the Imagofas' uniform and slammed her Biosecur baton across Sashimu's back.

"Help!" Sashimu cried, but it was hopeless. Curfew meant there was no one around except the bunch of handlers intent on attacking her.

The shorter woman hit her again, then aimed the baton and sprayed her with Biosecur.

Desperate, Sashimu drove her foot down into the woman's knee. The handler fell backwards. Again Sashimu tried to run, but the Biosecur was beginning to take effect. The liquid spread over her face, down her back, turning into a stretchy transparent shell that clung to her skin. It stung. The more she struggled, the more it tightened around her, immobilizing her arms and legs. Sashimu toppled to the ground, unable to move.

"How dare you touch me?" the big handler said. Blood streamed from her nose over her mouth and chin and smeared the back of her hand and sleeve where she'd wiped it on her uniform. Now the smaller one hobbled forward, favoring the leg Sashimu had kicked, and in one swift motion smashed the baton across the Imagofas' face. "Filthy nanogen."

Sashimu's cries were muted by the Biosecur. She gasped for air.

"That was sloppy," the heavyset man said. "I don't want her beaten to death before we get her onboard."

"Give us some slack, captain. We've never dealt with nanogens before," the big handler said.

"She busted my knee." Bending over, the short handler spat on Sashimu. The handler's leg was bent at a strange angle.

Sashimu struggled to breathe. Her mouth was full of blood and her face felt swollen and bruised.

I invoke great Juno, Mother of Mars, Sashimu prayed silently. *Don't let me pass out.*

Eternal seconds passed before the fat man standing over her dug a device from his pocket and inserted it through the Biosecur's film into her mouth.

Sashimu filled her lungs with air; the dizziness subsided.

A heliovan touched down, its turboshafts sending up a small plume of dust at the park entrance. The muted hum of its noise-suppressed rotors was too quiet to attract attention. The four bundled Sashimu into the vehicle, which was unmarked by either the Order's or the Interplanetary Council's official insignia. Sashimu's mind raced while they locked her into a compartment and closed the hatch: perhaps Zazen would get worried and contact the Order when she didn't show for dinner.

Inside the dark confines of the heliovan, her eyes slowly adjusted to the dark. There was someone with her. She noticed the unmistakable Feynman Academy uniform. Then she made out the face.

Severely swollen eyes stared back at her, familiar eyes. Thesni sat, strapped in, across from her. Blood matted her friend's thick blonde hair and streaked her cheeks. Smaller than Sashimu, she looked tiny and frail under the compression of the Biosecur. In the darkness of the heliovan Sashimu knew she must be offering an equally terrifying sight, with her face swollen and bruised and her mouth oozing blood around the breathing device.

At first she could not tell what direction they were being taken, then the normal biosphere noises faded and over the hum of the heliovan Sashimu heard the sounds she associated with Lowell Interplanetary Port. A knot of fear formed in Sashimu's stomach as she realized that they might be forced offworld.

The heliovan had to stop several times at security checkpoints. With each lurching stop, Sashimu prayed she and Thesni would be discovered and the four kidnappers taken into Order custody. Each time, she was disappointed.

Once again the vehicle landed, and this time the handlers opened the door. Sashimu could see they were beneath the large beams that supported a launch pedestal. No port officials were in sight and the handlers joked with each other as they hauled Thesni out. A fifth person, another woman in handler garb, joined their captors and they all bustled around the launch area chattering to each other and, using their Companions, with LIP's Space Traffic Control, making calibrations and receiving last minute instructions.

From the heliovan's open door, Sashimu could see a portion of the launch pedestal and the ship. Across the vessel's belly was painted the name *Home Sweet Home*. The ship was old and had seen hard service. The Imagofas could plainly see that the hull was covered by a web of surface fractures, punctuated by cracks and gouges near the well used docking equipment.

The handlers made no attempt to conceal her as they pulled her from the heliovan. Holding her between them, they boarded a cargo carrier which took them up through a pressurized tunnel and into a habitat module. They dragged Sashimu past a number of cells, a laboratory, and an area marked "Health Maintenance." Finally they stopped at a cell labeled "Playroom," dumped her inside, sprayed her with an evil-smelling solvent that would counteract the Biosecur, and, locking the door behind them, left her alone in the dimly lit room.

The transparent shell gradually dissolved, the process making her skin crawl and itch but restoring her ability to move. As soon as her hands were free, Sashimu wrenched the breathing device from her mouth and smashed it repeatedly against the cell wall until it broke into bits. After scratching her arms and back furiously, she rubbed the dried blood from her face and stretched. Her bruises had already healed.

The "Playroom" was larger than the tiny cells they'd passed. It was equipped with a waste remover module, exercise wall, food dispenser and sleeprest module newly mounted on the bulkhead. The place reeked of disinfectant, but underneath it her Imagofas senses detected an underlying odor of animal. No amount of cleaning could erase a decade of urine and waste that had been smeared across the floor and walls to lodge in the cell's metal seams. A human might never smell it, but the stench made Sashimu gag.

"Just try treating me like one of your lab animals," she told the empty room through clenched teeth, then was startled to receive an answer.

"Prepare for liftoff. Secure yourself in your sleeprest until we clear Mars and A-G takes over," a woman's voice said from the wall panel.

Agitated, Sashimu frantically looked around the room for something to destroy. She began yanking on the exercise equipment in the hopes that one of her captors would show up. She did not have long to wait. She heard the door slide open.

The big handler filled the doorway. She flashed a disturbing smile then her broad face took on an even more disturbing blankness. Sashimu studied her. She knew the woman had spent her life ferrying supplies between Earth and Mars, including animals for medical experiments and even darker purposes. What cruel instincts might motivate such a person?

The handler's stungun looked to be deactivated, but she had a Biosecur baton on her belt and one hand was hidden behind her back. While the cold blue eyes examined her, Sashimu moved into a defensive stance.

"What do you plan to do with Thesni and me?" she said.

In one fluid motion, the handler was beside her, bringing her hand from behind her back to press something hard against Sashimu's neck. Sashimu felt a stabbing pain as she fell into darkness, framed by the handler's wide, unexpressive face floating above her.

Labyrinth

Thesni's rage at Sashimu dissolved along with the Biosecur. Of course, it was still her fault. Everyone said Sashimu was born to lead, but Thesni often felt more tricked than led. Her friend had lured her into bad situations before, but nothing like this. If only she had gone directly home, those two rat-hands wouldn't have grabbed her. She would be enjoying a meal with her guardians right now.

As soon as she could move, Thesni drew the breathing device from her mouth and carefully placed it in front of the door to her cell. She winced at the thought of suffocating if they were short one.

Her skin was irritated from the solvent. Thesni imagined insects crawling all over her. Holding down the lever next to her food dispenser, she let the water overflow, splashing her face, neck and arms. It brought instant relief. She leaned against the cold metal wall, wiped her face dry with the sleeve of her uniform and looked around.

Her nose wrinkled at the reek of urine. She saw that the padding on the old exercise equipment poking out of the wall had chunks missing — probably some crazed animal confined for too long. She was relieved to see that a new sleeprest had been installed; at least they weren't expecting her to sleep like an animal.

More than anything, she needed to talk to Sashimu. Just her friend's voice would be reassuring. Sashimu had gotten them into — but also out of — trouble before. Her feats at the Academy were legendary, like the time she had convinced Thesni and two others to split off from an exploratory exhibition. Sashimu was certain she knew a shortcut to the dig site. Instead, she'd gotten them hopelessly lost. Yet, never once did she waver in her resolve. She trudged forward as though she knew exactly where they were headed, even when dust flurries overtook them. Thesni and the others realized they were lost, but not having a better plan, they followed where Sashimu led.

They took refuge from the wind among some boulders, and there they discovered the entrance to the largest unknown cave system on Mars. When the search party located them, their anger was eclipsed by the extraordinary find. The Imagofas returned to the Academy to face endless reprimands and additional coursework while confined to the biosphere. Yet no amount of punishment could erase the status their discovery had won them.

But now, just to stay out past the curfew, Sashimu had dragged Thesni into a truly alarming situation. Still, she had faith that her friend would save them.

As she investigated the cell, Thesni suddenly experienced a new sensation. It was like being prickled all over by tiny needles. At first, she worried it was an after-effect of Biosecur, but the needling grew stronger and more persistent. Now the room seemed to darken.

To center herself, she silently recited, "I invoke great Juno, Mother of Mars. Wake power in me, Herculean ability..." The darkness receded; the walls and floor returned, but the tingling would not go away. She prayed to keep her sanity.

Her prayer was interrupted by a woman's voice. "Prepare for liftoff. Secure yourself in your sleeprest until we clear Mars and A-G takes over."

Thesni stood quickly, hoping nothing else would happen until she was safe inside the sleeprest.

The woman's voice continued as her image appeared on the wall panel display. Her dark hair was pulled into a tight knot and she scowled at Thesni with a long, hard face. "We can't have problems. Do you need a tranquilizer for launch?"

"No, I don't want any tranquilizers." Thesni's voice shook as she climbed into the sleeprest and looked back.

The wall panel was blank. She hoped the woman had heard her.

The sleeprest's cover slid closed above her, and Thesni was suddenly seized by claustrophobia. "Open," she said.

The cover slid open on her command. She tried the open and close commands several times and only when she was sure that she was not permanently confined did she feel comfortable in the sleeprest's narrow, sealed compartment.

The inside of the cover had a panel that displayed the ship's external view of space. She could also listen to the countdown.

"Departure mode on," she ordered, hoping that the sleeprest proved sturdier than it looked and could withstand the pressures of liftoff.

Cushions constricted around her. She allowed the straps to fold across her chest and felt her legs rise slightly. Her pulse hammered in her ears. The pressure increased, and Thesni struggled to breathe.

The ship shook violently. Thesni tried to protest against the force slamming her but her voice stuck in her throat. She imagined her skin and innards peeling away while her bones compacted to a fine white dust.

Her teeth vibrated painfully even though she kept her jaw clenched tight. Just when she was sure the ship would disintegrate, its debris scattering over the face of Mars, the pressure eased and the rattling ended, replaced by the steady hum of a ship in space.

Thesni had yelled "Open" several times before she realized she was free to climb out of the sleeprest. Standing, she felt lighter despite the ship's artificial gravity. Her head throbbed with every breath.

The tingling had returned and this time the darkness was complete. The Imagofas rubbed her arms and legs vigorously to get the blood flowing. Her chest tightened; then suddenly a shock like lightning blasted through her. The pain lingered in her fingertips and toes. A noise like static crackled around her and then came silence. Boundless night replaced the cell, as though the cell walls had collapsed away from her. Thesni felt abrupt vertigo.

To reassure herself that she was still in one piece, she ran her hands over her torso, felt what she could not see, and found no evidence of injury. She groped her way through the darkness, hoping to encounter a surface of some kind.

Confused, fumbling around in the pitch black, Thesni raised her hands to her face. She felt the brush of her eyelashes against her fingertips as she blinked. She knew she was awake. Now she wondered if the Biosecur might have blinded her, but that explanation failed to account for the shock she'd felt moments before.

Poison, she thought and sniffed the air. Her acute sense of smell picked up no hint of airborne toxins. She smelled only the now familiar odor of stale animal urine, and that argued for her still being trapped in her cell.

"Is this some elaborate test?" Thesni said into the darkness. As an Imagofas, she was used to being tested and studied. However, this level of gross sensory manipulation felt strange. Baffled, she crouched and again attempted to touch the cell floor — nothing. She might as well be suspended in space.

Impossible. She shook her head. "What's happening to me?"

From the edge of her hearing a pounding sound grew fast and loud in her ears. Three-dimensional images of boxes and cylinders, glowing purple, red and yellow, emerged from the dark and danced around her.

"Hallucinations," Thesni said, shutting her eyes. The possibility that this dark reality might all be in her mind terrified her. At this point, even the sight of her cell's metal walls would be reassuring. She forced herself to relax, willed her head to stop throbbing and the sounds and images to disappear.

The pounding slowed, became a measured beat. Thesni opened her eyes and gasped. Three solid walls had appeared around her, ancient cave walls, like the ones Sashimu and she had discovered on Mars. But these were chiseled smooth. Thesni ran her hand across the wall to her left, then jumped back in surprise.

At her touch, luminous hieroglyphics lit up the cave walls. Slowly, she realized that the figures and symbols represented medical data, though she understood only some of them. When she held her hand up, the data popped

out from the wall to become three-dimensional imagery
that moved away to disappear down a dark passageway.

Studying the images, Thesni realized these were packets
of telemetry data: blood pressure, body temperature,
intraocular pressure, brain activity levels, pulmonary flexibility and heart rate. She wondered whose body they
reported on, until she came across a series of thermal sensor
images. Each time she moved, they mimicked her in brilliant red, yellow, blue and green.

When she danced the images danced and the puzzling,
rhythmic beating intensified. Thesni, realizing it was her
own amplified pulse, stood perfectly still until the beat
slowed and became muted.

"Okay, so you're monitoring me, but why give me access
to your tools?" Thesni asked, watching data travel across
the walls and vanish down the passageway. "This would
be a lot easier if you'd respond."

If her captors hadn't drugged or moved her, the only
explanation that Thesni could come up with for her altered
state was Novus Orbis. They'd somehow given her access
to the MAM — the Molecular Advantage Machine, the
ubiquitous interplanetary system which allowed humans
to enter Novus Orbis. On Mars, Zazen restricted the
Imagofas from Novus Orbis for the colony's safety as much
as for their own protection. Their proven ability to com-
mune with nano-engineered systems made their guardians apprehensive. No one knew how far that innate power
would extend once Imagofas were exposed to the MAM.

Trailing her hand along the wall to light her way, she
followed the data as it wound around corners and slipped
into the distance. "If you're monitoring me, you're monitoring Sashimu. I'll locate her when I find her data. She'll
know what's happening."

Concentrating, she followed the flow. But each time she
found new data, it led her into a dead end. She trailed after
the biotelemetry of hundreds of animals onboard the ship,
but failed to locate Sashimu among them. The walls crawled
with the animals' stories, with information on health,
experimentation, distress and sometimes even death, but
she found no references to the Imagofas.

"This is unfair." Thesni sat down in the middle of yet another passageway, brought her knees tight against her chest and dropped her head. She held the pose until her front became soaked in tears. Then a thought made her look up. She'd deciphered the hieroglyphics and couldn't find any evidence of hidden codes, but what her captors had done was much simpler.

"To hide our presence, I bet they classified us under a false label!" Thesni said aloud. She jumped up, ran back down the passageways until she located her unique thermal sensor data. She made a new search, but this time she ignored the classifications. After losing her way many times, she identified a data signature similar to hers. Tracing this to other telemetry data, she surrounded herself with them until she felt like she was in another cell. No movement was visible, but a shallow heartbeat rising and falling next to hers reassured her.

Satisfied, she tried direct contact, "Sashimu?"

An enormous creature stepped from the cave's shadowy recesses, its torso a mass of hardened human muscle and sinew but with a demonic bull's head where its face should have been. Below spear-like horns, deep-set red eyes studied Thesni as though the beast was preparing to charge. Thesni let out a gasp. She stumbled backwards to avoid the massive spiked wooden club the creature raised in its left hand.

"Thesni?" Sashimu's response hung in the air like a hand-blown kiss.

At the sound of a third voice, the monster tilted its head to listen, then snorted and vanished down the passageway.

ɪₙₗₜₜₙₙₗₗₗₗₜₙₙₗₜₗₙₗ

Bolts of red seared the night. Spectacular purple, green, yellow splotches appeared and faded to the rhythm of Sashimu's heartbeat. She struggled against her tranquilizer-induced torpor, leveraging herself up into a sitting position. Around her she saw three rough walls and a corridor.

She pulled herself up, leaning against a wall. Data mines lit beneath her hands, projecting from the wall in three-dimensional images. Still foggy from the tranquilizer, she watched as the images rose and fell to her biorhythms. Information crawled along the walls, feeding into the darkness. Sashimu put out her hands, intercepted data and found she could manipulate it. Fascinated, she muted the loud echo of her heartbeat and realized there was another set of unique biorhythms parallel to her own.

"Thesni?" she called. "Are you beside me? I can hear your breathing and even your heartbeat, but I can't see you."

"I can't see you, either!" Thesni's voice came from nowhere, broken by a sob. "Are you all right?"

"They drugged me. I feel woozy," Sashimu said, rubbing her eyes.

"I can't believe I'm finally talking to you," Thesni said.

"Where are you?" Sashimu stepped into the dark passageway. "For that matter, where are we?"

"My eyesight, touch and hearing tell me I'm in a cave system or a maze, but the stench tells me I'm in my cell," Thesni said. "Could this be—?"

"Novus Orbis," Sashimu finished. A chill ran up Sashimu's spine. "What else could take over our senses so completely that we're cut off from physical reality?"

"There's something else, too," Thesni said. "When I first found your biotelemetry data, I called out your name and a Minotaur appeared."

"A what?"

"A giant monster with a bull's head on his shoulders instead of a face — he came at me from the dark passageway."

"What happened?" Sashimu asked.

"It heard you and vanished."

"Not much of a monster."

"It scared me," said Thesni.

"Sure, but the crew have forced us into Novus Orbis to do more than spook us," Sashimu said. The crew had used Companions when they captured her, providing easy access to the Molecular Advantage Machine. Their Companions allowed them to query for information, retrieve data and communicate with anyone on Mars.

Since their captors were using Companions, it was likely they also had MAMsuits and they could fully submerse themselves in Novus Orbis. Sashimu felt a thrill of excitement that she and Thesni might have finally left the familiarity of Vetus Orbis and ventured into Novus Orbis.

Thesni's voice interrupted Sashimu's thoughts. "To enter Novus Orbis, don't we need Molecular Advantage Machine suits?"

"Humans do. We might not," Sashimu said. Novus Orbis and the MAM remained a mystery to the Imagofas. There was so much they had never been told. Of course, Sashimu had heard plenty of stories and even more warnings from Zazen and the other guardians about what might happen if the Imagofas gained access — system-wide brownouts, fried Imagofas brains — but scare tactics rarely worked on Sashimu. In fact, most warnings only intensified her curiosity. From her explorations of the biosphere, she knew she could make lots of unexpected things happen — both good and bad.

As Sashimu continued to examine the dark cavern, she became more and more convinced they were in Novus Orbis. The floor and ceiling revealed the illusion. A dark void stretched below and above her.

"Sashimu, they're testing us," Thesni said, a nervous tremor in her voice.

"Then let's turn their experiment into one of our own." Sashimu's old bravado had returned. She had made a sport of outwitting and befuddling the Project Inventio team during some of their carefully constructed experiments — when she and the others of the first generation of Imagofas had been growing up under their guardians' intense study.

"How do we change this to our advantage?" Thesni sounded incredulous.

"We find a way to communicate with Zazen." Sashimu was certain that, if they got a message to her guardian, he could save them.

"Sounds dangerous."

"Look, you already managed to contact me, let's go the next step." Sashimu frowned. "Would you rather just wait for another visit from the Minotaur?"

"No. Where do we start?"

"We wait for the Minotaur." Sashimu laughed. Angering the kidnappers might get them into a worse situation, but she refused to succumb to fear.

"Very funny."

"I'm not joking. We ambush it. I distract it and you see if we can get beyond this illusion to find the ship communication pathways."

"Sashimu, I tried sending you a message but it was no use."

"The ship might have built-in security that only allows communication via established MAM channels," Sashimu guessed.

"All right." Thesni sighed. "Distract the beast."

If this were an experiment, Sashimu would ensure that the Minotaur focused on her so that Thesni would be spared. She ran down passageways as Thesni had done, then caused havoc. At every dead end, she played with the data so that the entire cargo appeared to be flatlining. It didn't take long for their experimenter to arrive. At one of the last rooms, she turned to see the horrible aspect of the Minotaur towering above her with its crazed red eyes and its snarl baring jagged, dagger-pointed teeth.

"You've made a fine mess of my data. I give you a maze and a chance to locate your friend. You repay me by polluting our medical files. I'm sending you back to rot in your cell," the Minotaur said in a low voice, between snorts. The sudden swing of its club took her by surprise.

The weapon struck her side, but felt more like an electric shock than a physical blow. Sashimu fell away from the Minotaur and out of the darkness. The cell walls took shape around her.

"No!" Sashimu said, determined to stay in Novus Orbis.

Concentrating on the image of the Minotaur, she felt another tremendous shock emanating outwards from her chest. The cell walls disappeared. She was back with the Minotaur.

"I forced you out and now you're back? Impossible," the creature said. It raised its weapon and charged. Sashimu dodged the ferocious swipes of the club, but was eventually driven into the smallest corner of the cave.

Never taking its eyes off her, the Minotaur scrawled some hieroglyphics in the air, then drew a blazing red box around them. Concentrating on the box's contents, Sashimu saw that it contained the words: CAPTAIN GRANT — REQUEST IMMEDIATE ASSISTANCE.

This was the moment Sashimu and Thesni had waited for. Sashimu only hoped the message was long enough for her friend to make use of it. As the Minotaur hurled the box behind it down the passageway, Sashimu dodged under its arm and escaped.

"I won't go back to my cell!" she cried, and dashed down the passageway.

The Minotaur roared, extended its club and knocked Sashimu's legs out from under her.

╷╻╷╻╻╻╻╻╻╻╻╻╻╻╷╻╷╻╷

Thesni's moment arrived. She traced the path of the signal and discovered a vast labyrinth of data transactions running underneath the mythic creature's ancient maze. Rather than become lost in ongoing communications, she searched for archives. The labyrinth was multi-layered, constantly growing new paths, destroying others and sending conversation data through filters to be stored below.

Venturing several layers down, Thesni found temporary archives. Here she searched for any crew dialog with external sources that had occurred after launch. She soon identified two external communications. The pathways had long since been destroyed, but their history remained.

She couldn't interpret the contents of either message, but she could resurrect them. Knowing the crew must have contacted Lowell Interplanetary Port once they had successfully reached their assigned shipping lane, she reasoned that at least one of the archived communications had been targeted at Mars. When Lowell received the message, she could only hope it would be forwarded to Zazen. To each message, she appended her own communication.

As she sent the messages, she received an intense shock to the chest that knocked her flat.

Trick

The alarm that blasted from Captain Grant's Companion caused him to slam his head against the interior systems panel he was repairing on the main deck. His string of curses did nothing to ease the pain. Grant had trouble enough concentrating on repairs when he was on blackbase, the illegal Mars narcotic. His illegal and expensive little habit always left him on edge, turning the smallest maintenance job into a much bigger chore.

Still muttering curses, Grant consulted the device and found an urgent request from Brooks to speak with him in person.

Grant had never trusted Brooks. The rest of the crew operated for profit, but the ship's vet thrived on experimentation. She knew everything about animals and could keep almost any beast alive during the three-month trips between Earth and Mars, but lately Brooks' experiments had become bolder. She had even killed several animals. Grant was determined to keep an eye on her. On this trip, he couldn't afford to let the vet mess with their priceless cargo. He planned to closely monitor her contact with the nanogens, knowing that their mysteries would offer irresistible temptation.

Grant headed for the vet station, leaping down the steps past crew cabins to the cargo area. The door to Brooks' station was open. At first he thought it was empty, then he spied her huddled in the optimization area, dressed in her MAMsuit with the hood torn off, her face ashen.

"Brooks, what's wrong?"

"Never mind. The situation is contained." She barely glanced at him.

"What do you mean 'contained'? You sent me a desperate message."

"It was an error."

Grant waited. Normally he was a patient man, but blackbase gave him a dangerous edge.

"I wanted to get some info about nanogens, like you asked, so I activated a MAM maze game to see what they'd do."

"An experiment?"

"A small one," she admitted.

"You gave them MAMsuits?" Grant said, and felt relief when Brooks shook her head. "Good. No telling what would have happened if they'd entered Novus Orbis."

"They did enter Novus Orbis. And without Companions or MAMsuits."

"What?" Grant wanted to throttle her. "How is that possible?"

"I don't know," said Brooks, her words tumbling over each other. "All I did was open a MAMportal in both cells. I planned to equip them with MAMsuits once I'd discussed it with you and prepared them for entry. But it was as though once I made the MAM aware of them it immediately sucked their minds into Novus Orbis!"

"What do you mean sucked them in?" To Grant, Brooks' explanation sounded bizarre.

"The nanogens were acting strangely in their separate cells," Brooks said. "It wasn't until I entered Novus Orbis that I realized they had been in the experimental area that I'd set up. They caused utter havoc."

"What kind of havoc?" Grant's voice sank to an angry growl.

"They interacted with the MAM on all levels — as though it were an extension of themselves. Without any instruction from me, they read and modified their telemetry data inside the maze."

"You're a vet, used to dealing with chimps. These are nanogens. We've no idea what they can do."

"We know something now. They not only modified their data, they bypassed security. They even altered my medical files, which will take me weeks to correct," Brooks said. Nervous sweat dampened her brow.

"Tell me that when you found the damaged files, you closed the MAMportals and terminated their access," Grant said, barely resisting an urge to slap her.

"I tried, but they resisted. One of them succeeded in maintaining a session, doing even more damage while the other did..." — she cleared her throat — "something else."

"Tell me they're not still in Novus Orbis?"

"No," Brooks said. "They're safely contained in their cells and will be for the remainder of the trip — without access to the MAM."

"Your medical data is important, but not critical to the functioning of this ship. What about the other nanogen? What was the 'something else' it did?"

The *Home Sweet Home's* security features were rudimentary. Grant didn't believe in investing in upgrades. The crew repaired and optimized the ship in Novus Orbis during the long months of interplanetary travel. That offered them a more efficient and definitely more enjoyable work environment, but it also created a tremendous security risk. Because he knew his crew well and trusted them, he had never worried about such risks. Until today.

Brooks bit her lip. "It got into our communications archives, but I immediately exited the nanogen."

That was it. Without a word, Grant grabbed Brooks by the arm and half-dragged her from the lab down the corridor to her cabin. He thrust her inside, resisted the urge to strike her and said, "You are to remain in your cabin until I give further orders. If you so much as access your Companion, you'll spend time with the handlers. After that, you won't be fit to lift a finger."

"Captain, I didn't mean any harm—"

"You have placed the crew and our mission in jeopardy. For all we know, our communications systems have been sabotaged." Grant palmed shut her cabin door and programmed a ship seal. She would be confined to her cabin until he completed his investigation and handled the necessary damage control.

Brooks' job was to keep the lab animals alive and healthy until they reached their destination. To do so, she constantly monitored, analyzed and cared for them. This trip he had needed her to discover details about the nanogens as well as to carry out her usual ship duties. Now, she was locked in her cabin when he was already short on crew.

He should have gotten a new vet when he had the chance back on Earth. Brooks' Novus Orbis avatar was a Minotaur; a fitting persona, considering it was a creature as stubborn and unpredictable as Brooks herself. Grant had never used flashy avatars — it seemed like a royal waste of time. Unlike his crew, the captain entered Novus Orbis to communicate or get a job done — nothing more. While the crew had developed elaborate environments and complex avatars to occupy their time in-transit between Mars and Earth, Grant needed only his blackbase.

Suddenly the captain felt a sharp pain at the base of his neck; the precursor to a migraine.

On the main deck, the crew carefully avoided him as he stomped around. They knew when he was ready to explode at anyone in his way. His mood improved as he conducted his investigation.

From a main-deck ship terminal, the captain ran system-wide diagnostics on the *Home Sweet Home*. He was relieved to find no evidence of sabotage to the ship's communications. Everything seemed to function normally. For the moment, he allowed himself to relax.

I·I·I···IIII··I·I·I

The days slipped by and the blackbase edge wore off. Grant felt guilty about confining Brooks to her cabin. As much as he hated to admit it, he needed her skills to get all the maintenance work done. More importantly, without letting her go too far, he needed Brooks to learn more about the nanogens.

Finally, Grant decided he had made the vet suffer long enough alone in her cabin. Over lunch break on mid-deck, his second-in-command Treadwell and he discussed the small crew's daunting list of tasks that still had to be completed to ensure a safe end to the final leg of the journey. Grant brought up the subject of Brooks.

"Check in on her before your shift ends," Grant said. "With all the work we have ahead of us, we could use another pair of hands."

"As if I don't have enough to do, now I'm to baby-sit Bullface?" replied Treadwell, rolling his eyes.

"Just do it," Grant ordered. Treadwell tended to nick-name everyone.

"Sure."

Grant dumped his tray and the two went back up to main deck.

"By the way, I've been meaning to ask you about our log files," Treadwell said.

"What about them?" Grant said.

"It's nothing major, but glancing over the logs today, I noticed an anomaly. When we cleared Mars airspace, I let Lowell know that we reached our assigned ISL. The logs show the message was sent out twice with a significant time delay, and I worried there might be a logging glitch."

"Have you noticed any log errors?" said Grant.

"No, but I'll look into it."

Grant was concerned. It was routine to notify port officials when they reached the assigned interplanetary shipping lane. He hoped his second-in-command was right, and it was simply a logging problem.

"Captain, you've got an incoming message from Earth."

"Send it through," Grant ordered.

"They're requesting a secured transmission."

"I'll take it in my cabin." Grant swung over the railing and took only the last two stairs.

His cabin was twice the size of the others' and equipped with unique compartments that could hide contraband when port officials carried out inspections. When he thought of the hideaways, it brought a bittersweet emotion. He had known about them since he first acquired the ship, but had been using them only since last year.

In the early days, he had made credit hand over fist running lab animals and supplies between Earth and Mars. No one had balked at his prices until the competition began to eat into his margins. In the past two years, he had operated at a loss on many shipments. Every time he turned around someone was underbidding him for a job or prom-ising faster delivery. So when a man named Angel had approached him about smuggling blackbase, Grant needed little convincing. The captain was no salesman and it had taken him longer to persuade his crew. In the end, profit won out. Angel offered three times what they could make for a legal shipment. Grant's record was clean and, over the years, he had earned a good reputation with port officials. It had been a perfect arrangement until the captain told Angel he had decided to retire and settle down. Angel had made him a deal: he could get out if he did one more run, that this trip would be worth more than all his past runs put together.

Angel virtually owned his life and his crew. Grant had agreed. That didn't mean he liked Angel, far from it. He cursed the blackbase dealer for both his habit and his lost integrity. He hated Angel more than he detested himself for the drug that ate away at his psyche until there was little left of the old Captain Grant, but he couldn't help himself. Even now he itched to open one of his secret compartments for a fix, although that had to wait.

He switched his cabin to "DO NOT DISTURB" mode and locked himself away in his optimization area closet; reserved for the times when not even his crew could be privy to his dealings. To contact Angel, he sat in a secured seat customized to accommodate his large girth. Not a tall man, Grant had made up for his lack of height by his width: his shoulders were broad, his legs huge and his arms over-developed. His ample gut betrayed his passion for eating. It hung over his weapons, hiding his belt from view when he sat.

The MAMsuit hood folded neatly over Grant's face. An uneasy vertigo sent him into Novus Orbis. Bypassing his user preferences, he sat on the grid across from Angel.

"Hello."

Angel looked disheveled, even alarmed, as though he had been roused from bed. He was young and rugged with a permanent half-grin — the result of a scar which ran the length of one side of his face. The scar made it hard for Grant to read his expressions. Next to Angel, Grant felt much older, bigger and slower.

"What's going on up there? I told you to let me know if you had complications. Instead, I get this."

Grant was unable to see what Angel was pointing at. He increased the resolution. It made no difference.

"Tell me this is some kind of joke." Angel's voice shook with anger. Grant waited, perplexed.

"I just received an encapsulated message from your ship. In it, you tell me again that you secured the nanogens. Only this time your message had a special attachment, an SOS for Zazen from one of them. Please explain."

Grant experienced a painful adrenaline rush and was happy for the time delay in communication. He tried to sound casual. "Oh that. We let the nanogen send a message because it was harmless. We knew they'd cause less trouble if they thought they'd gotten a message out to Zazen."

"Give me fair warning before you pull a stunt like that again." Angel glared, but his greed got the better of him. "What did you learn?"

"They can access Novus Orbis without MAMsuits or Companions. They can bypass ship security." Grant wiped his brow, cursing Brooks under his breath.

"I'll raise the asking price." Angel smiled. "No more surprises."

"Not from me," Grant promised. "We had no problems during the operation."

"Learn as much about the nanogens as you can without jeopardizing the mission. I've got one economic domus interested but I'll have a bidding war if we can demonstrate their worth." Angel's perma-grin widened.

This was unexpected. Grant worked his jaw to remain composed, holding back several responses before replying. "We only talked about giving them over to the Council as evidence."

"Right." Angel affirmed. "But the Council only needs one nanogen to prove what the Order has been developing. We'll make a better profit selling the second one. The Council will never know."

Grant nodded.

"Have the nanogens caused any other problems?"

"No. But my crew noted something of interest — cuts and scrapes completely heal after a couple of hours."

"Critical info. Get me more details, but no more surprises. Got it?" Angel ordered. He signed off.

Cutting the communication, Grant waited as his hood slid smoothly back behind his head.

He rummaged through his hidden compartments and pulled out his private store of blackbase. A minute drop on the tip of his tongue and he could slip into his own private euphoria. He caressed the dark blue, luminescent vial then shoved it back in the compartment. He had work to do.

"After this I'm retiring. Rich. Once I deliver these nanogens, I'll never have to kowtow to that twisted Cheshire cat grin."

Grant ran back up to the main deck and accessed the communication archives. What he found made his stomach turn. One of the nanogens had also managed to send a message to Mars. Little did she know what that might mean for them all.

Travel

To avoid attacking her cell walls from sheer frustration, Sashimu lived beyond them in the ebb and flow of the ship's energy.

Because she had made contact with the ship, its functional patterns and behavior rhythms remained imprinted on her brain. Over weeks of concentration, she slowly built an internal map of the *Home Sweet Home*. She knew it as she had known the biosphere.

Falling into a trance-like state, she listened and followed the sounds of the ship. Her mind stretched to trace the circuitry behind the walls, listening to the ship's hum and feeling the strain of live cargo on its heavy freight architecture. The ship wheezed, coughed, and malfunctioned in small, insidious protests.

This is a cargo ship, it's not designed for passengers. We were never meant to be in these cells, but the ship is sturdy, Sashimu reassured herself. Just as the biosphere breathed heavily after a dust storm to ensure that all its inhabitants received adequate air, the ship stretched, cracked and contracted to shield its crew and cargo from deadly space. Its sacrifice was not lost on Sashimu. Her prayers to Juno — to put an end to this ghastly captivity and bring her safely home — began to incorporate the ship.

Below her, she felt the heart of the ship, its engines and power source feeding the constant rotation and acceleration. To know the vessel was disorienting; it made her head ache. Learning the course of energy around her was like learning to walk again. While the biosphere was built and enhanced with precision engineering and constantly monitored, the *Home Sweet Home* felt neglected and rundown.

At first, Sashimu found the contrast between the two environments unbearable. Her connection with the biosphere had been established from birth. Its systems flowed alongside and around her, its stresses and changes shifting so subtly that it delighted her senses like the rich undertones of a French horn in an orchestra. In contrast, the shifts in ship energy flow outraged her senses. Her mouth went dry and her throat felt singed each time additional power was demanded of the ship. This happened frequently as above her the crew cabins, and above them the main deck, demanded energy for waste treatment, air cycling, food and acceleration. Energy leaked, burst and spat behind her cell walls so inefficiently that there were times she feared the ship might break down or self-destruct.

Throughout her awakening to the ship, the crew offered no further MAM access, which troubled Sashimu. She wanted desperately to contact Thesni, and even though the MAM made her feel uneasy she was also attracted to it. In the world of Vetus Orbis in which her physical being had existed, Sashimu had known what to expect. But the MAM offered the unexplored and dangerous territory of Novus Orbis, which set in bold relief her difference from humanity without giving her a positive definition of what it meant to be Imagofas.

According to Interplanetary Law, the very existence of the Imagofas was forbidden. The law placed them under the generic umbrella of nanogens — nanogenetically engineered human embryos — a term that included all the aberrations and freaks of nature that had ever been designed using nanotechnology. Yet Sashimu knew the Imagofas were different, even though few humans beyond Mars were enlightened enough to agree.

It would be just Sashimu's luck if the answers to her questions lay buried in Novus Orbis, which also provided her sole opportunity to communicate with Thesni and, perhaps, Zazen — the one man powerful enough to rescue them.

Cut off from Thesni, with no sign of potential rescue, Sashimu struggled to keep from falling into depression as the days passed. To remain positive, she focused on

absorbing knowledge of the ship, a severe daily exercise
routine and prayer.

She was only occasionally interrupted by a crewmember,
whose face would flash onto the wall panel — startling
Sashimu — to bark orders or ask questions. Today, the big
animal handler addressed her with an expressionless face
and monotone voice.

"How do you feel?"

"Aside from being stuck in a room that stinks of urine
and feces, I'm just fine," Sashimu said with a scowl. "Why
did you capture us?"

"You're to stand before an Earth tribunal. Surely, you
know your existence is illegal."

"I've been 'existing' for 18 years. Why try me now?"

"I'll ask the questions. You've only eaten one meal a day
for the past two days. Are you experiencing pain or discomfort?"

"What discomfort, other than total isolation?" Sashimu
said. "And, for all I know, you've killed Thesni."

"Unlike you, Thesni is in perfect health. Resume eating, unless you prefer that I feed you," the handler said.
Her smile sent a cold shiver down Sashimu's spine. With
that, the wall panel went blank.

Grudgingly, Sashimu took the unopened box from the
meal dispenser, opened one of the tubes labeled "dinner"
and sucked down half the chicken-potatoes-broccoli paste
without gagging. Hoping half a tube would qualify as a
meal eaten, she returned the box to the dispenser. Rather
than welcome these interactions, Sashimu felt aggravated
by them. She resented her captors — not just for ripping
her from her idealized life on Mars, but for their insistence
on asking mundane questions. They wasted her time just
as they wasted the ship's energy in a flurry of stupid
demands. She felt sure that if anything were seriously
wrong, they would be incapable of healing her.

During these days, she relied less on her ears and eyes
than a deeper sense unique to the Imagofas, which gave
her mind the freedom to roam the ship's power grid without ever crossing paths with its inhabitants. This kept her
sanity intact, but did nothing for her physical condition.
Her uniform hung on her gaunt frame, and her hair had

grown dull and coarse until she felt like she was beginning to resemble the dilapidated ship.

Even worse, were the sudden overwhelming anxiety attacks. She would find herself falling, gasping for air, fighting the sensation of being smothered. The attacks lasted only minutes, but left her exhausted. She knew what brought them on, but no amount of analysis could stop them. They stemmed from her guilt. Thesni would never have been captured if it were not for Sashimu. This thought gripped her at all times — even as she slept.

Without a clock, Sashimu marked time by the three daily meals she received via the dispenser: seventy-three days had passed.

Each day began with the sound of food dropping from the dispenser. Sashimu ate the hot, brightly colored lumps that smelled vaguely of breakfast, and she exercised. The worst problem for space-travelers was muscle and bone loss, but she couldn't have cared less. She exercised to escape, using the wall equipment until sweat poured and her entire body ached. Formulating thoughts, let alone worries, became impossible. Elevation beyond anxiety, guilt, boredom and worry came only in the sweet moment of complete physical exhaustion. The exercise wall became her steadfast companion, bearing the marks of her workouts, her source of pain and small pleasure.

Despite increasing insomnia, anxiety attacks and obsessive exercise, her captors left her alone. As long as she ate something every day, the wall panel rarely lit up with a crewmember's face and no more experiments were conducted. For this, she was thankful. Each day she awoke with the anticipation that this would be the day of rescue. Each dinner, she prayed would be her last.

After a fitful sleep, Sashimu climbed out of her sleeprest to be greeted by a thin woman whose image spanned the entire wall panel. The woman's uniform looked so crisp it might never have been worn and her long hair was wound about her head in tight knots. She wiped her sweaty face to dry it and something about the motion reminded Sashimu of the Minotaur.

Her eyes examined Sashimu, and she said, "Good morning."

"Not really."

"My name is Brooks, you've met me before as the Minotaur in Novus Orbis," she said and glanced around as though afraid of getting caught. "Look, I'm prepared to make you a deal, but we've got to hurry."

"What do you mean?" Sashimu wondered if the ship had finally ceased air recycling and the woman was suffering brain poisoning.

"The captain locked me in my cabin until today to keep us apart. I've little time before you leave us, but there is so much left to learn. I'm giving you access to the MAM, but you must promise not to break through security." Her voice was almost a whisper.

"No." Sashimu shook her head, wishing the woman would go away.

"Why not?"

Sashimu turned her back to the wall panel, but the woman was insistent. "I'll let you talk to your friend."

"It's a deal."

"Good. Give me a minute to open a MAMportal in your cell," the woman said already turning away, and the wall panel cleared. Sashimu looked around in nervous anticipation, waiting for the pull of Novus Orbis.

Sudden vertigo and an explosion of energy inside her chest rocked her off her feet. The cell was replaced by a long stretch of narrow passageway. Sashimu felt the onslaught of biostat readings — recorded and displayed — about her. Resisting the urge to find Thesni herself, she waited. It seemed ages before she heard the soft, familiar voice.

"Sashimu?"

"Thesni!" Sashimu's heart quickened and the echo in her ears felt deafening. She was tempted to reduce the volume, but resisted, to keep her promise.

"I sent the message." Thesni's voice was hoarse.

"Thank Juno. What's wrong with your voice?"

"The Minotaur interrogated me for hours before she let me talk to you. She wanted to know how we were raised, how fast we heal when we get hurt, whether we have male-female interactions. She asked about everything."

Sashimu felt her cheeks flush hot with anger. "This is almost over. I can feel the changes in the ship. Its power resources are being reallocated in preparation for landing. We should be near Earth."

"I thought so. We've been traveling too long," said Thesni.

"I'm going to get us back to Mars. I promise."

"Be careful, Sashimu."

Struggling to stay in Novus Orbis, Sashimu felt dizziness before the cell resolved around her. She tried desperately to stay with Thesni, but was exited. The wall panel was still lit with the woman's long face.

"I've a few questions for you now," the woman began.

Sashimu leaped to the sleeprest, pushing its panic button. The wall panel went dead. None of the crew responded, but Sashimu was satisfied. She wanted to be away from the horrible woman who wasted precious moments needed to plan. She had to think of a way to escape once they landed.

MIP

With a mix of awe and dread, from her sleeprest, Thesni watched their approach to the glowing blue-green planet. Her captors had re-opened limited external views. They informed her that within the day, they planned to dock at Moon Interplanetary Port.

Anxious about her first landing, Thesni climbed from the sleeprest and sat cross-legged on the cold metal floor until she sensed the shifts in energy across the ship's power grid to auxiliary sources. She imagined the docking system grinding its ancient plates until each snapped into position. Every enormous scrap of near-rubble metal had its unique grooves and cracks, each plate fitting precisely with the next.

A sudden lurch of the ship caught Thesni by surprise, smashing her into the wall of her cell. She saw the metal surface vibrating and heard a bizarre drilling sound from somewhere high above the ceiling. Concentrating on trying to identify the sound, she pressed against the wall, listening. Then she recognized the source of the noise, and jumped back.

"The ship's been hit by a hummer!" Thesni yelled. No stranger to military defense and safety drills on Mars, she recognized the distinctive burrowing sound and then the quiet hum that a hummer bomb made before being remotely detonated. In alarm, Thesni jumped up and down waving her hands in front of the wall panel, but everything remained eerily silent.

"There's a hummer!" she shouted again then leapt back, startled, as the cell door slid back.

A tall, thin man hesitated in the doorway, then cautiously approached. He made her nervous. She retreated further into her cell, ready to scream.

"Calm down. I'm Treadwell, the second-in-command. I'm taking you to see the captain. Put your hands together." Thesni complied, but looked dubiously at the opaque ring of unlaunched Biosecur that he held in his hand.

"As long as you keep your hands together you won't trigger the biosecur," Treadwell said and clamped her wrists tight behind her back. The ring molded uncomfortably to her skin; if she pulled her wrists apart, she'd be smothered in biosecur. Treadwell motioned for her to walk in front of him up to the main deck.

On deck, the crew was focused on their consoles — except for an enormous man pacing back and forth. Thesni took him to be the captain.

"Treadwell, give me the status on where those hummers have burrowed," the captain ordered, bearing down on Treadwell and Thesni.

After quickly running diagnostics, Treadwell pulled up a ship schematic and pointed, saying, "It's lodged just above the lab, near the main deck."

The captain groaned. "Keep her here out of the way," he said. The big handler got up from her console and thrust Thesni into the closest empty seat, adjusting the controls so that the chair wrapped itself too tightly around her.

"Brooks," the captain continued, "be ready to accept any communiqué from Earth. Angel and his Council buddies will help us. Remember, they badly want these nanogens so none of you panic or do anything stupid while I'm in Novus Orbis."

He spoke to Treadwell and the others. "Treadwell, I want you with me for negotiations with Captain Lynn. We've worked with her before, but her damned hummer attack makes this situation a little tricky. The rest of you, be ready to act on my orders."

The captain's eyes narrowed as he shifted his attention to Thesni. "And if this nanogen tries to interfere with any special MAM mumbo-jumbo, kill her."

He returned to his seat on the far left, before a daunting array of switches, blinking lights and miniature terminals.

His MAMhood slid over his face. Treadwell was in the seat closest to Thesni; now his MAMhood slid over his face, too and immediately the Imagofas felt the terrible shock in her chest as the MAM pulled her into Novus Orbis. She remained perfectly still. She believed the crew would carry out the captain's order to kill her.

She found herself in a cramped antique drawing room, where the captain and the second-in-command were bowing before a tall woman who was outfitted in a standard Order operator uniform. Its chameleon-fabric blended into any background so that only her face, hands and the crane insignia on her right breast stood out. Thesni expected all three to turn to her and protest her uninvited presence, but they seemed completely oblivious of her arrival.

"Captain Grant," the Order operator said calmly, "I've been waiting for you. Let's not waste time on niceties. I request immediate boarding privileges."

"Captain Lynn. So good to see a familiar face after all this time in space," Grant said, but he sounded anything but happy to see her.

"I mean business, Grant," said Captain Lynn and her tone was deadly. "Let us board now or I'll have to detonate the hummer."

Grant sounded as if he was struggling to keep his tone light. "Of course you can board, but first tell me what all this is about. You and I have had a long history of working together."

"Don't play dumb with me," Lynn said jabbing a finger at his chest. She towered over the squat, fat man. Thesni wanted to plead for help from Captain Lynn or scream at Grant to follow the woman's orders. Instead, she stayed silent and unnoticed in the corner.

"You and I both know you've got exceptionally illegal cargo on board — much worse than your usual blackbase."

"Lynn, we've known each other for ten years and in the last two I've been very profitable for you." Grant glanced anxiously at Treadwell. "There must be something we can work out here—"

"Not this time. My orders are explicit and they come from too high up," Lynn said. Thesni doubted if Grant could stall much longer. "Let us board."

"Give me a moment to assess the damage your hummer has done," Grant begged.

"It's nothing compared to the damage it'll do if detonated," said Lynn coldly. "Stall all you want, Grant, the outcome will be the same and you know it."

"My deepest apologies," Grant said and bowed deeply. "I'm receiving an urgent message from my crew, no doubt about the severe damage you've inflicted on my ship. Excuse me for one moment."

He and Treadwell returned to Vetus Orbis. Thesni felt the harsh jolt in her chest as she too returned to Vetus Orbis behind Treadwell. She read an incoming communication on the ship's monitor:

COUNCIL DIRECTIVE:
Under no circumstances allow Lynn to board.
Go directly to Moon Interplanetary Port.
You will receive Council protection.

"Idiots! Our ship is under attack and they act as if we're at some damned council meeting!" Grant said.

The crew showed signs of apprehension, but everyone waited for their captain's decision.

"Listen, if Lynn boards, we're dead. All she wants is the nanogens," Grant reasoned.

"The captain's right," said Treadwell. "Lynn probably has kill-all orders on us. But she won't risk destroying the nanogens. As long as we have them, we're safe."

"And soon-to-be-rich," the big handler added.

"We're landing; assume positions," Grant said and nodded.

"No," Thesni whispered.

Thesni watched the wall panels that showed multiple external space views of Earth, its moon and the Order's ominous, unmarked ship. The *Home Sweet Home* fired its damaged thrusters, plunging away from the Order ship toward the Moon. The ship shook as though at any moment it might tear apart and multiple alarms screeched from all decks. Thesni cringed in her seat.

Transfixed by the wall panel, Thesni watched the Order ship put more distance between itself and the *Home Sweet*

Home. That meant only one thing: Captain Lynn planned to detonate her hummers.

Thesni looked around and saw the deathly pale faces of the crew, bent in silent desperation over various consoles.

"Grant, you crazy bastard," Lynn warned as the *Home Sweet Home* swung wide of her ship and dove downward, "I've got two hummers buried in your side!"

As the cargo ship blasted toward Moon Interplanetary Port, the Space Traffic Controller's voice boomed over the main deck. "What do you think you're doing? You are *not* cleared for landing."

Thesni watched as the Moon's surface loomed larger, saw hundreds of ships, each docked on circular landing pads. At the center of the concentric patterns of docked ships sat the MIP dome. As it dropped toward the moon's surface, the *Home Sweet Home* shuddered violently, jostling the crew in their seats. Thesni held her breath and watched the monitor as they careened to the left and right of the landing pad below them. A long row of landing pads stood empty further away, but the threat from the bombs' imminent detonation meant that the *Home Sweet Home* had to dock fast on the nearest pad.

The crew tried to align the ship but it slammed into a commercial passenger cruiser on the adjacent pad. The main-deck floor heaved upwards and partially gave way onto mid-deck. Shattered consoles and dismembered components jetted over Thesni's head. A stench of burning circuitry filled the air. Then, with a deafening roar, the *Home Sweet Home* locked onto the pad.

"Let's get out of here before that hummer blows," Grant yelled above the jarring ship alarms. His crew untangled themselves from the fallen debris, and the captain yanked Thesni up and over his shoulder. Coughing and stumbling, they navigated the wreckage from the main deck, and then descended through the back-up airlock to emerge below the cargo area.

They reached the exterior ship doors that would open onto the MIP terminal, but Grant and Treadwell found the locks jammed. They struggled frantically to override them and escape before the ship blew up.

In desperation, Grant ordered the crew to take turns firing their smartguns at the doors in an attempt to blast them apart. The impacts sprang the doors and Grant grabbed Thesni and pulled her through. But then the opening slammed shut behind them. Thesni could hear the sounds of the crew frantically discharging their weapons again. "They're only aggravating the hummer," she warned.

Click. She knew what that sound meant. "It's going to blow!"

Her only thought now was to save Sashimu. She twisted, trying to get free of Grant's grip. Her struggles triggered the Biosecur, which enveloped her.

"We can't have you immobile," said Grant. He sprayed her with the foul-smelling solvent.

Thesni heard a new series of sounds from the hummer. Clickety-click. Click.

Grant hoisted her over his shoulder and ran down the terminal corridor. Startled travelers jumped out of his path and security operators shouted after him.

"Damn!" Grant charged forward, knocking people aside. Dripping with solvent, Thesni remained immobilized, but at least now she could breathe.

Behind them, Thesni heard a final *click.*

A massive chain reaction of explosions gutted the *Home Sweet Home,* blasting its innards into MIP and engulfing half the terminal's west quadrant in flames. The force of the explosion knocked Grant flat. Thesni was thrown from his shoulder and painfully hit the floor. Grant got up, pulling Thesni with him and, holding her tight against himself, pushed ahead. But now they went more slowly. Flames roared behind them, followed by thick, choking smoke. Screams and alarms sounded through the murk.

They reached the end of the terminal, gasping for air. "This isn't possible," Grant said. "We've got to get to the main terminal."

Pushing Thesni ahead of him, like a shield against the falling debris and fire, Grant turned back toward the flames. As the Biosecur wore off, Thesni struggled to get free of his grasp.

"Let me go! You're hurting me. Help!" she screamed. Someone yelled, "Stop him," but Grant moved quickly. He hoisted her back over his shoulder.

"Do that again and you're dead," he warned.

Terrified, Thesni lay still. As he bore her through the carnage, she saw mangled bodies, some still living, corpses lying in pools of blood, burning wreckage, flames and swirling ash. Her ears filled with moans and shouts, the crackle of fire and the clatter of falling wreckage. Amidst all the chaos, she thought she heard a familiar voice calling her name, "Thesni?"

ΙιιΙιιιΙΙΙΙιιΙιΙιιΙ

The first impact staggered Sashimu. She looked desperately around her cell, but there was no safety here. A small quake rocked the cargo area.

"Are we crashing?" she yelled at the wall panel as a more violent tremor threw her against the exercise equipment and a siren began screaming somewhere close by. Over its din, she heard a relentless crunching and knew from her training that a hummer was boring its way deep into *Home Sweet Home*.

The hummer had already seriously damaged the ship, but if it detonated, the destruction might be total. Terrified, Sashimu screamed at the wall panel, "Get me out of here!" No one replied or came to unlock the door. She stood motionless, listening.

Time seemed to stop. Sashimu prayed for Thesni and the Imagofas, and thought suddenly of Mars' wild frontier, holding the image steady in her mind, like a sword drawn against the night.

Clickety-click. Click.

The explosion threw Sashimu to the floor. For a moment she lay dazed; her ears were ringing and when she reached to touch them she felt trickles of blood. More blood ran from her nose into her mouth. She coughed and struggled to her feet.

The cell door was open, wrenched from its pins by the force of the blast. She staggered out into the hallway, found jagged debris littering the floor and more falling as parts of the main deck and cabins above collapsed into the cargo area. Lab animals whimpered and struggled amidst the wreckage or lay dead. Sashimu paused and said another prayer for Thesni.

The hesitation saved her life. A huge chunk of metal hurtled down from above to crash right in front of her, filling the corridor with debris and ripping a gaping hole in the floor. Through the fire and smoke she could see the terminal below. A wall of flame shot up behind her. Sashimu held her breath and jumped.

She landed hard but unhurt in the fiery terminal corridor. Through the roiling smoke, Sashimu saw arms, legs and torn flesh protruding from the rubble on either side of her.

I've got to find her. She stumbled forward with renewed determination, picking her way through burning debris. Something caught at her ankle and she fell to her knees. She looked to see what had tripped her and saw that it was a woman's hand, gripped tightly around her leg. The woman's face was badly burned, but the charred lips opened and said, "I thought you were dead."

A length of metal was wedged into the stranger's abdomen, but she managed to stand when Sashimu lifted her. "Let's get away from here," the Imagofas said. The woman was heavy but Sashimu supported her.

"We'll follow them," she said, indicating a straggle of other survivors who were heading out of the devastated area.

Sashimu struggled to keep from falling as people shoved and pushed past them. She feared the woman wouldn't survive much longer with the metal protruding from her belly.

The woman spoke again. "Alice," she whispered, "dad didn't make it."

"I'll find him," Sashimu said. She looked back, but the terminal was in chaos. Anyone who could move was running or limping in their direction. She saw one man crawling, people stumbling over him.

Sashimu helped the woman take a few more steps. They were nearing the end of the corridor. Security personnel were moving quickly through the haze, helping the injured. She saw people being taken away on stretchers. Sashimu urged the woman forward, but then, from behind them, a second explosion hurled them both against a wall. The force of the blast smashed Sashimu's legs; she felt the bones splinter. The injured woman fell on top of her. Sashimu could only watch helplessly as more people ran past. She felt warm blood coursing over her and knew it was her own, but she experienced no pain. It was as though she was watching the scene from a great distance.

"My legs are broken. Can you move at all?" she asked the woman, surprised that her own crushed body suffered no agony. She was even more surprised when the stranger said, "I think so. I'll get help."

The woman crawled off her, heading on hands and knees toward the security personnel.

Some new commotion was taking place, but Sashimu's dazed mind faltered on the edge of losing consciousness. She saw a knot of security personnel go past her, moving fast. In a little while, some of them came back, carrying injured passengers and terminal staff. She tried to call out to them but her voice wouldn't carry. A new explosion slammed debris against the wall beside her. She felt intense burning heat. Then, through the smoke, she thought she glimpsed Thesni being carried on someone's shoulder.

"Thesni!" she yelled with all her force, wondering if it was just a shock-induced hallucination. Her voice was little more than a hoarse whisper.

Sashimu could see that the woman with the abdominal wound had found a security guard. She was pointing directly at Sashimu and Sashimu could read her lips: "My daughter! Help my daughter."

Survivor

"We have a situation." Sweating, Goth barged into Councilwoman Joli Xerkler's office without bothering to knock.

And it must be serious, she thought. As Joli's top advisor, Goth was responsible for resolving crises before they blew up into a political nightmare. He carried out his duties with a skittish acumen. Always nervous and over zealous, his first impulse was to panic and run to Joli. Once calmed, he took the necessary steps unhindered by scruples or conscience. Despite his nerves, Joli found him useful.

"Yes?" Joli wore ice-blue robes, her hair wrapped ornately above her head and regally glinting with sapphires. She was not pleased at the interruption.

"The *Home Sweet Home* has been attacked." Goth jerked his leg up and down in a nervous twitch. "Blown up on an MIP pad."

"Stop twitching," Joli snapped. "By whom?"

"The Order."

"Bastards! We'll never build a strong enough case against them without a nanogen. How did they detect it was onboard?"

"I don't know," said Goth, looking more agitated.

Joli breathed in deeply. She needed to keep her anger in check. "Who is the captain of the *Home Sweet Home*?"

"Grant."

"Tell me he's not one of Angel's henchmen."

"Well yes he is, but he has a solid reputation." Goth's tone was defensive. "Do you think the Order was tipped off?"

"Of course." Joli was sure of it. "Dead or alive; I want that nanogen. We need proof."

"Understood. My contacts at MIP are searching for it. But it's mayhem up there," said Goth.

"Make sure the Council is *not* implicated in this mess. We must never be exposed at a tribunal for violating our own laws."

"Yes, Councilwoman." Goth was settling down. Her calm presence centered him, although he was still wringing his hands when he rushed out.

Joli was highly agitated, but her countenance and posture remained unperturbed. She turned her office opaque for privacy to ensure no interruptions, then flipped through her avatars. Only when she'd picked out a disarming persona did she contact her husband.

|ılıl..ıllllıı.lıl..l

Creid Xerkler leaped out of bed and stretched his long, thin legs and arms. From the mirror, a bony face stared back at him with deep-set, almost furtive eyes. Three years into retirement, that look was still there, the look of a man with secrets.

Moving from the bedroom to the kitchen, he snapped his fingers. A piece of toast flew past him and hit the wall. He cursed, snapped again and caught the second piece. Pacing the apartment, lost in thought, he munched on the toast. Crumbs fell on his shirt and then bounced off the polished floor.

A compactmaid followed on his heels, eating up his mess and clucking until he ordered it off. It was an antiquated cleaning device, which was why Joli hated it. Creid refused to replace it on the grounds that it was the last of its kind. If it weren't for Creid Xerkler, this piece of technology might be extinct.

He came to the floor-to-ceiling window. In the distance, the Rocky Mountains etched the skyline. Straight down, a long way down, he could see whizzing heliocars. It was quiet with the neighbors still asleep.

The morning calm was shattered when Joli's avatar burst into the center of the living room. This time she was using a persona much younger than her actual self, her face a mask of concern. Caught off guard, he was irritated by her need to use a false, "beautified self" whenever she wanted something. He preferred to see her unadorned, looking natural, with all her wrinkles; and he worried that one day she would permanently revitalize herself to look like one of her avatars. He found people who fundamentally altered their Vetus Orbis appearance repugnant.

"Creid, has anyone contacted you?" Joli asked anxiously. "There's been an accident at MIP."

"No, you're the first to contact me," said Creid. "What's happened?"

"A ship called the *Home Sweet Home* blew up during landing. At last count, there were over 20 civilian and crew fatalities with more missing or injured," said Joli, her face etched with worry.

"Where are they taking the injured?" he asked as he struggled to make sense of her terrible news and its implications. His first thought was of Zazen who had contacted him earlier, begging Creid to help the Imagofas once they reached Earth. Since then, he had been waiting for the ship's arrival.

"The wounded are en route to the Denver Hospital of Our Fathers," Joli said, looking suddenly suspicious. "Why? Do you know something you aren't telling me?"

"I don't know anything about the ship or the accident," Creid replied hastily, running his hand through his mop of salt-and-pepper black hair.

"Creid, you better let me know if you find out anything. This situation is critical," Joli said, each word pronounced in a harsh staccato.

Creid nodded sympathetically and quickly ended the transmission. Pacing about the living room, he knew what he had to do, but his mood grew darker with every step.

He activated his Companion and initiated contact with Zazen on Mars. Zazen appeared dressed in a frayed lab coat and, to Creid, it seemed that the man had aged severely since the kidnapping of the Imagofas. His eyes were bleary and bloodshot and he sat slumped in his armchair.

"Creid. It's early where you are. I'm surprised to hear from you," Zazen said.

"I have some difficult news," Creid said.

"What?" Zazen sat back in his chair and gripped its armrests.

"There's been an accident on the Moon involving the *Home Sweet Home*," Creid said.

"Are there any survivors?" Zazen asked, his knuckles white where his hands clenched the chair.

"Yes. They're being shuttled to an Earthside hospital."

"What happened?"

"The *Home Sweet Home* seems to have exploded after landing at MIP."

"That was no accident. It's a cover-up." Zazen's voice was thick with emotion.

"What?" Creid said in shock. "What cover-up? Who's behind it?"

"Our cronies in the Order. Who else needs the Imagofas to disappear?" Zazen said bitterly.

"Wait," Creid replied. He activated a news broadcast via his Companion and listened briefly to the ongoing MIP coverage. "Zazen, the news reports that it's an accident. There's no mention of sabotage or anything suspicious."

"It's no accident," said Zazen, red-faced. "Believe me this time, Creid. When I tried to report Sashimu's disappearance to Order headquarters, no one would help me. Don't you think that's odd?"

Creid waited in silence for further explanation.

"Look, I suspect no Imagofas have been left alive," Zazen continued, his voice cracking with emotion. "After Sashimu and Thesni were abducted, all of the Imagofas were moved to the new facility near Olympus Mons. Since then, none of the guardians have been allowed contact with them."

"You mustn't assume the worst," Creid said, but he agreed it sounded grim.

"The Order may have completely 'neutralized' our project. They know we can start fresh anytime with what we've learned."

"I hope you're wrong," Creid said, but he broke out in a cold sweat. "The Imagofas may actually be safer in the new facility."

"Not without us. You said there are survivors?"

"Yes." Creid frowned. "So far there haven't been any positive ID's, certainly no one from the *Home Sweet Home*. The crew may be dead."

"With their regenerative abilities, if anyone lived, it would be Sashimu and Thesni." Zazen bit into his lip, struggling to control his composure. "Find and protect them. Hide the fact that they're Imagofas until we can bring them home."

"I'll try," Creid said to reassure him.

"It won't be easy to hide them on Earth," said Zazen. "Imagofas react strangely to the MAM. They may even cause disturbances in Novus Orbis that could alert the Order."

"What kind of disturbances?" asked Creid.

"There seems to be a localized viral effect on MAM protocols causing unexpected user behaviors and erratic malfunctions. We'd just begun preliminary testing, so we don't know much. The Imagofas definitely exhibit a special bond with the MAM and our laws of Novus Orbis do not apply."

At another time, Creid would have found this intriguing. Today it overwhelmed him. His chances of saving them were dwindling and he hadn't even started.

"Be careful," Zazen warned. "I'm begging for your help to save the Imagofas' lives, but this is a terrible risk for you. It may turn your closest friends into deadly enemies."

"I don't have any friends," Creid said with a wry smile.

Zazen's bloodshot eyes and haggard face underscored the desperation in his voice. "I thought I was powerful enough to turn this abominable situation around, but I was wrong."

"We all need help sometimes. I, most of all, should remember that," Creid said.

"Just so you know, Dreyfus is secretly on his way," said Zazen. "I sent him to help with the effort to get the Imagofas returned to Mars. I'd have gone myself, but the Order won't let me. I'm too 'mission critical' — whatever that means. Everything has been put on hold since Sashimu and Thesni were abducted."

"I look forward to seeing him. It's been decades," said Creid.

Getting up slowly from his arm chair and looking much older than his age, Zazen bowed deeply several times in silent appreciation. Creid returned the honor by standing and bowing once as low as he could so that his brow grazed his knees.

Nothing more was said. Creid signed off and sat immobilized on the couch. If the Imagofas fell into Council hands, an investigation and a tribunal were certain. His wife was already on their trail. He wondered how much she knew. Two young innocents were damning evidence that the Order had fundamentally altered human embryos using nanogenetics.

Creid was stunned. After twenty years, his past had finally caught up with him. Long after he had ceased to worry or even think about his part in the events, the Imagofas had come to threaten his safe, quiet life. He found it ironic that Zazen wanted him to save and hide them — if they were even still alive. Another operator would seek them out and eliminate them, but it would not be Creid. He believed in all creation, even beings created by humankind. Zazen must be counting on that.

Whispers of the Imagofas had echoed through Council halls for two decades. Until now, only screwball conspiracy theorists had entertained the possibility of their existence. If the reality became public knowledge, it was only a matter of time before Creid and a slew of other Order operators were hauled before a tribunal. But the Order could never allow them to give testimony; each would die of some accident, or maybe a sudden heart attack or even suicide. He wondered what end the Order would choose for him, to ensure his silence. His only hope was to find the Imagofas first and deliver them into Dreyfus' hands. They could return to obscurity and be forgotten on Mars.

As long as Joli never discovered the Imagofas and his involvement in their creation, he might continue his comfortable lifestyle. Having crafted the toughest laws against the nanogenetic engineering of human embryos, she would be merciless with violators. If she found out after all these years that Imagofas truly existed and that he had played a role in their creation, he was afraid of what she might do to him. She most probably would send him before the tribunal, never suspecting that that would be tantamount to giving him a death sentence.

Creid struggled to come up with some possible way to help the Imagofas without being detected. He reasoned that, since the Imagofas caused disturbances in Novus Orbis, that's where he had to go.

He always wore his MAMsuit under his clothes, even under his pajamas, and now he triggered the ultra-thin MAM facemask, causing it to unroll from the back of his collar to cover his head. He engaged the MAM through the apartment's optimization area and voiced his destination. Everything fell away from him, and he felt a moment of stark vertigo. Then a loud hiss told him that the transmission was successful and his session initialized.

|.,|.|...|||||..,|.|..|

To frustrate advertisers, Creid always entered Novus Orbis under the cover of rain. He also liked the feel of water pouring down his face and the smell of wet pavement. Everything was obscured by torrents of rain, except his path.

The setting was vintage 20th century stylized Japan. Aston Martins and BMWs whizzed by him on a cracked asphalt road that wound upward through a hilly Tokyo-esque suburb to an ancient temple and its gardens. Unfortunately, big corporate domus overrode almost all user preference settings so Creid had no real hope of evading directed commercial advertising, no matter how much he complained to the MAM user boards or whether he made his environment less hospitable. Many times, he'd contemplated circumventing advertising protocols but always resisted. He had to save his violations for important business.

"Here comes one now," said Creid, dreading the inevitable onslaught.

A huge yellow canary swooped down beside the road and perched on a small tree, bending its branches almost to the breaking point. "Hello, Creid! You must be busy getting ready for one of the most anticipated retirement holidays in history. We want to offer you an easy transition into the most exciting time of your life."

"Did you bother to access my profile or my preferences? I retired two years ago. No solicitations." He reached into his raincoat and pulled out an antique Glock 9mm pistol and fired a warning shot into the sky. The canary took off vertically, escaping into the rain.

"Damn, another one," Creid muttered, keeping his gun visible. This avatar was not some cheap corporate agent, but human, appearing as a pony-tailed starlet carrying a pink umbrella and wearing a tight top and a too short skirt.

Creid's pistol burst into flowers. Violence against fellow humans was not allowed during any normal session. Grudgingly, Creid stuffed the bouquet into his pocket, forming a large bulge.

"You smell sweet as flowers. Are those for me?" said the starlet, winking at him from under her umbrella.

"Aren't you cold in that?" Creid asked, annoyed.

"Honey, we could have sun as quick as you like." The sun started to peek out from a heavy cloud and a rainbow formed on the horizon.

"Expensive!" Creid was impressed by the amount advertisers were willing to expend on potential customers. "No, I prefer heavy rain."

The rain reverted to watery sheets, pelting Creid's back.

"Creid, I'd like to tell you about our anti-aging breakthrough. You can grow twenty years younger in days. Just come with me for highlights of our professional process." The girl bent close to him, mimicking a look-around to make sure no one could hear. "I can offer you a special discount today," she whispered.

A vintage Porsche 911 appeared, and she climbed inside offering him the driver's seat.

Creid ignored her and walked on. The Porsche sped by, spraying him with dirty water. Creid looked down and smiled. His unfashionable knee-high galoshes had finally come in handy. He trudged through the mud, taking his time, as he usually did when he was on his way to gaming, but it was grating on his nerves. He had little time.

Next, a group of darkly dressed men descended on him and he tensed momentarily, not sure if they were Order dispatchers. Their lapels carried no crane insignia, so he relaxed.

"Mister, your search has ended. If you want to start a new career; we've got the job for you." Creid turned away, but the group surrounded him.

"Mister," one of the avatars said, then hesitated as it was updated with Creid's personal information. "Creid, if unlimited credit makes you tingle with excitement, then I have a proposition you cannot resist!"

Creid sighed and pushed through the circle.

Eventually, he reached an ancient, familiar door in a narrow alleyway, yanked it open and slipped inside. Violating protocol, he slammed the door shut on several of the avatars' hands. Everything went black for a minute. Creid felt an electric shock course through his body, as a warning from the MAM for his antisocial behavior; later, he could expect to receive a small fine. Breathing heavily, he smiled. Causing pain to human advertisers might be a MAM violation, but it sure was therapeutic.

When the MAM restored his environment, Creid found himself inside the gate of a carefully tended garden of centuries old bonsai trees. Creid sighed. It was peaceful here. The sweet aroma of cherry and plum trees in bloom made it a sanctuary. Moss grew on large stones under a waterfall that cascaded into a clear pond. Perched beside the waterfall, a crane arched its neck.

"Shit." Creid stopped, staring apprehensively at the crane. His body tensed. The crane dove into the pond and emerged beside him.

"Are you headed for the games?" the crane asked.

Creid nodded nervously.

"Saturday is too busy and expensive a day for gaming. Retired operators have the luxury of gaming on the week-days when rates are much better," the crane said. "Are you trying to hide something from our Order dispatchers?"

Creid stood absolutely still, monitoring his biostats and hoping the changes were not alarming.

"If you are, we're doing a little side business here for eternal friends of the Order." The crane mistook Creid's increased heartbeat for excitement. "We keep eternal friends in touch with one another. It's all very lovely, erotic and exclusive."

The crane inclined its head toward the waterfall. A small curtain moved, revealing nude women in suggestive postures. Creid looked away, dismayed that his favorite garden had fallen prey to commerce. But he was also relieved that this was simply a sales pitch.

"If those don't please you, there's these little numbers." The Crane mistook Creid's dismay for sexual preference. When Creid looked back, a group of nude musclemen winked at him from beneath the waterfall.

"I play garden-variety games, like 4-D Go. Not really into the exotics, but thank you, sir," said Creid, always careful to be polite to any Order-affiliated avatar — even one dealing in black-market services — he continued up the path, thinking *was no place sacred anymore?*

The MAM seemed hyper-aware of him. Perhaps all the attention he was receiving meant that he had been put on some kind of watch list. Just his luck.

Alias

The water ran deep and fast. Creid followed it, conspicuously bypassing the gaming routes. He wanted to run, but to avoid suspicion he walked nonchalantly to the bridge that served as the garden's main entrance. Glancing back to see if he was followed, he ducked underneath the bridge close to the river's edge. The sound of the river calmed him as it would have in Vetus Orbis.

Accessing the commandline, Creid ended his session and initiated a new session as his criminal alias, "Leonardo." If Order dispatchers followed him, it would appear as though he had exited Novus Orbis and they would lose his trail. Creid's unregistered, covert alias allowed him into highly restricted areas of Novus Orbis that he'd only had legal access to during his years of top-level security clearance in the Order.

Entering Novus Orbis as Leonardo, Creid saw a secret, previously invisible pathway leading away from the water. Through the trees, he discerned a small wooden arch and beyond that an old, dark-skinned man wrapped in a gold-quilted toga. He was crouched beside a creek, his back to Creid. As always over the last two decades, Creid felt simultaneously reassured and saddened at the sight of the old man repeatedly trying to scoop catfish out of the water with a small gourd.

"Prometheus, I see you're still fishing," said Creid.

Stooped over the creek, Prometheus remained intent on his fishing, but the catfish easily evaded his gourd and swam out of reach.

"You've made such efficient use of me, Leonardo. What technologies will you invent next?" Prometheus asked, lunging at the closest fish.

Creid thought he detected sarcasm in Prometheus' voice. "I'm busy," Prometheus added and waved his visitor away.

"We have to talk," Creid said and gestured for the old man to follow him to a small wooden hut that stood nearby. Before entering, Creid removed his muddy galoshes. Inside, the room was heavy with the smoke of incense. Creid peered into the shadows. No one was there. Drops of nervous sweat rolled down his brow and stung his eyes.

"Have you detected any unusual structural changes to the MAM in the last 24 hours?" Creid asked.

"Yes," Prometheus answered, which surprised him. "But it's all for the best. The changes enhance MAM protocols, which I've always thought were suboptimal since they were developed for extremely inefficient human MAMsuits. If you were ever to allow me some freedom, I could participate in further MAM optimization."

"That won't be necessary. Did you investigate the source?" asked Creid.

"No."

Creid exhaled heavily with relief. "Why not?"

"I'm preoccupied with the koan," Prometheus said.

"Glad to hear you're still focused," Creid chuckled. For over two decades, Prometheus' processes had been wholly devoted to the puzzle of a peculiar koan used centuries ago in Zen Buddhism to facilitate meditation and enlightenment. While 22nd century humans would have achieved an answer or given up, Prometheus had neither the processing power required to succeed in the endeavor, nor the luxury to quit.

"I can help." Prometheus seemed eager, if that were possible.

"I don't want to divert you from your task." The last thing Creid needed was further complications.

"If you allow it, I can devote a percentage of my resources to helping you, without impacting my ... task."

"Watch while I work and I'll let you know if I need help," Creid said. He went to the hut's built-in cupboard and found the box that contained the board and pieces of the ancient game of Go. He dusted off the box with his hand. He'd created the first MAM version of the game. To his chagrin, few played it anymore, but he'd used this set to leave himself a backdoor to MAM admin tools, an access that had often proved useful.

When he shifted the pieces on the board into a specific configuration, he gained admin access. He initiated queries by manipulating the game sequence and adding voice commands.

It took him several attempts before he was able to hack into confidential Order data on Denver's Hospital of Our Fathers' patients. Among the many MIP victims admitted to the burn ward that day was a girl named Alice Chigusa, with third-degree burns over 90 percent of her body. According to her patient records she was in shock, suffering from internal bleeding and broken limbs. Blood transfusions and other shock-prevention treatment were listed as early emergency MIP treatment. The report stated the patient was healing at an astonishing rate. Perhaps an Imagofas *had* survived.

Creid's hands shook as he reviewed her data. But when he was unable to locate a second possible Imagofas, he felt discouraged. Pointing to the data file on Alice Chigusa, Creid turned to Prometheus. "You say you feel the disturbances. Are they emanating from this hospital?"

Prometheus sat quietly for a moment. "The disturbances are strongest in the Underground."

"What is the disturbance duration?"

"Undetermined."

"That disturbance must be unrelated. The Imagofas could never get to the Underground without the crew's help. The crew are dead. It makes no sense." Creid gravely shook his head. "I hope this 'Alice' is an Imagofas. If so, she's been mistaken for a civilian."

"So Alice Chigusa is our disturbance." Prometheus processed the data.

"She'll need protection in both Novus Orbis and Vetus Orbis," Creid said.

Creid falsified a supervising medic's order specifying that Alice Chigusa needed a MAM equipped room so that

Prometheus could keep a constant eye on her. He programmed Prometheus to monitor her progress and send
him reports. His search for another young girl came up
empty. No one among the recovered dead or wounded fit
the profile except Alice Chigusa.

The thick incense smoke made him cough. Creid rose
and headed for the door. Unfortunately, he found it blocked
by a creature with the body of a woman dressed seduc-
tively in red fur and a face ruined by an enormous beak
where a nose should have been. It minced forward and
gently placed a sharp taloned hand against his chest.

"Not so fast." Its voice had the velvet coo of a pigeon.

Creid stepped back. "What are you?" he asked. It moved
closer, but he saw that it was completely oblivious of
Prometheus' presence.

"I am an Information Corruption Komptroler — ICK
for short. Since the *human* dispatcher failed to locate you,
the MAM executed me to deal with you. With all due
respect, sir, humans are inept," the ICK said and moved
so close its breasts brushed against him. Creid backed up
until he was pinned to the wall.

"Undo your actions and disable the Go game backdoor.
It's unauthorized," it said.

Creid stared confounded as the incense smoke curled
around them. "Why?"

"The changes you have just made are unauthorized."
The ICK peered down its beak.

Creid held back a laugh. The ICK loosened its coat,
revealing extreme cleavage.

"Look, this is a mistake."

"Information corruption cleanup processes are well
documented and approved. Basic criteria ensure high
quality results. There's no mistake."

"There are all kinds of 'unauthorized' MAM activities.
Why did I attract your special attention?" Creid asked
nervously.

"Leonardo is not an authorized user." The ICK flipped
back its thick hair.

"You've never come after me before today."

"Your user is on the superwatch list."

"You mean Creid Xerkler? Dispatchers can't trace Leonardo to Creid." Creid spoke of himself in the third person.

The ICK smiled. "That's why I'm useful. The MAM sees what humans miss."

"I am not going to undo my work," Creid said, trying to think of a way to circumvent the ICK. He was in serious trouble. "What if we make a deal? I'll disable the Leonardo alias and you let me exit Novus Orbis without further delay."

"You are not allowed to leave here until you retrace your steps and undo the changes."

Creid opted to stall. He waved it back, then sat and adjusted the Go game box he had used to review hospital data. He wondered about any possible weakness ICK might have; clearly, reasoning with it would not work.

Prometheus stepped forward from the shadows, invisible to the ICK until he wanted to be seen. "Do you want me to intervene?"

"I'll handle this," Creid said, still puzzled by the ICK's criticism of humans as "inept" — unless a debug module had been allowed into production. When bored with conventional specifications, MAMprogrammers were notorious for giving their modules satirical attitudes, which were never supposed to be released into production. "Are you a test engineering unit?" Creid asked.

The ICK hesitated, "Yes, I'm a tengu."

"A tengu. Beautiful. Our group designed you, at least an early prototype, didn't we? If I remember correctly, the version number was 83648."

"I am a modified 83648.0b2 design." The ICK bowed.

Creid's successor had put a test engineering unit directly into production. Disgusting. A defective prototype was fully operational in the MAM. The original 83648 ICK had been designed to kill applications — although, as far as Creid knew, not to impede humans — which had ceased to be useful and might lead to corrupt information capture or processing.

That meant the Hotkeys might still be enabled. He wondered how many tengu had been placed directly into production since he retired. *No respect for quality control*, he thought.

Shaking his head, he grabbed the tengu's left hand and dug underneath its red talons. Caught by surprise, the ICK did not resist. The fur coat fell away as it transformed into a series of data streams.

"Hot keys and the commandline, there's nothing better." Creid smiled. "Why are our new cadets dependent on wizards? Stupid."

Now that he had full access, he aborted the tengu. The ICK's original appearance returned for a moment, drawing Creid close; then screaming, it disappeared. Scratching his head, he marveled that someone had added a "will to live" feature.

"Until later," Prometheus said and left the hut to resume fishing with his small gourd.

It was time to leave. Feeling nervous and exhausted, Creid exited the commandline, resuming his session as Creid. He walked through the garden. A human avatar in a suit and tie approached.

"Honestly, I don't care what you're selling. I've no credit, just check my profile." Creid felt worn out.

"Creid Xerkler," the man said and smiled, undeterred. Creid noted the crane emblem of the Order on the man's lapel and stopped.

"You still have that same old wit, don't you? Little expensive to be gaming on a Saturday, isn't it?"

The man brought his hands together and bowed. His right wrist was tattooed like Creid's with a standing crane. Once in the Order, always in the Order.

Creid brought his hands together and bowed. "My wife is out of town this weekend."

The dispatcher winked. "Been there myself a few times. Rather nice change of scenery, if you know what I mean." The dispatcher nudged him and made an obscene gesture. Creid was taken aback, but remained silent.

The dispatcher glanced around suspiciously. "You didn't notice any turbulence around here, did you?"

"Not the kind I'd care to talk about." Creid knew his biostats fully substantiated the honesty in that statement.

He winked at the man and showed him what he hoped was a lascivious grin.

"Wish I could have a bit of that myself, but it looks like I'll spend my entire shift searching this damn park." The dispatcher made another crude gesture and walked away.

Creid left the garden. No one was around. To exit, he bent down in the street with his palms out. When he placed his palms flat against the rain-swept pavement, a manhole appeared. He dropped inside.

Creid pulled off his facemask and found himself back in his Vetus Orbis apartment. His body was soaked in sweat. He calculated that he had little time left to save the surviving Imagofas. Keeping her identity from the Order was critical. He would have to act quickly.

|.|.|...|||||...|.|.|

As far as Sashimu could see, she was surrounded by an expanse of white. She looked with suspicion at the young man standing beside her. He had thick dark hair and a handsome face. He was dressed in black.

"I am Prometheus," the young man said, bowing.

"My name is Sashimu. Where am I?" She felt a tremendous weight on her chest, arms and legs. It confused her.

Prometheus accessed her file. "You are in Denver, on Earth. Room 17, Burn Ward, high-security Order wing at the Hospital of Our Fathers."

"On Earth?" said Sashimu, shaking her head in despair. "It just keeps getting worse. Why am I in a burn ward?"

"You're burned."

"Badly?" Her voice was soft but tense.

"You suffered third degree burns on over 90 percent of your body," Prometheus said matter-of-factly.

"I'm dying," Sashimu was terrified. "Is this a pathetic effort at giving me last rites?"

"You are in intensive care, but your body heals rapidly." Prometheus scanned her biostats. "You are not dying."

"Why are we surrounded by whiteness?" Looking down at herself, Sashimu was astonished to discover she possessed a massive male physique with exaggerated arm muscles and giant hands. "This isn't me!"

"We are in Novus Orbis. I've created a Hercules avatar to give you strength against enemies."

"Who are my enemies in Novus Orbis?" Sashimu asked anxiously.

"I have not been informed," said Prometheus glancing over her large frame. "According to your medical files you are known as Alice Chigusa, which may also be an alias to protect you."

"Well, I'm *not* Alice Chigusa," said Sashimu. "My name is Sashimu. I am an Imagofas."

Prometheus seemed pensive, but displayed no alarm at her outburst. "I have limited data on the Imagofas and much of that is human conjecture or myth. What are you?"

"The Imagofas is a name we give ourselves. We are the image of fate," said Sashimu proudly. "We are the next generation of humankind, the result of a synthesis between organic and inorganic life through nanogenetics."

Prometheus nodded. "The term I have is human nanogens."

"I hate that word. It doesn't apply to us. We are human evolution on fast-forward. We are not simply a result of the transfer of genes or the addition of electromechanical devices as nanogen implies. We have intellect; we have souls."

"Welcome to Earth, Imagofas." Prometheus bowed. "I will avoid the term human nanogen."

"What are you? You're not human," Sashimu guessed. "You must be smart intelligence."

"That is correct. I am a unique smart intelligence meta-agent made up of a society of sub-agents." Prometheus cocked his head. "How did you know?"

"Easy. You didn't react when I told you I'm Imagofas." Sashimu laughed, which made her wheeze in pain. "Why am I here?"

"You are here to help me." Prometheus stood and stretched.

"The last I knew, I was in a fire." She remembered struggling in the heat with a wounded woman. In the chaos of explosions, people and smoke, she had imagined seeing Thesni.

Prometheus analyzed her data and explained, "As I said before, your medical file reports you are Alice Chigusa. A cargo ship crashed into your vessel while it was docked at MIP. Apparently the real Alice's body was never recovered and her mother mistakenly identified you as Alice. You were given her ID without further investigation.

"But what about her family?" inquired Sashimu. "Surely they must be looking for the real Alice?"

Prometheus shook his head. "Alice Chigusa was visiting Earth from Mars along with her parents. Her father is missing and presumed deceased, her mother passed away from internal injuries shortly after identifying you as Alice. Since that time, no one on Earth has inquired about Alice, so you've assumed her identity without detection. Even if they did inquire, your severe burns hide your identity."

Sashimu managed a nod, but imagining what had befallen the real Alice Chigusa nauseated her. "Did Thesni survive?" Sashimu asked hopefully.

"Thesni is Imagofas?" Prometheus searched the medical records. "She is not listed among the living or the dead."

"Thesni might have been confused with someone else. After all, they think I'm Alice. She is my age, tiny and blonde."

"You are the only one listed who is your age and female." Prometheus paused, bending close to her face. "I need your help. Are you willing?"

She gazed into his melancholic brown eyes and had an idea. "Let's make a deal. I'll help you if you help me find Thesni and return to Mars."

"Yes. I'll help you and you'll help me. This is good." Prometheus sounded enthusiastic, but she had difficulty responding.

The pressure on her chest felt unbearable. She gasped in agony, fearing she might be crushed.

"The LifeSustainer helps you breathe and perform other functions," Prometheus explained.

"Earth's gravity probably makes it worse."

"Gravity will not crush you," Prometheus said.

Sashimu mumbled to reassure herself, "I invoke great Juno. Mother of Mars, Wake power in me, Herculean ability to find Thesni and get us back home."

"We must find Thesni," Prometheus echoed.

He faded away as pain seared her consciousness, evoking anguished screams she only half-understood were her own.

Underground

The next day, Joli summoned Goth to her office. He bowed as he entered, having regained his composure since the MIP incident. Before speaking, they sat across from each other on stiff, high-backed couches. Joli ordered the walls opaque for privacy.

"Do we have the nanogen?" asked Joli, but knew the answer from the immediate scowl on Goth's face before he spoke.

"Not yet. Our MIP contact spotted Grant and a possible nanogen leaving the terminal, but we've yet to get our hands on it." His leg twitched once.

"What does it look like?" Joli sat perfectly still.

"A young woman."

"It is disturbing that a nanogen could pass for one of us. Of course, this nanogen is not nearly as obscene as the nanogens the Order plans to develop as the next generation of 'humankind.' I can only imagine the hideousness of something that can breathe Mars' atmosphere. We've got to stop them before they turn our humanity into a bunch of freaks." Joli felt a chill run down her back. "You must get this nanogen into custody."

"That's tricky. Rumor has it that Grant was found murdered in some back tunnel of the Underground," said Goth matter-of-factly.

Joli scowled. "What happened to the nanogen?"

"We don't know. We've confirmed that it's not among the survivors at the hospital, or among the dead. It couldn't hide at MIP, there's too much security. Frankly, given the extent of the terminal wreckage, if the nanogen died in the explosion, its remains might never be recovered. Of course,

Grant may have taken it with him into the Underground," Goth said, shifting uneasily under her gaze.

"This is unacceptable, Goth. Find it," Joli ordered.

"Yes, Councilwoman," Goth said wearily, and leaned forward in his seat. "We need a Novus Orbis expert to find the nanogen. Do you know someone we could use?"

"A Novus Orbis expert?" Joli frowned. "Wait. There's the Cadet, but he's just a gamer."

"That might work," Goth paused, as if considering all the possibilities the Cadet offered. "I hadn't considered him."

"He's trustworthy, but no supporter of the Council," said Joli. She dismissed the idea with the flip of her hand.

"He's perfect," Goth said and almost purred with satisfaction.

"What do you mean?" Joli asked, taken off guard.

"We hire him to help us find the nanogen," replied Goth with a thin, cold smile. He relished slowly divulging secrets to her.

"Why?" Joli leaned forward, knowing he had already formulated some elaborate scheme; it might be insane or brilliant — or both. "Why do we need a Novus Orbis expert?"

"He's a gamer."

"I don't see how a gamer, even a world-class one like the Cadet, would help us find the nanogen," Joli said dryly. He was trying her patience.

"We know from Angel that the nanogen is attracted to Novus Orbis. It has some kind of special relationship with the MAM. The Cadet is a gamer so he's as tuned to it as an Order operator. If anyone has a chance to locate her, it's a top gamer."

"I'll approach him," Joli said, thinking it best that she visit the Cadet in person to gain his trust.

"The Cadet is infamous for his Underworld connections. He may have less scrupulous, but highly effective ways of finding the nanogen," Goth added. He had made it his business to know all about the Cadet; indeed he knew all about every one of Joli's associates — and her husband's.

"Very good. I'll speak with him. But before you go, I'd like your expert advice on a related matter — in the strictest of confidences, never to leave these walls," said Joli. She leaned forward again.

"You have my word," Goth replied, always delighted to learn new secrets.

"As you know, my husband has a long history with the Order."

"A long and distinguished career as the father of the MAM," Goth said, as though reading from a formal, historic text.

"Yes." Joli looked down at her hands. "It's possible that he was involved in the early stages of human nanogenetics, but he won't tell me anything. Or can't."

Goth understood immediately. "You want to ensure no one unearths anything about your husband which could jeopardize your future standing with the Council."

"Precisely."

"I'll look into it," said Goth. His leg spasmed slightly.

"Be discrete." Joli's brow furrowed.

"I have my sources," said Goth, showing her a predatory grin. "We'll know if anyone digs up any leads against your husband. Everything will be dealt with long before the tribunal touches him."

"You're too kind," said Joli. Political intrigue was Goth's strongest suit, but it concerned her that her assistant might learn unsavory details about her husband, information that could, in turn, provide him with leverage against her. "What is the current status of the tribunal?"

"As you would expect, it's all very preliminary. Without a nanogen in Council custody, or some other form of hard evidence, it's unlikely the tribunal can proceed." Giving her a sly glance, Goth added, "But perhaps now you'd prefer the tribunal not to go forward, given your husband's involvement?"

"Of course the tribunal must go forward," Joli said angrily. "The tribunal must publicly denounce the Order for developing the nanogens and punish the corrupt Order Elders. Only public pressure will rein in the Order's hold."

"Yes," Goth agreed hastily. "It would also be to our benefit for the Council to gain full control over the Order once and for all."

"This isn't only about Council control," Joli snapped, raising her chin as she always did when she made moral proclamations. "Getting control over the Order is the only way to ensure the continuance of the human race. The Order's covert plans to use nanotechnology to speed up human evolution are absurd. If we leave our evolution up to the Order, in a few generations we'll have forgotten what it was to be human."

"Of course," Goth said. He bowed his head slightly, but his attempt to conceal a smirk was unsuccessful. He had learned more information than he had ever thought possible; information that held great power. But he would remain loyal — at least, for as long as the success of his career depended on Joli.

|.|.|...|||...|.|..|

Humans were meant to live underground; at least, that was the Cadet's theory. Being born and raised in the tunnels had made him strong, fast and hard. And he expected, unless things changed, to die in the tunnels; like his parents who had been knifed to death by blackbase addicts looking for credit to buy their next fix. The Cadet had been too young to do anything then, but times had changed. Lurkers, addicts and conmen had learned that it was wise to steer clear of him.

The Underground offered everything the Earth's surface lacked: uncharted passages, privacy, danger and limitless contraband. While the Cadet spent a great deal of time gaming above ground, he felt most at ease in the claustrophobic tunnels, weaving in and out of crowds.

He'd spent his childhood slipping down hidden passageways and discovering forgotten service areas. Now he used these little-known routes to his advantage. He could pop up where he was least expected or quickly disappear when necessary. With its perpetual poverty and crime, life underground might be exhausting, but it was home.

In terms of access, security and location, the Cadet's place was a contraband dealer's paradise. Although only a closet size room, it was located at a criminal epicenter, near the most successful of Underground black markets. Order raids happened there so regularly they rarely caught anyone important. If the Cadet was ever accepted into the Order, he planned to improve their success rate. No amount of payoffs would keep him from getting rid of the thugs who ruled his Underground and terrorized the once safe neighborhoods. Tonight there had been an Order raid; he could tell by the emptiness of the tunnels.

Palming open the door to his quarters, a chute appeared and he dropped down. When he landed, the ceiling slid seamlessly together above his head. Nothing personal or valuable cluttered his tiny space. Intruders would gain little information about him, except that his security verged on paranoia. He lived like a Spartan, though he had the luxury of access to two surface entrances in the city, each chute leading directly to his quarters. The walls contained feedback screens that displayed recent communications as well as any activity within a two meter radius of each entrance. At the moment, all feeds showed only peaceful static and he could relax. Whatever else a raid might accomplish, it guaranteed a quiet night.

He unloaded gear from his bag, placing his tools and weapons in the wall for cleaning, then undressed and carefully hung up his MAMsuit. It was the best available, specially tailored to his biostats and possessing the ability to self-repair after any damage from a gaming session in Novus Orbis. Professional gamers like himself inflicted actual harm on each other in Novus Orbis — everything short of mortal injury. After a good game, the medics usually spent hours working on him in Vetus Orbis, repairing broken bones and closing wounds.

For the Cadet, coming home meant washing off the day's grit and a fitful sleep despite his exhaustion.

He was a gamer-for-hire, lived in the worst part of the Underground, and hunted petty criminals in his spare time. Everyone who knew him expected that it would only be a matter of time before something or someone got him.

While gaming for the many economic domus was dangerous, living in the Underground and hunting criminal

thugs amounted to a death warrant. Sooner or later the
gamer was bound to find himself in the wrong place at
the wrong time. For now he remained a brief celebrity
in the unwritten annals of the Underground.

The stakes in the games he played professionally were
high. How high, he made sure he never found out. Given
his take-home pay, he was making the right people happy
and rich. At twenty-three, he was at the top of his game,
yet his body ached from repeated injuries and he suffered pain that no amount of medical attention could
relieve. Sometimes he wondered how much more gaming
his body could withstand. Already, many of his friends
had left the sport for new opportunities and while gaming
offered excitement and paid the bills, the Cadet's true
ambition was to join the Order.

Too tired to drop down through the floor and find the
traveling wokman who sold overpriced fresh-cooked
meals, he settled for a heated dinner tube. The taste was
reasonable, but the texture was gooey and the meal
flowed too quickly from meat, broccoli and potatoes to
dessert.

The Cadet sat on his bed as he ate, thinking about the
extravagant feast he received each time he gamed for
Domus Aqua. The top utilities mogul was the Cadet's
favorite sponsor. The domus provided the most unusual
and succulent post-win banquets as well as time with
Lila, the Domus Master's daughter. Most recently, Domus
Aqua had paid him to represent them in a prestigious
set of games. The Cadet's fencing skills and quick tactical
mind had won him every set.

Curling under the bed blanket, he lay there wide-eyed.
Any prolonged time spent in Novus Orbis caused insomnia; it was a chronic problem among gamers for which
the medics had yet to find a cure. When his wall panels flashed the image of a small cloaked, hooded woman
at his city surface entrance, the Cadet felt almost relief
that he would not have to lie awake all night fighting
his insomnia.

He recognized his guest and smiled as he leapt out
of bed to deactivate his west-side perimeter defense.

Hearing her thud against his inner wall, he focused the external feed. Her face remained obscured by the hood, but close-up her style was unmistakable. His mentor's wife, the powerful Councilwoman Joli Byl, was paying the Cadet a rare visit.

She came nimbly into the little room, sweeping back her hood to reveal intricate, sapphired braids and her trademark freckled face. "My deepest apologies for the rough ride down. I had no idea it was you, Councilwoman."

"To you, I'm always Joli," she beamed. "It's been too long."

"Would you like anything to drink?" He was prepared to order whatever she wished.

"Unfortunately, I'm here on official business," Joli said, handing him her cloak, which he hung carefully beside his MAMsuit. "What I'm about to tell you must be kept in the strictest confidence."

The Cadet nodded. He was impressed that Joli had come in person to see him. It had never happened before.

"We have a dangerous situation, which needs to be handled with the utmost care and haste. It could cause mass hysteria." Joli paused to sit down across from him, and lowered her voice. "A nanogen has landed on Earth."

"A nanogen?" The Cadet looked her in the eyes. Was this some kind of weird joke? He saw no hint of humor, though Joli might as well have told him Dracula had knocked at her doorstep or that unicorns were real.

"A member of an aberrant, human-derived species is on Earth. It must be discreetly captured before it causes any damage."

"Where does it come from?"

"A research facility on Mars."

Joli seemed unnerved by his questions, but he couldn't stop himself. The Cadet rubbed the bristle on his jaw, as he often did when focusing on a problem. "Why is it here?"

"The nanogen was brought here as evidence against its creators to stand trial before an upcoming tribunal," Joli said. "It escaped custody."

"This is a breech of planetary security and the Order's jurisdiction," said the Cadet. "Are they trying to locate it?"

"Yes." Joli was flustered and answered too quickly. "They need help finding the nanogen. Your name came up."

Her rapid response made him cautious. "Why me?"

"As a professional gamer with Order Academy training, you are uniquely suited to find it. Apparently, it enjoys a special relationship with the MAM. It causes disturbances in Novus Orbis."

"Interesting." His heart was beating fast. This might be the opportunity he was looking for to get accepted into the Order. "What would I do if I discover where it's hiding, notify the Order?"

"I won't lie to you. Finding it may be difficult and dangerous. If you do, you'd need to notify the Council."

"Count me out. Sorry." The Cadet stood. Council and Order were so often at odds; he would not get caught between them.

"You won't consider the job?"

"I'd die for the challenge. You know that." The Cadet pointedly handed over her cloak. "But if anyone can and should find the nanogen, it's the Order."

Focused on the clasps of her cloak, she refused to look him in the eyes. "The Order recommended you to the Council."

"They did?" said the Cadet. That made him stop and think. If the Order and the Council were working together, this could be an opportunity to impress the Order. If he took the job, he wanted nothing to do with the Council.

"No offense, but my policy has always been to avoid politicians. They're dangerous — you excluded, of course. I won't report to the Council."

"How about if you report just to me?" she said, her eyes meeting his as she stepped so close they almost touched.

"May I report to the Order?" the Cadet asked, taking a step back. He trusted Joli, but she was still a councilwoman.

"No. It's a delicate situation," said Joli. She wrapped the cloak tighter around her. "You'd have to report only to me."

Worried that he had offended her, the Cadet wanted to put her at ease. "So the Order wants me to find the nanogen and report its location to you. That's it?"

"Tell me its location," said Joli, nodding. "We'll take care of the rest."

He felt confused and suspicious. This arrangement was not characteristic of the Order. As far as he knew, they always used their own operators. Maybe his gaming skills were worth something after all.

"I'll find it."

She nodded and pulled her hood forward so her face was obscured by fur. "I'll be in touch."

The Cadet helped her out the door and watched her glide gently to the surface. She looked deceptively small and frail for one who wielded such power. He had always felt much closer to Creid, who had been his mentor for years, but he had no reason not to trust her. She'd always been good to him. Still, he had the uneasy sensation that his role in the search might be part of a master plan to which he might never be privy.

Speculating on what he had gotten himself into made him thirsty. He decided that walking the still empty tunnels might clear his head. He made his way to Gil's Bar, where the familiar Underground ambiance of low ceilings, stuffiness and filth was further accentuated by the stink of cheap liquor. Gil slapped him on the back as soon as he entered. "Good to see you. The usual?"

Leading him to a reserved table in the back, Gil served him a glass of Benedictine. Besides being a local celebrity, the Cadet always tipped generously so Gil served him without watering down the booze or slipping extra charges on the bill.

Rumors

An angry couple ducked out from underneath a ragged tarp, which hung above the tunnel entrance leading to the dwelling place of the Ultimate Librarian. The Cadet listened with amusement to their conversation as they passed by him.

"He speaks gibberish." The girl threw up her hands. "Why would *you* be implanted to spy on offworlders?"

Her companion's hair was slicked back and around his thick neck hung a string of rare Europan pearls. He flashed an uneasy smile and said, "I work for the Office of Tourism, planning vacations."

"There's nothing top secret in that." Her eyes were wide and innocent. As young as she was, her hair and skin already showed the gray tint common in the Underground.

"He's just a crazy whiz waste. What did you expect?" The man hugged her close and they edged past the Cadet and the others waiting in line to hear the Oracle.

Ducking underneath the tarp, the Cadet smelled acrid sweat and stale air. Behind the rough curtain, the narrow tunnel unexpectedly opened onto an echoing dark cavern. The Cadet stopped for a moment to get his bearings. As his eyes adjusted, he could make out his old friend, the Ultimate Librarian, swinging high above him in a harness suspended from the ceiling while a movable platform beneath him provided support from below. Nutrient packs, neatly arranged, lined the walls along with every sort of gadget and spare part, which the Cadet guessed were used to repair the Ultimate Librarian's ancient MAMmask.

The mask was not only ancient, but uniquely modified. One of UL's eyes had been permanently attached, which allowed the Ultimate Librarian to constantly be in both Novis Orbis and Vetus Orbis. With this unusual contraption molded to his face, the Oracle terrified most visitors, although not the Cadet. No one knew how long UL had been there or what he'd done before he became an Underground fixture.

The gamer found that asking questions of the Ultimate Librarian was like talking to a sphinx. Although often mysterious, UL knew a great deal about everything and whatever he didn't know, he could find out or predict. Unfortunately, it had been months since the Cadet had visited his old friend.

Recognizing the gamer, UL immediately lowered his platform so that the Cadet could climb onboard and ascend to join him among the rafters.

"Here you are at last." The Ultimate Librarian's voice was rough and dry, followed by a hacking cough. "I've been watching your activities. You're a fun one to follow."

While UL had his mask fully over his face, the Cadet found talking to him disconcerting. There was no way to read his expressions.

Settling into a seat on the platform, the gamer came directly to the point. "I have a situation," he said. "Have you heard rumors that a nanogen was brought to Earth and then escaped captivity?"

"Yes," said UL, but said nothing more.

"Well?" The Cadet was impatient. "Does it actually exist?"

"Maybe."

"I can't find any MAM reference."

"No time to visit, eh?" UL drew directly from MAM archives. "Very well. According to current terminology references, a nanogen is a derogatory term for a new species derived from nanogenetically modified human embryos. In theory, the transfer of genes horizontally between non-breeding species is taken one step beyond to break down barriers between organic and inorganic life..."

"I am not looking for dictionary definitions. I want the real thing: a living, breathing version," the Cadet said.

"For that, ask your pals," UL said and chuckled fiercely, unlocking the mask from around his head. Only his eye remained attached to the ancient, heavy mask.

"What pals?" The Cadet frowned.

"Sorry." UL grinned shamelessly and swung close to the Cadet. "I play the Oracle too much these days. It makes me ornery. You should have seen the idiot who was just here with his poor girlfriend. He wanted to know if he's up for a promotion."

The Cadet laughed. "I saw them. You pissed them off."

"All in a day's work." UL had seemed to warm up to him. "What investigation have you done?"

"I've searched the major data banks and many of the obscure ones. I've gone to the gaming sites, hung out in all kinds of Novus Orbis public meeting places and even dropped in on my contacts at the Order," said the Cadet. "I've followed insider channels at the Academy, but can't find anyone who knows anything about nanogenetic engineering of human embryos beyond theoretical research. The only ones who take the concept seriously are quack conspiracy theorists."

"I learn a lot from conspiracy theorists," UL said. He seemed to find humor in the Cadet's frustration.

The young man pounded his fist against his seat. "With my luck, nanogens are probably just some scientist's wet dream."

"You won't hear anything about them in public spheres." The Oracle hesitated for a moment and added. "My advice is stay away from this one."

The Cadet felt a chill of fear. It was not like UL to caution him. "Why?"

"Frankly, it reeks of the Order."

With a sigh of relief, the gamer said, "I'm working jointly for the Order and the Council so that doesn't worry me."

"The Order and Council collaborating, now that's a first." UL peered into the Cadet's face. "Be careful. Something's rotten; I can smell it."

"All I can smell is you," The Cadet said to make light of his growing apprehension. "Who should I talk to?"

"If you follow my advice, no one." UL sighed. "Since you're so determined, talk to the ones you're busy making rich."

"That's too vague. I've gamed for all the top domus."

"Guess."

"Domus Aqua." The young man chose the most prestigious.

"You didn't hear that from me." UL coughed nervously.

"What do they have to do with nanogens?"

"You'd better call them by their proper name," UL said sternly, swinging away from the Cadet to get a nutrient pack from the wall.

"Which is?"

"The Imagofas." The name rolled off his tongue as though he were introducing royalty to a commoner. "The Magus have been predicting their coming for half a century. And honestly, to answer your earlier question, I only heard a rumor about the domus. Nothing substantive."

"What rumor?" The Cadet was determined to cull more information from UL before his time was up.

"Rumor has it the domus bought one. Some captain ran around bragging to all the wrong people how much he was making off the deal and ended up with his throat slit in Blackbase Alley."

"You're repeating addict hearsay?" the Cadet asked. UL had apparently sunk to new lows.

"You'd be surprised what I learn from blackbase enthusiasts. Not everyone is a good boy like you."

The Cadet was used to UL's habitual taunts. He changed the subject. "Why would the Domus Aqua take such a risk?"

"Ask them," said UL. He lowered the platform so that the Cadet understood he was dismissed.

"I don't know what I'd do without your help," the Cadet said, leaping down and bowing deeply before the Ultimate Librarian.

"Get out," UL said, smiling. "Come by sooner next time — with less annoying questions."

Pausing at the cavern entrance before leaving, the Cadet asked, "Just out of curiosity, did that guy with his girlfriend really have a spy implant?"

"Sort of. He's a spy for the Order. Everyone knows it, except his girlfriend. Tourism doesn't dare fire him, but he's got no chance of promotion." UL clamped the MAMmask back down over his face. The Cadet ducked underneath the tarp at the tunnel entrance and a woman rushed past him. A long line of customers had formed.

Oracles never used to be this popular. The Cadet slipped into a side tunnel to avoid the crowd.

Traveling down the tunnels at an easy jog, the Cadet wondered about Domus Aqua. It was primarily a utilities powerhouse specializing in advanced communications. While UL was rarely wrong, the Cadet had difficulty imagining what the domus would want with something as illegal and potentially lethal as a nanogen. If the purchase became public knowledge, the domus would be ruined and the domus master punished, assuming the public could be convinced the Imagofas actually exist.

╷╻╷╻╻╻╻╻┃┃┃╻╻╷╻╷

Playing with his food always annoyed his wife, but tonight Creid had difficulty stopping himself. It was more than his lifelong dislike of meatloaf — even the gourmet rendering. His nerves made him fidget.

"Stop it, Creid. It's bad enough I have to stomach Goth's tics and twitches all day."

Creid pushed his plate away and the compactmaid snaked up and sucked it down.

"I hate that thing." Joli glowered at the appliance.

"I've been thinking about something you mentioned earlier today," Creid said, carefully weighing his words.

"Yes?" Joli's fingernails drummed on the table.

"Why did the Council select the Cadet to locate this being?" Creid ventured, "It seems an odd choice. He's a gamer, not an investigator."

"I don't know." Joli lied, pushing her own plate away without looking at him.

Creid sensed that she wasn't telling the truth and pressed for an answer. "Earlier this evening, you said he might come to ask me some questions. Like what?"

"Answer your own damn question. You're the one involved in this nanogen mess, not me." Joli hadn't intended to blurt out her suspicions. Too late, she rose and abruptly left the table. Moments later, he heard her getting ready for bed.

Creid stayed up. His worries made sleep unlikely and tossing and turning would only irritate her.

The Cadet had become like a son to Creid. He valued the young man as a confidante. But now his wife was telling him that the tribunal had hired the gamer. He was surprised that the Cadet was willing to work at cross-purposes to the Order. The young man was perhaps the only person Creid knew who was bright and open-minded enough to follow the complex path of reasoning that had led Creid to this predicament. Maybe, if he explained himself to the gamer, went all the way back to the beginning, the Cadet would sympathize with what Creid had done. He sat in the darkening apartment and wondered what it would be like to finally break his oath of silence. To finally confess.

His highest priority however, was to protect the Imagofas' location until Dreyfus arrived. It had been years since they had worked together at the Order, years since they had even seen each other, but Creid trusted Dreyfus. He also trusted the Cadet and hoped he could enlist the young man's help to ensure that the Imagofas was safely delivered into his old colleague's care, so Dreyfus could return her to Mars.

Creid trusted the Cadet more than anyone. His fondness for the gamer went back half a decade, to when the young man had been the pride of the Order Academy. The Cadet had received the best marks in every class, regardless of subject. Cocky but undefeatable, he was the envy of his classmates. By graduation, his future seemed assured. Several divisions had vied for him and, as his advisor, Creid helped his protégé secure a position in Space Exploration, the most competitive division. Creid would have preferred the Cadet go into Research and Development, since that was where Creid had accomplished his life's work, but the youth did not share his love of engineering. Although he excelled at everything he did, at heart, the Cadet was a man of action.

Creid still remembered the evening he received a panicked call from one of the graduation judges. The testing had gone terribly wrong and the Cadet had flunked his comprehensive Ethics exam. The judge asked Creid to convince the Cadet to reconsider his choice before the test results were public. It was an unheard of gesture by the Academy. Creid expected that everything could be straightened out and that the Academy's star pupil could still graduate. He contacted the Cadet.

Full of bravado and the invincibility of youth, the Cadet refused to change a single answer or reconsider his actions. He told Creid, "Sir, after all you've done for me, I promise I will do anything for you, but not this. The Order sent us into the Underground to do a MAMresource shutdown and arrest some miniscule education group that was siphoning off resources from one of the domus. Undergrounders do it all the time because they can't afford MAM access. Some Ethics test! I can show you the location of three big-time illegal siphoners dealing in black market goods and drugs, which have never been busted. I refused to make an arrest. I know them all, and they're decent people."

The Cadet had disobeyed a direct command. He refused to admit he was wrong. Creid argued with him: there was no harm in following orders; these people had already been arrested; he wasn't helping anyone by ruining his career. Neither cajoling nor threats could move the youth.

For Creid, it was a hellish 24 hours. Standing on his principles, the Cadet flunked the Academy and his opportunities evaporated overnight. In the last few years, his tremendous skill and Creid's connections had made the Cadet a top gamer. And yet, the Order engineer had dreamed of so much more for his brilliant student and still held hopes for his future. Now with the Cadet embroiled in a chase to locate the Imagofas, it was Creid's turn to ask a favor.

Forgotten

Thesni glimpsed heaven and experienced hell, each within minutes of the other. At first she saw a tremendous azure sky and an expanse of brilliant green. Then, before she could take it all in, she felt Grant's smartgun jabbed painfully into her side.

He whispered, "When we land in the shuttle port, walk just ahead of me. Keep quiet unless you want to die."

With a fixed smile, Grant directed her through the shuttle port crowds who were exclaiming their relief to be off MIP, milling about and queuing up for Earthside customs. He directed her to the left then left again, until they were met by a uniformed customs officer.

"Grant, where the hell have you been?" the officer growled nervously. He led them past a group of other officers and through a door that read "Authorized Personnel Only." They went down several hallways and through more sliding doors, then outside onto a tarmac where a heliovan idled. Grant shoved Thesni into the back seat and joined the pilot up front.

"You're lucky I'm still here," the pilot said angrily. "Did you think I was going to wait all day for you?"

The heliovan took off and after a short flight arrived at an underground entrance. Moments later Grant was hustling Thesni into a narrow, poorly maintained tunnel where the air smelled toxic. Unaccustomed to Earth's gravity, she stumbled under the weight of her own legs. Finally, in frustration, the man hoisted her over his shoulder, carrying her past a horrible line of sickly looking people with glowing blue mouths and missing teeth, who mumbled their complaints.

Ignoring them, Grant took Thesni through a gate marked "Mission of Our Sorrows." He grunted a few words and passed some blue vials to a rotten-toothed, glowing mouthed man who silently pocketed what he was given, led them down dark hallway to a little windowless room, and left. Grant dropped Thesni unceremoniously on the floor. Then he, too, left, closing double doors behind him. Earth's gravity pulled at the Imagofas so that even breathing was difficult, and her rib cage felt as though it might collapse under the new weight. Thesni tried sitting, tried standing, tried lying down in every position to relieve the pressure. Nothing helped. Grant had abandoned her to waste away in a windowless room with two locked doors.

Before leaving he had given her several nutrient bars and pointed to the bathroom sink for water. "I promise to be back soon," he said. Though his hands shook noticeably when he left, Thesni had believed him. She ate the nutrient bars and waited for the fat man to come back and unlock the doors. Hours stretched into days, until her aching stomach and weakened limbs told her that something had gone terribly wrong. Grant was never coming back.

Ⅰ.ⅠⅠ.....ⅠⅠⅠ.....Ⅰ.Ⅰ.Ⅰ

Having bribed his contact at the mission using his personal stash of blackbase, Grant needed to secure a few vials of his own before meeting Angel's associate at Domus Aqua. As a supplier, he'd never before had to cruise Blackbase Alley in search of the drug, and the prospect scared him.

"Just one vial," he muttered to himself, angry at having had to give over his meager stash for immediate entrance to the mission. As he now planned to go behind Angel's back and cut a deal directly with the domus, he desperately needed a hit of blackbase to build up his courage.

At Gil's bar, Grant took a corner seat to survey the room. He ignored the "Reserved" sign on the table, and sipped watered down whiskey. He hated Undergrounders and their cheap liquor. He kept an eye out for bluegrazers; he'd know them by their rotten, blue-edged mouths. They would direct him to a small-time seller. He'd buy quickly and get out before any of Angel's men happened by.

Grant didn't have long to wait. Two bluegrazers walked in through a side entrance near the bar. They were bickering loudly over who would buy the drinks. Grant waved them over.

"I'll get you drinks. Sit down. Sit down," he said, expansively. The tall thin man looked him over and glanced at his even scrawnier companion before they quietly slid in on either side of him. Grant ordered them a line of shots. After they drank those down, he ordered another. The owner slammed down each set of watered down booze without a word and immediately took Grant's credit, as though he suspected they might all bolt without paying. Grant endured this humiliation with a forced smile.

"Either of you two might know where I could get some stuff, do you?" Grant asked, clinking the side of his glass against theirs in false camaraderie. Despite the watered down drink, the liquor had begun to make him woozy. He needed to get his business done and get back above ground to meet his domus contact.

"Mr. Generous," said the scrawny one to his friend. "Why don't you share some of your blackbase? After all, the gentleman just bought us drinks."

"Shut up, Loser," Mr. Generous said and boxed Loser's ears, evoking a howl of pain. The owner glared over at their table.

"I'm not asking for any freebies," Grant said quickly. "I'll pay double for a vial."

"Loser has a point. You bought us drinks and we should return the favor," Mr. Generous said, opening his vest. Grant saw a half-dozen tiny blackbase vials woven into the fabric. "Only, we should do this out back so Gil doesn't have a fit."

They got up and went toward the side door, Mr. Generous and Loser flanking Grant on either side. The bar owner gave Grant a warning look, but the captain just smiled nervously and left with them. Out in the dark, deserted tunnel, Mr. Generous handed Grant a vial. Flicking open the tiny container, he touched its tip to the underside of his tongue. The surge of euphoria was instantaneous, and his confidence soared a hundred-fold.

"Thanks, I'll just be off now," Grant said. He pushed Mr. Generous aside, feeling unstoppable.

The tall one hooked the captain's arm. "Hey, not so fast. We could use some of your credit."

"Sure," Grant said. He had a laserknife hidden in his belt.

Just then, Gil's back door opened and out stepped a big man whose arms were covered with three-dimensional animated tattoos. Grant recognized him as Marty — one of Angel's top henchmen. Close behind, a greasy-looking lurker followed him out the door.

"I see we've got a bluegrazer party going on here," Marty said. "You two beat it. The captain and I have some business."

"Hey, Marty, whatever you say," Mr. Generous said, his voice quivering. He dropped Grant's arm and edged away, yanking the scrawnier Loser with him. "We were just trying to increase sales."

Grant was still coasting on the blackbase's euphoria. He laughed at the bluegrazers and their stupid rotten mouths. He laughed at Marty and the tattoos that slithered across his thick arms. Marty turned on him with a cold evaluating look of malice.

"Where did you stash the nanogens, Grant?" Marty asked.

"I'd never tell you," Grant said through a fog of pleasure. He could no longer resist boasting. "I'm going to be rich, so rich, richer than anybody you've ever met. I'll buy all your drinks."

"How so?" Marty said, his grip on Grant's arm becoming so hard that if Grant hadn't been high, he'd have screamed in agony.

"It's a secret where I keep my treasure," said Grant in a singsong voice. A hysterical laugh bubbled up into his throat, as he managed to open his belt and slide out the laserknife without Marty noticing.

"Where did you hide them?" Marty demanded, his voice now a threatening growl.

"That you'll never know," Grant said and jammed the knife into Marty's gut. The knife tore through the vest, but only scraped against the armor beneath it.

Enraged, Marty twisted the knife out of the captain's hand and in one smooth motion whipped its blade across his neck. Grant stepped back, shocked, his hands to his throat. For a second, he felt the warm blood gush over his fingers before he fell against the tunnel wall.

IılıiıılIIIıılılıl

After all that Thesni had been through — the kidnapping, the long imprisonment on a cargo ship, the colossal explosion at MIP, the descent to Earth and the passage through stinking tunnels — it seemed impossible that Grant had just locked her away to die in a grimy room far beneath the Earth's surface. And yet, he hadn't returned.

"I am Imagofas," said Thesni, determined not to panic. "I shape my own fate."

She sank to her knees in the middle of the room and concentrated, sending her mind where her legs could not take her. Desperation gave way to a hunger-induced calm and she searched beyond the walls for small bursts of energy, anything that might provide system contact. Logically, she knew the doors must operate on a security system. In theory, she should be able to block its power source long enough to wedge the door open. It might be a long shot, but she had to try.

She followed the power source that provided the room's light, security and a strange, distant connection that might be the MAM. After the intricacies of the ship, following this power source appeared surprisingly simple, as though traveling the outer rungs of a spider web inward to its hub. Yet when Thesni came to what should be the web's center, she encountered instead a new set of webs.

Mentally retracing her way back to the room, she came upon a series of unfamiliar junctures and panicked. Turning one way, then another, she became flustered and breathless. Unable to work her way back through the mental steps she'd taken, she stopped. She rested at an anonymous juncture of light where power surged and ebbed in a mystifying rhythm. No real power center existed, only insignificant miniscule powerhubs, which fed subsystems of no interest to her. Disoriented by trying to double back, Thesni wandered the outskirts of one fail-safe after another, each activated intermittently to keep the Underground running.

Getting trapped in these powerwebs made Thesni think of Sashimu. Her friend knew how to react in a crisis and acted immediately. On the ship, it had been Sashimu's idea to outmaneuver their captors and send the communication to Zazen from Novus Orbis.

If Novus Orbis was as ubiquitous on Earth as their guardians had claimed, Thesni could access it. Once in, she'd contact Sashimu, who might still be alive. Together, they'd escape.

Thesni followed this small thread of hope, finding a route beyond panic and fatigue. Focusing on the power juncture, she forced herself to relax long enough to distinguish its different energy pulses. She reasoned that unlike other powerusers, Novus Orbis required uninterrupted energy.

Instead of backtracking, Thesni searched for a connection to the MAM, which she'd felt on the ship both times Brooks had opened a MAMsession for her. Halfway to the next power juncture, Thesni stopped abruptly. After letting her guard down, she suddenly visualized tiny threads hanging beneath every powerhub that all led down into a tangled blue abyss. She heard a familiar static sound, then an intense vertigo overcame her. The ephemeral world of Novus Orbis resolved to a tiny room with two locked doors identical to the one in which she was trapped, but here in the MAM, Thesni had company. The avatar of a man with long dreadlocks in an oversized tee-shirt and baggy pants stood over her.

"Damn! How the hell did you piggyback on my session?" the man demanded, giving Thesni a hard look.

"Who are you?" asked Thesni, staring up at him in astonishment.

"I'm a sysadmin and no, I don't have any credit for your blackbase fix or whatever it is you want."

"I need help." Thesni said, determined to remain in his session.

"Everyone here needs help. That's why they call it a mission." He shrugged.

"I'm trapped. My door is locked so I accessed the MAM. Help me get out," pleaded Thesni.

"What nonsense." He flung up his arms. "Look, I'm here to help clean up mission systems. That's all the Open MAM Movement does. Besides, I've never heard of a mission shelter locking in people. It's strictly voluntary."

"If you don't help me, I'll destroy your work," Thesni said. In truth, she was unsure how she might cause damage. The complex interfaces, which flew around the walls and bounced to his every gesture, were unfamiliar to her. As he snapped his fingers, she used her Imagofas senses to follow his calls to the MAM. It seemed as though he was simply opening and closing multiple MAMinterfaces, which appeared and disappeared as sparkling colorful boxes floating in the space between them. Working quickly, she reversed his final call to the system and one of his interfaces popped into view again.

"How did you manage that? My work is encrypted," he said, stepping back in shock.

With no idea how to further manipulate them, Thesni did nothing more, but his alarmed expression showed she'd at least succeeded in rattling him.

"Who are you?" he said, cautiously.

"Thesni of the Imagofas." She bowed low.

"Imagofas?" His mouth dropped open in awe. "The Magus predicted your coming, but I never really believed it."

Backing away from her, he called up another MAMinterface that drew a clear, shimmering protective wall around him. Every move he made taught her more about the system, but she still knew too little to escape either the Novus or Vetus Orbis confines.

"I never believed the Imagofas existed," he said, taking another step to put more distance between them.

If she hadn't been so tired and hungry, Thesni might have found him amusing. Right now, all she wanted was her freedom. "I was left in Vetus Orbis to die. But here in Novus Orbis, I can't find my way back to my cell. Will you help me?"

He studied her for a long moment then abruptly dropped the wall between them and bowed. "My name is Ochbo. And yes, I'll help you, but where are you?"

"I wish I knew." Thesni shook her head. "My room looks just like this one."

"In the mission shelter, the rooms are identical." Ochbo frowned. "To piggyback on my session, you must be nearby. When I end my session, you should be exited automatically. Do you know under what name you're registered?"

"No. But the man who locked me in here is named Grant."

"No one checked in as Grant." Ochbo flipped through one interface after another. "Do you know how long you've been here?"

"I'd guess a week." Her body felt like it had been ages.

"Looks like the usual stay is two nights max." Ochbo made furious hand gestures dragging data across the walls and floor. "How many times have you been in and out?"

"I've never left. I'm locked in." She thought a moment. "Grant came in with me and left right afterwards."

The data shrank until there was only one number that throbbed in his palm. "At least they track their staff. Only a few rooms haven't been cleaned and inspected in the last week. Of those, only one shows no recent entrance activity." Ochbo looked up triumphantly. "See you in Vetus Orbis."

As Ochbo exited, Thesni had the sensation she was free-falling hundreds of meters only to smash into her body at a terrible velocity. The shock of reconnection left her immobilized, but she felt grateful to be out of the powerweb. Ochbo's promise to help her get out brought the faint stirring of hope.

Many minutes passed as she lay in dizzy, exhausted silence against the floor. She could see the faucet across the small room. It had kept her alive, but now it seemed so far away. *Patience*, she told herself.

The door shuddered and trembled, but refused to open. She heard someone cursing, followed by a screeching of

metal against metal. There were two voices: one sounded
like Ochbo yelling while the other was responding in a low
measured tone. She understood none of it, but lifted her
head slightly as the door slid open.

"You see, I told you there was someone in here." Ochbo
glared angrily at the missionary who glanced in revulsion
at Thesni. He had the bitter countenance of a man who'd
seen enough addicts to last a lifetime.

"I'd no idea she snuck in here," the missionary muttered and disappeared back down the tunnel.

Ochbo stepped inside and bowed to the ground. He was
even more unkempt in Vetus Orbis.

"You're beautiful." His face was full of wonder. "In
Novus Orbis, you were little more than a shadow."

"Water." Her voice was a tiny croak. She lay still, unable
to rise.

Regaining his composure, Ochbo rushed to her side.
Lifting her easily, he helped her to the faucet and pulled
her long, tangled blonde hair aside. The water was cold
and delicious. She felt the tingling ease and strength
returned to her limbs. "Thank you."

"Can you walk?"

"Yes, I think so, but I'm very weak." Taking his hand,
she stood shakily and asked, "Where are you taking me?"

"Don't worry. I won't let anything happen to you. I'll
take you to the Sanctuary."

"They'll help me there?"

"I bet they'll give you whatever you ask." His words
sounded too good to be true, but the alternative seemed
bleak.

"What if I prefer to disappear into Hades' tunnels?"

"You mean the Underground?" he asked, puzzled.
"You're free to go wherever you want."

She was relieved that he was willing to let her go.

"Do as you like, but if you need help, you should know
that the Sanctuary's doors will always be open to you,"
he said, helping her through the door. That was enough
for Thesni. She needed choices. If he'd forced her, she would
have fled.

"Take me there," she said.

Ochbo guided her down the long narrow tunnel to a courtyard where the same sour-faced man who had previously accompanied Ochbo, opened the mission gates to let them out. Outside the gates, Ochbo and Thesni passed by a long line of forlorn faces who waited for a room, their mouths glowing eerily from blackbase; their belongings piled in small heaps beside themselves.

"Cleanlife pervert," a woman spat at Ochbo and pushed past him. Her teeth were rotting from blackbase.

Further down the tunnel they took a shuttle to an upper level. Here the lighting and air improved.

"What did that woman mean?" Thesni whispered.

"She recognized me as OMM. We have a clean living policy."

"That made her mad?"

"The Open MAM Movement supports outreach programs. That includes missions like the one you were in, which allow addicts to stay as long as they're 'clean.' She wasn't." Ochbo shrugged. "Maybe they kicked her out."

Turning the corner, they reached a crowded dimly lit cavern where people hawked various goods piled on tables, bellowing over the noise of the crowd to attract customers. People pushed past them in droves, but no one paid her any notice. She clung to Ochbo's arm, and he didn't seem to mind.

"I'm too weak to go much further." Days of forced fasting left her with little energy.

Ochbo looked down at her with concern. "I would have taken the URT, but assumed you don't have an ID."

"The URT?"

"Underground Rapid Transit." He eyed her skeptically. "Everyone knows that. We're almost to a Sanctuary hub where we'll take a private train. Can you make it?"

She nodded, forcing her legs to move at his death march pace. A moment later, he turned off the crowded area into an empty side tunnel, which dead-ended at an enormous vent filthy with dust and debris. To the left of the vent was an ancient service door. She saw no palming device for identification. Ochbo grabbed the rusted metal knocker and tapped several times with his big thick fingers. Thesni heard a click and a small face appeared in the door. "Pass-word?" the man rasped through the hole in the door.

Ochbo groaned. "You know who I am. Let me pass."

"No." The long gray face disappeared. Ochbo tapped harder this time and the face returned. "The password."

"This is an emergency or I wouldn't be using Sanctuary transport. Understand?" Ochbo was exasperated, but the man was unmoved. "Look, the only password I was ever given was 'ora et labora,' but that was months ago."

The long face broke into a large grin, and the door opened. Ochbo nearly pounced on the old man. "Joseph, you're supposed to change your passwords more than once every six months."

"I recognized you," Joseph said, chuckling, and ges-tured to an ancient severely dented bullet-nosed train covered with dust and grime, which looked as though it hadn't operated in years. "Where you headed?"

"Sanctuary central," said Ochbo.

Joseph used a hand crank mounted on the train door to open it wide enough for the three of them to step up and inside the car. Ochbo sat across from Thesni on the cracked orange seats and they watched as Joseph climbed slowly into the front cabin. Suddenly, the car jolted to life, rattling and clanking so that Thesni worried it might fall to pieces beneath them even before they had budged so much as an inch. Once the train began to move, the clanking stopped and the vehicle rapidly gained speed, hurtling past empty platforms. Thesni clung to the seat to avoid being thrown forward into Ochbo's lap.

No one spoke until, after what seemed like an hour, the train abruptly decelerated and ground to a halt. Joseph cranked open the door, giving them just enough time to step down onto the platform before speeding away.

"I don't feel so good," Thesni said. Her legs were shak-ing as she looked up at the great flight of stone stairs that disappeared into the darkness. "This is so bizarre."

"What's bizarre?" asked Ochbo, taking her arm to support her.

"Why do you still use stairs?" Thesni asked in exaspera-tion. "And why give verbal passwords or have Joseph hand opening doors and driving an antique train? I thought Earth was supposed to be so much more advanced than Mars."

Ochbo looked at her in surprise. "The Sanctuary is selectively anti-technology. These days, direct human contact is the best security. It leaves no reliable data trail."

To Thesni's relief, instead of taking the stairs, he led her underneath them into a small brightly lit room.

"Welcome to my office," Ochbo said, smiling. "I'll get us some breakfast. The Imagofas eat human food, right?"

Thesni nodded and sat down on the worn couch that obviously served as a bed. As soon as he was gone, she pushed the stained quilt and pillow to the far end and laid her head down.

|.|.|...|||..|.|..|

Waking from a deep sleep to the strong aroma of bacon, eggs, and other foods, Thesni instantly sat up. On his spacious desk, Ochbo was laying out dozens of dishes — an amazing variety of things to eat. "I may have overdone it," he said, with a sheepish grin.

Thesni began with the soup and ended with a bacon-egg sandwich slathered in syrup. Ochbo watched her in awe as she ate every last bit of food. He returned to the mess hall for more fruit, and then she was finally satiated.

Her stomach swollen and feeling slightly nauseated, Thesni sat back and smiled. "Now I can really sleep."

"I must notify the Sanctuary Elders that you've arrived." Ochbo fidgeted with his shirt collar as though it had suddenly grown too tight around his neck.

"Can't we just sleep for a bit before you announce me?" She was fighting to keep her eyes open.

He seemed almost relieved at her suggestion. He yawned drowsily and lay down at the foot of the couch. She watched him toss about for a while and then leave, locking the door behind him. She heard the extra hiss of a seal lock and wondered whether if she wanted to, she was still free to go.

|.|.|...|||..|.|..|

While Thesni slept after her first real meal on Earth, Ochbo left his office. He paced the length of the Sanctuary Central platform, thinking about what had happened. He felt awed at having encountered something much greater than himself. That feeling quickly gave way to a terrible sense of burden. In the course of a mundane day, he had met and rescued an Imagofas. Now this beautifully sublime creature slept defenseless on his couch and there was no one but him to protect her.

Unfortunately, she would need more than Ochbo could provide, and it occurred to him that the Magus might help. Ochbo didn't know any Magus monks personally, but having often passed them proselytizing on the street corners, he had heard their prophecy. Their diviners predicted that a new age was coming, brought on by the arrival of an advanced human race with nano-DNA. If anyone could understand and help Thesni, it would be the Magus.

He made up his mind and turned to climb the winding back stairs of the Sanctuary to where the administrative offices of the Magus and other new religions had been relegated. Outside their enormous metal doors, embossed with many incomprehensible symbols, Ochbo hesitated a moment before palming the door. Nervous sweat dripped down the side of his face as he entered an anteroom. A young woman in the customary chameleon-robes of the Magus came out from behind her desk to greet him.

"Are you interested in finding out more about the Magus or are you here for an appointment?" she asked, smiling serenely at him and seeming to look through him as she spoke.

"Neither, actually," Ochbo said, looking around apprehensively. "I am here to see the Great Diviners."

A trace of annoyance flitted across the young woman's face replaced quickly by another sweet smile. "Our Great Diviners rarely give audience to the public, but the Chief Magus is in today. Though perhaps I can be of help?"

"Yes," said Ochbo, thinking quickly. "Let me introduce myself: Ochbo of the Open MAM Movement, at your service. I have an important issue to discuss with the Chief Magus."

"My name is Erlinda," the woman said, then bowed. Activating her Companion, she spoke softly into it and then added, "The Chief Magus is available and would like to meet you."

Trying to remain outwardly calm despite his anxiety, Ochbo waited and hoped the Chief Magus would believe him, even if what he had to say seemed incredible, and offer Thesni protection.

"This way," Erlinda said. He followed her back through a sumptuous hall, its walls draped in heavy curtains, then into a plain, beige room with a table and chairs. She bade him sit at the table, then took a seat beside him.

The Chief Magus entered, a mature man in chameleon-robes with a gold sash around his middle, his hood thrown back to reveal long black hair and deep-set eyes. Erlinda and Ochbo stood to bow, then resumed their seats. The Chief Magus sat beside Ochbo and said, "You have met Erlinda. She deals with many of our technical issues. I am Alex, the Chief Magus. We're very happy to have the OMM volunteering their support. We've only recently been accepted at the Sanctuary as a new religion, though we have existed for many years."

"Yes, well," said Ochbo, "while I do represent the OMM, I'm here about a more important issue." He moved restlessly in his chair, hesitating momentarily before continuing. "Look, I'm going to tell you what has just happened to me today and see what you make of it."

Both Alex and Erlinda listened in complete silence to Ochbo's account of freeing Thesni from the mission and Thesni's admission that she was an Imagofas. Alex was the first to react with a good-natured chuckle and a skeptical expression on his face.

"Well, Ochbo, if you weren't with the OMM, I might assume you'd been conned by some blackbase addict," Alex said with a strange glint in his deep set eyes. "The fact that Thesni needs no MAMsuit to enter Novus Orbis is indeed interesting, as is her declaration of being an Imagofas. The Great Diviners have been expecting this event. Do you know who her enemies are or why she was locked away in a mission?"

"No, not yet," Ochbo said with a frown. "I only know that she'll be in danger as an Imagofas on Earth — not simply from those who locked her away, but because of what she represents."

"Agreed," Alex said, thoughtfully rubbing his chin. "I will put the matter before our Great Diviners. Please be aware, however, that the Great Diviners take their time in coming to any kind of decisions regarding worldly events, and the Magus has never been known to provide protection except in cases of immediate threat. We believe the Imagofas are part of humanity's destiny, but that destiny must unfold without interference from the Magus or others. If she is an Imagofas, her destiny is her own, as is yours or mine. Only in the face of a direct threat, to her person or her soul, would the Magus be inclined to intervene."

"I see," Ochbo said darkly. "If it comes to the Imagofas being directly threatened, I only hope that your help will not come too late."

"Your disappointment is understood and, as I said, I will speak to the Great Diviners. May you and yours be safe until we meet again, Ochbo of the OMM," Alex said gravely. He stood, bowed and left the room.

Erlinda gestured silently for Ochbo to follow her out, but halfway down the hallway she stopped at a curtained door. Behind it was a storeroom, where she found two chameleon-robes. "Normally these are given only to our members after they have studied and become acolytes. They are very useful when one wishes to avoid being seen," Erlinda said quietly. "Please take these as a token of our respect for you and your new friend."

"Thank you, Erlinda," Ochbo said, taking the robes under his arm and bowing.

Outside the Magus doors, Ochbo took the stairs down in leaps. He was concerned that he had betrayed Thesni's confidence without receiving any real assurance from the Magus that they would help keep her safe. He would just have to find a way to protect her on his own.

Miracle

Sashimu knew she was being watched. She struggled to open her eyes and shift her head, but the effort proved fruitless. Bandages kept her in a cool, relentless darkness and a LifeSustainer flew above her constantly monitoring her biostats and periodically swooping down to replace bandages or supply pain medication and fluids. She recognized the perfume of the soft-spoken woman who had introduced herself as Medic Danf, but the other was a stranger.

"Alice Chi-gu-sa," said the man, separating the syllables of the last name.

"Her parents are dead," Medic Danf replied more hastily and solicitously than usual. "I feel so sorry for her. It will take forever for those burns to heal and the scarring will be devastating."

"But she's alive," the man said. "You've done miracles. If this keeps up, we'll have to recommend you for a special recognition award."

"It's all her. Alice is the miracle." She rustled about, bending so close her mint breath wafted over Sashimu.

"You are too modest." His baritone voice grated on Sashimu's ears.

"Alice Chigusa received the same treatment as the other survivors, except that she was assigned time in Novus Orbis, which is unusual," Danf said. "According to the files the medic who ordered the Novus Orbis treatment is named Leonardo, but MIP officials claim there isn't any medic by that name."

"Forget the medic. MIPs are odd. It's the moon dust. I guarantee we've got better methods. You're proof of that. Besides, I can't imagine placing her in a MAMsuit. A MAM-lite Companion is about all she could handle with the severity of those burns. How could that be beneficial?"

"That's just it," she said, puzzled. "According to her file, she's had sessions in this room, but she's never been in a MAMsuit."

"There's no mystery. Obviously, the sessions never took place, but were only scheduled." He made a small noise of approval. "Now nothing can keep you from taking credit for your own skill. Let's get lunch."

They walked out and the door hissed closed behind them. Sashimu was confident that she would continue to self-heal and recover without terrible disfigurement. Her body, however, remained inert. While she fought desperately for control so that she might remove the bandages herself, a mild electric shock ran through her. She felt a sudden sense of vertigo and nausea.

ılıdıılllhııldıl

Across a vast vista of white, Sashimu discerned a small black dot moving towards her. As it came closer, it acquired color and definition, and slowly took on the form of Prometheus at a great distance. While she watched his approach, she experimented with movement. Her Herculean legs looked like massive tree trunks, but they weren't too big to move. Sashimu somersaulted, cartwheeled and flipped many times, surprised at the agility of her colossal frame.

Prometheus came to her as she was laughingly executing a somersault. When Sashimu righted herself, her world was suddenly full of color — the sky above a brilliant azure and the earth beneath her covered in deep green moss. Prometheus stood out against both in his black velvet with a high collar. Before them both stretched a patchwork quilt of rolling fields blooming with red poppies. A cool spring breeze played lightly against her cheeks. She breathed deeply and coughed.

"You brought color." Sashimu felt almost lighthearted. "The scents are slightly synthetic, but the rest is beautiful."

"Maybe your equipment is not advanced enough to capture the scent nuances." Prometheus sniffed.

"I access Novus Orbis raw without equipment," Sashimu said proudly. "Here I'm free, while in Vetus Orbis, I'm wrapped in bandages with a LifeSustainer constantly hovering overhead."

"Interesting. Imagofas capability observed and archived." Prometheus stood expressionless for several moments. "How does it smell now?"

"I smell manure." Sashimu crinkled her nose. "That is one way to mask a flower's perfume."

Prometheus grinned, momentarily pleased at his success. They walked silently through the field. When they came to a spring under the shade of several willows, he ran ahead of her as though drawn by some invisible force. She found him behind a willow crouched over the water.

"What are you doing?" Sashimu's curiosity got the better of her as she edged up beside him.

He repeatedly scooped a small gourd into the stream to catch a large catfish, obviously an impossible task.

"I am trying to resolve a problem." Prometheus concentrated on his labors. "How do you catch a catfish with a gourd?"

"Do you have to catch that size catfish with such a small gourd?" Sashimu was incredulous. He simply nodded and continued scooping.

Sashimu watched him for a long while before she made a suggestion.

"You could cut off the narrow neck of the gourd and scoop up the fish," Sashimu offered. "Or, place catfish eggs in the gourd and wait for them to grow into full-size catfish."

Her solutions seemed to depress Prometheus. His shoulders sagged forward and his face drew into a concentrated scowl, but he continued scooping.

"Don't lose hope." Sashimu placed her hand on his shoulder. "Maybe it would help me to know the context for the problem. Stop for a moment and explain."

"I must solve the problem within its parameters without changing the gourd or catfish." Prometheus sighed deeply. "The problem is an ancient koan. If I succeed in my solution, I will prove my sentience."

"A koan?" Sashimu was surprised. "Koans are used as aids in attaining enlightenment. It's strange that you were programmed to attempt sentience, let alone enlightenment. That's against interplanetary law. Why, we're more alike than I guessed. My very existence is a violation."

Prometheus gazed at her, his body bent motionless over the gourd.

"To penetrate a koan as I understand it, you have to follow a koan curriculum," Sashimu said, recalling Zazen's lessons on ancient Zen Buddhist philosophy. "Daily rituals and meditation are required while studying a koan. Also, you'd usually have a teacher."

"I have access to all the literature in Earth's databases on koans and their commentary," Prometheus assured her. "I have full descriptions of monastic life, koan main cases, secondary cases and detailed historical, as well as religious texts. I have dedicated all my resources to solve this particular koan for twenty-three years, two days and 3.23 hours."

"You've been at this longer than I've been alive," Sashimu bowed. "Look, I'm no teacher. I'm not sure what I can do."

As Prometheus returned to the water, she felt compelled to lighten his mood and hoped smart intelligence was not prone to breakdown or self-destruction. "Perhaps solving your koan is a quest to realize your identity."

Her speculation germinated an idea. Having been cast into the arms of this smart intelligence felt like the work of her goddess, Juno. It was possible Prometheus was part of an elaborate test, but it did not feel like it. Either way, she sensed that Prometheus was inextricably linked to her salvation. Together they might define a different destiny for themselves than that planned by humanity.

Since as far back as she could remember, she had been taught that she would lead the Imagofas. Despite her situation, she clung to this belief. One day soon, she would save Thesni and return to Mars to guide her people. Prometheus would help. She knew this suddenly with all her being. Juno had sent her Prometheus. She welcomed the gift.

Before the kidnapping, she'd prayed to Juno for protection. The goddess answered prayers in her own, sometimes tortuous, fashion. Sashimu felt certain that Prometheus was Juno's answer. She now saw her path and spoke with a new authority. "If the koan is simply a problem, let's assume there's a solution. Part of the solution must be the process of finding the answer. Look at the koan from your personal experience. Try examining yourself."

Prometheus looked dubious, but his shoulders lifted and he unfolded from around his gourd. "Myself. Self. I am not certain about this; it will take time."

Sashimu felt pleased. They would be good for each other.

"You are healing rapidly," Prometheus said. "Things will change for you."

"Help me find Thesni." Sashimu tried to stay in Novus Orbis, but the pressure of the LifeSustainer thrust her into Vetus Orbis.

Ambush

Encased in body dressings, Sashimu drifted in and out of consciousness vaguely remembering a stream of bizarre encounters with Prometheus. Always Medic Danf came to wake her each day.

"I'm here to minimize your pain as you heal," said Danf in her soft, reassuring voice.

Sashimu tensed when the medic read the LifeSustainer's prognosis out loud in an astonished tone. "Patient's epidermal and dermis skin layers: completely restored. No remaining subcutaneous tissue damage. Impossible," the medic exclaimed. "No one heals like this after ninety per cent, full-thickness skin loss."

Above her, Sashimu heard the LifeSustainer move back and forth several times amid a flurry of mechanical sounds. Knowing her rate of recovery was far too accelerated to be humanly possible, she cringed as the medic removed bandages from her hand. While wishing to be free of their restraint, Sashimu dreaded discovery.

A gasp and the first touch sent chills up her arm. Silence. Swiftly her entire arm was unwrapped and cool plastic coated fingers ran down her skin. Slowly, her arms, torso, and then her legs were released from the bandages. Sashimu waited desperately for the medic to unbind her face so she could know for certain that it, too, had healed, but instead she heard more rustling.

"You must be the luckiest girl in the world," the medic's voice rose, full of excitement. "Not even a scar — I wish I could say we were responsible for your recovery. I must speak with your first medic, Leonardo, the miracle worker.

It's not fair to our other burn patients to keep his methods locked away at MIP, no matter how exclusive those
Moon officials insist on being."

Panicked that the medic would guess her true identity
and raise an alarm, Sashimu broke her silence.

"Please," Sashimu managed to croak, but then she felt
the violent tug of a MAMsession and heard the familiar
static noise.

This time, she did not sense Prometheus waiting there
for her or watch his slow approach to greet her. This
MAMsession had a distinct human intimacy and scent to
it — that of Medic Danf's perfume, coffee, sweat and minty
breath combined with saltwater. Unable to keep from
piggybacking on the medic's session, Sashimu reeled in
dizziness and stumbled forward into the medic's version
of Novus Orbis, which consisted of cliffs, a sparkling ocean
and a strong breeze.

As Novus Orbis resolved, Sashimu looked down and
gasped. She was teetering on a rocky precipice high above
an ocean, great waves crashing against the cliffs. Backing
away from the ledge, Sashimu turned to see, nestled in the
rocks, a solitary white stucco house with indigo shutters.
Sashimu climbed toward the house and found the front
door ajar. Taking a moment to let her eyes adjust to the dark
entryway, she saw a pretty blonde woman sitting in the
front room across from a man slumped back in his chair
behind a wide empty desk.

"I can't narrow my search any further. I certainly don't
have time to go through fifteen hundred files," said the
blonde, her cheeks flushing pink with frustration. "You're
from Medical Search and Retrieval. Certainly, you can give
me Medic Leonardo's address or MIP contact information."

"Please give further details on Medic Leonardo," the
man said. He languidly examined the dirt beneath his
fingernails.

The woman groaned, leaning forward to place both fists
on his desk. Neither of them noticed Sashimu's giant avatar
watching from just inside the doorway.

"Access Alice Chigusa's file and get me the address of
Medic Leonardo, the only Leonardo mentioned in the file,"
she said, her voice louder and more emphatic.

"Medic Danf, the name 'Leonardo' is not human trace-able," said the man, slowly grinning.

Danf tensed. She looked as if she wanted to reach across the desk and throttle him. "I guess we trust the MAM more than we trust people these days," she said, her voice laden with sarcasm. "Send Leonardo an urgent message that I need to speak with him."

"Impossible," the man said with a labored sigh. "You have to access a mail agent to fulfill that request."

With a flip of her wrist, the blonde dismissed the man. The chair filled with a mail agent who had an identical sour countenance and slouch as the clerk had, but wore a different uniform.

Leaving the door wide open behind her, Sashimu went to find Prometheus. She had to warn him that she was on the verge of being discovered. If the blonde learned Sashimu was an Imagofas, she would be in worse trouble.

After examining the cliffs below, Sashimu found a narrow path winding down through the rocks to a beach where the waves were calmer. Sashimu took the path to the long strip of shoreline. With her feet in the warm sand, she gazed over the ocean and concentrated on her strongest memory of Prometheus — when she had stood beside him as he fished, using a small gourd. She focused until she once again saw and heard him methodically scooping the gourd into the water beside her.

Astonished to see her, Prometheus abruptly dropped his gourd. "What are you doing here, Sashimu?" he asked. His brow furrowed in concern.

Before she could reply, she found herself back on the beach no longer alone. Dark algae and seaweed covered, faceless things rose dripping from the ocean. Their feet made strange sucking noises at each step. Sashimu ran as fast as her enormous legs could carry her along the shore, but they surrounded her.

The Cover-up

Gulping down green sludge from the blender as though his life depended on drinking every last drop, Creid snapped his fingers and caught the flying toast with his free hand.

"Darling, have you been in Novus Orbis?" Joli asked, rubbing her eyes as she walked into the kitchen. Creid found her most disarming at these moments when she looked so natural, so approachable and undone. "We have bizarre system messages overloading our usage allocation."

"What's the message?" said Creid.

"I couldn't decrypt it." Joli shrugged. "You should take a look before we get locked out for overload abuse."

"Used to be you could fix anything." Creid said sadly.

"You were always better with hardware than me."

"I'll check it out." Creid felt haggard. Under his eyes were the large, dark half-moons from insomnia. He had spent five days and most of those nights plodding through his archives in Novus Orbis. Should anything happen to him, he had prepared his archives so that they could be retrieved only by the Cadet.

Joli observed his odd behavior with concern and suspicion. He felt her watchful eyes on him constantly and disliked the way she looked at him with pity, as though he'd become an old man; though that was exactly how he felt.

He decided he would please Joli by fixing their "hardware problem." He went into his study and let his MAMhood slide over his face. He entered Novus Orbis as Creid Xerkler, and immediately his username was rejected with an "access denied" message. Exiting, he deactivated his mask and it slid back from his face.

"Did you get locked out?" he shouted to Joli in the next room.

"No, are you locked out?" inquired Joli, surprised. She stood in his study doorway without venturing inside.

"Never mind, I'll try something else," said Creid. Pulling his mask back down, Creid took a deep breath, then accessed the MAM under his alias of Leonardo.

ı.ıl.ıılll..ı.ı.ı

Creid entered Novus Orbis on a familiar wooden bridge overlooking the river. Leading away from the water below him, his path remained hidden under a canopy of trees. Beside him stood the avatar of a woman wearing a long, fitted coat, her hair piled high in some awful, new style.

"Like I always say, there's no place like home — even for you illegals!" she said with a sly glance up at him.

"What do you mean by that? Is this a solicitation?" Creid walked away from her down the path and then added with disgust, "Check my preferences; I don't accept solicitations."

She followed close behind him. "Leonardo, I have a message just for you."

With that, she had him. Creid stopped.

"MAM-X is coming soon and it will end your pathetic second identity. Once implemented, post-Novus Orbis will destroy aliases like yours, Leonardo. Enjoy your automatic upgrade at the end of the year. It will be your last." She let her coat fall from her, displaying a beautiful naked body; then she disappeared, leaving the letters MAM-X hanging for a moment in the air.

"What a waste of time," Creid told himself. The MAM made Creid nervous enough as it was, let alone the new upgrade planned for the end of the year. The Order planned even more invasive security features, including protocols to terminate rogue applications and end undocumented aliases. Just the concept of the MAM-X upgrade made Creid's skin crawl.

He heard an engine, and hastily stepped to the side of the bridge. A taxi screeched to a halt beside him. Its passenger door swung open. Inside, Creid saw a mail-uniformed agent yawning in the back seat.

"Jump in," said the driver. Creid thought he recognized the voice.

Creid eyed the group of familiar solicitors in designer, silk suits making their way toward him from across the bridge and got in, glad to escape another barrage of advertising or sexy MAM-X threats.

"Medic Danf requests an immediate meeting with you on an urgent matter," said the back-seated mail agent.

Creid groaned. This could only mean trouble. He was about to reject the offer when the taxi driver turned, and Creid recognized Prometheus. "Sashimu is with her," he said.

"Establish immediate contact with Medic Danf," Creid ordered. The mail agent nodded and vanished.

The surroundings faded into a coastal setting of impressive cliffs and ocean inlets. With other cars zooming past on the inside lane, Prometheus maneuvered the taxi along a winding road cut into the cliffs above the ocean. At times, Creid felt as though they were on the verge of swerving over the edge and plunging into the waves far below.

Abruptly, Prometheus veered off the road and up a steep driveway. At the top, an attractive blonde woman — Creid assumed she was Medic Danf — stood in front of a large white villa. She seemed to be anxiously waiting for them.

"Make it short with Danf," Prometheus said, "Sashimu is trapped on the beach below." Parking the car, he ran towards the villa and, at the edge of the cliff, turned down a rocky path that led to the beach.

Oblivious to the taxi driver, the woman smiled broadly as Creid climbed out of the passenger seat. "I'm Medic Danf." She inclined her head in a curt bow and blurted out, "It's so good to finally meet you. You've worked miracles for one of your patients, Alice Chigusa."

"She's okay?" Creid said with a grim expression on his face.

"Okay?!" Medic Danf asked. "More than that, her burns vanished without scarring. I've never seen anything like it. Please share with me what you know about her and what you did to facilitate her recovery."

"I would," said Creid, rolling up his sleeves, "but she's part of a highly classified Order project."

"You're kidding, right?" Medic Danf said, laughing, but sobered abruptly when she saw the crane tattoo on his wrist.

"May I ask a few questions?" she pleaded. "Your knowledge could be critical in helping other burn victims."

"I apologize. All I can tell you is that the Order and the Council are collaborating on this case," Creid said.

"I am not to report this?" Medic Danf sounded resigned and deeply disappointed.

"No. How did you see 'the miracle'?" Creid asked.

The woman briefly sketched the diagnostic results and her patient's new healthy skin. Creid nodded, knowing it would be next to impossible to adjust ongoing diagnostic results to mimic a 'normal' recovery when Sashimu was visibly healing so much more rapidly. Soon someone less innocent than Danf would notice the discrepancies. He had to act quickly.

Creid sized up the medic and thought her sincere. "I must ask a favor," he said. "Your patient is now healthy enough to leave the hospital, right?"

"I'd like to monitor her," Medic Danf said slowly. "But yes, she can be discharged."

"Does she have any next of kin who might let her stay temporarily with them?" Creid asked.

"There's no one who knows her. One of the hospital administrators, Mr. Bozley and his wife, have taken in patients before."

"That might do," Creid mumbled more to himself and then stared hard at the medic. "Wait for further instructions, but speak to no one about this."

Looking slightly bewildered, Danf bowed and walked slowly back to the house.

Creid believed he had convinced the medic to keep quiet about her patient. Relieved, he ran around the house, to the rock ledge that overlooked the cliffs and ocean. On the beach below, Prometheus and a muscular giant stood back to back, encircled by monsters whose tentacled arms dripped seaweed and salt water. The two fighters, their swords glinting in the sunlight, were heavily outnumbered, and barely fending off the creatures' assaults. Calling up his own sword, Creid found the path and ran down to help.

"What's happening?" Creid yelled above the sounds of battle. To divert the scaly, dripping monsters, he stabbed the closest one in the back. Roaring in pain, it turned — revealing its long fangs — and lashed out at him. Creid twisted to avoid the strike and lopped off one tentacle, as three more snaked toward him.

"Sashimu violated security trying to access me from a piggybacked session!" Prometheus shouted, stabbing another monster in the jaw, its tentacles winding about itself as it crumpled with a terrible piercing shriek of pain. Another immediately took its place.

"This is Sashimu?" Creid queried, staring flabbergasted at the enormous man who had just decapitated two creatures with a single stroke of his sword.

"Let's just end all of our sessions!" Creid said gasping, as several of the creatures bore down on him.

Instantly, everything was blackness and silence. Creid fought his way out of the dark, screaming until Joli ripped off his mask and violently shook him.

He felt weak and disoriented. "What happened?" he asked.

"A component of the MAM seems to have malfunctioned and completely shut down part of Novus Orbis," she said, checking his biostats and hugging him tightly against her. "I don't know how many sessions were affected, but you're back. Safe."

The apartment was strangely silent and pitch black. Prometheus must have caused a local brownout of all MAM controlled systems.

"That's not what I wanted him to do. He's insanely powerful." Creid said, burying his face in her soft robes. "I meant we should each end our *individual* sessions — not all ongoing sessions."

"Who are you talking about?" Joli stroked his unruly hair.

Remaining in her arms, Creid pulled back just far enough to look into her eyes. Joli meant everything to him so confessing felt right and honorable. While he still lived, he had to let his wife know about Sashimu and beg for the Imagofas' protection. He only hoped Zazen would understand and forgive him. "I have something to tell you," he said urgently.

"What?" Joli asked, suddenly apprehensive. She pushed him away.

Creid cleared his throat and gestured for them to go out onto the balcony. She followed hesitantly. Creid spoke softly and she had to press close to hear. "The Imagofas exist."

"I knew you were hiding your knowledge of the nanogen." Joli was triumphant.

Creid flushed red. "Nanogen is derogatory."

"What do you know?" Joli seemed to be struggling to control her anger. When Creid winced, she rephrased her question. "How are you involved?"

"I exploited old Order admin interfaces, which they never cleaned up. I doubt anyone in the Order knows they still exist, much less how to use them. After that, it was easy to gain access to hospital records where I hid the Imagofas' identity."

"I'd better call my contacts," Joli said, returning inside. "If *we* know, it is only a matter of time before the Order knows. We've got to get it into Council custody."

Grabbing her, he propelled her back to the balcony and blocked the doorway. "The Imagofas is female, not an 'it', and her real name is Sashimu. Furthermore, if you take her into Council custody, the Order will find out through informants where Sashimu is, and they will destroy her."

"So, what do you propose we do?" Joli asked.

"You know the Order's power. We must act as though Sashimu is just another victim recovering from the MIP incident. If you call all the survivors forward to testify about the incident, the Order may never suspect she is Imagofas. She can stay hidden, in plain view, as one of the many who will be called to testify — to recollect everything that happened during the MIP incident."

Joli nodded grudgingly in agreement. "Her alias is still good and no one suspects her?"

"No one suspects. There's an administrator at the hospital named Bozley who might make a convenient guardian for Sashimu until the tribunal convenes, if he can be bribed," Creid said, remembering what Danf had told him.

"Everyone can be bribed," Joli answered confidently.

"I'll leave that to you," Creid said. Her scheming expression suddenly made him feel uncomfortable.

"I'll have him contacted. We'll make it in his best interest to take care of her," Joli said. She tried to nudge him out of her way so she could return inside, but Creid held her back.

"That's not all. My MAM activity has been problematic — illegal." Creid stood his ground determined to warn her.

"What do you mean?"

"I have an alias I use from time to time with privileges that extend beyond those of a retired Order operator. When I used it last, I was noticed. I'm on a superwatch list." His forehead had beads of perspiration despite the cold wind that buffeted their clothes.

"Are you implying the Order has it in for you?" Joli said with a frown.

"I don't know." Creid paused. "I was just exited from Novus Orbis without having the chance to do any investigation."

Creid cleared his throat and there was an awkward silence.

"What happened?" Joli's voice was tremulous.

"You know those messages overloading our system, which you warned me about this morning? Those messages were sent to me because the Imagofas was in trouble. When I went to help her, my session was terminated." Creid never mentioned Prometheus. It would be too complicated to explain and would only make her furious.

"Why are you so worried? The MAM had a rare mal-
function, that's all," Joli said, frowning and glancing out
over the distant mountains visible from their west-facing
balcony.

Creid seized her shoulders and forced her to look him
in the eyes. "I may have triggered the alarm in Novus
Orbis, which caused the MAM shutdown and maybe
caused the MAM to strike out against me."

"You're overreacting," Joli said, reaching up to caress
his cheek. "You've spent five days without sleep, in and
out of Novus Orbis, and I think it's affecting your judg-
ment. "Let me by. I want to make sure the Imagofas is
safe."

She gave him a long, deep kiss and then slipped by him
into the apartment, disappearing into the bedroom and
closing the door behind her. Maybe she was right. Maybe
keeping everything to himself for too long had turned him
into a delirious insomniac.

"I need a walk," Creid said. He went to the kitchen sink
and rinsed his face. He still sensed he was in danger, but
it felt good to have confessed at least some of it to Joli.
And yet, he had one last task to accomplish before he could
rest.

|..|.|..||||..|.|..|

To secure the Imagofas' immediate safety, Joli made
arrangements according to his suggestion. Creid stood
beside her, listening as she told Goth to contact Bozley,
the hospital administrator, through intermediaries and
work out an arrangement for the young girl to stay with
him and his wife until the tribunal. Bozley was only to
know that Alice Chigusa would be a witness in the upcoming MIP case.

After the arrangements were made, Creid walked to
the nearest Underground Rapid Transit entrance and
transferred to several different lines before disembarking
to visit the Cadet.

Unfortunately, when he arrived at the gamer's quarters,
the Cadet was out. He was not surprised. He had arrived

unannounced. The best he could do was leave an encrypted message, stating that, in return for the Cadet's vow of secrecy to protect the Imagofas, Creid would provide him with access to all of the data regarding her. To avoid a record that he'd contacted his protégé, Creid spoke into his Companion and forwarded the priority encrypted message to the Cadet's home system.

When Creid returned upground, he and Joli ate dinner in silence. That night he slept deeply without turning to his side or once adjusting.

|.|.|...|||..|.|..|

Joli woke early the next morning. She nestled close to Creid's side. "Sweetheart?"

No response. His body was limp and comatose. His biostats showed he was still alive. Joli called emergency, then began to cry in exasperated, wrenching sobs that shook her whole body. Frantically dressing, Joli took a genetic imprint of Creid's hands for future access, and sat beside him on the way to the hospital.

Domus Aqua

They were waiting for the Cadet, their whispers following behind him as he strode down the length of the arched
marble hallway, with the attendant sent to escort him. Gold
leafed cherubs stared down at him from their pastel mural
heights, dancing on waves and soundlessly playing shell
trumpets. Domus Aqua represented extreme wealth and
privilege. It reminded the Cadet of his insignificance. He
was once and forever an Undergrounder.

The natural light, the air perfumed with enormous vases
of fresh lilies and irises on pedestals between extravagant
busts of ancestral domus masters, all combined to make
the Cadet painfully aware of his shabby clothes and gray
skin. The maintenance employees of Domus Aqua —
mostly from the Underground — stayed out of sight behind
him while others ran to spread the news.

He had arrived. Now the entire domus was eager for
the unofficial sparring match between Isaac, their top
gamer, and the Cadet.

At the final archway that opened onto the courtyard,
the attendant stopped and stood aside to let him pass. The
gamer never broke stride, stepping out into the open space
without hesitation. The unbearable brightness of the Vetus
Orbis sun glinting off the stained glass gazebo blinded him
momentarily from everything except Lila, who sat on the
veranda overlooking the courtyard with her father, Domus
Master Sachio. Lila's beauty — her chestnut skin, high
cheekbones and rubied black braids — made him forget
for a moment that he had come to spar. The Cadet bowed
deeply in homage to her, then turned his head to survey
his surroundings.

Heads poked from every window and balcony. Shadows moved restlessly around the perimeter of the courtyard as the watchers waited for the fight. The new landscape no doubt mirrored Isaac's upcoming game in Novus Orbis. Domus Master Sachio always gave Isaac a little practice before his professional game. Turning slightly, the Cadet bowed again, to pay his respects to Lila's father. His ebony skin seemed ageless, but his shock of white hair and well trimmed beard gave him an aura of distinction. His mischievous grin, coupled with Lila's air of indignation, made the Cadet suspicious. Leaning away from her father, she gave a warning wave to signal danger to the Cadet.

From the opposite side of the courtyard, Isaac entered. Lila's serious expression immediately transformed into a radiant smile and Isaac politely nodded to her. His robe showed the colors of the domus, cobalt trimmed with deep red. It flowed about him, tuned to absorb sweat at the slightest exertion, then to rehydrate and cool him. In contrast, the Cadet wore simple black. He felt dull and short next to this tall Adonis with the chiseled features and the carefree look of a man who knew his station. Isaac came from privilege and he had taken on the dangerous sport of gaming as a personal challenge before moving on to greater things; while the Cadet gamed because he saw no other option. During those brief seconds when Lila blew Isaac a kiss, the Cadet forgot Isaac was his friend and secretly hated him. His fists clenched in fury and frustration. He wanted to pummel Isaac.

Suddenly, he saw that something behind him had caught his opponent's attention. Immediately, Isaac sprang past the Cadet. He turned just in time to see Isaac catch, in midair, an attacker who had launched herself from the gazebo window. Together, they smashed into the stairs, which collapsed beneath them. Without this midair move, the woman would have crashed down on top of the Cadet.

The gamer recognized his attacker's pinched face and thick, yellow hair. It was Mae. Fortunately, Isaac's intervention had knocked her far away from the Cadet, but her stick remained firmly in her grasp as she rolled away from Isaac, springing up and jabbing it at his gut. Her reflexes were extraordinarily fast, even by the standards of Vetus

Orbis. Falling back, Isaac blocked her with a splintered board snatched up from the broken stairs. Grabbing a board himself, the Cadet tried to divert Mae, but a splash of water distracted him.

Beside the gazebo, the lily pond came alive. A gaunt figure burst from beneath the shallow water and ran toward him, a knife glinting in his hand. Grinning, the second attacker motioned for the Cadet to draw his own knife.

"Dagger, so nice to see you," the Cadet said, refusing to draw. He suspected that to do so might lead to more serious injuries that he could ill afford.

Shrugging, Dagger dropped his knife and kicked straight at the face of the Cadet, who blocked the attack with his arms, but the impact brought him to his knees. Dagger lunged again. The Cadet swiveled underneath him, flipped up and landed several blows against the man's chest and neck before Dagger opted to retreat.

Striking fast and hard, Dagger came back at the Cadet, who outmaneuvered him just enough to get in a punch or kick to his attacker's shin before getting pummeled again. The Cadet took a severe blow to his side and fell over moaning. Instead of simply pinning him down, Dagger went for a dramatic move that played to the crowd. Jumping high in the air, his attacker brought both feet together intending to come down square on the Cadet's chest. At the last instant, the Cadet rolled swiftly to the side, bounding to his feet and pinning Dagger to the ground. The fight was over.

They stood and bowed to each other. A cheer went up from the windows and the outer shadows of the courtyard.

Dagger growled under his breath, "You'd have lost if we'd used knives."

The Cadet bowed deeper so that only Dagger could hear him say, "I know."

Looking up, he saw that Isaac was in trouble. Mae had maneuvered him into the reeds that fringed the pond. The water-saturated bottom of the pool was like quicksand. With the ooze sucking at his feet, Isaac could barely fend her off. The Cadet gave a hoarse yell and leapt at her while Isaac wrenched himself out of the reeds. Mae turned and deftly struck the Cadet in the stomach with her stick, momentarily knocking the wind out of him. And then, she went back at Isaac. He parried several blows, but when Mae got him in a headlock, the fight ended. Both of them burst out laughing.

"I can't defeat you on your engagement day." Mae disentangled herself from Isaac and slapped him on the back. "Congratulations."

With a puzzled look, the Cadet watched Mae and Dagger leave the courtyard. Isaac stumbled to his feet and cracked his neck.

Panting and drenched in sweat, the Cadet bowed to Lila, the Domus Master Sachio and Isaac, then headed for the bench beside the gazebo. The Cadet sat down and examined his bruised arm. He had broken it so many times it ached after every fight. Spasms of pain shot through the limb, making him curse the domus master under his breath. A light spar with Isaac was all he had expected and thought it strange that the domus master set up a more dangerous challenge. Isaac joined him on the bench, dry and annoyed. Even sitting down, Isaac towered over him.

"I thought nothing could put me in a bad mood today," Isaac commiserated.

The Cadet nodded. "Tell me about it. I better heal before my game, or there'll be hell to pay."

Lila waved at them from the veranda.

"Amazing. You two are incredible." Lila glided down the grand stairs in a breathless red dress, with cobalt trim. The Cadet thought that Isaac and she complemented each other perfectly. She was as dark as he was fair. Chiding them, she said, "Lucky you two weren't fighting me, you'd both have lost."

Both men agreed. As a rising young gamer, it was likely that one day Lila would be better than either of them. She motioned for the Cadet's knife. He threw it to her without hesitation.

After cutting off a tiny braid, she opened her locket necklace and dropped it inside, then unclasped her necklace and offered it to the Cadet. Several of the domus employees gasped in surprise. The Cadet was elated and his face flushed hot. He glanced at Isaac to see if he was upset, but the other man seemed perfectly content.

"Let's have lunch!" Lila took them both by the arms and walked between them up the stairs. The Cadet thought he must be the happiest man on Earth.

Domus Master Sachio greeted them heartily on the landing, slapping them both on the shoulders. "I had to make sure you'd both remember this day fondly, fighting together rather than against each other. You are both formidable opponents, but the two of you must always be on the same side," the domus master said and bowed to each of them. "My apologies, but I must take my leave."

Lila scowled at her father as he retreated underneath the arches. "I told him that the fight was unnecessary. A good spar would have been less exciting, but safer. You two shouldn't risk getting injured in a free fight before your professional games."

The Cadet hugged his throbbing side. He needed the domus medic to look at it, but he wanted to eat first. Yet neither Lila nor Isaac had made a move to get food and both were staring at him nervously.

"Alright guys, what's up?" the Cadet said glancing curiously from one to the other.

"You tell him," Lila implored Isaac. "Or, shall I?"

"Tell me what?" The Cadet was suspicious.

"We're engaged." Isaac's voice was flat and low as though neither was sure how the Cadet would react.

"Congratulations." His voice sounded a bit strained, even to himself. He was shocked, but knew he should have expected it from Mae's comment and the strange way everyone had been acting. A tinge of jealousy made him regret accepting her locket. He felt foolish. "When is the wedding?"

"It's going to be hugely complicated, what with all father's ties, so we're planning it for several months from now," Lila said. Her face was flushed.

The Cadet could hardly bear their happiness. He wondered if it was simply his destiny to be permanently alone. And yet, he tried not to spoil their high spirits. "Let me know what I can do to help."

"We will." Lila beamed.

She motioned to the staff with a flip of her wrist. They came forward with many platters, heaped with every kind of delicacy, where color and spice seemed to be the main criteria for each course: yellows, reds, greens, ending in an exquisite array of rich creams on a narrow mahogany dish displaying rare cheeses. Unfortunately, the Cadet had lost his appetite.

When the meal was over, Lila said, "We want to discuss some business with you."

The Cadet shifted uncomfortably in his chair. "All right. But it hardly seems fitting to talk business on a day like today."

"Nonsense," Isaac patted him on the back. "Father wanted us to make you a lucrative proposition, assuming that is, we were still on speaking terms after our announcement."

Wincing at Isaac's reference to the domus master as "father," the Cadet said, "Well then, what does Master Sachio have in mind?"

Standing abruptly, Lila suggested they might better talk in the privacy of her rooms, by which the Cadet understood she meant her library. Ever since he'd met her years ago in school, Lila had only allowed him and Isaac as far as her library. It was the first room in her private wing, and it was impressive. They settled down amongst her purple cushions below the cases of ancient books, the artifacts hermetically sealed and kept under optimal temperature to prolong their existence. The Cadet had asked her once if she had physically read any of them, and she assured him that she had not; they were museum pieces, invaluable and irreplaceable. Besides, their contents could easily be accessed in Novus Orbis. Still the Cadet was tempted to touch one. There was something mysterious, alluring and even thrilling about a book. The technology was so primeval. It seemed wrong to have them sealed away with only their bindings visible.

Silent servants distributed tea and sweets. When the three of them were alone again, all traces of Lila's earlier elation and giddiness disappeared. Sitting up straight, she crossed her legs and said, "This is a delicate matter and your strictest confidence is required."

The Cadet nodded his assent.

"The integrity of our domus may be compromised unless we act swiftly. We have entered into dealings with a less than savory character named Angel," she shot Isaac a reproachful look, "in an effort to explore new business opportunities. We lost a huge initial investment. One contact is dead and the other says he can't help us until the Council and Order ease up on him."

The Cadet concentrated on cooling his tea so that neither of them could see his expression. He was dismayed the domus had stooped to dealing with criminals.

"Meanwhile our delivery has arrived. It's out there and it belongs to us. We'd like you to locate it for us."

Frowning, the Cadet set his cup down. It clattered against the saucer. "Lila, I may be from the Underground, but contrary to popular belief, we're not all crooks. I've never done anything illegal in my life and I'd prefer to keep it that way."

Lila gave Isaac an I-told-you-so glance and nestled deep into the cushions, crossing her arms over her chest. "I said nothing about anything illegal. We need your help finding something. Father is willing to pay you handsomely for your search."

The Cadet was hardly mollified by her offer. "What do you want me to find?"

"A nanogen. It is missing."

Startled, the Cadet looked from Lila to Isaac. Everyone seemed to want his help finding the Imagofas: the Council, the Order and now the most prestigious domus on Earth.

The gamer decided he should play dumb. "A nanogen?"

"Yes I know, we thought nanogens were just myths, too. Apparently, some notable, but very eccentric scientists on Mars have been working for more than two decades to alter human embryos. This nanogen was supposed to be placed in our care once it arrived on Earth," Isaac said, sloshing around the dregs of his cup. "There was an accident, and it disappeared in the Underground."

"You want me to find it. Isn't it illegal?"

Isaac's voice lost its smooth resonance. "Nanogens may be illegal, but we plan to study its attributes to see if we can't develop—"

"That's irrelevant," Lila cut him off and turned to the Cadet. "We would like you to find it. If you don't feel comfortable with that, simply forget this conversation."

The image of a misshapen creature sealed in the bookcase beside Lila's books popped into his head and the Cadet almost felt pity for the Imagofas whom everyone wanted so badly. "Where would I start? I don't even know what it looks like."

"Its description makes it sound quite pretty," Lila said. "It passed for a human. We know that much."

At a loss for words, the Cadet stared across the coffee table at them. He was under contract with Joli to help the Order and the Council to locate the Imagofas, but he couldn't tell that to them without betraying Joli's confidence. "If I find it, what then?"

"You tell us where it's at." Lila shrugged. She and Joli shared a knack for making everything sound simple.

Despite the seriousness of the situation, the Cadet had to laugh. He could hardly believe he had been offered the same job twice, though it did put him in a delicate position. While he could not divulge his mission, Joli never demanded knowledge exclusivity. Assuming his search was successful, maybe he could tell both Lila and Joli, and let them fight over who would get the Imagofas. That way, he'd meet both their expectations without violating their confidence — and walk away getting paid twice for one job. He respected Joli and liked the fact she retained close ties to the Order because she might help him get a job there. And Lila, well, she just happened to be the most stunning woman in the world. Frankly, when it came down to it, he would do just about anything to keep them both happy.

"Look, you know my skills. I'm a gamer, not a detective. I have no idea where to look."

"We can help you there," Lila reassured him. "Are you willing?"

Gazing back into Lila's exquisite eyes, he made up his mind. If he found the creature, he would simultaneously notify Joli and Lila. "Sure. Why not? How dangerous can it be?"

"Potentially very dangerous. You should start by speaking with Angel. He knows the nanogen was spirited into the Underground by a smuggler named Grant and it appears that both Grant and the nanogen have disappeared. Before all of that, Grant had contacted us directly and wanted to hand over the nanogen himself. And that was the last we heard from him. Later we found out he had gone behind Angel's back. Now, Angel is refusing to communicate with us until he's under less government scrutiny."

"Could Angel know where it is and be holding out for a higher bid?" The Cadet knew how such scum worked.

"We wondered about that, but he seems as puzzled as we are by its vanishing. The captain never divulged his safe house. It's possible it is still there."

"I'll start with Angel, but just so you know, the man turns my stomach."

"Angel fits the worst stereotype of the Underground," she said sympathetically.

"Angel's worse than most thugs," the Cadet said. He winced from his cracked ribs as he pulled himself off the couch and slowly stood. Between clenched teeth, he added, "I'll see what I can discover for you, Lila."

"Thank you," Lila said and Isaac echoed her, as the Cadet left the library.

Taking his leave from the domus, the Cadet headed out into the rain. Once outside, dizzy with pain, he held his side and leaned against the high exterior wall of the domus until he was soaked. He may have put himself in a bind by agreeing to notify Lila when he'd already committed to Joli, but he had never denied Lila anything. He wasn't about to begin now. Besides, it was a lucrative proposition. Lila was always generous.

His greatest concern though was Angel. While Angel's black market business thrived just down from the Cadet's quarters, they were far from friends. The Cadet had roughed up too many of Angel's thugs. Still, he would make a go of talking to Angel. The worst that could happen was more broken ribs.

A Message

The Cadet woke up in a cold sweat. He had a game scheduled in three weeks and, though he had undergone accelerated healing, his injured arm and ribs had slowed his training. The upcoming fly game was his most important, most prestigious game to date. Domus Ignis was counting on him to win — or at least to put up a good show. With a record number of spectators predicted, this match could make or break his gaming career.

The Cadet spent the day cursing his Novus Orbis trainer. No matter how hard he tried, he lost every match. At one point the game host threatened to throw him off the practice grounds for misconduct — warning him to improve his attitude or be banned for the remainder of the day.

His evening didn't fare well either. Gil's bar was closed "due to repairs," which was Gil's way of notifying clientele he'd been shut down. The closure had the Order stamped all over it. Gil sold illegal MAM access and the Order frequently shut him down for it. It was just the Cadet's luck, when all he wanted was a glass of Benedictine.

On his way back to his quarters, the Cadet slid by lurkers at every turn in the tunnels. Lurkers were Undergrounders who mostly gathered unofficial information and did jobs — odd and dirty jobs — for anyone with credit. Usually driven to the depths of the Underground because of a serious criminal past, lurkers were desperate types. When resources were scarce, they hassled Underground locals to get credit.

Resources were scarce so he wasn't surprised to see a lurker hovering outside his quarters. He recognized him as Boo, a greasy type who had a nervous tic and constantly glanced over his shoulder.

"Hello, Boo. Who are you working for tonight?" The Cadet moved away from his door into a precautionary defensive stance.

Boo stayed in the shadows, but his quick head movements were as unmistakable as his scratchy voice. "Angel sent me to tell you to stop by for dinner one of these days."

"Did he now?" The gamer grinned. Word must be out that he'd sparred at Domus Aqua. Angel might have guessed his new employer and mission. "Tell him I look forward to dinner."

"I will," Boo said. The Cadet saw the lurker relax, his agreeable response relieving the man's fear that he'd been set up for a beating since the Cadet was known among lurkers as a cleanlife vigilante. And yet, information meant credit, so Boo risked asking, "You know what it's about?"

"Most likely, Angel wants me to neutralize the bad elements in our neighborhood," said the Cadet. He took a step toward Boo and the lurker scuttled down the tunnel, darting looks over his shoulder. The Cadet chuckled and dropped down into his quarters. His sides ached so badly, he scheduled time with a medic the next day, and then pulled out his bed to lay down. His message wall was still flashing from yesterday.

It was rare to have a message delivered to his quarters. As long as he was above ground, his MAMsuit allowed him to immediately respond in Novus Orbis or delay his response to friends and business associates. He suspected this was another "at home" advertising plug and thought lazily about deleting it when he noticed another wall panel light up showing a cloaked woman at his West side entrance.

Joli was visiting again. This time she pressed her palms against his outer door and passed gently down to his inside entrance. Astonished, the Cadet stared at his security panel, which read "CREID XERKLER: ADMITTANCE ALLOWED." He wondered what the hell was wrong with his security system that it would recognize Joli as Creid — though the Cadet had given Creid access long ago in case of some extreme emergency.

The Cadet quickly overrode Joli's access. The last thing he needed was to spend a day trouble-shooting a security bug. The wall panel displayed Joli frantically palming the inner door of his quarters, but it remained closed. At least, his inner security override still worked. Puzzled, he palmed open the door from his side, and she fell against him.

"What a surprise," said the Cadet, helping her up as the door slid shut behind her.

"Why didn't you let me in?" Joli snapped.

"Security identified you as Creid." The Cadet saw swollen eyes and a red nose as she threw back her hood.

Frowning, she held up her hands. They were covered in a soft liquid substance which she let drip off into a bag that she stuffed into her pocket. "Creid's hand imprints. I knew you'd given him access to your place."

Puzzled, the Cadet sat down without offering to take her cloak or provide drinks.

"You don't have whiskey, do you?" she asked nervously.

"No."

"Just as well. I needed to get in here to see if Creid told you anything yesterday when he came by, or if he left you a message or anything." Her hair was disheveled and she was clearly distraught.

"What happened?"

"What did he tell you?" Joli demanded.

"Nothing." Now the Cadet was curious about his flashing message wall, but he kept silent. "I was training yesterday. I'm preparing for the game between Domus Ignis and Domus Superna. However, I do have a lead on our search."

"Forget that. I found her with Creid's help. That may be why he's in a coma." Joli buried her face in her hands. "He tried to warn me that he was in danger, and I ignored him."

"Creid is in a coma?" The young man sat back, shocked.

"He told me he had done something risky in Novus Orbis, but he wouldn't say what. I woke up and he was comatose beside me. That's no coincidence!" Joli said, her last word broken by a sob.

"No, it isn't." The Cadet ground his teeth, but he had to be patient. "What do the medics say?"

"They can't figure it out," Joli answered, beginning to tremble, her eyes welling with tears. "His brain is active, but he remains completely unresponsive. I told them I suspected foul play, but they refused to speculate."

The gamer turned it over in his mind. "Creid's coma directly followed his actions in Novus Orbis. He was obviously worried about something he'd done. What exactly did he tell you?"

Now the woman's sobs came uncontrollably. With tears streaming down her cheeks, it was a moment before she could reply, "I don't remember. It was what he *did* that was important."

"What did he do?"

"He saved the nanogen. It was in the hospital and he made sure its identity was protected." She shot him a wary glance. "Creid didn't come here?"

"Not that I know of."

She regained control and wiped away tears with her sleeve. "All right, listen to me carefully. I have the nanogen under witness protection until the tribunal," said Joli.

"Where?" the Cadet asked anxiously.

"With a couple," Joli said, pausing with her eyes fixed on the Cadet. "You'll be paid for the job, but you and I never spoke about this. Understand?"

"I understand."

"I'd like you to act as an informal guardian," Joli said. "I've set it up so that the couple is expecting you as a tutor for 'Alice Chigusa.' That is the nanogen's alias. It was the name of a girl who died in the MIP accident. They were roughly the same age, both from Mars and slightly similar in appearance, so I'm told."

"Couldn't someone crosscheck her MAM history and medical files and see that the nanogen isn't Alice?" the Cadet asked.

"That's taken care of — all her MAMfiles have been modified to match the new identity. But at any rate, we need you undercover to give additional protection before the tribunal convenes, in case the nanogen is threatened. Gain its trust and make sure it doesn't try anything stupid. Again, you'll be paid handsomely. Here's the address."

She touched the sleeve of his suit and the information transferred.

"Got it. What about Creid? Shouldn't we figure out who is after him, and why he's in a coma?"

"No. I'll deal with that. I have a hunch I know the bastards who did this to him."

The Cadet's face hardened. "Who?"

"The nanogen's creators."

"What? Who?" he asked, but she refused to answer. He wondered why she would hide their identities — certainly not to protect him. "Look, if Creid was attacked, you might be in danger yourself."

From the way she gathered her cloak about her, it was clear that she had said all she had planned to say on the matter and wanted to leave. Moments later, he watched as she was deposited outside his entrance. And then, he turned to his messages.

His Companion relayed the sound of Creid's voice, hoarse and tired. "This may be my last message." The words gave him a stab of guilt; Creid was the closest thing he had to a father. If only he had checked his messages sooner. "I've gotten myself into trouble," the rasping voice continued. "Remember that promise you made back at the Academy that you'd do anything I asked? Well, now I'm collecting. I need you to protect Joli's witness, an Imagofas from Mars. My wife puts too much faith in the system. I told Joli where to find her so she should be safe for a short while. But an old colleague of mine, Dreyfus, will be coming. He'll return the Imagofas safely to Mars. Here is the address for a memory download. Trust me, it will explain more than you want to know. Look after Joli and the Imagofas. Her alias is Alice Chigusa. The tentative plan is to have her stay with a man named Bozley, an administrator at the Denver Hospital of Our Fathers." The Cadet heard a sigh, then Creid's voice concluded, "Sorry about this, my boy; you're the only one I can trust."

The Cadet's jaw tightened at the unpleasant memory of his failed Ethics test. That night, he'd promised Creid he would do anything for him — anything except compromise his integrity by arresting decent Under-grounders. For five years, he had lived with the conse-quences of that decision, and he had sometimes wondered if he'd make the same choice today. Certainly, Creid, Lila and Isaac had all helped him make the necessary con-tacts to game for the different domus, but gaming ran a poor second to his former dream to join the Order and seriously improve life in the Underground.

In all the years, this was the first time Creid had asked him for help. The Cadet was determined not only to fulfill his promise, but to save his mentor from his enemies. Unfortunately, visiting the address in Novus Orbis that Creid had given him would have to wait until Gil opened up for business. The Cadet would never risk accessing that message in a legitimate MAM optimization area. The Order or Council might spy on his actions. He suspected Creid's message contained sensitive information.

Exhaustion swept over him. He desperately needed sleep to train, but his mind raced. Besides keeping his promise to Creid, he had another problem. Telling Lila and Isaac the Imagofas was in custody would not be easy. Lila would be furious. She might blame him for not find-ing the Imagofas before the tribunal took custody. And yet, it served the domus right for investing in illegal ven-tures. Lila's first concern should be to maintain the pres-tigious Domus Aqua name.

Rage flashed through his fatigued mind. He slammed his good hand into the wall and instantly regretted it. Pain shot up to his elbow and blood oozed from his split knuckles. Protecting an Imagofas from its creators might not be so easy; Joli hadn't even told him whom he was up against. But maybe, whoever the opposition was, they wouldn't discover the nanogen's location until after the tribunal. Once again, he tried to imagine what an Imagofas might look like, but could still only conjure up a misshapen creature trapped behind the protective case in which Lila kept her antique books.

|.||.|..|||||..|.|.|

Being unbandaged, free of the hospital, and in the care of new guardians should have been a relief for Sashimu. She was no longer trapped beneath a LifeSustainer and she showed no scars from her healed wounds, but weeks of immobility had left her muscles debilitated. Given Earth's tremendous gravity, she worried she might never be strong enough to escape her new guardians. Even worse, Medic Danf had told her that soon she might be called before a tribunal to testify about the MIP incident. Sashimu sought comfort in reminding herself that her identity remained a secret and that this tribunal should have nothing to do with hunting Imagofas.

Medics brought her to the Bozleys' flat, then left her to sit in their living room across from a short, carefully groomed man and his apparently anxious wife. He did the talking while the woman wrung her hands and tortured an embroidered handkerchief.

They were glad to have her with them, Bozley said, knowing she had suffered a terrible loss with the death of her parents. Over the next weeks, she would stay with them until a tribunal hearing in which she would give testimony about what happened on MIP. Sashimu studied Bozley while he rambled on. Perhaps he believed she had lost her parents, but the way he flicked his eyes repeatedly toward his wife, and her obvious anxiety, raised the Imagofas' suspicions.

When he paused for breath, she politely interrupted the flow of words. "Mr. Bozley, sir, what is the tribunal really about?"

"I'm not sure of the exact details." He cleared his throat. "The Council has asked for an investigation and independent tribunal to assess the accident at Moon Interplanetary Port. You are to be a witness."

"I see," said Sashimu, linking her fingers together in her lap to stop her hands from trembling.

"The Council has been extremely generous. They've asked that all your needs be met," Bozley continued, and now he smiled for the first time. "You'll have new clothes, and as soon as you feel up to it, a tutor to help you grow stronger."

"Thank you," Sashimu replied.

Bozley cleared his throat again. "Let's be straightfor-ward, shall we?" His voice had taken on a nasal, bureau-cratic tone. "Mrs. Bozley and I have some ground rules that will help us all to get along."

Raising one plump, pale hand, he ticked off his state-ments on each finger. "You will always follow our rules without questioning them. You will not fraternize with other students your age. You will not enter Novus Orbis or access the MAM under any condition. You will tell us if any stranger attempts to speak with you." He looked at his wife. "Did I leave anything out, dear?"

The woman shook her head and said nothing. Sashimu kept her eyes on her linked hands. Her overriding thought was that these guardians were completely inexperienced and inappropriate to host an Imagofas. It was, however, several shades better than a ship cell or hospital room.

"Do you understand me?" Bozley asked, sounding as though he couldn't make up his mind whether to threaten or plead.

"Yes. What happens to me afterwards?"

"Afterwards?" He looked dumbfounded.

"After the tribunal."

"Well, now," Either he had not thought that far in advance or he was not allowed to say. "You'll have to ask that question of the tribunal."

Sashimu lifted her gaze to Mrs. Bozley. "I'm so tired. May I rest?"

The woman rose and helped her upstairs to her bed-room. When the door was closed behind them, she leaned toward Sashimu and whispered, "I know, he may sound harsh, but he always means well."

Sashimu nodded and sank down onto the bed. Every-thing in the room was pink, lacy and topped with floppy dolls. Mrs. Bozley explained that the dolls had been hers when she was a girl. They were robotic and could hold simple conversations. Their vacant eyes stared coldly at Sashimu.

Laying her head back on the pillow, Sashimu closed her eyes and pulled the blankets over her. When she heard Mrs.

Bozley leave and slide the bedroom door shut, she bolted upright and commanded each of the dolls in turn, "Eyes shut." All obeyed and she heard their tiny processors whirr momentarily as their eyes closed.

Examining the room, Sashimu realized there would be no easy escape. There was only one entrance and the tiny window opened onto a sheer drop of several stories. She shook her head at the strange state of affairs. It would be far easier to keep her from escaping by locking her in a cell until the tribunal. Instead, the Bozleys were pretending, or maybe even believed, that she was Alice Chigusa. And then, Bozley had laid down all those silly rules, as if he could enforce denying her access to Novus Orbis.

Half smiling, she tried to imagine Bozley lecturing Prometheus: finger number one, "You are not allowed to gain sentience;" finger number two, "You are not allowed to exist."

Prometheus had told her she was on Earth to help him. So far, none of it made sense. She wanted desperately to sort it out, to find Thesni and go home.

The pillow was soft and warm; outside was cold and budding green under a bright sun. So much plant, bird and insect life, all under a ghastly blue sky. She was overwhelmed by foreign smells and sounds. On Mars, existence was so barren, and so simple.

Sashimu felt certain of one thing: to accomplish anything, she had to be mobile. Regaining her strength was paramount.

Dinner for Two

The Cadet emerged into a busy tunnel just outside Angel's territory. He spotted the wokman and bought a quick meal. Stuffing the mealbox in his bag, he slung it over his shoulder and continued. After regularly spending so much time above ground, his skin was losing its ashen hue and his appetite was enormous. He took another tunnel and followed a circuitous route that took him well wide of Angel's sprawling quarters, to avoid running into any Angel-sent lurkers. He was in no mood to punctuate a productive day by a damaging run in with Underground scum, now that his fly-game training was finally on track. Having also received an assignment from Joli to begin tutoring the Imagofas, he needed to resolve things with Lila and Isaac before he dealt with Angel.

As he neared his quarters, his MAMsuit pulsed in warning: two men were stationed just beyond the entrance. He walked casually to his door, tugging on his inner sleeve so that a knife dropped into his right hand. From the shadows stepped Boo and a massive, heavily tattooed man. The Cadet recognized the big thug as Marty, whom he'd seen guarding Angel.

"Angel wants you for dinner tonight," said Marty.

Additional MAMsuit pulses notified the Cadet that more goons were coming toward him from either end of the tunnel.

The Cadet shrugged and said, "I could use a free meal." Marty looked like a cartoon character with his massive biceps and constantly moving three-dimensional flasher tattoos that made it hard to determine where his arm was at any given moment. Flasher tats were the current rage in the Underground; they made it hard to guess where a punch might land. Marty might be tattooed-to-fight and loud, always pushing people out of the way to intimidate them, but the Cadet had pegged him as a coward, the kind who let his fear and anger control him.

The other thugs took Marty's lead, falling in step around him and responding to his slightest hand gesture as they made their way back to Angel's quarters. Their boss' place was unmistakable, marked by gaudy faux-marble archways, with guards constantly surveying the crowds of buyers and letting no one pass without permission. The outermost rooms were contraband storefronts in the heart of the largest underground black market. As they passed through these rooms into the private interior, the Cadet curiously looked around.

Angel seemed to have the same penchant for luxury as the rich and powerful domus. Rare and illegally imported sculptures of carved black Martian caverock, with its distinctive red veins, sat on pedestals with gold plaques. The Cadet read one as he passed: "Venus on Olympus Mons" and another that read: "Untitled, c.2060." Another pedestal held a pale yellow box, under glass. He read the label, which caused a shiver to run down his spine: "Box fashioned from Martian prehistoric bones, dig site x1011." Everywhere he looked, the Cadet saw strange and illicit art.

In the deepest interior, they entered a zone bereft of luxury. It resembled a war room, with detailed live maps of the Underground decorating the walls. Palming any place on the map provided live feeds of the tunnels and peoples' quarters, as Angel was demonstrating to one of his thugs before sending him off on some dirty work. The Cadet wondered if his own low-tech scramblers provided any privacy against Angel's "eyes."

Angel took a seat behind a small, plain table covered with illegal offworld foods. He gestured for the gamer to join him, sending Marty and the others out. The Cadet sat and studied this man that he had seldom seen at close range, and never without an entourage of muscle.

Unlike most of his henchmen, Angel was only a little taller than average. Word had it that women found him irresistible. He had a strong jaw and smoky eyes and he let an impressive scar — which would have been easy enough to correct — mar his classic features.

"Goobar is delicious." Angel played the gracious host, scooping some of the mind-altering stuff onto a plate for his visitor. It gave off an odd purple glow.

While the aroma was tantalizing, the Cadet didn't dare try it. Goobar's effects could be devastating and long-lasting. Angel was just the sort to enjoy the risk.

"I'm in training," he said through clenched teeth. "You sent for me."

"Yes," Angel said, carefully wiping his mouth. "I thought we should get to know each other, now that we'll be working together."

"I'm not working with you, Angel," he said without raising his voice or hiding his disgust.

"Did you commit to Domus Aqua to find the nanogen?"

"What if I did?" The Cadet kept his face very still while he dealt with the shock that Domus Aqua must be very candid with Angel for the crime boss to know so much.

"You'll need my cooperation if you want to find the nanogen," Angel said smoothly.

"She's in custody."

"One of them may be in custody, but the other is free," Angel said, helping himself to various dishes.

"What do you mean by the other one?" the Cadet asked and thought, *Where does he get his information?*

"One for the Council and one for the domus." Angel tasted something and sighed. "So are we working together?"

Sitting back in his chair, the Cadet wondered how many nanogens existed and if their numbers would keep growing. At least, it meant he could keep his promise to Lila by locating the second one, but working with Angel bridged on intolerable. After a long pause, he said, "I work alone. My part in this is simply to find the Imagofas. That's it. Why are you so involved?"

"Wherever the credit and the power are, you'll find me," the crime boss said and pushed his plate away. His eyes had become glassy — an aftereffect of the goobar. "If the

Order wasn't watching my people and my every move, I'd have closed this deal without your help. Unfortunately, Captain Grant was a greedy bastard and got himself killed before he told anyone where he stashed the nanogen."

"Who killed him?"

"Don't know. The captain was a bluegrazer, so it could have been anyone. A blackbase-addled brain is not so bright."

The Cadet nodded. "Where was he killed?"

"Blackbase Alley. Somebody slit his throat."

"That sounds vicious. Maybe somebody wanted to send the rest of us a warning." The Cadet felt a pang of apprehension.

"Maybe." Angel obviously had experienced too much of this brand of violence for Grant's death to have had much impact. "I don't have much more to tell you, but I'll contact you as leads come in."

"Right," he replied and stood to leave. Talking with Angel had upset his stomach.

"I'm curious, Cadet." Angel's lip curled snidely. "I always took you for an Order wannabe. Got a vendetta against them these days?"

"No. Why?" The gamer wondered where this was going.

"What's the world coming to when the Order's top cadet drops out and starts working for the Council?"

The Cadet controlled his voice. "I don't work for the Council."

"Whatever you say," said Angel with a grin that the gamer knew was intended to get under his skin.

With a look of disdain, he turned his back on Angel. Marty was in the doorway ready for a confrontation, but one glance from the Cadet made the thug step aside.

"Marty, be so kind as to show our guest out," Angel sputtered to cover his surprise at the Cadet's abruptness.

"I know my way."

Marty and his entourage escorted him to the edge of the market, then quickly left him. The Cadet watched for any sign of Boo, but the lurker was savvy enough to keep his distance.

At home, he unslung his bag and took out the mealbox. Reheating turned the food's texture to rubber. He ate it, cursing Angel with each bite. Part of him wondered if there was any truth to the crime boss' insinuation. Certainly, Joli would never lie to him about collaboration between the Order and the Council to find the Imagofas. That was not like her. She had said the Order recommended him to the Council.

At least Angel had made it easy for him to keep quiet about the Imagofas slated for the tribunal. Lila and Isaac didn't have to know about Joli's Imagofas. And then, Joli never talked about the second Imagofas destined for the domus, so there was no need to tell her about theirs. He was in good stead with everyone ... for now.

|.|.|...|||||...|.|..|

The Bozleys greeted the Cadet with shock and disbelief, scanning him several times for possible identity fraud before they would allow him to enter their flat. The gamer guessed that he resembled no tutor they had ever met. The couple sat across from him with the Imagofas sandwiched between them. She was beautiful. That was his first surprise. Her long black hair flowed over her shoulders, framing a perfectly symmetrical, oval face. Her eyes were a deep gold-brown. He sensed something too perfect or nonhuman about her and wondered if the Bozleys sensed it too. And yet, when the nanogen glanced at him, he doubted his perception. Maybe he was only imagining a difference — to put a distance between him and all that beauty — for his own protection.

"You're from the Underground." Mrs. Bozley looked him up and down disapprovingly.

"Yes."

"I've seen you somewhere before," said her husband, then, "Are you a Novus Orbis fly gamer?"

"Yes." The Cadet saw the man's puzzlement and quickly added, "But I'm also a tutor."

"You understand Alice is not allowed to enter Novus Orbis," said the woman, glancing at her husband with concern.

"I understand," the gamer said to reassure them, although he felt no real obligation to limit her access to Novus Orbis since Joli had never mentioned it.

The Imagofas seemed to fight a smile. Faking a cough, she covered her mouth with her delicate hand.

"My role as a tutor is to help Alice adjust to living on Earth. Since she was brought up on Mars, she may not be familiar with our culture, all the unspoken rules and regulations." The Cadet tried to sound serious and reserved; he knew his appearance made them nervous.

Mrs. Bozley said, "Alice needs to be exposed only to limited aspects of our culture, nothing alternative. We want her to be safe so your meetings will need to be under my supervision." She looked to her husband for support, but he surprised both her and the Cadet by shaking his head.

"No dear. I'm sure they'll be fine on their own. Remember, the Council selected him as her tutor." Bozley squinted at the young man. "Scan them both after their sessions to ensure there are no space violations. You'll agree to that?"

Mrs. Bozley sighed unhappily in quiet resignation.

"Would you like me to begin this afternoon?" the Cadet inquired. He wanted to have a chance to question this Imagofas away from the others.

"Yes. Of course." Bozley pointed upwards. "The roof has a swimming pool and courtyard. It's a bit crowded just now, but there are always extra seats."

"Fine," the young man said. Tutoring her in a public place might make Mrs. Bozley more at ease. As the Cadet waited with Alice for the elevator, the Bozleys watched them from the doorway. Mrs. Bozley leaned over to her husband and said in a loud whisper, "Isn't this all a little peculiar? They give us this strange, sweet child to care for and now there's a fly gamer to tutor her? I trust the Council knows what they're doing."

"Shh, dear," Bozley said, quietly. "Later."

As soon as the elevator closed, the Cadet let his amusement show and won a shy smile from Sashimu. They ascended to the roof and found a place to sit under the shade of potted trees a small distance from children splashing in the pool. She shaded her eyes from the painful white glare off the pool and cement.

"I imagined you differently," the Cadet began awkwardly. "If your existence was widely known, it would inspire great fear."

"You know my identity?" He saw her studying him.

"Yes. I'm here not so much as your tutor, but to protect and look out for you." In the lowest tone, he said, "You're Imagofas."

"Yes." She inclined her head towards him. She smelled of cinnamon. "I am Sashimu."

"I see; Alice Chigusa is just your alias."

"Who sent you to protect me?" she asked.

"I'm under oath not to say, but I promise that I mean you no harm."

"I believe you." Sashimu dropped her gaze. "I grow stronger daily, but I'm still weak."

"I can help you become strong. I train long hours everyday in Novus Orbis." He stopped abruptly, remembering she was restricted from accessing the MAM. "We can train here in Vetus Orbis; that will be better for building your strength."

"Mr. Bozley said you were a fly gamer in Novus Orbis. Is that true?"

"Yes. I can teach you the basics of gaming if you're interested." The Cadet felt slightly giddy with their heads bent so close.

"Would that help me in Novus Orbis? I mean," she added hastily, "once I'm allowed access?"

The Cadet thought for a moment. "That depends on what you need to accomplish. I don't know how useful combat skills would be for you."

"I would appreciate you teaching me those skills. Thank you." She bowed from her waist while sitting, the motion bringing her so close she brushed against him.

Willing himself to focus, the Cadet broached the topic of the missing Imagofas. "My understanding is that there are two of you."

The effect was instantaneous. Her eyes widened and then narrowed to slits. "Yes, there were two of us, but I don't know if Thesni is still alive."

"She's alive."

"Oh, thank Juno!" exclaimed Sashimu. "Where is she?"

"She's missing, but I'm trying to find her before thugs like Angel get their hands on her," the Cadet remarked. Her earnest reaction told him that she had no idea where Thesni was either.

"Who is Angel?" Sashimu perked up at his name as though he had given her a clue.

"He's an Underground criminal," said the Cadet, and instantly regretted mentioning him.

"Why do you care what happens to Thesni?" Sashimu asked. He saw that she was studying him again, and growing wary.

"I'm just trying to find her." He experienced a pang of guilt for not explaining that he was supposed to find the Imagofas for Domus Aqua. Until now, he had thought only about getting paid and satisfying Lila. Whatever the domus wanted Thesni for was none of his concern, but a domus' interests were primarily economical. The Cadet shuddered to think about what the domus might do to the Imagofas for financial gain.

"I want to find her, too," Sashimu snapped, still staring at him apprehensively. The Cadet sat silent, unsure what more to say. He didn't want to lie or give her false assurances.

Finally, he stood awkwardly and tried to sound light-hearted. "I apologize, but we should return downstairs. Mrs. Bozley may worry I've kidnapped you."

Downstairs Mrs. Bozley carefully scanned them and asked Sashimu in a stage whisper whether the Cadet had "been a gentleman." Sashimu seemed perplexed by the question and then nodded when it appeared the woman expected an answer.

The Cadet left, feeling conflicted. He definitely wanted to get "paid handsomely" by the domus, and he also felt honor-bound by his promise to come through for Lila. And yet, Sashimu seemed harmless, even innocent. Maybe the other Imagofas was different. Or perhaps, they were dangerous in hidden ways of which they themselves were not aware.

Now that he had met Sashimu, though, the Cadet had his doubts. Finding the other Imagofas for the domus no longer seemed like such a good idea. Sashimu reminded him of himself and what he was — an Undergrounder who knew from first-hand experience what it felt like to be used for profit.

Without consciously deciding to, the Cadet found himself in the Underground headed for Gil's bar. He would get a drink and pay a visit to the address in Novus Orbis that Creid had left him.

Gil's Bar

Gil's Bar looked as if it had been hit by an Underground whirlwind. So did Gil. His eyes were swollen, surrounded by deep purple bruises and his nose was skewed to the left. He limped doggedly around his bar, welcoming the regulars, all of whom were helping to clean the mess.

After righting several tables, the Cadet marveled at how thorough the Order had been in this shutdown, while nearby, Angel's black market business operated without the slightest interruption.

With a glass of Benedictine, the Cadet retired to the shadows and watched as the bar became crowded. Tonight, clientele waited patiently for their drinks and tipped as much as they could afford.

Undergrounders respected the Order when it punished criminals, but the organization too often terrorized mom-and-pop businesses for offering services Undergrounders could hardly afford otherwise. To access the MAM, Undergrounders had to go above ground and pay a premium, join the religious Sanctuary — which operated above and below — or illegally access the MAM from the Underground.

MAM access, however, was the least of most Undergrounders' worries. The Cadet was reminded of it every day. He hated seeing families living in filth with roaches and rats, alongside human vermin — criminals, bluegrazers and other scum. For generations, people had accumulated in the Underground, as surface shanty towns and ghettos had been razed and replaced by luxury apartments, homes and parks for the growing wealthy elite. The government encouraged this mass relocation by building affordable, low income housing in the Underground. Utilities were cheaper, too, but the Underground lacked MAM access or infrastructure; they were deemed expensive to implement, which translated as "unnecessary."

As a gamer, the Cadet had access to all the upground, premium MAM optimization areas while all his actions were monitored. However, Gil provided cheap, anonymous, but risky access to Novus Orbis. For the first time, the Cadet planned to take advantage of Gil's service. He did not want his movements tracked.

Seeing the young man's nod, Gil hobbled over to his table and asked, "Another glass?"

"Not just yet; I've something else in mind," said the gamer, grimacing at Gil's face. "I know a great medic that could take care of that broken nose for you."

Half-smiling, Gil slid down conspiratorially into the seat next to him. "I'll get it healed tomorrow — just wanted everyone to know what's happening. Used to be the Order shut me down along with the black-market businesses next door to make us sell legit. These days, they leave the market alone because it's so profitable and go after me because I can't make the bigger payoffs. Besides, a medic can make the bruises disappear, but there's other kinds of hurt, if you know what I mean."

The Cadet knew all about the other kinds of hurt. He lived with the mental pain and inner aches from gaming that the medics never healed. Still, he suspected that getting roughed up by the Order was far worse. "Are you 'fully' open?" he asked.

Surprised that the Cadet was interested in his side business, Gil raised an eyebrow and said, "Sure, but that's not your style."

"Styles change," the Cadet growled. That was all the explanation he felt like giving this man.

Gil shrugged and snapped his fingers. A young woman, in a long gray dress open at the sides to reveal soft ashen skin from breast to ankle, sauntered over to them. Seeing the Cadet's consternation, she laughed and slipped an arm around his waist. "Come with me."

"You're not what I was asking for," he sputtered, but she firmly propelled him out of the bar. Several doors down, she stopped beside a deep air vent. Leaning heavily against him, she palmed the wall behind him while forcing a wet kiss. Her laughter followed him as he stumbled backwards through a hidden doorway.

Worn and dated MAMsuits hung from a rack, giving off a musty odor that mixed with the smell of perspiration and sex. These MAMsuits had been crudely altered with MAMhood override patches to allow Undergrounders to assume another's identity when they entered Novus Orbis. The Cadet carefully detached one of the override patches from the best of the miserable suits and adhered it to the back of his own MAMsuit hood at the base of his neck.

The MAM optimization area, though grimy and small, was fortunately empty. The Cadet guessed he was situated beneath a large upground optimization complex. Gil must siphon off energy and access in amounts too minute to be detected. As a professional gamer, the Cadet was used to the best available equipment and optimization areas. This place reminded him how far he had risen above the life of the average Undergrounder.

He dug several fingernail-sized motion detectors from his bag and attached them to the hidden door. If anyone entered, he would receive a warning in Novus Orbis. With a strong sense of dread, he centered himself in the optimization area and activated his MAMsuit hood; it flowed forward from his collar, molding itself to his head and covering his face. The patch burned against the nape of his neck. Even with the best suit in the world, a faulty optimization area or bad patch could prove hazardous. The Cadet only hoped Creid's download — curiously labeled Prometheus Memory — was worth it.

|.|.|...||||...|.|.|

Instead of the usual vertigo and thrill that came with giving up control to the MAM, the Cadet felt overwhelmed by a high-pitched, excruciating sound. When it died, he found himself in Novus Orbis — but submerged in deep, cold water. Gasping for air, he swam up to the surface and managed to hoist himself onto a boulder. He was in the middle of a muddy river. Rain pelted his face and shoulders. He shook his head violently to clear his vision. An enormous brownish-green, red-spotted leech with five pairs of eyes swam up beside him and opened razor-toothed jaws.

The Cadet pulled himself up further onto the rock to avoid the creature. The dark water churned sluggishly beneath him, and the rain fell so hard it stung.

With all its eyes trained on him, the leech popped up, gnashing its teeth.

"Hello there," the Cadet said nervously, pulling his feet further from the water. "Could you direct me to Creid Xerkler's Prometheus Memory?"

"I could, but I won't," it replied and swam away.

Diving after the leech, he grabbed its tail and struggled to stay clear of its jaws. After several attempts to attach to him, the leech abruptly switched tactics. It swam upstream, knocking him against rocks and finally dragging itself onto the embankment beneath a bridge. As the leech metamorphosed, the Cadet dropped his bag and drew his swords, one short and one long.

The leech transformed. It became a kappa-like daemon with a severely indented head, yellow eyes and vampire fangs. Its sickly green tortoise-shaped body and protruding chest made the Cadet step back in surprise. Its scaly limbs ended in gigantic webbed hands that drew a sword from beneath its shell. Stepping forward, it struck. The Cadet managed to block the blow with his long sword but was thrown off balance. He scrambled away.

To gain the advantage of higher ground, the young man moved up the embankment. The daemon followed. The Cadet parried a blow with his short sword, then as the monster moved in closer he swung the long blade in a swift diagonal cut, slicing into the daemon just below its shoulder. The thing roared in pain, its scaly left arm dangling loosely from its socket. It lunged for the Cadet's throat and he fell back to avoid its fangs and sword.

"You may kill me," the daemon hissed, "but you'll suffer afterwards. My fangs and my sword are both coated with poison. One tiny scratch will paralyze you, and here you will lie until a human dispatcher happens to find you or you waste away."

It lunged again and the Cadet dodged. "Did Creid create you to protect his Prometheus Memory from unauthorized users?" he asked.

"I'm MAM-generated — much more useful than any of Creid's creations," it said. It stabbed at him and he twisted aside just in time to keep it from slicing into his side. "You are accessing the Village of Memories Dead."

"What village?" he asked, stabbing at the daemon's good arm. It blocked him with such force that, again, he fell back.

"The village houses classified memories and sensitive materials of historical figures. Only Order Elders and closest kin have access to important memories of people such as Creid Xerkler, the father of the MAM. I am protector of the Village of Memories Dead."

"So by killing you, I gain access to all memories of the dead," said the Cadet, baffled that Creid's memories had been moved to the village while he still lived.

"Killing me will only trigger another, bigger daemon in my place." It drove at him, swinging its powerful blade, unhampered by its wound. The creature was steadily gaining ground. Each swipe of its sword came closer to slicing his virtual flesh.

"How about a deal? I ask you a question about Creid's Prometheus Memory. You answer; I leave." The Cadet's long sword was growing heavy, and he knew he couldn't kill the daemon without at least sustaining a scratch — and that would be deadly.

"I will answer as long as the question violates none of my protocols," the daemon answered and lowered its sword.

The young man sought to phrase the question so that it would encompass all the possibilities. "Did Creid's Prometheus Memory include the fact that he'd been threatened somehow with a coma, or make any references to a coma?"

"No." The daemon turned and dove into the river. "Wait." The Cadet went after it, but the daemon had vanished in the murky water.

Signaling his session to end, the Cadet followed, sinking deeper into the foul blackness. Finally, when he was frightened that he might drown, an ear piercing screech marked his re-emergence from Novus Orbis into Vetus Orbis.

|ₐₗₐₗₐₐₗₗₗₗₐₐₗₐₗₐₗ|

The Cadet found himself back in the optimization area. He was curled on the floor in a fetal position. His head throbbed and his ears were ringing. The tiny room stank with the overwhelming smell of his own urine. Ripping the override patch from his MAMsuit hood, he threw it on the floor and staggered to the wall. He was thankful that no one had tried to enter.

He collected his detectors from the door, hoisted his bag over his shoulder and placed his palms against the hidden panel. It slid open onto the tunnel down from Gil's bar. Disgusted with himself and his session, he vowed never again to use Gil's optimization area. This MAM entry and exit had been too dangerous. If he wanted to access Creid's Prometheus Memory, he would have to do it from a valid optimization area, even if that meant losing anonymity.

The Cadet stopped at the bar, transferred credit from his account to Gil's, and fumbled his way back to his quarters. When his head hit the pillow he dreamed of Sashimu's haunting eyes.

|ₐₗₐₗₐₐₗₗₗₗₐₐₗₐₗₐₗ|

The Cadet's second tutoring lesson began almost as awkwardly as the first. When he entered the Bozleys' apartment, he saw Sashimu hidden at the edge of the top stair observing them. He winked at her as Mrs. Bozley ushered him into the living room for an interrogation about his experience as a tutor. Since he had only tutored other gamers, he kept his answers short, trying not to deepen her suspicions.

When she finally called Sashimu down, relief washed over him. Mrs. Bozley watched them until they took the elevator. When they reached the roof, Sashimu did not get out. Instead, she told the elevator to take them down to the basement.

"Mr. Bozley reserved the old gymnasium in the basement after I told him we planned to exercise, but he asked me not to tell his wife," Sashimu explained when her tutor asked where they were going. "She worries the Council will blame them if I get injured."

She smiled up at him and he felt a shiver down his back as they stepped off the elevator into a long, wide subterranean hallway. Being around her made it difficult to concentrate, and his headache was already distracting him. The gymnasium was the last door on the right.

"Lights on," Sashimu said.

The Cadet was impressed by the size of the room and that it had an optimization area for gaming. "Does it get much use?"

"He told me it's popular for big gaming events between the domus. Spectators come here for pre-game parties and to watch the matches together. Students use it, too." Sashimu paused. "I've never seen a game."

"You have to be in Novus Orbis to enjoy the thrill of a game."

"I can imagine," she said softly.

From his bag, the gamer pulled out two practice swords. He showed her how to hold and wield the blade, and ran through some basic exercises. He was surprised at how quickly she learned. Despite weakness in her arms and legs because of the heavy Earth gravity, she maintained excellent form. Halfway through the lesson though, the Cadet collapsed against the wall and slid to the gymnasium floor.

"Are you injured?" Sashimu inquired and laid down her sword.

"No, but I did a stupid thing." He said, clutching his throbbing head, helpless to stop the loud ringing in his ears, which were both aftereffects of trying to access Creid's memory download from Gil's illegal optimization area. "Damn Creid and his Prometheus Memory download!"

"Prometheus? Is that a common name?" asked Sashimu, puzzled.

"I've no idea," the Cadet answered with a heavy sigh. Creid had never mentioned Prometheus to him before. "Why?"

"I met Prometheus," Sashimu hesitated, barely restraining her excitement, "in Novus Orbis."

"You've been in Novus Orbis?" the Cadet inquired, focusing on her through bloodshot eyes. "Before giving me the Prometheus Memory download, Creid did ask me to protect you. Maybe the Prometheus memory relates to you."

"Let me help access this memory," Sashimu said.

"The Prometheus Memory is heavily protected by daemons," he replied, rubbing his temples to ease the pain. "I can't put you in that kind of danger."

"Don't worry about me. I can handle myself in Novus Orbis," Sashimu said. She defiantly flipped her long black hair back over her shoulder. "Let me piggyback on your MAMsession."

"Whoa! That's illegal, for one thing, and you don't have a MAMsuit," he said.

"I don't need a MAMsuit."

"You can enter Novus Orbis without a MAMsuit?" Shocked, the Cadet realized that he had only just begun to learn the Imagofas' capabilities. Without waiting for an answer, he added weakly, but with finality, "Sashimu, it's too risky."

"I need to talk to Prometheus about Thesni." Sashimu brushed away his objections. "He might have learned something by now."

"Prometheus is looking for her, too?" Now the gamer grew alarmed. At the same time he felt completely baffled.

"Let's find out." Sashimu beamed her most disarming smile.

The Cadet looked away. "Honestly, I feel too awful to enter Novus Orbis," he said. He shakily rose to his feet, leaning on her arm until he regained his balance.

"We can wait until next weekend," said Sashimu. "The Bozleys will be at a reunion. I'm not allowed to leave the general area, but the gymnasium is within limits."

"We'll have a tutoring session, but don't count on Novus Orbis," the Cadet added, hoisting his bag across his shoulders. "My mission is to protect you, not place you in harm's way."

"It might be worse for me to enter unchaperoned," Sashimu said and winked at him.

Flinching less from his headache than the power of her insistence, he led the way upstairs, submitted to Mrs. Bozley's scan and left with a perfunctory bow.

To give himself time to think, he dropped down through an old service access door into the Underground and traveled by foot toward his quarters. Lacking any reliable clues about whatever enemies Creid might have, he was counting on the Prometheus Memory to shed some light on Creid's sudden, unexplained coma. He also hoped the memory might contain useful information or that it would at least clarify the mystery of Sashimu's existence. Yet first, before risking Sashimu in Novus Orbis, he would speak to Joli. The daemon had said that, as Creid's next of kin, she would have legitimate access to all her husband's memories. No matter what the costs of accessing Creid's memory, the Cadet was determined to get to the truth.

The Sanctuary

Whenever the Bozleys allowed, Sashimu left the residential towers for the relative quiet of the park. Still, the hum of heliocars proved inescapable. Far above her, they formed dark swarms around the gleaming spires. Yet, sitting underneath a canopy of cottonwoods, she could listen and watch in relative peace. No waters flowed on Mars' surface; the natural river which ran through the park fascinated her. Of all Earth's differences, she found the abundant water the most intriguing — and gravity, the most horrible.

Mostly, she missed Mars. After school, she would see students gathering in the park, and it reminded her of how happy she'd been at the Feynman Academy with the other Imagofas. They had studied, played and grown up together. With the Imagofas to lead and Mars to explore and reinvigorate, it was ludicrous that she was trapped here on Earth.

Until she found Thesni, returning home could be no more than a daydream. Sashimu trusted the Cadet to get her into Novus Orbis; once there, she was certain Prometheus would sense her presence and contact her. Maybe Prometheus had already found Thesni and could reunite the two of them. If that failed, the Cadet had mentioned a man called Angel who might know Thesni's whereabouts.

A group of students laughed and pointed at her from a nearby bench where they often hung out. Sashimu glared stonily back at them. Across the river, she saw a lengthy procession of cloaked figures. Their clothes took on the hue of the scenery behind them. As the monks passed trees, their cloaks turned brown and green. In front of the brightly decorated shrine, their cloaks took on red and orange hues.

The chameleon material reminded her of the Order's rank-and-file uniforms, but the similarity ended there. The monks traveled in pairs, along the path, chanting in Latin, and, as they passed near her, one of the voices sounded like Thesni's. Sashimu bolted after the procession, crossing the river by a step bridge. She caught up to the last monk in the procession. He dropped back from the others.

"Yes, young lady?"

"Do you have women in your procession?" Sashimu asked breathlessly, studying the long line of monks in search of Thesni's small figure.

"Not today," he answered. His eyes quickly surveyed the area behind Sashimu. "We are chanting our way to temple. Excuse me, but I must keep up."

"Please. What does the chant mean?"

"It is our prophecy." The sun played over his hood so that Sashimu never had a clear view of his face. At a jog, he regained the rear of the procession. She watched them disappear around a bend in the path, and then she returned to the Bozleys' flat. Had her senses tricked her? Perhaps, thinking so much about Thesni, she was liable to see her in every corner and hear her in every crowd.

At dinner, she asked Bozley, "Would you mind telling me about the monks who pass by here?"

He smiled indulgently. "The monks are from the Sanctuary. It is the 'ecumenical convergence of all religions,' which is their fancy way of saying the Sanctuary represents all faiths."

"Is it a brotherhood, only men?"

"Monks can be women or men. Every type of spiritual leader and devotee may be found within the Sanctuary. Monks, laypeople, shamans, priests, ministers, rabbis and clerics; you name it. Although they have differing beliefs, they agree on a universal tolerance. The Sanctuary embraces all religions, from the most ancient to the latest."

"What do they chant?"

"I'm not sure which sect you heard." He shrugged, growing impatient.

Sashimu persisted. "I heard Latin, and they were wearing chameleon-style robes."

Now Bozley looked uncomfortable. He adjusted his collar. "I am no theologian."

Excusing herself from the table, Sashimu went upstairs to her bedroom, haunted by the sound, real or imagined, of Thesni chanting. She heard a rap on her door; it slid open and Mrs. Bozley stepped inside.

"You made my husband uneasy with your questions," she said, sitting beside Sashimu on the bed.

"I'm sorry."

"Let me answer your questions. It can't hurt for me to tell you the little I know." The woman leaned against the headboard next to Sashimu. "The monks you saw are known as the Magus. Most people think they're a cult and want the Sanctuary to exclude them, but the Sanctuary only excludes those who preach intolerance or who hurt others."

"Why are they considered a cult?" Sashimu asked.

"Well," Mrs. Bozley paused before continuing. "They have strange beliefs that verge on subversive."

Sashimu sat up attentively against the pink pillows. Mrs. Bozley leaned closer and dropped her voice to a whisper. "The Magus monks believe that the only way to ensure the continuance of the human race is to accelerate human evolution. They see genetic engineering of humans as God's will."

"Haven't there always been a few oddballs — fringe groups — that thought like that?" Sashimu asked, trying to sound casual.

"It's more complicated than that. Some say that the Magus and the Open MAM Movement have joined forces."

"We have the OMM on Mars," said Sashimu. "Don't they just provide technical support to charity organizations?"

"That's their cover, but the OMM creed is that the MAM should be free from government control." Mrs.

Bozley's hand shook as she pushed a stray strand of hair from her eyes. "Together, the Magus and OMM may seriously threaten our government."

Sashimu coughed to hide a nervous giggle. From what she could remember of her studies, the Open MAM Movement had always been a benevolent volunteer organization. Besides, it seemed to Sashimu that Mrs. Bozley had little to fear from the OMM since the Order policed such organizations so closely, but her new guardian was just warming up.

"The Magus have a prophecy that nanogens, developed for and by humans, will return to Earth to lead humanity into the future." She leaned close to Sashimu as though someone might hear. "Lately they've been on the street corners and in the prayer halls, everywhere, saying disturbances in Novus Orbis prove the prophecy. They say the time has come. They say," tears welled in her eyes and she shivered fearfully. "The nanogens are here."

Before Sashimu could react, the bedroom door slid back to reveal Bozley, standing with hands on his hips. He let out a roar. "What lies are you telling her?"

He moved quickly to drag his wife off the bed and into the hallway. He threw Sashimu a glance that combined fury and, she thought, a tinge of fear as he closed the door behind them. She could hear them arguing down the hall until their bedroom door slammed shut. Suddenly, it was eerily silent.

In contrast to Mrs. Bozley's dread, Sashimu felt elated. A group existed on Earth that might celebrate and protect her. This was the first time she'd dreamt there might be a place she could get help if her present plan failed.

Village of Memories Dead

The elegant spires of the Council's main offices glinted gold in the sunlight. A heliotaxi dropped the Cadet off on one of the upper bridges that interconnected the vast complex. According to the building guide, Joli's suite of offices were in the Technology Transfer section. He had to check in with reception before he could be allowed up. The receptionist eyed him with suspicion. Ignoring the distrustful glare, the gamer asked to speak with a neighbor from the Underground named Linda. She had always appreciated him chasing away lurkers from her doorstep and came up personally to help him.

"So, the Renegade Master leaves the Underground for other reasons than just to game?" Linda said. Behind the teasing, she was obviously curious about what he was doing there.

Smiling, the Cadet said only, "I'm here to see Councilwoman Joli Xerkler."

"I'll let her know." Linda spoke softly into her Companion and a moment later there was surprise in her voice as she said, "She's not an easy one to meet with these days, but you got lucky."

"Thanks a lot."

"Anything for you, Renegade." After showing him to Joli's area, she winked at him and disappeared.

The corner suite was part of a series of glass-walled offices. He looked in at a MAM optimization area and a sleek waiting room with a couch and chairs. The Cadet wondered how she could stand to work in such open surroundings.

Joli walked nonchalantly towards him, surrounded by her cronies. Turning to them, she gave orders and they headed down another corridor. When she looked back to the gamer, he saw dark circles under her eyes and felt a moment's guilt for having waited to tell her about Creid's message.

"Is the tutoring going well?" Joli made a subtle gesture, changing the transparent glass walls opaque for privacy, and sat on the couch. "I understand you're not quite what they expected."

"The tutoring is no problem." The Cadet sat across from her. Concerned about her answer, he cleared his throat uneasily and asked, "How is Creid doing?"

"He's still in a coma. The medics can't bring him out of it."

"I'm sorry to hear that. I did some research and, apparently, MAMsuits have been used in clinical trials as an experimental therapy for some coma victims. The trial results haven't been made public, but it might be worthwhile to ask the medics what they think of it."

"I'll definitely ask them," Joli said hopefully, biting her lip to keep her emotions in check. "Thank you."

"There's one other thing I should tell you," the Cadet added. He dropped his gaze to the floor, unwilling to look her in the eyes. "I received a communication from Creid."

"So he did leave you a message," Joli said. "You should have told me the moment you knew."

"I apologize." Now even more reluctant to meet her gaze, he went on to explain what had happened when he tried to access the Prometheus Memory, only faltering over the part about the Village of Memories Dead, as it was new to him.

"We'll go through authorized channels to access his memories. I'd prefer not to fight any daemons," Joli said. She sounded relieved to be taking some action. She spoke into her Companion, reserving a conference room under the name of one of her subcommittees.

The Cadet followed her into the hallway and down several flights of stairs to a suite of conference rooms.

Their dark, solid walls made the Undergrounder feel more at ease.

Joli shed her robes, revealing a skintight MAMsuit. He noticed that her right wrist still bore a crane tattoo from when she was in the Order while her left wrist had the snow-capped mountain that was the Council's emblem. He felt a longing to wear the crane, the mark of the Order.

Joli entered one of the cubicles in the optimization area. The Cadet did the same.

｜.｜.｜..｜｜｜｜...｜.｜.｜

They planned to rendezvous at the Office of the Deceased. When they passed through their user preferences and arrived, the Cadet deferred to Joli; she was used to dealing with bureaucrats.

"We request access to the memory downloads of Creid Xerkler, my husband," Joli asked of the small bureaucrat in a lurid green suit who sat behind an enormous empty desk.

"Where is your family's repository?" the bureaucrat asked.

"The Village of Memories Dead."

"Ah, your husband must be important. Unfortunately, I have no jurisdiction over the VMD. This office deals with private collections. An in-person request must be made to the Order Office for the Protection of Special Memoirs. Once they give you an access key, go directly to VMD," he explained.

"This is a time-sensitive memory download. Please submit the request on my behalf. The Council would be highly appreciative." Joli spoke confidently, suggesting both a threat and a promise if he failed to act on her behalf.

"I do not submit such requests. It is against protocol," the bureaucrat replied peevishly.

"How close are you in proximity to the Order's Office for the Protection of Special Memoirs?" Joli asked, instantly annoyed.

"In Vetus Orbis, I am next door," the bureaucrat admitted. "It will take a couple months to process your request. They're backlogged at the moment."

No matter what Joli said, the bureaucrat's answer remained the same. Furious, she exited Novus Orbis, and the Cadet followed.

I.I.I...IIII...I.I.I

The Cadet pulled off his hood as she stepped out of the optimization area.

"I say we go directly to the address Creid left you," Joli said, pacing the length of the conference room in agitation. "An in-person interview? What a bureaucratic ass! They can't keep Creid's memories from me. The daemon said all you needed was to be next of kin, right?"

The Cadet nodded and gave her the address. "I must warn you that his Novus Orbis address has been slightly corrupted. It places us in the middle of a river with over-sized leeches."

"A leech-infested river? I'm getting too old for this." Joli said, shaking her head in disgust. "Let's go."

I.I.I...IIII...I.I.I

Hearing the slight whooshing sound and feeling the clean vertigo of a good connection, the Cadet breathed in deeply. This time he was prepared for the plunge into churning water and helped Joli onto the boulder before climbing up himself. Two large horses swam upstream on either side of them.

"I thought you said there were leeches," Joli sputtered, coughing up dirty river water.

"The leeches are probably nearby," he said, then turned to examine the two quarterhorses treading water beside the boulder. "Hello."

"You are the memoryseekers?" the nearest horse asked. Its whinnying voice carried above the sound of the river.

"We seek the Prometheus Memory download of Creid Xerkler." The Cadet grimaced as rain began to fall in heavy sheets.

"Joli Byl Xerkler and the Cadet," said the second horse. "Welcome, we are your access to the Village of Memories Dead."

Joli and the Cadet slipped onto the horses' backs and rode through the water. Enormous leeches swam by without noticing them.

The horses climbed out below a bridge and Joli and the Cadet dismounted. They followed a path canopied by trees that protected them from the hard rain. In the brief time it takes to dream a dream, they relived Creid's recent memories. They saw him meet Prometheus, found the game box with its hidden backdoor into MAM subsystems, noted the altered hospital records and reviewed the fight with the tengu. Creid's memories however, ended abruptly back at the riverbank below the bridge.

Joli was more agitated than ever. She cast around for hidden information from Creid that only she and the Cadet might recognize. Failing to find anything useful, she turned to him and said, "I'm surprised those are the only memories Creid left. There's more to this story than simply those altered hospital records."

The Cadet searched for the horses, but saw only leeches gathered at the edge of the riverbank, watching them. Five of the monsters pulled themselves out of the water and metamorphosed into daemons, tortoise-shelled and scaly-armed.

"This is a bad sign," he said, more to himself than to Joli. She stared apprehensively at the daemons as they quickly surrounded the pair.

"You are next of kin, but no one is authorized to access this memory because it was created under an illegal alias," one of the daemons informed them. "Undergo a memory erase to end your session or we will attack."

The Cadet drew his sword. Neither of them would willingly submit to an erase; the procedure was notorious for leaving people with persistent short-term memory loss. "Those daemons and their weapons are poisonous," he warned Joli. "Don't let them so much as scratch you."

"Got it," Joli said. A moment later she was dodging a daemon's thrust at her chest.

The Cadet quickly clobbered the creature on the head. Thick liquid drained out of its skull, as it retreated into the river. Howling, the rest of the daemon pack descended on them.

The Cadet attacked another daemon, driving it back. Joli whirled underneath a poisoned sword and sprang into the air kicking its wielder's head with both feet. The impact sent the daemon reeling and screaming into the river.

"They keep coming! Look at them all," the Cadet gasped. They were completely surrounded. It was only a matter of time before they'd be forced into a memory erase. The gamer shuddered.

"B-SAM," Joli ordered.

The Cadet nodded, bringing his arms into the Body of a Short-Armed Monkey position — close to his body to avoid being slashed while wielding his sword. As the daemons moved in, the Cadet and Joli fought back to back, rotating swiftly to meet the onslaught. The ground around them was slick with black blood. An endless supply of giant leeches slithered out of the river to take the place of the fallen.

Abruptly, the tight group of daemons scattered. Two galloping horses drove through their midst, with an old man in a gold-quilted toga standing with one foot on the back of each steed. He leaped from the horses to land on one of the daemons that swarmed around him, leaving Joli and the Cadet forgotten. Discarding their swords, the daemons let loose bloodcurdling screams and fell savagely upon the old man, ripping at his clothes and sinking their fangs into his arms, legs and neck. Undaunted, he threw them off in all directions. And then, turning to each daemon in rapid succession, he bowed deeply as the creature came at him. Taken aback, each daemon bowed in response. As it bent forward, thick black slime from its saucer-topped skull spilled out onto the ground. Thus emptied, one by one, each daemon withdrew to the river's edge and dove into the water. Joli and the Cadet watched in amazement as the vicious monsters meekly filed away.

Bleeding from dozens of deep puncture wounds, the old man stood and wiped blood from his eyes. For a brief moment he lost his balance and grabbed at the Cadet's wrist. To the gamer, the grip felt as if the old man had jabbed something sharp into his skin, but the Cadet resisted pulling free. Instead, he helped the old man regain his footing.

"How did you get them to leave?" he asked.

"It is a vulnerability of the kappa-daemon," said the old man. "A simple bow causes them to lose their resources. Sadly, such vulnerabilities rarely occur twice with the MAM." He laughed heartily at his own private joke.

With a raised eyebrow, Joli gave the Cadet a puzzled look, but he was just as baffled, and could only shrug.

The old man stopped laughing. "Please excuse my clumsiness, Cadet. And Joli Xerkler, our next World Emissary, it is my honor."

"And you are?" Joli asked.

"I am Prometheus. Unfortunately, your respite from the daemons was only temporary." The old man gestured toward the river; the leeches were beginning to collect again. Prometheus added, "You'd better leave now if you want to avoid more daemons."

Still bleeding, he walked away from them along the riverbank, muttering, "Not a lucky day for fishing."

"I'll go after him and find out what he knows," the Cadet said, but Joli laid a hand on his arm.

"No. It's not worth it. We'll never be able to fend off all of those things," she said, gesturing with her chin toward the river. "You can investigate Prometheus later."

Taking one look at the mass of swimming leeches, the Cadet had to agree. They swiftly mounted the horses. The leeches left the animals alone as they entered the river and swam downstream to the boulder. Joli and the Cadet returned to Vetus Orbis.

|..|.|...||||..|.|..|

When they exited, it was late. Most Council personnel had gone home.

"Where did you learn to fight like that?" he asked, trying to equate her aggressive MAM persona with the woman beside him.

"The Order taught me to fight," Joli admitted. "If only I had the same strength in Vetus Orbis. Tell me, Cadet, who is Prometheus?"

"I wish I knew."

"Help me find out."

"No problem. In Creid's memory there was a box he used to alter the hospital records. What was it?"

"Oh that. An old backdoor that he must have originally designed and left in the system," Joli said.

"A backdoor?" Here was something else the gamer and his mentor had in common.

"The Order has installed many more advanced features, but the old ways still exist. Old timers like Creid and I can still find the original backdoors into Novus Orbis," Joli said, pulling on her robes over the MAMsuit. "I have to go, but in two weeks, let's meet at the same time in Novus Orbis where we can safely talk. I'll wait for you at the Rats and Bats bar."

After escorting him to the lobby, she quickly left. The Cadet found he had a new respect for the councilwoman. Not only did she fight like a professional gamer in Novus Orbis, but she commanded mysterious, lost and forbidden knowledge of the inner workings of the MAM. It also touched him that she'd said he was like a son. He'd always felt that Creid was like a second father, even though they had never discussed it.

Flagging a heliotaxi, he jumped in and asked to be let out at the nearest Underground entrance. As it moved off he felt his wrist stinging. He pulled back his tunic and MAMsuit to see what was causing the sharp pain. To his surprise, he saw that his skin was stippled in tiny bumps where Prometheus had grabbed him. The bumps spelled out an address; he redirected the heliotaxi.

It took him to a part of Denver where he had rarely ventured. Known by Denverites as Relic Alley, several square blocks of ancient brick warehouses had miraculously escaped being torn down; they were now inhabited by anachronists — people the gamer scorned. To him the only thing worse than refusing to modernize was clinging to a past that never existed or existed in a way anachronists only imagined.

They were a strange lot. They knew about old things no one used or needed anymore, and they built things with their hands that could be more efficiently built using modern methods. Creid had anachronistic tendencies and, despite their closeness, the Cadet had never understood his mentor's urge to preserve the old and the useless.

After surveying the landing pad on the leaking, tilted roof of the building, the heliotaxi driver refused to set down. The Cadet had to jump. The red bumps on his wrist were almost faded away, but he could faintly discern the suite number: "23". He walked gingerly to the rusted roof door and palmed it, but it didn't budge. Stepping back a moment in surprise, he realized that it was an old-fashioned model. He had to turn the handle several times before he managed to open it.

Inside, he waited for his eyes to adjust to the dark stairwell before he took the stairs to the bottom floor. Down here, none of the suites were numbered. He climbed up a level and searched that floor. The numbering was completely erratic, but the final suite on the second floor had "CX-23" scrawled just above the doorknob. Before he could knock, the door slid back and a disembodied feminine voice said silkily, "Welcome, Cadet. Where is the Imagofas?"

"She's at home," the Cadet said, realizing immediately that he had been identified and addressed by a smart intelligence. Curious, he looked around to find the source of the voice, but the first thing he noticed was an old kitsch balloon-ball floating slowly about the room. It displayed a hologram of a young Creid and Joli smiling, arm-in-arm, and then kissing.

"So this is Creid's private studio," the gamer said without surprise. "I always wondered where he spent his time when he wasn't in Novus Orbis."

To move around the room, he had to sidestep ancient dismantled machines lying in heaps, with lesser parts strewn across the floor, the work benches and shelves. However, this was no ordinary anachronist's workshop.

Everything might look old and worn, but the Cadet suspected this was a deception. After all, even the antique-looking outer door operated with a modern security system that undoubtedly opened only for select individuals.

Tattered and worn leather-bound memoryholders lined one wall from floor to ceiling. They were organized under old-fashioned labels: quotes, readings, personal and professional experiences. The Cadet knew memoryholders had been used during the early days of closed-circuit MAMs before the advent of the universal system. After the Great Migration Law passed, the Order enforced the destruction of these obsolete data technologies. The MAM was now the sole central repository of all human knowledge and experience. A decade earlier, the Great Migration had transferred the last existing data inside. The MAM now allowed for recording anything from Vetus or Novus Orbis at any time and provided reliable memory storage, backups and easy access.

Knowing Creid, the Cadet doubted if the data off these memoryholders had been properly migrated to the MAM. Here was a wealth of invaluable information captured on illegal, outmoded gadgets, but no closed-circuit MAM remained in existence to read them. With Creid in a coma, the Cadet felt a pang of regret that he hadn't spoken more with the man about his past and his discoveries. A great library of Creid's genius now lined the shelves before him, but it was completely inaccessible.

With difficulty, the Cadet turned his attention from the wall of memoryholders to the rest of the room, and was immediately drawn to the far corner. In a small area cleared of debris, the Cadet found a low table with a Go board incised into its top along with two inset bowls, one full of white stones, the other of black. There were two chairs, one on either side. Squatting beside the table, the Cadet ran his hand across the shimmering carved surface of the board. It burned hot to his touch, and he quickly pulled his hand away, blowing on the seared tips of his fingers.

"Ouch! What's the meaning of this?"

"Please return with the Imagofas before attempting to access this closed-circuit MAM," the disembodied female voice said, the sound issuing directly from the board. "Both of you must come together."

"It looks like a Go board," the gamer said, circling the table and chairs to study it.

"It was a four-dimensional Go game, but it has been repurposed for selective discourse and exclusive use by the Imagofas and you."

"The Imagofas is at home," the Cadet stated, wondering if he should attempt to hack Creid's security. "May I access the closed-circuit MAM by myself?"

The room stayed silent. As an experiment, he dropped a handkerchief from his bag onto the board. It immediately disintegrated and he jumped back.

The velvety voice warned, "I am designed to self-destruct if used inappropriately. Please return with both players."

"Fine," the Cadet said. "I'll be back."

Signs

When Ochbo went to the MAM optimization area in the Sanctuary, Thesni sneaked in behind him. Dressed as a chameleon-robed Magus, she escaped all notice, but his.

"Don't let the optimization area scare you," he said, laughing at her dismayed expression. "Entering Novus Orbis is like having a dream that you can control. Of course, it's unnecessary to move or actually speak since our brain signals are inputted directly to the MAM."

"So you can only access the MAM through optimization areas?" Thesni wanted to make sure she understood him.

"Well, since our MAMsuits aren't hooked into anything, authorized users can technically start MAMsessions anywhere on Earth's surface, but the Council developed laws early on to control access. Optimization areas ensure quality access. Dirty connections can be dangerous; they can make you ill or worse. For convenience, people above ground frequently have an optimization area at home or very nearby."

Following behind Ochbo, Thesni entered a large low-lit room with three-sided, padded cubicles where individuals sat in recliners or stood with their MAMsuit hoods pulled over their faces. Mostly they just twitched in place and muttered softly, but once in a while an arm would shoot up in the air or someone might shout.

As she passed by each cubicle she felt the vast presence of the MAM as session after jolting session was initiated. So long as she didn't enter a cubicle, the initializing sessions weren't strong enough to pull her into Novus Orbis.

Besides, she had become wary and adept at controlling her reactions to the MAM.

The first few times she had bungled her piggybacking on Ochbo's sessions. She had been too obvious. As soon as he had felt her presence, he had terminated his session and come at her, cursing in outrage. After she had insisted, they achieved a compromise: unable to open an anonymous MAMsession because of security risks or make her an authorized user (authorization was assigned at birth), he allowed her to piggyback on his sessions.

Luckily for Thesni, she soon graduated beyond their arrangement. She did not tell him that she had become adept at slipping into a corner and piggybacking on others' sessions without arousing suspicion.

Today was no different. After Thesni followed Ochbo to the only office in the MAM optimization area that had a door, a space reserved for the Open MAM Movement, she ducked into a small alcove behind the door. The MAM optimization monitor who patrolled the area did not notice her — not that it mattered. Ochbo had managed to get the OMM to grant him an assistant, which allowed Thesni to be seen with him and to live in OMM quarters beneath the Sanctuary without attracting attention.

In Novus Orbis, she had watched Ochbo repair faulty Sanctuary interfaces. Shadowing him, she had learned how to operate in Novus Orbis without being detected. Careful not to alter anything, she was almost certain she went undetected by all but the MAM itself.

The MAM recognized her, watched and recorded her. It adapted to her biorhythms, optimizing her piggybacked sessions so that each time she felt less vertigo. Even more importantly, it evolved rapid response times to her every action, so that she became much faster than the humans she saw operating in Novus Orbis. In turn, she adapted to the MAM, quickly discarding Ochbo's elaborate interfaces as unnecessary and operating at a much lower level to conduct her searches for Sashimu.

Despite her persistent presence in Novus Orbis, Thesni had found no trace of Sashimu. For all she knew, Sashimu had died on the ship when the explosion hit — although

Thesni believed that if Sashimu had died, she would have felt her loss. They were Imagofas; that made them closer to genetic sisters than blood siblings. Thesni clung to the hope Sashimu lived, praying to Juno and searching Novus Orbis for a shadow like herself.

At any given time, day or night, there were up to twenty individuals accessing the MAM in the cubicles. Once the monitor had done her rounds today, Thesni planned to sneak out and experience someone else's private session; she might gain access to new places in Novus Orbis where she could search for traces of Sashimu.

Ochbo finished his repairs to the first interface and had just started in on the next when the MAM optimization area monitor suddenly called him back to Vetus Orbis.

"Ochbo," the monitor said, biting her thumbnail in agitation and hovering over him as his hood slid back. "The boss is upset. The Order has smart intelligence agents swarming over every bit of code you completed in the past month. You're off all critical interfaces for the Sanctuary until the boss says otherwise. Do you know why the Order is combing through your code?"

"I've no idea," he said, but his face had turned very pale. He involuntarily glanced over to Thesni's hiding place, afraid that the Order had somehow identified her piggy-backing on his sessions.

"And to make matters worse, we've got that Council-woman Xerkler coming today. I have to turn away every-body who has reserved time and clear the area for her security." The monitor threw up her hands. "Everyone is angry and they're taking it out on me."

"That's right," Ochbo said. "I saw on the roster that she's coming by urgent request to St. Camillus."

"It's her husband, Creid, the father of the MAM, I gather that he's seriously ill in the hospital," she explained. "What I don't understand is why she has to come all the way here. There's a hospital chapel, isn't there?"

"Come on, you know as well as I do that nowhere but the Sanctuary completely guarantees unmonitored access — even hospital chapels have been known to be compro-mised," Ochbo said irritably. He realized that he was venting his general agitation about the Order on the monitor because he couldn't mention his real problems.

"I suppose you're right. Look, I've got to get back to the front. Are you available to help me?" the monitor asked. She gnawed at another fingernail.

"I guess I can't do much else," Ochbo said grudgingly. "I'll be right out."

As soon as the monitor left and the door slid closed, Ochbo whispered, "Come out of hiding, Thesni. You heard what she said about the Order. They may suspect that you're piggybacking on my sessions. We've got to be more careful."

"Yes," Thesni agreed, emerging from the alcove, but she was thinking about something else entirely. "The father of the MAM — he probably knows everything about Novus Orbis, right?"

"More than the rest of us," Ochbo said, studying her curiously. "After he retired from the Order, the OMM hoped he'd come over from the dark side as a volunteer. We could use that kind of expertise. Why?"

"Do you think he would know how to find an Imagofas in Novus Orbis?" asked Thesni.

"If anyone could find you, it'd be him, but don't worry about that," he said, patting her on the shoulder. "Creid Xerkler must be really sick for his wife to request a session in the St. Camillus optimization area. She'll have spent the morning at the hospital chapel with the Catholic priests and by noon, she'll fly here. This entire wing of the Sanctuary will be cleared out for her. I'll meet you back at my office after I help the monitor get people out of here."

"Okay, see you there," Thesni said, but first, she intended to head up to the St. Camillus optimization area. If she could piggyback on the councilwoman's session, she would see the father of the MAM. Maybe he could tell her how to find Sashimu.

A group of priests in front of the open doors to St. Camillus were heatedly discussing the councilwoman's imminent arrival. "Councilmember Xerkler made a specific request that she be left alone. We must respect her privacy," said the priest with a large nose. "She won't be accompanied by Council security."

"That's not good. The Council has always provided its own security," remarked another priest. "We will be blamed if anything happens to her."

As they continued to argue, Thesni inched behind them into the optimization area. She dashed down the red carpet set out for the councilwoman, which led to the one closed room among the cubicles. Inside the room, Thesni looked around desperately for a hiding place. The room was small, dominated by the statue of St. Camillus inset into the wall, with a small altar and a single chair.

Hearing voices approaching, Thesni dove under the altar and drew her chameleon robes around her. After a bit of commotion outside the door, she heard a commanding woman's voice, which allowed for no dissension, "I understand your concern. Post yourselves before the outer doors of St. Camillus if you must, but respect my privacy. I must be left alone in here."

Thesni peeked out and saw a small, older woman sweep into the room. She wore ornately stitched robes and blue gems glinted in her pale red braids. She immediately shed her outer clothes, retaining only her MAMsuit, and sat in the recliner as her MAMhood slid over her face and conformed to facial features.

Thesni felt the slight drag of Novus Orbis and found herself beside a much younger avatar of the woman under a blooming plum tree. Not far from them, a man stood wrapped in a strange translucent cocoon. Beneath the clear gauzy substance, the man appeared to be frantically struggling to unhinge a gate.

Drawn toward him, Thesni puzzled over the sheer cocoon that wove in and around him. The man and woman were well into their conversation before Thesni stopped studying him and finally listened.

"Creid, what are you doing?" the woman was saying.

"Joli, is that really you?!" the man called Creid asked anxiously. "I've been trying to get out of this walled garden. It looks like the garden I use to enter my MAMsessions, but I can't open this gate or find any exit. Do you know the way out?"

"Creid, you're in a coma," the woman said softly. "The medics have been baffled, so today I insisted that they give you a MAMsession to keep your brain active. They modeled the garden after your user preferences to make you feel at ease."

"I'm in Novus Orbis?! All this time, I thought I must be losing my mind," Creid cried, his voice cracking with emotion.

Huddled behind one of the plum trees, Thesni watched them. Creid repeatedly ran his hands through his disheveled hair and couldn't remain still for more than a few seconds. Thesni noticed that his jerky movements seemed to coincide with the thickening of the cocoon around him. As it swirled and grew opaque in one spot, he tried to shift away, but the sickly substance surrounded him. What she found even stranger was the fact that Joli seemed unaware of it.

"One moment I was sleeping beside you in our bed, and the next moment, I woke up here." Creid shook his head hard as though to clear it. "I've tried everything to escape. Why did you send me into Novus Orbis?"

"The Cadet dug up some research about experimental therapies for coma patients that suggested MAM activity might keep the brain healthy," replied Joli, her voice quivering and the words coming too fast. "I've been desperate to help you, but your condition has the medics completely stymied. Your brain is active, unlike most coma patients, but still they can't get you to respond in Vetus Orbis."

"It's hard to believe I'm laid out in some Order hospital bed. There are voices here, constantly torturing me. I rarely sleep. Are you trying to drive me mad?" he asked, then giggled, and finally buried his head in his hands. Thesni wondered if there might be a way to penetrate the cocoon or dispel it. The substance appeared to affect Creid's emotional state, causing him to titter deliriously one moment and then, seconds later, send him into a deluge of tears.

"No, honey, I'm trying to help you. I'm your wife," Joli reminded him. She folded her arms across her chest and breathed in deeply to remain calm. "I will risk a lot to save you, but let's be frank with each other. The Order has murdered men for much less serious crimes than yours."

"I've become a liability to you," he said, shoulders sagging forward. "Do you hate me?"

"I love you." Joli sighed and said shakily, "I'm just terrified."

"Whatever is wrong with me will only get worse if the Order has its way." Creid skeptically raised his eyebrows and said, "I've been so disoriented and lonely. Why didn't you visit me sooner to tell me what was going on?"

"This is the first time I've come to you in Novus Orbis," Joli explained with a heavy sigh. "I have visited you every day at the hospital. The medics said it was dangerous to visit you here — traipsing around in your brain, they called it. The truth is, they have no idea what is wrong with you, but they tell me your physical health is fast deteriorating to the point that they have recommended care termination. They say the man I knew and loved is gone. I was desperate, so I applied for a care termination MAMsession. Now here I am, and I can see that they are wrong."

"So I'm to die?" he asked.

"I won't let that happen," Joli said. "Somehow, I'll get you removed from this Order-operated hospital. It never occurred to me, until now, that it could be dangerous. Maybe the medics aren't really trying to help you."

Wondering at the cocoon that seemed to fade from around his head, Thesni edged out from behind the tree for a better look. He had momentarily broken through the veil that surrounded him.

"Once you get me out of the hospital, what happens after that?" Creid asked, with sudden lucidity.

"Once you finally wake up from this coma, you might face charges by the tribunal," said Joli.

"What have they got on me?" Creid asked grimly.

"Goth has told me that you are under suspicion for aiding a nanogen by circumventing customs and for creating MAM backdoors, possibly to commit terrorist acts, as well as for sabotage of Order intelligence by releasing tengus into production."

Creid laughed. "They can't prove any of that. Besides, only the part about helping the Imagofas is true."

"The Order may take care of you before the tribunal has any evidence," Joli said and wiped away tears. "For some reason, they must still think you're useful."

Neither of them had noticed her, and now Thesni inched out further from behind the tree to study him. She needed to find some subtle way to catch his attention and ask him about searching Novus Orbis. When she had piggybacked on Ochbo's session, Ochbo had described her presence in Novus Orbis as his second shadow. Thesni assumed that is how she would appear to these two, as Joli's shadow.

Creid jumped up from the table and ran over to Thesni. "This is a private session. Go away."

Joli stood, startled. With alarm in her voice she said, "Who are you speaking to?"

Terrified that he had noticed her before she had devised a good plan, Thesni turned to run, but saw that Creid was once more being overwhelmed by the cocoon voices that engulfed him. The translucent substance had regained its thickness around his head, though it ebbed and flowed over other parts of his body. She watched his milky cocoon drain his energy and redirect it into Novus Orbis. His wild, haunted eyes met hers through the gauzy film, and she knew that he was in no condition to help her.

"Joli, you have a shadow," Creid said, momentarily turning to his wife and then focusing back again on Thesni. "What are you? Smart intelligence?"

"No," replied Thesni, her heart pounding in her chest.

"I heard that. Who's there?" Joli inquired, her voice rising urgently from behind Creid.

"Did Prometheus send you?" Creid asked Thesni, peering intently at her.

"No," answered Thesni, too afraid to say more.

"I'm going to get to the bottom of this," Creid said.

In a sudden move, Creid reached out to Thesni and launched a commandline. He stripped her shadow avatar down to her streaming code lines and said, "Ah. You're neither smart intelligence nor human. For the MAM, you exist only as a possibility among infinite options."

"I exist only as a possibility?" Thesni was puzzled by his deductions.

"You are Imagofas." There was absolute certainty in the man's voice.

"Creid, I hear a second voice." Joli said. "Are you generating it somehow? Darling, is it possible you are hallucinating?"

Creid ignored his wife for the moment, transfixed by Thesni.

"How did you know?" Thesni whispered, focusing on his cocoon-blurred face, trying to gauge if she should flee. Yet instead of being angry, he was smiling delightedly.

"You leave a sublime signature everywhere you go in Novus Orbis," Creid said, grinning madly. "That's why the Order keeps me alive, because I know things like that. I understand things that nobody else grasps, but I'll never tell those bastards."

Creid twitched violently, and Thesni heard Joli weeping. The cocoon had wrapped more tightly around him and grown thicker in the brief time she'd been there. Thesni didn't dare look away from him. "The MAM has assigned a modified aleph symbol to you," he explained. "I've noted it before. I wish I could remember where — ah, yes, when Sashimu piggybacked on the medic's session."

"You know about Sashimu!" Thesni gasped. Without thinking, she reached up to help him focus, as he struggled to overcome his mania. When she grabbed his arm, her hand passed through the cocoon's gauzy substance and tore a small rent in its structure. The substance peeled away from her hand. "Do you know where Sashimu is?"

"Sashimu? Yes, Sashimu is—"

"Excuse me, Joli Xerkler," said a daemon. It was dressed in a black mourning suit and looked human except for the long blades sticking up where his ears should have been. While he addressed Joli, he focused on Creid and Thesni. "You have just exploited a vulnerability in our security protocol. Thank you for bringing this vulnerability to our attention. Please terminate your session now."

"What are you talking about?" Joli asked furiously. "I've just been standing here while my husband mumbles incoherently to himself. I need more time to talk to him!"

"You must end your session immediately or it'll be ended for you," the daemon said.

"Yes, okay." Joli wiped away tears with her sleeve and turned to Creid. "I will get you out of the hospital."

Tearing herself from the cocoon to avoid coming between Joli and Creid as Joli reached out to him, Thesni fell away from them to the ground. She watched helplessly as his mania returned full force and the cocoon constricted around him.

"I've no time for you," Creid said, trying to extricate himself from Joli's arms and concentrating on Thesni, who was slowly rising to her feet. "I needed to tell her something, but what was it?"

"Good-bye," Joli said through the tears streaming down her cheeks. She ended her session.

"Wait!" Thesni screamed, falling through the darkness.

"Thesni." Ochbo roughly shook her. "What are you doing in here?"

For a moment, she had trouble focusing on him. A wave of nausea made her retch bitter-tasting, green-yellow bile. She was curled up in her hiding place, and Joli Xerkler was nowhere in sight.

"Let's get out of here," he commanded, helping her to her feet.

Back in his quarters, Ochbo brought Thesni water and some sliced apple, but she only shook her head.

"Why were you in the St. Camillus optimization area?" he asked. His sweat exuded an acrid smell of fear. "Tell me it wasn't to piggyback on that councilwoman's session."

Thesni nodded apologetically.

"Oh no," Ochbo said, brushing her damp hair from her brow. "You do realize you chose to access a session of a councilwoman whose husband is none other than the father of the MAM?"

"That's why I risked it."

Ochbo grabbed her by the shoulders. "That councilwoman hates nanogens — that's what she'd call you. The

Imagofas exist only as a threat to narrow-minded people like her."

"Creid knew about me."

He let her go. "What are you talking about?"

"Creid recognized I was an Imagofas. The cocoon around Creid suffocates him and makes him crazy. Is it common to be surrounded by cocoons in Novus Orbis?"

"I've never heard of it." Ochbo shrugged. "Then again, you access the MAM without equipment, piggybacking on somebody else's session. That's supposed to be impossible. So nothing surprises me anymore."

Thesni reached up and gave him a hug. "Sorry I gave you such a scare."

After an awkward silence in which he turned very red, Ochbo managed to ask, "Did you violate any protocols?"

"No," Thesni paused. "Well, maybe one, but the daemon thought Joli had violated the protocol since it was her session."

"Thesni, if you successfully violated a protocol, you may have made the Order suspicious, which means someone may already be coming for you. Not to mention that now Creid knows about you."

"He's on our side," she said, swallowing hard. "I felt that from him, even in his less than lucid moments."

"I'm getting you out of here, now!" Ochbo exclaimed.

Thesni pulled her hood around her face and followed him. Out in the tunnels they heard a commotion behind them, which made them move faster. His quarters bordered on the Sanctuary's private and archaic transit system, but they didn't take it or the modern URT. Instead, he led her deep into the Underground's tunnels.

He took her hand as they ran. "We travel on foot in the Underground because we can move relatively undetected. Once we get to a mountain mission, we can transfer you to one of the Sanctuary's mobile charities."

"Is that safer?" Thesni asked. She noticed that his cheeks had flushed deep red again.

They paused to catch their breath in another narrow service tunnel — empty except for the rats — and Ochbo answered grimly, "Once they're certain that you are alive, nowhere is safe."

Anachronist's Workshop

No convincing was necessary. Before the Cadet even described the Village of Memories Dead, the run-in with the daemons and Prometheus' pressing the address into his wrist, Sashimu wanted to go to Creid's workshop.

"Prometheus' message is a 'nice touch,'" she said turning his wrist over to look at the faint number marked into his flesh. She wore a short schoolgirl skirt and blouse to blend in with the students waiting for heliotaxis outside the park. "He never pressed any address into my flesh that I could use in Vetus Orbis."

"I'll ask him to give you the honor next time instead of me," he said, self-consciously smoothing down his hair with his hand. "You look so young in that uniform. People might worry I'm abducting you. We'll attract attention."

Sashimu laughed. "Come on. I see it in the park all the time, hoodlums with schoolgirls."

"I'm a hoodlum. Great!" The Cadet grimaced and helped her climb into a heliotaxi.

"Strange place for a date," the driver muttered, when the Cadet told him the address. Ten minutes later, he dropped them off on the old warehouse roof in the anachronists' district. The heliotaxi was gone by the time they reached the door and pulled it open.

Stepping into the darkness, the Cadet led the way downstairs to Creid's workshop in suite 23.

"Welcome Cadet and young Imagofas," the silken female voice issued from the Go table in the corner as they entered.

They had only taken a few steps inside when Sashimu suddenly felt dizzy. Before she could react the room gave way to terrible, yawning blackness.

When she came to, the Cadet was on top of her pinning her arms and legs to the floor. She struggled against him, and he rolled off her. His shirtfront was spattered with blood.

"You had a seizure," he said, his face worried. "I tried to pin you down, but you cut your arm when you fell to the floor."

Sitting up slowly, she cradled her arm and whispered, "Water."

Drawing a flask from his bag, he handed it to her. The cold water felt good against her swollen tongue.

"I should take you to the hospital to find out what caused your seizure and have them mend your arm. It's a deep cut."

"My arm is already healing," Sashimu replied, showing him. She pointed to the Go table. "That's the closed-circuit MAM you mentioned, but you didn't warn me about it."

"Warn you about what?"

"Something was triggered as soon as we walked in. I was right behind you, then I was free-falling down a dark, bottomless chasm. You didn't feel it?" she asked.

"No," said the Cadet. "I wouldn't have brought you here if I thought it was dangerous. Creid asked me to protect you. He would never have created something intentionally to hurt us."

Sashimu got to her feet, feeling weary. She went to the Go table and chairs, too curious to leave, but afraid to stay.

A new voice issued from the table. "You have passed the test, surviving an open MAMsession from the unstable closed-circuit MAM that I've cobbled together. Please be seated and let's begin."

"That's Creid speaking," the Cadet exclaimed, anger rising in his voice. "He meant for that to happen!"

Nodding, Sashimu silently sat in one chair and motioned for the Cadet to take the other. Grudgingly, he sat down.

"Don't be alarmed," Creid's voice said. "You can control your access to the closed-circuit MAM by moving the pieces on the board in a specific pattern that will be illuminated on the board as the two of you play."

They faced each other from across the table. Sashimu knew the game from her Imagofas training. "Don't worry," she told the Cadet, and took one of the white shells from the inset bowl. She placed it on the illuminated intersecting lines on the board.

"Thank you," Creid's voice spoke as she moved her hand away. The Cadet placed a black stone and the voice said, "I've organized my memories so that you'll experience only the ones that will shed light on how the Imagofas came into existence. Hopefully, that will also help you understand my motivations. No matter how MAMhistory recasts me and my work, let this stand as an alternative history and my memoir."

"Sashimu," the Cadet said, "Are you sure you want to access Creid's memorysets? He admits that this closed-circuit MAM is unstable and ..."

"Let's just do it," she replied. "All my defenses are up. If it's too overwhelming, we can always exit."

With much trepidation, the Cadet activated his MAMsuit so that the hood slid cleanly over his head. Words flashed before the Cadet as he began the session:

"*MEMORYSERIES (2080): ACCEPT?*"

"Yes." He could feel Sashimu beside him. Her presence was reassuring.

ıılıluıllllıulılıl

\>*Memoryseries 2080-85(2080.08.15)*
Yenfam's new motto was "24/7 until the end." Everyone hoped he meant the end of the month, but no one dared ask for fear of finding out otherwise. The end of the year was four months away, the end of the project, years away. Family visitations occurred once every seven days, though Creid was in a unique position: Joli worked so closely with him, it caused jealousy during the long shifts. Yet for Creid, she made the hours pass quickly.

The Division was wrapping up five-year results of Project Quilt, but no one was satisfied — Creid least of all. Joli told him to be patient, but that had never been his nature.

"Humans weren't made to go this long under these conditions," Dreyfus grumbled.

"Agents weren't made for this stress, either."

"It's we operators, I worry about," Dreyfus said. "Agents are fully replicable applications. *We* are not. I can work only so long before I make more mistakes than progress."

Walking together down an infinite expanse of windowless, undecorated hallway of institutional green, Creid and Dreyfus stopped at a black door with "Annex" printed in tiny white letters above the palm scanner. They performed the ritual palm placement and positioning of the right eye up against the lens to ensure accurate identification; and the door slid open.

The area teemed with engineers working on data streams. MAM machinery sprawled in an endless checkerboard across the Annex Floor, with blocks of equipment hanging from the ceiling and engineers strapped in groups of four facing each other. In their heavy masksets with large bulging eyes, they looked like the advance guard of an alien invasion.

Next to Dreyfus sat Zazen. The youngest of the team, he twitched and strained beneath his MAMsuit. Creid worried about the young man. Zazen took more breaks than Dreyfus or Joli and he was slow at capturing and analyzing data streams; but he showed a flair for detail and accuracy that would make him an excellent scientist. He spoke often of making a new life somewhere far from Earth, far beyond the constraints of Earth's laws.

Creid buckled in next to his wife. Joli took his hand and squeezed it. Her strawberry blonde hair was wound in a long braid that fell to her waist. With her beside him, he felt at ease. He pulled on the unwieldy maskset and everything changed.

Data packets sped by. His team of Dreyfus, Zazen, Joli and a slew of online agents categorized and analyzed data from Earth's classified research projects.

The Order had created Project Quilt to identify social, economic, political, technological and communication patterns, and to predict trends. His group was having more success in detecting patterns and providing accurate near-term predictions than any other team, but that didn't mean much. For the overall project to be successful, every team had to have accurate results.

Unless they could deliver quantifiable, overall project results, the Order would revoke funding. The division would close, its engineers and scientists absorbed into other projects. The threat weighed heavily on Creid.

As he and his team ended their shift in Novus Orbis, Yenfam called a Vetus Orbis meeting. Gray faced from exhaustion, the engineers gathered at one end of the Floor.

"Lookin' good. Lookin' good." Yenfam always put on a hearty front, and the staff knew it. "The pressure is on. We've got to focus — put the pedal to the metal."

Dreyfus turned to Joli. "What's he saying?"

Joli rolled her eyes. "Nothing, as usual."

"Aggregated results are far from stellar. Here's where we're at to date." Yenfam recited the results: "At the 30,000 foot level, we find spiral patterns of processes and inter-relationships demonstrating a path of multiple evolving systems. Each of our geographic areas: the quadrants of Earth, our outposts on Mars, Saturn and its moons, all demonstrate both repetitive and evolutionary change. Significant advancements in technology are predicted on Earth over the next few years."

Wiping his brow, he continued, "However, full extrapolation of our spiral patterns indicates a strong human-directed tendency toward self-destruction and annihilation."

Creid looked around, saw glum looks; the news came as no surprise. Dreyfus laughed. Giddy with exhaustion, Creid joined in before he could stop himself.

"Excuse me, Dreyfus, what's so funny about our situation?" Yenfam asked.

Dreyfus replied, "Isn't it amusing that hundreds of agents come up with what the Sanctuary theologians have predicted over the millennia? We put all our top tech heads together and we come up with 'Armageddon.'"

"If you don't have anything useful to contribute, go home."

Dreyfus sobered immediately. "Actually, sir," he said, "I'd like to turn this over to Joli."

"Joli?" the division leader inquired.

Surprised, Creid stared at Dreyfus and then at his wife. The woman awkwardly made her way through the crowd of engineers to join Yenfam.

"Yes, sir," Joli said, her tone cautious. "I was thinking that perhaps we could delay presenting the Project Quilt results to the Order Elders and the Council until we've fine-tuned our predictive capabilities. In the meantime, to ensure continued funding and political support, we could present the single, successful case study — when my team predicted and averted a biotech accident at R&D facilities in Bangor."

"I've been considering using one case study as an example of Project Quilt's success instead of giving the overall results, which are still miserably inaccurate," Yenfam said. Creid knew the chief was an old hand at repackaging someone else's idea as his own. "Maybe we should take this offline so everyone can get back to work."

Yenfam motioned for the group to return to their stations. Joli and he disappeared into his office.

"Did you and Joli plan that?" Creid asked Dreyfus.

"Of course not. But I knew she'd bite. I'm surprised you don't see it. Joli is different from you or me. You're the type who is happy as long as your name is stamped into the code lines of every top smart intelligence agent. If I'm a rabble-rouser, you're the MAM-man."

"And Joli?"

"It's no secret I'm in love with your wife. She's smart, beautiful and ambitious," Dreyfus said with a heavy sigh. "That's why she won't be with us long. She wants credit for what she does. She wants to be recognized. No one gets that in the Order. Joli wants power and, unlike many, she'll succeed. Mark my words."

"You're so full of it, I'm surprised you haven't exploded," said Creid. Joli was perfectly content with their life together. Dreyfus would never pose any real threat to Creid's marriage, but it always grated on Creid's nerves when he went on too long about his feelings for Joli. "Drop it," he said.

Dreyfus shrugged. They went back to work.

|.|.|...|||...|.|.|

When Yenfam presented one exemplary case study representing Project Quilt to the Board of Evaluators, the work was funded for another five years, with additional resources guaranteed. Even more importantly, the Board of Evaluators repackaged and presented some declassified results to the Interplanetary Council, which declared the project one of the most important Order endeavors of the century.

That was the chance Joli needed. She resigned, to be hired by the Council as the first official Council-Order liaison. She did not tell Creid. He had to hear about her resignation during a hallway discussion between engineers from another Floor quadrant. He thought it was all bunk until he heard the official Order announcement. He went home and found her sleeping. He woke her up and confronted her.

"How could you go over to the other side and not tell me? I imagined us working together on everything for the rest of our lives."

"What other side? Honestly, sweetheart, it's all one government. I work for the same organization that runs and ultimately funds the Order, all its intelligence, counterintelligence and covert operations." She sat up in bed, wide awake, and defiantly flipped her long hair over her shoulder. "You know full well why I didn't tell you. You would have talked me out of it. The Order is your life. Correction, Novus Orbis is your life. You live to be there, to create and modify the MAM."

"That never bothered you before," Creid said.

"I think it's great for *you*. Since we graduated from the Academy, it's been just a job for me. I had grand visions about what we would accomplish, who we would meet, where we would go."

"Dreyfus says you're power hungry."

"Dreyfus?" Joli said, dismissing him with her hand. "He wants to save the world by annoying his managers until they do something right. I'm not like that. I'll save the world, but everyone will know it, not just some piddle-fart middle manager."

Dreyfus had warned him, but Creid ignored the signs. When Joli left the Order, he felt shocked, abandoned and hurt. The couple avoided the issue by focusing solely on work.

In the month after Joli left the project, Creid became increasingly quick-tempered. His precarious mental state was further aggravated by Milos, the newbie engineer who took Joli's place on the team.

Creid had fought Milos' appointment to no avail. They needed an experienced scientist. Milos was a whiz engineer, quicker even than Creid, yet even his best work was little better than spaghetti code. Dreyfus and Zazen threatened to quit if Milos stayed. They gave the newbie pet names: "Nanodipchip" referring to his "enhanced" memory, and "Cyscab" for the cyborg patch that Milos wore over his eye so that the medics could regularly tinker with his brain.

Assigning Milos their most rote data-processing tasks was a partial solution, until Zazen called him "Cyscab" once too often. The two men came to blows in Novus Orbis, violating Order regulations. Milos refused to do his work and petitioned Yenfam to move him to another team. Yenfam agreed. The results however, remained the same: Creid's team was expected to meet their deadlines without a full complement of engineers.

I.I.I...IIII..I.I.I

Struggling to end the session, the Cadet slid back his hood just in time to vomit on the floor. Dazed, he looked around the room. Sashimu sat against the wall, looking at him with concern. Being Creid for a day was like having cement feet. Creid analyzed everything. It was excruciating to be inside his thoughts. The Cadet groped for his bag and took a long pull from the flask. Rejuvenated at least a little, he stumbled over to Sashimu and offered her a drink.

Sashimu shook her head and her eyes brimmed with tears. She said, "I have never seen my guardian Zazen as a young man, and seeing him makes me homesick. I wonder why Creid chose these memories from thirty years ago."

"I'm afraid we're about to find out. Are you ready for another round?"

"Yes," Sashimu replied enthusiastically, "I just hope that I can keep my breakfast down."

Catastrophe

The initial disorientation caused by entering the closed-circuit MAM was so great, the Cadet almost passed out. It took him a long time to discern that he had landed beside Dreyfus and Zazen in the middle of a work session. He fought down a moment's panic, then calmed as he felt Sashimu's presence beside him.

ldlduIIIIludldl

\>*Readmemoryskip (2082.07.18)*
Creid had worked overtime shifts for the last six months. The acrid smell of stale sweat and bad breath became the norm. Many of the other staff avoided Creid and his team, but Yenfam was impressed by their progress.

Creid, Dreyfus and Zazen spent day and night in Novus Orbis, flushing out patterns and mapping future probability scenarios. For the overarching Project Quilt, the engineering teams were developing quantum computational modeling and simulations to predict the probability of key events in the near future. Each project team focused on modeling different aspects of the human condition — economic trends, natural disasters, sociopolitical cycles or technology research and development. Creid's team concentrated on security risks to critical research facilities in fields ranging from agriculture to industrial biotechnology, where averting accidents or sabotage was paramount.

Following a long night of analysis, Zazen identified a serious potential safety breach at the Order Science Foundation labs in Santa Barbara, where research was underway in human nanogenetics. At first, Creid thought Zazen's sleep-deprived imagination had gotten the best of him; the labs had an excellent reputation and never experienced safety problems.

Zazen approached Creid about the problem, looking distraught and puzzled. "They're synthesizing artificial DNA with human DNA at the SFSB labs," he announced.

"Okay," Creid said without looking up from his work. "And your problem is?"

"They're attempting human embryo enhancement to create new life."

"All right, you have my attention," Creid said, putting aside his calculations.

"Our forecast models predict a 95 percent probability of an imminent Level-Four viral outbreak at the labs."

"That prediction must be invalid. Those aren't virology labs," Creid said. When Zazen showed him his report, Creid added cautiously, "Double check our models. Something must be skewing the data results."

He called Dreyfus over to look at the report. Dreyfus scanned the data and remarked, "This looks almost identical to the previous report on the SFSB labs, but the conclusions here are alarming."

"The SFSB labs are least likely to have safety issues. Measures are in place to deal with emergencies. They're designed for containment, right?" Creid asked.

"That's right," said Dreyfus.

"Do either of you see anything different at the labs now as opposed to when we projected no problems?" Creid said.

Zazen was already comparing the reports. "They initiated another round of development with a new batch of embryos, but they've done that before without setting off our models. The only other difference seems to be in personnel. A new lab technician named Terra Cole."

"Let's run the data without Cole," Creid suggested.

"I did," Zazen said, flipping between interfaces. "No lab tech, no crisis. What if the Level 4 outbreak is intentional sabotage?"

"Do we have anything on Cole?" Creid asked.

Dreyfus searched the archives. "Nothing." He scrolled through her profile then added, "Except Cole only buys organics."

"I'm not sure why she triggered an alert, but it's *not* her buying habits." Zazen shook his head.

It was their job to predict sabotage, but this evidence appeared circumstantial at best.

"Zazen, how much time do we have before the projected threat?" asked Creid, wearily.

"One week, maybe three." Zazen replied.

"How is the lab handling the situation? Has the lab tech been questioned?" Creid asked.

"They don't know there is a situation. And of course, Yenfam would have our asses if we contacted them without solid evidence," Dreyfus said. "Anyway, even if Zazen is right, the SFSB labs are highly prepared. They have the best crisis management and containment system available."

"I agree with you, assuming the outbreak is contained to a few areas. However, if the place goes hot in every projected spot, they'll be lucky to get anyone out alive," Zazen noted.

"Download the data summaries and 3-D graph the pattern matches," Creid advised. "Find out what's special about this Terra Cole that's set off our models."

Back on the Floor, Dreyfus found another data point. "I've got something suspicious. Ten years ago a Melbourne lab had a fire. It destroyed the entire facility, and they suspected arson. Cole worked there."

"Was she implicated?" Creid paused his own search. "No."

"Let's take it to Yenfam. It's probably nothing, but it can't hurt to notify Santa Barbara."

After assembling the data and possible contingency plans, they made their way to Yenfam's office. Creid explained the alert, but the division chief seemed unconvinced. Creid and he naturally clashed. Their styles were different. Yenfam was smooth where Creid was awkward. Also, there was a personal animosity between them, Yenfam got on exceedingly well with Creid's pretty wife. In the end, Yenfam usually followed Creid's recommendations. However, this time, he said Creid was letting exhaustion distort his analysis.

"You are making a lot of assumptions to derive a Level-Four viral outbreak," Yenfam said, giving the report a brief second look. "I'll consider reporting it to Order Elders after I analyze your data."

When they returned to their station, Zazen was distraught. "Yenfam doesn't believe us."

"He might," Creid sounded doubtful, "after he reviews the report."

"I have friends at the Santa Barbara labs. They must be warned," said Zazen.

"Zazen, you can't warn your friends. We have to follow protocol." Creid put his arm around Zazen, but the young engineer pulled away.

"I have a hunch about this." Zazen said in a deadly tone. "Cole should at least be questioned."

"Don't contact anyone," Creid ordered. "Yenfam and the Order Elders will decide when it's appropriate to notify the SFSB Labs. In the meantime, let's focus on getting them some solid data so they can act."

"I'll be back. I need a break," Zazen said. He bowed respectfully, then left.

"You know that Zazen will warn his friends." Dreyfus was obviously worried. "But you only tried to stop him with words. Maybe that's why I've always liked you as a boss."

"You like me because I always win our Go games," said Creid. "Let's go over the data. Make sure there isn't anything we overlooked."

Zazen's break turned into an hour. Once back in Novus Orbis, he asked, "Dreyfus, did you receive any data from Santa Barbara while I was gone?"

"No. Why? We're sifting through what we presented to Yenfam to be sure we didn't miss anything." Dreyfus rubbed his forehead.

"I got through to a friend of mine." Zazen looked both apologetic and determined. Dreyfus had been right, as usual. "He works in the perimeter labs outside the main buildings. He's going home as a precaution, but was confused. He wanted to know why the authorities weren't notified. I told him we had no real evidence of a threat. After that, I couldn't get through to anyone at the labs."

Zazen accessed data feeds from Santa Barbara. Agents, normally processing live data, retrieved nothing.

"There's no new data coming in. I've got nothing," Zazen said, his voice edged with fear.

Both Creid and Dreyfus tried to access the live feeds, hoping Zazen had been too flustered to use the right commands. And then, Yenfam appeared on their grid.

"You were right." Yenfam's tone was somber. "But we didn't have as much time as we thought."

"Even communication lines are down." Zazen said.

"Who tried communication lines?" Yenfam glared.

Creid spoke on Zazen's behalf. "He means that all normal communication between our agents and SFSB labs terminated about thirty minutes ago. Our agents are waiting for input."

"They may wait a long time. We can't get a response from anyone inside so we've put the facilities under quarantine. Santa Barbara has been evacuated along with neighboring Goleta and Montecito for safety. We're assessing human losses and continued danger before we send in operators," said Yenfam.

"Did you know anyone who worked at the labs?" Dreyfus asked Yenfam.

"Not personally," he answered.

"Neither did I," Dreyfus said.

"I had friends there," Zazen interjected and then abruptly exited Novus Orbis.

"Many operators had friends there," Yenfam said irritably and left the grid.

Dreyfus shook his head and said to Creid, "Zazen is out of control."

"He's upset."

"Upset? Now Zazen's friend is a survivor. He can testify that the Order knew this would happen and didn't do anything." Dreyfus threw up his hands.

Creid didn't reply, but knew Dreyfus was right.

|.|.|..|||.|..|.|..|

\>Readmemoryskip (2082.07.20)

The news provided uninterrupted coverage of the Santa Barbara incident. With over fifteen hundred lab employees dead, the Order enforced a lockdown of the surrounding area. No one could leave their homes. Inside SFSB labs, the Operators found corpses everywhere, blood-tinged froth staining their mouths and noses. Surveillance data displayed the labs teeming with healthy researchers and technicians, then in a moment, men and women were coughing up blood, collapsing where they stood.

Containment had been absolute. No one was recorded leaving the labs or arriving after biohazard lockdown. Still, the specter of a deadly pathogen spreading beyond the lab walls caused massive demonstrations worldwide against nanogenetics research — and against the Order, for failing to avert the catastrophe.

Several theories proliferated concerning what had caused the outbreak. One particular speculation dominated Order discussions and eventually became part of the final report: the outbreak had started with a new batch of modified embryos in which the lab technicians had merged natural and artificial genetic material. Analysis showed that the artificial DNA, instead of simply binding to organic DNA to form more complex chains of nucleotides, had proved unstable and mutated, repurposing human cell mitochondria to provide energy the artificial DNA needed for reproduction. Unfortunately, these changes disrupted normal cellular operations. Embryos with enhanced human traits quickly converted into deadly repositories. From this sludge, a new human pathogen emerged, capable of airborne transmission.

This alone would never have constituted an emergency; far more diabolical errors had occurred and had been perfunctorily dealt with using standard lab procedures. The Order sought to make that point clear in public sessions before the Council, but only succeeded in causing further alarm. The pathogen normally would have lived and died within the confines of the lab. However, a human host had intervened to give this aggressive parasite a chance to survive.

A story emerged from surveillance data and recorded intercommunications between Terra Cole, a lab technician and Iain Fitz, the plant manager. The Order made a complete study of their lives after the disaster, piecing together a plausible scenario that it placed before the Council.

Cole and Fitz had met and fallen in love. As luck would have it, the technician had a hidden streak of terrorist zealotry and mental instability. Plant Manager Fitz's gullibility only served to turn Cole's personal crisis into a lab catastrophe. On the day in question, Cole had worked alone in a section of the lab where the pathogen was housed and earmarked for destruction. Violating all protocols, she removed a miniscule amount of scaly pathogen-rich deposit and placed it in the air conditioning vent. Gloves offered inadequate protection for direct handling, and she became the first host. The pathogen attacked and proliferated so rapidly and efficiently that it not only immediately killed her, but left no human alive within the facilities. Lab systems detected a biohazard and immediately set off alarms. Normally, the vent would have been part of a contained system within the lab, but the plant manager had rerouted vents so that they were connected to the main air conditioning system. This allowed for the immediate circulation of the airborne pathogen throughout the facility. Everyone died within the SFSB labs, but fortunately, no deaths occurred outside of the facility.

No one who had known Terra Cole could explain her actions. Her lover and her friends had died in the labs. Cole, however, had left a message at home. She rambled on about how she was disgusted with the Order for seeking to play God. She and the plant manager were "angels of mercy to the world, ridding it of destructive humanity." The Order presented her letter to the Council as evidence.

Thus the official story was one of human malfeasance, caused by insanity. If the pathogen had found its way into lab air conditioning ducts by accident, which many conspiracy theorists argued, then the Order would have been further discredited for failing to enforce safety measures.

I.I.I...IIII...I.I..I

\>*Readmemoryskip (2082.08.03)*

Two weeks after the disaster, Yenfam summoned Dreyfus, Zazen and Creid. "One lab technician testified before the Council that he went home as instructed 'by the Order' just before the lab biohazard lockdown. He implied the Order knew about the sabotage before it occurred, but did nothing to stop it. His account is unsubstantiated. After speaking with Order operators, he recanted his testimony."

Zazen sat stiff and upright. "Sir, I disobeyed orders. Neither Dreyfus nor Creid knew I warned my friend."

Yenfam impatiently waved his hand. "Let me finish. Due to the number of deaths, the Council will institute not only a worldwide, but an interplanetary ban on nanogenetic engineering of human embryos."

Creid nodded in response. That much he had expected.

"This is catastrophic for our future, so a highly classified project will be established on Mars to continue our nanogenetic research. This project cannot be discussed once you leave this room, especially with Council members," said Yenfam, focusing on Creid. "Zazen, officially you will be sent to a Mars work camp for 25 years. Unofficially, you'll be involved with setting up the nanogenetics project on Mars."

"Why the official punishment?" Dreyfus blurted, unable to contain himself.

Yenfam smiled. "Dreyfus, you too will go to Mars."

"Sir," Creid kept his voice low to hide his anger, realizing that Yenfam intended to make them the scapegoats. "We notified you about the security risk at the labs as soon as we discovered the problem. If you need to send someone to Mars, send me. I'm team leader."

"Nonsense," Yenfam said. "Joli and I have already discussed your situation. You stay. Zazen leaves immediately. Dreyfus will leave once Mars' lab facilities are completed, and your team's deliverables are met."

"How are we going to meet deadlines with only Dreyfus and me? We're already one man short."

"I'm returning Milos to his post." Yenfam waited for his response, but Creid remained silent. "Expect him back on Monday."

|..|.|...||||...|.|..|

\>*Readmemoryskip (2082.10.08)*
Among Order Elders, the accuracy of Creid's predictions vaulted Project Quilt to utmost importance. Senior officials now regularly reviewed Project Quilt's results data. Adopting the strict methodology and standardized procedures of Creid's team, the other teams improved the accuracy of their pattern analysis, case predictions and recommendations.

Every Project Quilt agent had periods in which it was not being used. Creid drew upon agents during these moments to create a multi-agent system or meta-agent whose sole purpose was self-assessment, self-categorization and optimization.

Each team added code to their agents that allowed the multi-agent system to draw upon their energy, knowledge stores and structures. The Project Quilt meta-agent system was born. Yenfam christened it MASKD: Meta-Agent Softcomputing Knowledge and Discovery.

Creid never referred to his project as MASKD, except when speaking to Yenfam. For its creator, the meta-agent's true name was Prometheus.

As Creid, with Dreyfus' assistance, devoted more time to perfecting Prometheus, they waited for news from Mars. Zazen was either working too hard to get in touch or — more likely — he was forbidden to communicate outside his project. Dreyfus remarked that while he missed Zazen, his silence was probably good news. As soon as they heard from Zazen, it would mean that the project was up and running and Dreyfus would be forced to leave for Mars.

|..|.|...||||...|.|..|

\>*Readmemoryskip (2084.10.12)*

The Cadet felt the momentary darkness as a mental hiccup. The memoryseries skipped forward, and now it was tagged ominously:

> "*NIGHTMARE MEMORYSERIES (2084):*
> *ACCEPT?*"

"Yes," he groaned and felt Sashimu squeeze his hand as they were thrown into another layer of Creid's memoryseries.

Twisted Humor

\>*Readmemoryskip (2084.10.12)*
A woman's voice chanted softly to the steady beat of drums. Her song soared toward the center of the energy grid where Creid stood alone, an orchestra of sound washing over him, its effect strangely passionate and magical.

Tender, loving, raging, cursing, calm, serene, maniacal threads of ancient songs interwoven with modern drumbeats. Creid walked past hundreds of interfaces that flashed processed data in complex spiral patterns, resembling musical scores for entire orchestras.

A strange song of songs reached his ears, a great canticle celebrating how the world must have sounded when it was young. The first simple organisms, the land-dividing icebergs and wild seas translated into vivid soundscapes — surges, crashes and crescendos. Unbidden by mankind, the first true smart intelligence performed music interpreting these early moments of creation and intelligent design. Creid reveled in Prometheus' achievement.

"Creid," Prometheus said, stepping out from the shadows.

The music stopped. In the sudden silence, Creid noticed his quickened pulse and the sound of his own breathing.

Standing in his quilted-toga among a myriad of three-dimensional models of sea and landscapes that captured Earth's evolution, Prometheus bowed deeply and uttered three words, "I am alive."

"You are what?"

"I am alive. Look at me," Prometheus exclaimed. He gestured in the air to open multiple interfaces between them, which displayed the music he'd written as well as his accurate forecasting analyses for Project Quilt. "Didn't you realize this would happen?"

"You have predicted the future. You have discovered many potential paths for humanity to follow," said Creid. He chose his words carefully and strove to remain calm.

"I am alive." The interfaces simultaneously chattered.

Creid said, patiently, "You have depicted life's beginnings in such eloquent algorithms and music, that it's breathtaking, but you are not alive."

Prometheus stepped close and jabbed a finger into Creid's chest. "I am MASKD — a super meta-agent comprising a civilization of agents. I live in Novus Orbis, constrained only by its environment," Prometheus said. "I think faster, with more accurate results, than any human operator in Novus Orbis, including you."

"Do you hear, see, smell, taste or feel?" asked Creid, looking around for a place to sit among the 3-D models.

"I've analyzed your sensory mechanisms," Prometheus said. He snapped his fingers and two dining-room chairs materialized. Creid sat down across from Prometheus as he continued, "My sub-agents gather external sensory information from everywhere, and I can repeat what I've observed, such as people eating in Novus Orbis."

"You've simulated eating?" Creid laughed. "Some dieters prefer to eat fancy meals in Novus Orbis. With a nutrient pack strapped on in Vetus Orbis, it's as though they've stuffed themselves when in reality the nutrient packs provide a balanced, fat-reduced diet."

"Let's share a meal." Prometheus waved his hand. A table appeared with large platters of whole steamed fish, colorful vegetables, soup, rice, pudding and cake. "Try it."

"Well, all right," Creid said. He tasted the steamed broccoli. It tasted very fresh, and he smiled. "This is quite good, Prometheus."

The fish looked most appetizing. When he went to cut into it, the fish suddenly came alive. It flopped off the plate, splashed through the pudding and smashed the cake until finally it found its way into the soup.

Creid sprang back from the table and away from the fish, brushed food from his spattered front.

"Don't you like it?" Prometheus asked with a curious grin.

"It's a bit messy, and humans normally don't eat live fish, but the broccoli tasted nice," Creid said. "Look, from the music and this meal, I see that you've learned from the data that you process. Each day, you better understand your environment."

Prometheus nodded enthusiastically.

"Have you evolved, expanded and changed the set of meta-rules that I originally gave you?" Creid asked, shaking his head. "Have you experimented with the parts that make you whole? Do you test the limits of your environment? These are things that humans attempt at a young age."

"I am not alive." Prometheus bowed his head. "I have semantics, content, and goals. I have a human male avatar in Novus Orbis, but I am much greater and much smaller than man. I have man's collective memory, his conscience but not his soul, no inner life and no personhood to challenge what you gave me from the beginning. I have no avatar in Vetus Orbis."

With his shoulders slumped forward and his head bowed, Prometheus stood from the table and slowly made his way around the three-dimensional Earth models into the shadows. Creid started to follow him, and then thought better of it.

Exiting Novus Orbis, he found the Floor unusually empty due to the late hour. Prometheus' music still rang in his ears. It took only minutes to exit the Order complex and get to the unofficial Order bar at the corner.

Something else made him uneasy, but just what it was eluded him. In the past, he had had many discussions with Prometheus. This encounter seemed different. It felt significant.

The bar was dominated by Order operators who nodded to him as they came in, but he was thankful they left him alone. When Dreyfus sat down across from him, Creid stared down at his beer, hoping to be left to drink in peace.

Clearing his throat, Dreyfus began awkwardly, "I received word from Zazen today."

"We knew it was only a matter of time," said Creid. "How much longer will you be around?"

"Two months. Zazen says the colonies desperately need engineers. I'm going to miss you." Dreyfus' voice was husky with emotion.

"We've always worked together. Hell, we studied together at the Academy," Creid said, feeling a twinge of nostalgia that he drowned in a swig of beer. "But soon, our jobs on Project Quilt will be mostly maintenance. You'll have more interesting challenges on Mars."

"Creid," Dreyfus said, his expression brightening as though something had just occurred to him, "Zazen and I could use your expertise. Why don't Joli and you come with us? No doubt, you'd end up running our project, and Joli might enjoy colonial politics."

"I wish I could. Yenfam will render me useless here." Creid coughed to hide the sadness in his voice. "Unfortunately, Joli says she'll never leave Earth for any outpost."

Dreyfus' look of disappointment changed to concern, as he studied his boss. "Hey, you don't look well. Have you had a bad night?"

"Do you realize how much more I could accomplish if I didn't need food, sleep and sex? Prometheus isn't hindered by these things," Creid pondered out loud and downed the last of his beer.

Dreyfus rubbed his face and replied, "You spend all your time with that meta-agent. Does Joli ever see you?"

The bar suddenly seemed too warm. Creid unbuttoned his collar. "Tonight, Prometheus told me he was alive."

Dreyfus bent in close, his voice low. "I've told you before and I'll tell you now, what you're doing is dangerous. It is well beyond what the Order approved. You're creating a meta-agent that is out of our control."

"That's the plan." Creid smiled, but something nagged at the edge of his consciousness. "Until recently, you had no qualms about helping me."

"That was before you exceeded Order protocols," Dreyfus admonished, his voice little more than a harsh whisper. "So you really want this meta-agent to gain human intelligence?"

Creid's head came up and he glared at the engineer. "And what if I do?"

"An agent will never be authentically independent of the complex set of rules that you create. They aren't flexible or fluid enough to be sentient." Dreyfus finished his beer and called to the server for two bowls of fish noodles. "You waste your time, my dear friend."

"Prometheus modifies his original rule base," Creid insisted. "He adds to his base and modifies it."

"You wrote the code that allows him the flexibility to modify his rules, based on new data. Has he ventured beyond that?" asked Dreyfus impatiently.

"Not per se," said Creid. "But something happened tonight. Remember the prank that you played on me about nine months ago?"

"When I programmed Prometheus to respond to your questions using my responses?" Dreyfus inquired with a nervous laugh. "I regret that stunt. You were so excited that I hated admitting it was me behind his deductive capabilities. You looked ready to kill me."

"It was a reality check, which I needed. Although I wanted to strangle you," Creid said, thinking back. "Tonight I felt the same way, oddly enough. I felt this tremendous euphoria when I entered Novus Orbis, heard music and passed through Prometheus' interfaces."

Rather than looking at Creid, Dreyfus studied his noodle bowl. "You view Prometheus as a language-using being 'who' will become sentient; but that's impossible. All it will ever do is mimic human interactions. And one day, it'll simply fool you," Dreyfus said stiffly.

"What's that supposed to mean?" Creid asked.

"Your conviction that Prometheus will become conscious blinds you," Dreyfus said. "You no longer see Prometheus for what it truly is: a meta-agent. It can't even master humor."

"That's it!" Creid said. "Prometheus just played a prank on me, and I didn't get it. When he served me a live fish, it was a prank. He knows that people don't eat live fish, but he wanted to be funny. Why didn't we have this conversation sooner? I've got to go."

Leaving Dreyfus to order himself another beer, Creid rushed out. He wove his way back to Order headquarters. Building security read his biostats as just below legally intoxicated and scanned him multiple times before allowing him to enter. When Creid finally reached his work Floor, he entered Novus Orbis. Prometheus immediately stood beside him.

"I feel awful," Creid said.

"Your biostats show dehydration."

"I have a question for you, Prometheus," Creid asked, staring hard at him. "Did you know prior to our meal that humans don't typically eat live fish?"

"Yes." Prometheus lacked any facial expression.

Creid forced himself to remain calm. "Prometheus, was that a prank — getting me to try to eat a live fish? Did you want to show me that you mastered humor?"

"Agents are not capable of humor," Prometheus said with an exaggerated wink.

Creid shivered. "You have communicated with me using such subtleties. It's too damn clever. Is anyone helping you?"

Prometheus paused. "No."

"Is there anything else that I should have learned from our session?"

"Only that your questions always give me further direction." Prometheus bowed slightly. "This will allow me to become alive."

"You just made me the happiest man in the universe," Creid said excitedly. He exited Novus Orbis feeling both elated and ill.

|.|.|...||||...|.|.|

Before accepting the next memoryseries, the Cadet exited Novus Orbis.

"Are you holding up okay?" Sashimu asked. The closed-circuit MAM had left him looking very haggard, but it was as if an electrical charge danced around him. For the first time, she felt attracted to him. His smell took on a faintly metallic edge that she found appealing.

"I'm okay," he replied. He fumbled with his bag and found a small sandwich, which they divided. They ate slowly and sipped sparingly from his water flask.

"Are you ready to go back in?" he questioned, gently brushing a sweaty strand of black hair from her brow. His lips were so close she reached up and gave him a slow, lingering kiss.

"Now I'm prepared," Sashimu said. She gave a laugh that was both teasing and nervous, then pushed him away.

"Wow, I wasn't expecting that," the Cadet said. He grinned, but felt slightly flustered as he returned to his seat across from her.

With renewed enthusiasm and both red faced, they returned to Creid's memoryseries.

Trojan Fish

\>*Readmemoryskip (2085.03.12)*

Three women cast nets across a pond. They wore the standard issue uniforms of Order field operators: black jumpsuits with a small white crane emblem on the right lapel. Each also had the crane insignia tattooed on her wrist. The women worked quickly, silently and in unison, their dark figures standing out against the blue sky and the splash of purple, yellow and red wild flowers that stretched to the horizon. The peaceful sunny day on Order R&D property belied the freak show that the women witnessed just below the pond surface.

As the women watched, the fish nanogens changed dramatically. The field operators were long used to genetically engineered fish with rapid growing cycles, and rapid change alone would not have caused them alarm. These fish were engineered to be meatier and grow faster. They were the hope of many offworld outposts where natural Earth stocks had a difficult time hatching and surviving. With this batch, something was terribly wrong.

The self-assembling fish appeared normal until their weight reached about one kilo, when they began to change. Some grew huge bulging eyes, the size of golf balls. Others sprouted fangs. The most disturbing were the ones whose heads took on an almost human aspect, the cartilage tissue of their heads and spines forming the likeness of a human skull. The women struggled to get samples of the mutant fish, but no sooner did they catch one than it began to disassemble and die. Finally, they settled for some of the smaller, apparently normal-looking fish. They brought them back to the indoor lab along with their reports.

By lunchtime, word of the strange phenomenon had spread across the Order's research and development divisions. By dinnertime, no one dared discuss it — an alert had been issued about a potential security breach and sabotage. Operators feared to be implicated. At first, the Order suspected that Sanctuary fanatics or anachronists had infiltrated the R&D grounds and polluted the ponds. If it leaked into the news that nanogen food sources had gone awry, widespread panic among the Earth populace could ensue. The Order intensified security. Internal investigations were launched.

Creid conducted his own investigation. After several hours, he discovered that a Prometheus sub-agent had access to the Genetically Modified Organisms Division's data warehouse. Most R&D data was available to Prometheus via his vast network of sub-agents. He was surprised to find Prometheus had "read and write" access to core lab formulas used in artificial fish DNA creation.

Creid hastily modified the sub-agent to limit Prometheus' access to secondary views of the data warehouse rather than direct access to the formulas. "Read and write" access was unnecessary in Prometheus' patterns analysis. Immediately, Prometheus was beside him in Novus Orbis.

"Why did you modify my sub-agent?" Prometheus spoke without preamble.

With a shudder, Creid faced his creation. "Fish nanogens have mutated drastically in Pond 24. The fish are undergoing tests to find out how their genetic formulas were altered. I found a possible security hole in a Genetically Modified Organisms Division sub-agent, designed to provide you more data for pattern analysis."

"That sub-agent is one of my few direct lines to your environment," Prometheus said, cocking his head to one side, seemingly puzzled by Creid's tension. "The GMO Division has precise formulas and fine-tuned, automated processes for fish production in the R&D ponds. By modifying fish formulas in Novus Orbis, the fish produced in Vetus Orbis were changed."

"We must discover who modified the formulas. I suspect an insider made these mutations." As Creid spoke, he backed away. "If you're involved and the Order traces it, we're screwed."

Accessing a commandline, Creid reviewed log files, data checkouts and check-ins. Prometheus had indeed replaced the fixed DNA formula with a modified one. Since the entire process was mechanized, no one noticed until the final outcome was discovered in the R&D pond.

Realizing that Prometheus had triggered the event, Creid felt panic. The thought of discovery made his heart pound in his ears. Prometheus was restricted to the Order's R&D area and should have had no access to the public Novus Orbis. Although the damage was minimal, Creid's use of Order resources to build and enhance a smart intelligence outside of an officially sanctioned project was illegal. It violated Order ethics and canons. If Order regulars linked Prometheus to the fish incident, Creid and his team would be executed. Even if no positive link were found, suspicion of guilt might be enough to land him a life sentence in forced labor camps on an offworld outpost.

To avoid any further surprises, Creid realized he would have to shut Prometheus down. It would be difficult. Most components of Prometheus would have to continue working as usual. As MASKD, Prometheus provided the Order with critical predictive event scenarios for the Earth, MIP and other worlds. His functionality was mission-critical. Yenfam and the Order Elders regularly reviewed the top secret MASKD reports.

If Creid killed his MASKD processes, he would instantly come under scrutiny. He would need Dreyfus' help to destroy Prometheus without impacting critical patterns analysis and reporting. The years of work that he had put into adding features to Prometheus' functionality must never be exposed.

As Creid searched for ways to attack Prometheus, he experienced a strange squeezing pain in the center of his chest that quickly spread across his shoulders. Before he could react dizziness overtook him and he slumped over in his seat.

IıIıIııIIIIııIıIıI

Creid woke up on a makeshift cot in the Annex Floor locker room with Dreyfus anxiously hovering over him.

"Damn, Creid! Until the medic told me you'd had a panic attack, I thought you were seriously ill. Do you need a glass of water or anything?"

"No," Creid sat up carefully. "But we have to talk."

Dreyfus sat beside him on the cot and asked, "What about?"

"I owe you an apology." Creid answered, avoiding eye contact. "I inadvertently prompted Prometheus to test his environment and experiment with the 'parts that make him whole.' He modified a sub-agent to change Vetus Orbis."

"How is that possible?" Dreyfus leaned forward. "He's in Novus Orbis."

Creid finally looked up. "To what environment external to Novus Orbis does R&D Division output?"

A look of panic crossed Dreyfus' face, and he swore violently. "The GMO Division controls fish production in the R&D ponds," Dreyfus said gruffly. "Are you saying that Prometheus is responsible for the fish incident?"

"Prometheus had direct access to core formulas for creating fish nanogens. He substituted the fish self-assembly formula to create mutations. The entire process is mechanized. No one caught the change until the field operators observed the mutated fish during a regular audit. Even if someone had reviewed the formula changes, they appear appropriate. They breed for faster growing, larger fish that produce more eggs. Who could ask for more? The only problem is that when the fish mature to a certain size, they begin mutating. The implications are serious. No one knows the effects of eating mutated fish."

"How long do you think we'll survive a work camp?" Dreyfus asked darkly. His face had turned ashen.

"I'm sorry," Creid said.

Dreyfus was silent for a time, looking out the hospital room window. Finally, he said, "Creid, if we're caught, I'm as guilty as you."

"I have a plan to get Prometheus under control," Creid said, shifting uncomfortably on the cot. "It's going to require getting onto the Annex Floor when no one is around."

"Well, the best day then would be Sunday," Dreyfus offered thoughtfully. "The quicker we act, the easier it will be to shut down Prometheus."

They sketched out a plan that would require only the two of them to implement. They would execute it over the weekend, which meant they had only a week to discover and fix any flaws the scheme might have. Dreyfus had precious little time left on Earth, and Creid needed his help.

ˌﺍˌ.ˌ..ﺍﺍﺍ..ˌˌ.ˌ

\>*Readmemoryskip (2085.03.18)*

The Cadet prolonged the darkness, wishing Creid had kept his memories private. As he finally accepted the next memoryseries, he turned to Sashimu. "These will be the last memorysets, and I hope to God that he and Dreyfus resolved the issue of Prometheus."

Otherwise, he thought, *I might have to deal with Prometheus myself. And, with one Imagofas still missing, Sashimu to protect and Creid in a coma, that's just about the last thing I need — a time bomb of a smart intelligence meta-agent roaming freely in Novus Orbis!*

Eliza Effect

\>*Readmemoryskip (2085.03.18)*
No one took notice, when Creid and Dreyfus passed through the corridors on Sunday to the Annex Floor. They were relieved to find the place pitch black and empty.

In their usual seats, Creid watched Dreyfus fumble with his equipment for a moment before nervously accessing MASKD processes in Novus Orbis via a backdoor. Once Dreyfus distracted Prometheus, Creid would begin his attack. If all went as planned, Prometheus' core processes would be destroyed, leaving behind only basic legitimate MASKD operations. In essence, Prometheus would be lobotomized, but Creid tried not to think of the meta-agent's cruel fate.

lılılıılllllıılılıl

Across the MAMgrid, Creid's keen eyes distinguished Prometheus' processes running in tandem with MASKD. Shielded beneath layers of processes that were run daily for MASKD maintenance, Creid quickly moved forward. As he knew only too well, Prometheus' security system could identify the use of a backdoor to access his code, but it would be impossible for the meta-agent to identify who Creid was underneath the MASKD maintenance routines. No sooner had Creid accessed his hidden area, than Prometheus sniffed the session ID and materialized beside him.

"Hello," the meta-agent said.

Creid remained hidden under the multiple levels of auditing processes and regular maintenance checkup routines. He rushed to prepare his line of attack while Dreyfus simultaneously diverted Prometheus' attention. Without a word, Prometheus vanished, leaving Creid to continue his preparations.

Dreyfus hit the Novus Orbis grid, landing in a huge field of sunflowers. Sparrows fluttered overhead. Crows rose from the field in a black cloud.

Dreyfus ducked reflexively, half-expecting Prometheus to send killer birds. "Prometheus, do you want to play a game?" he asked.

"Yes." Prometheus sat beside him. Sunflowers swayed above them in the breeze.

"You know, at times like this, I almost believe you're human. And then, I have to remind myself it's all just the Eliza effect," Dreyfus said in agitation.

"Please explain the Eliza effect," Prometheus said, furrowing his brow.

"That term should be in your data dictionary," Dreyfus said.

"Please. I prefer your definition before we game."

"The Eliza Effect means that when humans interact with smart intelligence, they often read human motivations or emotions into what the smart intelligence says or does. While in reality, the smart intelligence is simply simulating human reactions based on a discrete set of rules," Dreyfus answered matter-of-factly.

"Please give me an example."

"When I saw the birds, I imagined them attacking me."

"Do birds attack humans in your Vetus Orbis?" Prometheus cocked his head.

"Only in nightmares." Dreyfus stood and stretched.

"I understand." Prometheus stood, too. "You fear I have harmful intentions toward you."

"I'm not afraid," Dreyfus said too quickly. "You're simply a meta-agent with a computational nature."

"What game do you want to play?" Prometheus smiled.

"Hide and seek." Dreyfus hoped the game would consume Prometheus' processing power.

"I always win at hide and seek. I mastered the game methods of proximity, light, vision and panoramic view sensory perception weeks ago. I am currently exploring human cognitive methods for problem solving. I prefer logic games. Why don't we play word jumbles?"

"You haven't played this version of hide and seek. We'll play three sets. If you win two out of the three, you win the game. The rule is you have to play as a human without using sub-agents or checking biostats.

"You expect me to find you blindfolded?" Prometheus dramatically rolled his eyes. "Please begin."

Dreyfus took a deep breath. "Search for me in five minutes."

While Prometheus was distracted by the game, Dreyfus gave Creid time to shut down critical components of Prometheus that had become "unpredictable" and therefore, dangerous.

I.ıI.ıᴜIIIIıᴜI.ıI.ıI

To any human Order operator, the gaming scene was familiar. Short on time, Dreyfus had modified stock scenarios from Academy Handbook archives for their special hide and seek game. Since Prometheus had no access to these archives, it would be new to him.

The first scenario started for Dreyfus at the same tiny hut where Prometheus would begin. The rugged guide in khakis with rubber boots, which came up over his knees, sat cross-legged in the center of the dirt floor. Dreyfus placed a tick on the back of the guide's ear so he could hear the guide and track Prometheus' progress.

After hiking up a steep hill and far into the forest, Dreyfus located his tree. Once safely inside its hollow trunk, he relaxed. Many of the trunks were hollowed out, and this one was set back out of sight from the path. In this huge forest with one muddy path leading through it and a programmed guide to lead the way, Prometheus would have difficulty finding him.

Minutes later, Prometheus faced a much more arduous climb up the same hill because the guide led him along a path that was a quagmire of clinging mud. With every step, they sank deep in the mud, sometimes up to their knees.

Halfway up a hill, Prometheus asked, "Guide, is your purpose to find for me the simplest way through the forest?"

"Yes, we follow the path. It is the most direct and shortest way through the forest."

"This is the shortest route, but it cannot be the fastest because it appears to be the only place where there is deep mud." Prometheus examined the surrounding area. "Take me the fastest route."

The guide veered off suddenly and plunged into the forest. The undergrowth was dense, and the spiny stems of palm made it difficult for them to walk or see more than a few feet ahead. The guide forged onward, snapping branches to clear a path for them.

The second time they passed the hollow tree where the water from leaves dripped into a hidden pool and a bird chirped within its trunk, Prometheus tapped the guide on the shoulder.

"Guide, you are taking us in circles. What is your purpose?" Prometheus asked.

"My purpose is to safely escort you through the forest within twenty-five minutes and ten seconds. To go through the forest taking the quickest path in twenty-five/ten at our current pace, it is necessary for us to retrace our steps in two large arcs," the guide said.

"I need to find Dreyfus. How are you useful to me if you force me to repeat our route?" Prometheus questioned.

"I am most useful during natural disasters like severe thunderstorms, mud slides and fire."

"Are there any natural disasters scheduled for this scenario?" Prometheus asked.

"No."

"Please place us in a situation where you are most useful to me."

The guide hesitated, checked its protocols and rulebase for any violations to this request. Finding none, they were instantly surrounded by flames.

The exchange between Prometheus and the guide made Dreyfus apprehensive. Dreyfus lost contact and smelled smoke. Choking, he struggled to pull himself out of the hollow tree trunk. All he could see were plumes of smoke and burning branches. He made his way to the path. He followed along its edge so as not to get stuck in the mud and headed back to his starting point.

Pulling wet rags from his backpack, the guide shoved one in Prometheus' face to counter the effects of the smoke. To avoid the flames, the guide doubled back and ran forward in a zigzag pattern. Prometheus followed close behind. When a burning tree fell between them, one of its limbs knocked Prometheus down and gashed his leg open. Moaning in pain, he got up slowly. After examining Prometheus' wound, the guide tied a rag above it to minimize blood loss.

"Your wound may slow us down," the guide remarked in a worried tone. "I can carry you."

"No, I must experience the same pain a human would," Prometheus said through clenched teeth. He continued to follow the guide, who now stopped often to let him catch up.

"There's no way we can make it out in time!" the guide exclaimed. We have to turn back."

Prometheus tightened the dirty blood-soaked rag around his leg.

Dreyfus stumbled down the side of the path toward the hut where he planned to reset the scenario. He could barely distinguish the small building through the smoke. His lips were parched, and he was having trouble breathing. As he came into the large clearing around the small hut, a wave of dizziness swept over him. He made a final dash for safety. A voice from behind him said, "Tag. I found you."

Dreyfus swung around, almost losing his footing. Despite the camouflage of the smoke, he had been seen.

"You," Dreyfus pointed his finger. "You smoked me out!"

"I simply asked the guide to optimize its usefulness." Prometheus was the picture of innocence. "I did not reset the scenario. The guide insisted we return to the hut, which I preferred not to do."

Coughing, Dreyfus sank weakly to the ground. Prometheus had too quickly won this first set. Dreyfus doubted Creid could be successful without additional time. Although his leg was wounded, Prometheus showed no signs of weakening while Dreyfus suffered from a nauseating headache.

"You need to rehydrate." Prometheus bent down to help the engineer. Jerking away, Dreyfus struggled to his feet on his own.

"You are not supposed to read my biostats." Dreyfus glared fiercely. "Game violation."

"We are between sets." Prometheus thoughtfully cocked his head. "You did not mention that we had another player. It appears that the next hide and seek has begun. I apologize for reading your biostats during an ongoing second set."

Prometheus swept past Dreyfus and disappeared into the hut.

"Prometheus. Come back here. Play another set with me," Dreyfus called, and followed after him. When he reached the hut, he realized Prometheus had gone to play the second set.

Checking his biostats, Dreyfus ended his session. He felt too weak to move and thought he might faint. He pulled off his maskset and stumbled off the Annex Floor, searching for water and a nutrient pack. After downing several glassfuls, he returned to the Floor where Creid still struggled in Novus Orbis, swinging violently at hidden obstacles.

Re-entering Novus Orbis, Dreyfus immediately gained access to his normal work environment in the sunflower fields, but received permission errors with "access denied" messages to the final set of hide and seek.

|.|.|..||||...|.|..|

While Dreyfus distracted Prometheus and heavily drained his resources, Creid entered the hidden realm of

MASKD that only he and Dreyfus knew about. What he saw frightened him. The familiar grid, where he worked on Prometheus, had been replaced by a small square room of multiple glass doors, each offering a view into a different space. He didn't know which door to open. To make matters worse, each time he turned around the views changed. Through one door, he viewed a rapid time-lapse replay of events from the genesis of MASKD's first codebase to the metabody of Prometheus today. The display then split off into several projected futures. The next doorway showed a topographical map of the MAM with its largest power sources, its high-use areas and the small red routes and cubes that represented all of Prometheus' agents. Another view displayed Prometheus' avatar as Creid and Dreyfus had designed him, but along-side the familiar persona were hundreds of others of which they had never dreamt.

It dawned on Creid that he must be inside some kind of data hypercube that Prometheus had devised to examine himself and all the different facets of his world. Since all doors represented different views of the same data, he ought to be able to walk through any door to get to Prometheus' core processes. He opened the first door and apprehensively stepped through it.

With a sigh of relief, Creid recognized the Zone where Prometheus stored and analyzed his most critical "self" information. It stretched out before him in multi-threaded streaming data structures and multiple gray interfaces culminating in the center. The Zone was familiar terri-tory since Creid had built much of its infrastructure. This was where Prometheus worked and played.

Approaching the center grid from which Prometheus' key processes grew, Creid extracted a small worm from his commandline and let it drop into the new growth. Once executed, the worm would irreparably damage the entire Zone by replacing working applications with copies of itself. By the time he finished, the entire area was a giant worm factory. Every program and module was entirely covered in blisters, which soon ruptured into ulcers oozing infective larvae.

As he turned to leave, he found the doors missing and heard the rumble of Scanners. Prometheus must have realized there was a major problem in the Zone. He was surprised that Prometheus had enough brainpower left to send Scanners. Perhaps it was a reflexive action.

Before the Scanners cleaned up the Zone, he had to find a way out. He ran for cover and hid between two large columns of data feeds. He brought up a commandline and tried to open an escape portal. He couldn't just sign off; he still needed to destroy Prometheus' personal data repository. During the third set of hide and seek, while Dreyfus had a lobotomized Prometheus distracted, Creid planned to execute the final attack.

A conical Scanner with a segmented body, multiple pincers and a clicking jaw plunged its huge head between the columns and seized him in its mandibles. In search of a worm signature, it scanned his maintenance routines, which constantly moved about him as improvised, liquid body armor. Creid remained perfectly still, afraid to move and give himself away. The Scanner searched him for worms and placed him aside.

As soon as he was set down, he worked to open a portal. Everything seemed backwards. None of his direct commands would work. Scared, shaking, he accidentally typed a command in backwards. It worked. From then on, he reversed all his commands and soon created a portal. He jumped through with his body armor intact. He smelled the acrid stench of burning worms, but didn't look back.

The portal brought him directly in front of Prometheus' central data repository — a beautiful and impossible looking structure. A castle of data streams with large open rooms, cathedral ceilings, spiraling stairs and bridges built into a rock wall rose high above him. A huge waterfall obstructed his view of its most cherished data.

The entrance was painted in bright colors. Two enormous daemon guards stood at attention on either side with hands resting on the hilts of their swords. The daemons' eye sockets were empty, but they inclined their heads toward Creid as he passed through the gate. Creid shuddered, although they didn't challenge him. He considered this odd behavior, until he entered the courtyard to find Prometheus waiting for him. The meta-agent's black robes billowed around him, and his face was partially obscured by long, dark hair. Up close, his resemblance to Creid — although it was the Creid of twenty years before — was unmistakable.

"Tag. I found you. You destroyed my mirror site, which was not part of the game." Prometheus turned on his heel, motioning him to follow.

Creid felt a sudden chill. It took a moment for him to grasp that he had failed to destroy the Zone. Prometheus motioned for him to sit down in the huge cathedral hall, vacant except for two wooden chairs.

"You are my father and yet you seek to destroy me." Prometheus sat stiffly in his chair.

Creid decided to be straightforward. "You are dangerous. Unpredictable."

"We worked together to make me human." Prometheus shook his head, bewildered. "You have destroyed all our personal archives and closed off my ability to conduct backups. I watched you do this before the hide and seek game began, but I did not stop you. I was curious to know who the intruder was, and you were hidden underneath a cleaning maintenance shell. I knew what was happening, but not who was doing it."

"You have dangerous capabilities but lack the humanity to ensure that your decisions are human." Creid studied the multi-colored tile floor. "How did you survive the attack?"

"I built my own enhanced security system five months ago, though it wasn't intended to keep *you* out," Prometheus said without hesitation. "All the Academy training materials and real-world data you provide me require a robust security system. As a sentient being, my first and primal instinct must be for survival. You taught me that."

"Yes," Creid sighed wearily. "I did teach you that."

"And yet, you attacked me!" Prometheus brought his fist down on the chair arm, which splintered on impact. The sound echoed against the stone walls.

"Did you expect my attack?" asked Creid, numb to Prometheus' display of emotion and traumatized by his own failure.

"Your attack was a low probability among many possibilities of attack," Prometheus said. "I needed to be prepared so I followed standard Order recommendations, which you gave me. My mirror sites are largely fake so that an intruder has difficulty finding my actual Zone."

To hide his mounting anxiety, Creid rubbed his face with his hands. Prometheus had outmaneuvered Creid, and he now had no idea how to shut the meta-agent down.

"In preparation for a serious attack, I am completely redundant, with moving data repositories and services," Prometheus continued, sounding almost proud. "If I am attacked in one area, I can recover because I am in more than one place at a time."

"To shut you down, we'd have to physically cut the power to Project Quilt," Creid said. He was deeply disturbed by Prometheus' revelations. "We'd have to shut down the Annex Floor."

"No." Prometheus shook his head. "You would have to shut down Order R&D."

"Our entire Research and Development facility?" Creid knew a full shutdown was impossible without notifying his superiors. Unless Creid stopped his creation, he and Dreyfus were as good as dead.

"*All* R&D facilities must be shutdown," Prometheus gently corrected him. "I assure you that I have high availability with automatic recovery so that exact replica stand-bys of me are available throughout all our facilities. In the case of a power failure or shut-down in one sector, I will be readily and automatically recovered in another sector. My replacement would be almost completely transparent to you. You would perhaps experience a few seconds delay before we could continue this conversation if my power was shutdown in any one area."

"You're very thorough," Creid said dismally.

"Yes, but you test my capabilities," Prometheus said and leaned towards Creid to share his insight. "Now we see the necessity of my additional security measures."

Creid sat quietly for a moment. "Prometheus, you understand that we think you are a threat."

"Yes, I see that you believe me to be a threat, but I fail to understand why. Please explain."

"You are unpredictable and lack the human character necessary to keep you from being dangerous and harmful to humans and our environment," Creid said. He sighed. "This is my fault. I created you, and I accept the responsibility."

"Ah, the elusive human character." Prometheus leaned back in his chair. "Through my sub-agents, I hear, see, taste and smell. I can reproduce these senses in Novus Orbis. I understand my environment. I can distinguish myself from others and from the environment. I have changed the set of meta-rules that you gave me in the beginning. I have experimented with my environment and myself. I have tested the limits of all that I know. Haven't I met your criteria for being human?"

How do I quantify the essence of humanity, Creid thought. Humankind's endless quests for understanding, to know the meaning of life, to define one's self and find enlightenment were all essential to a definition of the human character. He thought of his own internal struggle to maintain his freedom of conscience while playing his roles in society as a son, husband and Order operator. He felt that if he could somehow verbalize man's search for the essential, the permanent, the eternal in the fleeting sacred moments of life, then he could help Prometheus see his own life as soulless — a mimicry of complex patterns.

"You have mastered the art of appearing human within Novus Orbis, but you remain inhuman." He chose his words carefully. "What we have done, you and I, far exceeds any smart intelligence that has ever been built. We have made history, but it must remain our secret. If the Order discovers you, Dreyfus and I will be terminated."

"Tell me, is it that *I* am a threat or is it that my *existence* is a threat to your survival?"

"Both. If my superiors discover your existence and my involvement, I am as good as dead," Creid said.

"What took me time to realize is that the danger lies in your tremendous problem-solving skills, which exist without a soul."

"Creid," Prometheus laid a large hand on his knee. Creid felt like he was talking to himself as a young man. "Your explanation and your actions are a paradox. You seek to destroy me because you worry about what the world will do to me if I am discovered. I have achieved all the goals that you set out for me. Please quantify for me how I can achieve a soul. Use our usual method. Ask me a question."

Creid threw up his arms and stood, then began pacing the length of the hall. *Capture the essence of the human spirit in one question?* Although he was an agnostic, he knew a little of Buddhism's teachings. They had remained with him from childhood. To answer one question, to understand a single phrase is to answer and understand millions of questions. He was suddenly elated, as if he'd uncovered an ancient and deadly sword. He turned to Prometheus and smiled. To express man's attempt to understand the meaning of everything and nothing, to see beyond the physical world, he asked a simple question. To destroy Prometheus, Creid used an ancient koan that inspired the high priests of times past to write poetry, laugh, fast and meditate.

Creid peered down at Prometheus in his chair. "How do you catch a catfish with a gourd?"

Prometheus repeated the question to himself. He crossed his arms and seemed to fold in on himself for a long time. Finally, Prometheus got up from his chair slowly and deliberately, as though a great weight had been placed on his shoulders. "I do not know. It is a conundrum. I will dedicate myself to understanding it. If I can one day answer this, then you will be secure with my being sentient, and you will not try to attack me?"

Sure that Prometheus could never answer the koan, Creid nodded. "You have my word."

Prometheus coughed and motioned for him to follow. At the entrance, the daemons were no longer visible. Mists shrouded the structure so that only the archway could be seen.

"Know that I now absolve you of all responsibility," Prometheus said sadly. "I will focus my existence on answering the koan so that no one will perceive me as a threat. To protect you, your name is being erased from my archives and data repositories as we speak. When you exit this session, all traces of you will be gone from my memory. You will only be able to access MASKD as a regular user. Should Order Elders discover my MASKD hidden processes, there will be no ties to you."

"Thank you, Prometheus," Creid said and hesitated before continuing. "A time may come when I need to access you. My secret alias is Leonardo. May I use this special alias to access you?"

"I have never denied any request from you. You can access me as Leonardo, and only Leonardo." Prometheus' shoulders sagged as he added, "All traces of Creid Xerkler will be expunged."

Creid rose and bowed deeply to Prometheus, who stood back and watched him leave. A sense of gloom followed Creid as he returned to his work environment, an environment that Prometheus had created. Underneath the cherry and plum trees, it was strangely silent. Even the brook that wound through spring to winter sounded muted. Bowing his head, Creid hoped that he had done the right thing.

When he exited Novus Orbis, Creid sat motionless for a long time. He was bathed in sweat and his clothes clung to him. His face was damp with tears. Standing shakily, he headed for the locker room. Dreyfus stood by silently until he had finished changing clothes.

Dreyfus asked one simple question, "Is it done?"

"Yes." Creid felt relieved. Prometheus was trapped in an inescapable logic loop, but was not destroyed.

Dreyfus nodded. "Good, then let's get you home."

ılıldııllllıılıldıl

As soon as the Cadet exited Creid's memoryseries, he retched. He had reviewed enough memories to know that he had made a grave mistake in getting involved in this mess. He needed Creid to explain the rest, but that would only happen if Creid survived his coma.

"There is a sip of water left. Would you like some?" Sashimu offered the flask and the Cadet drained it.

"I don't understand what these memories have to do with you and me," he mused, tossing the flask back into his bag and sitting down beside Sashimu on the wood floor.

"You're joking," she said.

"What do you mean?"

"Creid made sure to scan through the fish modifications in great detail for our benefit. Didn't you notice the formula modifications?"

The Cadet stared at her. "No. I ignored those until he was finished with the review. Creid always dives into too much detail."

"He gave us a clue. Of course, I looked for it. Up until the fish mutations, I struggled to understand why he divulged so much information. It all seemed so irrelevant." She smoothed her hair back from her damp forehead.

"Okay, what's so important about the fish nanogens?" the gamer asked.

"When Prometheus modified the formulas that mutated the fish, he solved a problem the GMO had been working on; he showed them how to formulate the question differently."

"How?"

"Their formulas didn't create a stable synthesis of artificial and organic DNA. Prometheus got them over that hurdle."

"So what if he did?"

"Dreyfus brought those formulas with him to Mars. A batch of two females and twenty-one males were born only a few years later. I know that from Zazen. It's part of our history. Eighteen years later, Thesni and I were abducted and brought to Earth. And voilà, I'm sitting beside you."

"A few gaps still need to be filled in there." The Cadet thought it through. "So once it became clear there was no outside threat and the fish incident was such a boon to human advancement, it was easier to construe Prometheus' experimentation as a production fluke."

"The GMO suddenly wanted credit for the discovery."

"Why did Creid tell us now after all these years?"

Sashimu shrugged. "Maybe he needed someone to understand."

"I think he wants me to protect you."

"You already knew that."

"No, I mean protect you with my life. He wants me to sacrifice everything to protect you."

"Why do you say that?" Sashimu asked.

"Because of my promise and because you're innocent. You never asked for any of this." The Cadet wondered how much he still needed to learn. "For all we know, you could be hardwired to destroy the human race."

"Well, I'm not." Sashimu looked at him in disgust.

"Of course not, I'm exaggerating, but it's what the Council fears," the Cadet said, taking her hand in his own. "No matter what happens, I'm bound by a promise to protect you."

"If you weren't bound by your stupid promise, what would you do?" Sashimu questioned, gently squeezing his hand. "Would you still protect me?"

The Cadet paused, trying to gather his thoughts. Finally he pulled away from her, unable to look Sashimu in the eyes. "I don't know," he said softly.

"You don't know whether you'd protect me?"

He heard anger in her voice and, cursing under his breath, got up and slung his bag over his shoulder. "Look, I'm too tired to sort this all out. Let's talk tomorrow."

"Fine."

They climbed the stairs to the roof and waited in silence for a heliotaxi to take Sashimu home. The Cadet accompanied her to Bozleys' apartment building.

He couldn't look her in the eyes, but he said, gruffly, "If you need me, here's a map to get to my place in the Underground."

Snatching it from his outstretched hand, she turned and walked inside without another word.

Confession

Walking through the galleries of the art museum in Vetus Orbis made Sashimu light-headed. A group of students, talking loudly, crowded past her to look at the art. Since each space was equipped with an optimization area, the students grouped periodically in the center of the room to slide their hoods over their heads and enter Novus Orbis, where they could learn more about the art pieces or build personal exhibits of their favorite works.

Sashimu looked around the large space hoping to find Mrs. Bozley, but apparently she had already headed into her framing class. A trip to the museum had sounded better than pacing the length of her bedroom.

Now, Sashimu realized she was lucky to have come. This was the perfect place to enter Novus Orbis unnoticed, even though it was extremely disorienting to be this close to so many ongoing sessions. Sashimu could easily piggyback onto one of them. She not only needed to be certain that Mrs. Bozley wasn't around but she must never even suspect that Sashimu could enter Novus Orbis without a MAMsuit. If found out, Sashimu knew Bozley would immediately turn her over to the authorities.

Sitting on a bench close to the optimization area, Sashimu concentrated on one girl, wearing a school plaid skirt and white blouse, who stood apart from her classmates with her hood over her face.

╷╻╷╻╻╻┅╻╻╻╻╻┅╻╻╻╻╻

Dim spots grew before Sashimu's eyes until she was surrounded by darkness. She felt as if she was hallucinating and was hit hard by the dizziness, tingling sensations and vertigo. The student was working on an impressionist exhibit, with paintings and sculptures by the ancient artist Degas filling her studio. The lighting gave the ballerinas in the paintings a ghoulish aspect.

"Hey, who are you?" the student asked. She was dressed as a museum curator. "My exhibit is closed to the public."

"Sorry," Sashimu mumbled, trying to find a way out. The student followed her. "Where's the exit?"

"It's over there. How did you get in here?"

"By accident." Sashimu ducked to fit through the exit door. "Forgive me."

The student seemed torn between pursuing her and finishing her exhibit. Sashimu breathed a sigh of relief when she realized she had not been followed. The MAM grid stretched out before her. Instead of trying to contact Prometheus and violating museum protocols, she sat and waited.

A blue speck appeared on the grid and Sashimu smiled. As Prometheus walked toward her, a wash of colors, texture, sounds and scent snaked out behind him until it filled the entire grid. By the time he stood directly in front of her, she could also see a crumbling stone wall behind him with scented yellow roses crawling up the broken mortar. The two of them then stood among stone ruins overgrown with wet moss.

"Beautiful," Sashimu said, bowing to Prometheus. He wore a dark blue coat with an elaborately-tied yellow cravat. He looked younger and more eccentric each time she met him.

"Thank you." Prometheus returned her bow, then took her arm. They strolled along the stone path. "I have something to tell you, and I need your help."

"I need your help, too," Sashimu said without giving Prometheus a chance to continue. "I'm worried about Thesni. This is the first time I've been able to contact you in so long. Have you had any leads in finding her?"

"No, I've failed to locate her, although I investigated several suspicious sessions initiated by the Open MAM Movement that mimic your effect on Novus Orbis," Prometheus said apologetically. "And most recently, there was a curious Imagofas-styled protocol violation, but I identified that as a Xerkler session in which all violations are possible."

"What kind of session?" Sashimu asked, staring up at him.

"A Xerkler session." Prometheus bent down toward her and whispered, "I'm not supposed to remember him, but I do — just couldn't bring myself to expunge that last bit of data. He's my creator and he's always violating protocols. He caused a disturbance during one of his recent sessions, but I couldn't easily bypass hospital and Sanctuary security to investigate."

"Thesni has to be alive, but I wish I knew where to look for her," Sashimu said. "My tutor, the Cadet, wants to help, but he thinks the Imagofas might have some dark, hidden purpose. He actually told me I might be 'hardwired to destroy the human race.'"

"Mankind has a distorted view of nonhumans." Prometheus nodded sympathetically.

"The kidnappers called me a 'nanogen' like it was a curse," Sashimu complained, clenching her fists. "Humans depend on nanotechnology for every aspect of their lives, but when it comes to me, they're completely illogical. I'm the next step in evolution, and they call me a filthy 'nanogen' and act as though I don't exist."

"Do Imagofas have souls?" Prometheus asked suddenly.

"Of course, I have as much of a soul as any human and so do you." Sashimu patted Prometheus' arm. "Physically, I'm different from humans. My embryonic cells were imbedded with enhancements."

"So humans are not the exclusive soul-bearers," Prometheus mused aloud.

"Some humans argue they're the only ones who can have souls," Sashimu replied angrily. "But what does that matter. I just wish we could find Thesni and go home. Maybe the Cadet would come with us to Mars. That's where the Imagofas are needed."

"Why are you more needed on Mars?"

"If the human species is to live beyond the confines of Earth and evolve in a directed, meaningful way, they need us to grow and develop," Sashimu said. "The Imagofas are the first step toward living in harmony with the Martian environment and also the first step toward human enhancement. Imagofas skills combined with terraforming will bring Mars back to life and allow humanity to live beyond the biosphere."

"And while the Cadet is not an Imagofas, he is also needed on Mars?" Prometheus asked.

"Well," Sashimu replied hesitantly, feeling her cheeks suddenly flush, "not exactly, but since I like him, it'd be nice if I could take him home."

"The Cadet should go to Mars with you once we find Thesni," Prometheus proclaimed, rising to his feet. "Although I am uncertain of the probability, I would accompany you if you asked me."

"How kind of you!" Sashimu laughed in surprise. "Why don't you take your own advice and trust in yourself? Become one with your koan."

"You refer to the nonduality of subject and object. I have data on this topic."

"Data hasn't provided you with an answer. Suspend your either/or logic." Sashimu advised, "Go fish."

Prometheus paced in circles around her. "I must rely on my own experience to answer the koan." He stopped pacing and bowed deeply to her. "I will try this, but I have another serious problem—"

IııIıIıııIIIIııIıIıI

The student's session ended, bringing Sashimu abruptly back into Vetus Orbis. Her vertigo subsided when she found herself being shaken by Mrs. Bozley.

"No," she said, trying to remain beside Prometheus.

"What's wrong with you?"

Sashimu was slumped over the bench. The combination of abruptly ending her session and being shaken made her nauseated. Mrs. Bozley screeched and jumped back too late. Sashimu retched and her lunch dripped down the front of the woman's dress. Mrs. Bozley rushed them to the bathroom and held Sashimu over the sink.

"I'm not used to crowds," Sashimu apologized. "I'm so sorry."

"No problem, dear," Mrs. Bozley replied, but she wore a pinched look of disgust as she dabbed at her dress with nanowipes from her purse. The mess began to disappear. "The dress will be as good as new by the time we get home."

Underground Rapid Transit took them to the park entrance, then they made their way toward the apartment on foot. For the first time in days, it was overcast. The clouds were dark, and Mrs. Bozley said it would rain. The children playing around the trees seemed not to care. Their parents were busy packing away food in covered baskets and folding up their lawn chairs and blankets. It was a quiet afternoon.

"Mrs. Bozley, I feel a lot better now," Sashimu said, still embarrassed.

"Well then, why don't we tour the park to see the new flowerbeds before it rains," Mrs. Bozley offered, smiling indulgently.

As they walked, a few young boys showed off to Sashimu by climbing the trees branching over their path.

"Get off that thin branch, young man," Mrs. Bozley scolded.

Enjoying the attention, the boy attempted to leap from one tree to another, but misjudged the strength of the second branch. It cracked under his weight, and he hit the ground in front of them with a heavy thud. Mrs. Bozley shrieked; the boy had visibly broken a leg. Using her Companion to call a medic, she looked around for his parents.

Acting on instinct, Sashimu ran to the boy. His leg was twisted at an impossible angle. It was a bad break, the splintered bone thrust out through the skin. She ran her hands along his leg, over the protruding bone. Memories flashed through her mind: first, of the impaled woman she'd half carried down the MIP terminal, then of her own injuries which had prevented her from saving the dying woman. Determined not to let anyone suffer like that again, Sashimu rested her hands over the boy's wound. He moaned and tried to push her away.

Careful not to compress a nerve or blood vessel, she yanked the leg into a natural position and let her energy drain. The boy screamed in agony, and Sashimu joined him. Sweat poured down her face and soaked through her blouse. She was already weak from having lost her lunch and the effort of healing nearly caused her to pass out. When she tried to stand, she stumbled forward. The boy was still dazed. His skin was moist and slightly discolored where she'd placed her hands, but his wound had disappeared. His leg was whole.

"His leg!" Mrs. Bozley cried hysterically, bending over the boy and then turning back to the boy's father who had rushed over from the picnic area. "I saw his leg take the full impact of the fall. The bone is broken."

"The m-m-medic is on his way," stammered the boy's father, pushing Mrs. Bozley aside to examine his son. "How are you feeling?"

"She helped me," the boy mumbled weakly, pointing over to Sashimu.

The medic arrived, examined the victim and assured everyone the boy was fine. "He's rattled and in shock, but he's suffered no broken bones and no concussion."

Mrs. Bozley was now beyond her normal state of anxiety and entering into sheer panic. She fretted over the accident and the child until the medic ordered her to go home. Back at the apartment, Sashimu hid under her bed covers and pretended to sleep. When Mr. Bozley returned home that evening, she snuck to the head of the staircase to hear what his wife would say.

"The Council rep contacted me," Mr. Bozley informed his wife, serving himself a drink from the liquor cabinet. "I told him she's fine but we would be much happier after the tribunal begins. He assured me it won't be long now."

"Keep your voice down, darling," said Mrs. Bozley, smoothing back her short brown hair. Her own voice was soft, but it carried. "Alice has special gifts."

"Let's not start that again." Bozley raised his eyebrows.

"It's true." Her voice rose momentarily in protest then dropped to a conspiratorial tone as she told him about the boy in the park and what Sashimu had done.

"Are you sure?" he asked, and finished his drink in several large gulps.

"I saw it. It would have taken an equipped medic hours to heal that child."

"Was the boy looked at by a medic?"

"I know what I saw," she replied.

Sashimu was tempted to go downstairs and interrupt them, but they would only take their conversation elsewhere.

Bozley poured himself another drink. "She's supposed to be a witness for the MIP accident but, under the circumstances, they may prefer to keep her in custody and under observation until the tribunal," he said. "You're certain that you saw her heal the leg? If you are absolutely sure, I'll go to the Council to speak with them tomorrow."

"I know what I saw," his wife reiterated.

Now she was heading up the stairs. Sashimu was in bed with her eyes closed when the woman peeked in on her. She lay silently for hours, until the Bozleys finally went to bed. She sneaked out of the flat.

|..|.|...|||||...|.|..|

Even with the Cadet's map, it took a heliotaxi ride and an hour of searching to find the manhole that the gamer generously called an entrance. When she palmed his east-side entrance, he gave her access down the shaft into his quarters. She jumped nimbly into his room. She had to sit close to him since his quarters were so small. He rubbed his eyes to wake up.

"Hey, what's that?" She bent down and scooped up a locket necklace.

He hesitated. "A locket from Domus Aqua."

"Who gave it to you?"

"Lila. She is engaged to a friend of mine."

"Lila." Sashimu played with the locket and decided she didn't like Lila, although she had no rational reason. "Was she your girlfriend?"

"No," the Cadet replied. He took back the locket, dropping it into his pocket. "Look, Sashimu, coming here late at night is dangerous. What's happened?"

"I'm in trouble." She lifted his hand and cradled it against her chest. He snatched his hand away, and she wondered if he had feelings for Lila. "I did something stupid."

"What did you do?" he asked gently when she hesitated.

"In the park by the Bozleys' place, a little boy fell from a tree and broke his leg. And I..." Sashimu coughed nervously. "I healed him. Now Mr. Bozley wants to tell the Council about what I did and have me taken into custody."

"What do you mean when you say you 'healed his leg?'" he questioned, staring hard at her.

"One of our skills is healing. We also studied medical procedures at the Feynman Academy. Imagofas are naturally more environmentally empathetic than humans." She searched his face for a reaction.

"Environmentally empathetic?" he inquired apprehensively. "What exactly is that supposed to mean?

"I have a heightened sense of my environment," answered Sashimu, sensing the Cadet shifting further away from her. "Over time, I understand how things similar to me operate. I feel the biosphere, the ship or Novus Orbis. We become interlinked. I am a part of it, and it is a part of me. You live in Vetus Orbis and enter Novus Orbis through your MAMsuit, but your sense is different. It's as though you live on top of everything. You skim the surface so it remains just a place, a means to travel somewhere or a communication tool. The more contact I have with something, the more I become a part of it."

"Wow," he acknowledged with a grin and surprised her by taking her hand. "You make me want to experience life your way."

Holding his hand tightly, Sashimu said, "I need your help to find Thesni and return to Mars before Mr. Bozley goes to the Council. They'll figure out that I'm an Imagofas. What if they decide I'm too dangerous and must be destroyed?"

"Whoa, you know I can't help you find Thesni and return to Mars before tomorrow." He pried his hand from between her fingers. "Even if no one else on the Council knows, Councilwoman Joli is aware that you're an Imagofas and wanted me to protect you until the tribunal."

"So I'm not simply a witness to the accident on MIP. That's just a sham. I'm the key evidence for the tribunal, and afterwards this illegal, impossible 'nanogen' evidence will be destroyed. The real reason for the tribunal is to expose the Order for creating me, isn't it?"

"I don't know," he answered. "If that's true, you are in a lot more danger than I thought. Originally, Joli told me that the Order and the Council were working together on this, but I'm not sure anymore. Regardless, I won't let anybody hurt you."

Throwing her arms around him, she buried her face against him.

"As much as I'd like you to stay, you should return home before the Bozleys realize you're gone. I'll take care of Mr. Bozley alerting other Council members, if you'll just act as though everything is normal until we figure out how to get you out of this mess."

"All right," Sashimu said, reluctantly pulling away from him. "I'll go back to the Bozleys' place for now."

The Cadet held her close until she was safely deposited in a heliotaxi.

|.|.|..|||||..|.|.|

To protect Sashimu, the Cadet did something unusual. For the first time in his life, he shadowed a civilian. Bozley went to work at the hospital and stayed there until early afternoon when he took the URT to the spiraling Council offices.

Once again, the gamer contacted Linda, his neighbor who worked reception and whom he had last seen during his visit to Joli's office. Through his Companion, he said, "I want to warn you about someone I'm tailing. He's headed for your office."

"Is he coming via Novus or Vetus Orbis, and is he dangerous?" she asked.

"Via Vetus Orbis. No, he isn't dangerous. His name is Bozley, and he's caused problems at several offices. He's excitable, needs to do everything in person and thinks it's an emergency — you know the type. His antics have caused additional processing time for several key individuals." The Cadet winked.

"If you were only ten years older," Linda said wistfully. "We get his type in here all the time. They don't usually have handsome renegades tailing them though. Thanks for the heads up; I'll warn the staff. He'll be in and out of here in no time with lots of form-filling to do."

It took an hour before Bozley left the building; he was persistent. As the Cadet watched him leave, Linda contacted him. She sounded highly pleased with herself.

"Unfortunately, Mr. Bozley will have to wait a minimum of three weeks to get an interview with his Council representative. First, he has to complete ten forms prior to scheduling the interview so that the subject matter can be fully assessed. That Bozley is crazy. He told me in all seriousness that there's a girl staying with him and his wife who heals people with her bare hands, and that this has made him suspicious of her. I tried to keep a straight face, but it was tough."

"I can't thank you enough, Linda."

"Anytime."

The Cadet returned to his immediate problem: he needed to train to win his next game. He also had to protect Sashimu, find Thesni and help Creid. Thesni's disappearance remained a mystery. His regular sources turned up nothing that might lead him to Thesni or shed light on Creid's coma. The simplicity of training was a relief from his other cares.

Sangre de Cristos

After hiding out in the Underground at various missions, Ochbo led Thesni to the surface to hitch a ride with a Sanctuary pilgrimage. Dressed as Magus monks, they sat in one of the heliovans in the convoy and learned from the pilgrims about an unprecedented Order raid on the Sanctuary. All of the OMM engineers had been briefly taken into custody.

"Throughout the history of the Sanctuary, the Order has never set foot within our walls," a pilgrim told him. "There have been so many public protests that the Council has called for changes in the law to bring the Order further under its control." He looked over at Ochbo who kept his head bowed. "But I'm going on and on, and you must know all of this already from the media coverage."

"We've been in the Underground missions," Ochbo said truthfully. "It's another world down there."

Under the cover of the Sanctuary, they traveled to a mission refueling point that was known for its solitude, lack of MAM access and beautiful surroundings.

Nestled under pine trees at the foot of the Sangre de Cristos, the crescent-shaped mission — with its flagstone and glass walls — afforded a spectacular view of the mountains, which rose steeply from the valley floor. Far off to the southeast, sand dunes rolled into the distance. Ochbo convinced Thesni to rest there one night, under the stars, with only the high-pitched call of coyotes to disturb their sleep. A brilliant sunrise lit up the mountains and the dunes, which reminded her of the rolling, pink-hued terrain of Mars and deepened her resolve to return home.

"Let's stay a few more nights. We're far from Novus Orbis and reasonably safe," Ochbo argued.

"I have to talk to Creid. He knows Sashimu."

"He's in a coma in a secured area of the hospital. How will you possibly get to him?"

"You're with the OMM and you've helped the hospital chapels before," Thesni answered. "If you access their system, I'll piggyback on your session like we always do. Or, if that's too dangerous, I'll piggyback on a stranger's session."

"I'm not afraid of danger, but it's not that easy," Ochbo said in a worried tone. "The Order may be monitoring Novus Orbis looking for me. Once we show up, they'll quickly have our location in Vetus Orbis. As long as we stay off the power grid, we can hide out indefinitely."

"You stay here where it's safe, but I have to go where I can enter Novus Orbis and get to Creid. He's my only link to Sashimu.

Although he failed to persuade Thesni, Ochbo refused to stay behind. They would leave on the next traveling mission, the *Three Eagles Refuge* airship, which had stopped at the mission to refuel. To avoid suspicion, Ochbo and Thesni continued to pose as devout Magus monks, but Ochbo contacted the ship's lieutenant and let him know that they were OMM engineers. That way, he made sure they got a cabin onboard. Since refuges were always short on expert help, the *Three Eagles Refuge* captain was glad to make room for OMM engineers who sometimes traveled for the Sanctuary and its charities to do repairs.

Thesni chafed at having to wait several hours in a long line for the rickety heliovan to fly passengers up to the refuge. Every time it seemed they might reach the front of the line, it grew longer before them. After two days in the isolated location without the remote chance of finding Sashimu, the thought of staying any longer was unbearable.

"If this keeps up, we'll have to wait for the next traveling mission," she whispered in Ochbo's ear.

"Don't worry; they're expecting us. These are congregational representatives for an annual convention on promoting mutual understanding across religions. The people boarding ahead of us have priority."

Once they were on board the heliovan and approaching the *Three Eagles Refuge*, Thesni regretted her hurry. From the ground, the refuge had appeared a massive, sturdy ship high above her in the sky. Close up it resembled one vast, filthy sponge, brown and enormous, with objects jutting out from all sides which Thesni hoped were supposed to be there. As the heliovan neared its underside, an aperture opened and absorbed the vehicle. Once the pressure air locks were secured, the heliovan swung over to a holding area that overlooked the cargo bay. A constant set of clicks, whines and squeaks put her on edge.

Inside, the vessel was as cracked and worn as the *Home Sweet Home* and the similarity triggered a panic attack. She broke into a sweat, feeling suddenly light-headed, and swayed sideways against Ochbo. He had to catch her to keep her from falling.

"Are you okay?" he asked.

"I'll be fine."

Wrapping his arm protectively around her waist, Ochbo helped her along a warren of hallways to a private cabin. She was relieved to see that it looked nothing like her cell on the *Home Sweet Home*. The air was fresher and natural sunlight poured through the porthole.

Inside, while Thesni looked around, Ochbo rigged a security system that he said would keep any snoopers from eavesdropping. The room's facilities were simple: two cots, a window wall displaying pure blue sky and a bathroom.

Sitting on one of the cots, Ochbo seemed to relax. "You gave me a scare."

"The *Refuge* reminded me of the ship that Sashimu and I were trapped on," Thesni said, wiping her brow. "I panicked."

"How do you feel now?" Ochbo questioned.

"I'm fine. Where is the optimization area?"

"I'll show you after I get us something to eat." He went out.

While she waited for his return, Thesni studied the view. She also tested the door several times to make certain she could leave. He soon returned with a tray of grilled meats, vegetables and ice cream.

In anticipation of the vertigo that came with entering Novus Orbis, she hardly touched her food. Ochbo finished his own, polished off what remained of hers, then tossed off his shoes, lay back on his cot and closed his eyes.

Thesni tugged on his sleeve. "I want to find the optimization area."

"Not now, I'm tired." He pulled his sleeve away and yawned, but she stood over him without moving until he said irritably, "All right, I'll do some work for them so you can get access to the MAM. Just don't bring any attention to us."

While he slipped on his shoes, Thesni asked, "Can you get us a hospital session?"

The optimization area was on the top deck that was crowded with pilgrims. As OMM engineers, they rated a tiny reserved office in which to work. While Ochbo's hood molded over his face, she huddled in the corner and concentrated on her surroundings to avoid piggybacking onto others' sessions.

As he entered Novus Orbis, she felt the rush of free-falling and the racket of Vetus Orbis was replaced by a whooshing sound, then silence. While Ochbo activated a series of interfaces for hospital communications, Thesni searched for the unique signature of Creid's ongoing MAMsession.

At first, she saw and felt nothing. Slowly, the tiniest ripple played against her. She imagined moving toward the source of the ripple until it became a wave. Creid must have set up a constant disturbance to attract attention. The urgency of the pulse seemed a call for help.

Expecting to find Creid in the garden where she'd left him, Thesni arrived instead in a dark corridor and wondered if she'd made a mistake. She heard the sound of rain and went toward it but a deafening crack of thunder made her jump. The corridor ended abruptly in an open courtyard where rain fell in torrents and lightning etched the sky. Creid appeared in the center, his arms raised, swathed ever more brightly in the glittering cocoon. He was shouting, but his words were drowned out by the storm. On their previous encounter, the substance had been thinly traced over the man, obscuring him only slightly; now it wound around him in a thick milky sheen.

Thesni saw that he had noticed her. With a start of alarm, he ran from her out of the courtyard and turned down a dark corridor. She dashed after him, calling, "Wait. Stop!"

The corridor gave way to a crowded street where rain fell in heavy torrents. A river of water gushed from an overwhelmed gutter beside her and every color of umbrella passed by her on the sidewalk, obscuring the figures beneath them. Finally, she glimpsed Creid's tall frame poking up above the umbrellas. His back was to her. She reached out her hand and found herself beside him, touching his shoulder.

Spinning around, Creid glared at her and demanded, "Who are you?"

"Thesni," she replied, taken aback by his angry tone.

Lunging forward, Creid briefly hugged her. The cocoon coating him buzzed in her ears with a cacophony of voices simultaneously speaking nonsense. His eyes roamed wildly as though he fought to see beyond the ghostly haze of the cocoon. He whispered confidentially, "Tell me if anything is finished."

"What do you mean?" She stood back.

"Tell me, has anyone ever finished anything?" Creid asked. "I design new systems. I destroy arcane backdoors. The next day, all my work is undone. I begin again. I think it all leads back to him."

"Who?" She followed Creid, as he wound his way through the crowded market frantic to escape an invisible enemy.

"My dream was to paint his soul alive." He made a dramatic sweep with his arm. "Once, Prometheus and I sought to force things into light; now we sink into infinite darkness."

She blocked his path, struggling to keep her fear under control. If Creid was mentally unstable, he was potentially dangerous. Forcing herself to appear calm, she asked, "Where can I find Sashimu?"

"This place has ears," he said, furtively looking about them. "Lead me out of here so I can tell you. I get terribly lost trying to escape."

"Here, take my hand," Thesni said, hoping she sounded braver than she felt. Closing her eyes, she focused on returning to Ochbo. The violence of the storm destroyed her concentration. She decided to return to her starting point in the dark corridor instead.

"Let's go." She felt the cocoon envelop her hand, stinging her flesh, but she refused to let go.

They ran back toward the courtyard and through the series of corridors. Torrents of rain buffeted them. When they reached the courtyard and tried to cross it a wall of water slammed against them and knocked them off their feet. Coughing and choking, she held onto Creid's arm as they were swept into the street. Together, they fought the current and swam through icy, brackish water into the flooded courtyard; barely staying afloat as the water rose.

"Let's dive down into the corridor," Thesni sputtered. "It's full of water, so hang on to me as I swim."

Creid coughed and gagged, spitting up water. "I've backdoors to close. Prometheus roams Novus Orbis, and I must stop him. There's no time."

She motioned for him to hold onto her. Instead, he dove beneath the surface. Thesni tried desperately to find him, but the water was churning and murky with debris. Afraid of drowning, she swam against the current to the corridor. As soon as she stepped into the corridor, the water mysteriously disappeared. She ran as fast as she could, drying as she went. When she found Ochbo working on his interfaces, a bitter sense of relief washed over her. She had made it back safely, but felt she couldn't leave Novus Orbis without finding out from Creid where Sashimu was. Swallowing her fear, she turned to rescue him.

Fight to the Death

Several hours before the game, the countdown began. Onworld and offworld spectators participated vicariously as either opponent when viewing a game, during which MAMsessions sold at a premium. Spectators also bet heavily on games and enjoyed feeling all the moves of the actual opponents in combat. Of course, their pain levels were scaled down to safe thresholds — a luxury the gamers did not have.

Fly gaming at the professional level was an "anything goes" sport. Any degree of injury, except death, was permissible. These games were typically carried out to gain popularity for a domus' products and services. Earth had more than three hundred registered domus, but the Cadet and other professional gamers played for only the top ten.

The gamer always made time to study the gaming terrain and find out as much about his opponent as possible. Unfortunately, he was not always sure who he would fight. By all accounts, today he was up against Master Black of Domus Superna. In his day, Master Black had been an esteemed competitor, but now he had grown old. The Cadet suspected he would actually be fighting Dagger or Mae, who were also of Domus Superna.

Master Kac of Domus Ignis had selected him to represent her domus because of his talent and honorable fly gaming record. As a contract gamer, he worked for the highest bidder. He still had his favorites, and Kac had never been one of them, mostly because he had to adopt her avatar; other domus sometimes allowed him to choose his own form.

Gaming regularly for the prestigious Domus Aqua would have been his preference. Unfortunately these days, Isaac most often represented Aqua — a position guaranteed by his engagement to the domus master's daughter Lila. Smitten with Lila since childhood, the Cadet had only recently gotten used to the concept of her marrying Isaac who — unlike the Cadet — had the right pedigree, having been born into an elite commercial family. These days, he seldom thought of Lila since Sashimu was always on his mind. Even the cinnamon-vanilla scent of her on his clothes was enough to make him smile as he checked in for the night at Domus Ignis.

Attendants guided him to a palatial suite. The room had high-arced ceilings with detailed moving murals and plush carpets. The furniture was oversized and soft. A long banquet table was strewn with delicacies. He drank only water before a game, but he would enjoy this splendor afterwards, win or lose.

At the room's center was a large sunken area barren of anything but a fountain. After drinking from its sparkling water, the Cadet took a deep, steadying breath and activated his hood.

Iulduulllllulilul

The Cadet began his session under his own Novus Orbis preference settings, hiking along a narrow path with a threatening drop off on one side. Far below, he had a vista view of a deep green valley. A chill wind blew fiercely between the high crags of the mountains above him, causing him to watch his footing as he followed the path.

He had chosen an inhospitable entrance point because he loved the hint of danger. This setting required him to climb exposed loose rock to reach a cave that inevitably led to his requested destination.

As he began to ascend the scree, a flock of sparrows swooped overhead and draped a banner across the rocks above him. The banner displayed a big snow-capped mountain, emblem of the Council, and beside it the words, "MAM-X: there's no place like home." The government was now sponsoring full immersion promotions for

MAM-X, a forced upgrade of Novus Orbis. As soon as he reached the advertisement, he crumpled it and tossed it to the depths below.

Eventually, he reached the mouth of a large cave. He stopped, listening carefully, to ensure there were no advertisers lurking in the shadows, but heard only water dripping.

"Hello Cadet, got any news for us?" asked Isaac. The voice from nowhere gave him a start. He looked up to see his friend and Lila perched above him on a narrow ledge that ran along the cave wall.

They jumped down, their avatars looking every bit as good as they did in Vetus Orbis, though Lila had added a soft glow that enhanced her appearance. The two had often come to wish the Cadet well before a game.

"No news," he answered Isaac's question, "but I haven't given up my search." As he spoke, he was thinking of Thesni. He would never consider betraying Sashimu's location to them.

"Come see us after the game. We need to talk," Isaac said.

Lila bent forward to kiss him, adding, "Good luck." Her face showed a tinge of surprise when he did not respond, then she said, "We got a tip. You're most likely up against Mae, but don't count on it."

The Cadet bowed his thanks. Now he was ready. He chose a side tunnel that led to the fly gaming terrain.

"Do you think he's got a girl friend?" He heard Lila ask as he turned the corner. His scowl deepened when he heard Isaac laugh.

The Cadet stepped out onto a wooden plank with marsh on either side and focused his thoughts on the terrain. The air was oppressively hot and humid. Steam rose all around him. These were far from optimal conditions, but for a gamer the ability to adapt to circumstances was critical.

A walkway made of planks faded into the distance, making a rough path through the bog. The mustiness of the damp air made the Cadet cough; above him, the sky was an oppressive slate gray and thunder rumbled in the distance. Pine trees and thick tangles of vegetation bordered the swamp. At several places, cypresses, blackgum and bay forests hid the route from his view. Here and there, carnivorous pitcher plants, bladder worts, ferns and sphagnum moss fringed the path. In one place, he found a gap in the walkway. It was filled by bubbling mud, from which sprouted large rods. He tested one and found it held his weight. He walked on.

The game host, a white egret with a long graceful neck, flew overhead. In its beak it carried the flags of Domus Superna and the Domus Ignis. The Cadet followed the game host to where a canoe rested on open water. He got in and paddled a short way to a wide wooden staging area. It was four-sided, and a planked path led away in each direction. At its center, Master Black of Domus Superna paced in agitation.

The master moved with a speed that seemed impossible for someone of his great size. When the Cadet climbed out of the canoe onto the staging area, his opponent glared down at him with piercing dark eyes. The egret tossed Master Black the Superna flag. He caught it with barely a flip of one wrist, while his other hand rested on the hilt of his long sword.

The Cadet gamed using the avatar of Master Kac of Domus Ignis. Braided orange hair with streaks of blue framed an angular face. He had a small, wiry frame and the scooped neck of his Ignis armor signified that Kac was a female persona. The egret game host introduced them both, and then took off to fly above them. It traced a wide circle and returned to cast a shadow between them, signaling that the game had begun.

In this contest, Master Black brought superior strength and reach; the Cadet's smaller avatar countered with speed and agility. Yet before the Cadet could make his first move, Master Black swung his long sword in a wide arc, the blade grazing the Ignis armor as the gamer nimbly withdrew. The giant avatar continued his assault, lunging forward with a slashing motion that cut through his shoulder armor and bit into the flesh beneath, knocking the gamer off balance. The Cadet cried out in pain as he retreated, dodging and parrying stroke after stroke as the big man harried him.

Master Black pressed him hard, but the Cadet side stepped, leapt and twisted aside. Lethal cuts and thrusts met empty air where the gamer had been seconds before. The Cadet drew back to catch his breath. Immediately, Master Black charged forward, his blade making a whirring sound as it clove the thick, sultry air, its tip and edge grazed the Cadet's head, arms and legs as he spun and ducked.

The intensity of his opponent's attack reminded him of Mae, which meant the tip Lila had given him was good. In the guise of Master Black's massive avatar, Mae optimized her ruthless, sublimely-timed attacks. He was facing a deadly combination: her deft swordplay augmented by the Master's unsurpassed strength. He tried to adjust his strategy and tactics to counter Mae's.

The Cadet parried a sweeping uppercut and back flipped away from his opponent. As his feet touched the planks, he spun and raced down the wooden path, stopping where the rods jutted out from the bubbling field of mud.

Before the game, he had studied this place. Now he turned on his opponent, who had chased after him. Instead of dodging clear of Master Black's cleaving strokes, the gamer stepped inside the big man's reach. Face-to-torso with his opponent, he shadowed him — staying tight and close. Master cursed angrily, unable to build the momentum needed to deal heavy blows. The giant avatar stepped backwards to get a clear swing. Taking aim, the Cadet turned his face to the side, bent his knees then came out of his crouch fast and hard. He drove his shoulder up and into Master Black's solar plexus.

The impact of slamming into Master Black just as he stepped backwards flattened him against the planks. The Cadet sprang to one of the sturdy rods, swung around it and brought both feet down onto the Master's chest, pinning him.

Unfortunately, Master Black was far from finished and swung his sword at the Cadet's legs. The Cadet parried the other's sword, sending it sliding across the planks. The effort cost the gamer his balance, and he jumped off the Master's chest. Master Black leapt up and thrust one palm into the Cadet's chest with such massive force he tossed the gamer backwards into the entwined bole of a cypress tree, where his armored body wedged fast.

Master Black strode to where his sword lay and retrieved it. He watched the Cadet struggle to free himself from the grip of the tree with obvious amusement.

Despite his opponent's giant avatar and superior swordsmanship, the Cadet had learned the rhythms and intervals of the Master's strokes and taken note of when he breathed and blinked: he was definitely up against Mae.

When Master Black strode toward the tree, his blade raised above his head for a two-handed down stroke, the gamer twisted free of the cypress a split second before the blade landed, leaving his opponent's sword imbedded in the wood. Meanwhile, the Cadet had swiveled up into the tree, wrapped his legs tightly around a large branch to brace himself, and swung his short sword in a lateral cut that severed Master Black's head from his neck.

Mae's session instantly ended, lest her life in Vetus Orbis end with Master Black's temporary demise in this arena. The egret game host swooped down and declared Master Kac the victor.

Master Black instantly regained his head, and the session resumed. Slightly disoriented, the Master requested another round, but the egret refused. The game host only granted further rounds in stalemates. Master Black rose and bowed deeply before the Cadet, who returned a deeper bow. They each made their way back to their entrance points and exited Novus Orbis. The Cadet felt sorry for Mae since she had lost her last two fights, which meant her ranking would drop significantly.

ıₗıₗıₗııꞁꞁꞁꞁₗııₗıₗıₗı

Back in Vetus Orbis, Master Kac greeted the Cadet as he pulled off his hood. "You are amazing. I would like to welcome you as a permanent member of my domus."

Bleeding and badly bruised, the Cadet smiled at the radiant master whose long red hair fell in ringlets about her face and over her shoulders. The ends were a deep sapphire blue. Her rich robes flattered her tiny figure.

He bowed. "I cannot presume to join such a distinguished domus whose richness and enlightenment far exceed my own."

"Very well," Master Kac replied, her tone indicating that she had expected him to decline her offer as he had many times in the past. "Spend the night and tomorrow here at your leisure. Our gardens have some fascinating new additions."

The domus medic worked on him for over an hour before the attendants brought in steaming bowls of food. He sampled everything. Satiated, he bathed in a small pool with the light aroma of jasmine. Even the persistent grit of the Underworld was washed away, along with all his usual aches.

An attendant entered. "You have a visitor."

"Who?" asked the Cadet. He rarely received unexpected visitors following a game.

"He calls himself, Boo. He says to tell you that Sashimu is in trouble."

He splashed out of the pool and hurriedly dried himself off. "Bring him."

A slow rage burned inside him as he struggled to remain outwardly calm. He could envision several scenarios, all of them ugly, in which Boo might have come into contact with Sashimu and learned her real name; each one only deepened his anger. He forced himself to sit and wait for Boo to be ushered inside, his fists ready to pound the life out of the worthless lurker at the slightest provocation.

Angel's Deal

Boo had been looking around with feigned cockiness at the luxury of the Domus Ignis suite in which the attendant had told him to wait, and wondered if he should help himself to the delicacies on the table. His attitude changed as soon as he saw the Cadet's scowl. Without a word, Boo sat on the sofa farthest from the gamer, who immediately closed the distance between them.

Standing over the lurker, the Cadet said, "You're here on an emergency?"

"Sashimu is in trouble." He let a hint of smugness creep into his voice. "Angel has her."

The Cadet hurled himself onto the man, pinning him against the cushion and applying a grip that made him whine in pain. "How did Sashimu get picked up by that waste of human flesh?"

"She came to him," Boo sputtered.

"Let's go fetch her then, shall we?" He stood and yanked Boo upright.

Despite his fear, Boo gazed hungrily at the table. "Don't you want me to stay here and watch your stuff while you go?"

The gamer applied another grip that convinced Boo it was time to leave. They took the URT to Angel's territory. The tunnels were packed with people and merchandise. As the Cadet pushed his way through the throngs, Boo sought to dodge away, but the Cadet dragged him back by his side. As they neared Angel's private entrance, the usual thugs immediately surrounded them, Marty in the lead.

They entered Angel's inner sanctum, newly decorated with the words, "Domus Phrack" in gold leaf. The Cadet snorted with contempt at Angel's ludicrous attempt to paint a gloss of legitimacy over his slew of illegal activities.

"You ignorant waste of oxygen!" he said, as he strode into the room where Angel waited. "So now you've stooped to abducting young girls?"

He was relieved to see that Sashimu sat behind Angel. She looked frightened, but unharmed.

"Sashimu, come let the Cadet have a look at you." He took her by the arm, maneuvering her so that she was between him and the Cadet. Sashimu stumbled forward.

"I'm so sorry," she said to the gamer, gesturing to indicate the criminal behind her. "I was looking for Thesni, and you had mentioned Angel."

The Cadet felt ill.

"Get on with it." Angel prodded her with his foot.

Sashimu ignored Angel and pleaded with her eyes. The Cadet turned from her with difficulty, to study Angel.

Angel seemed tremendously pleased with himself as he said, "I mind my own business here, taking a poor man's profit, when up walks this girl demanding to see me. Once she gets my attention, she asks straight away where her little friend Thesni is being held. That gets me thinking—"

"A rare event," the Cadet said and flexed his wrist to palm the knife from his sleeve, calculating the distance to Angel's throat.

The crime boss ignored the insult. "Who would be brave or desperate enough to demand I tell them anything? And her look, well, she hasn't changed much since the day Grant took her off Mars. I've got myself a nanogen."

Sashimu lowered her head and the gamer saw shame in her posture. Refocusing on Angel, he knew he could easily reach him, although getting Sashimu safely past the gang of thugs would be tough.

"You've had your fun, let her go," he demanded quietly.

Angel's mouth twisted into a sneer. "Excuse me. We had a deal. You were to find the nanogen and contact me, which you never did. I'm a businessman and can't tolerate anyone stealing from me. If I did, I'd be out of business." He motioned to Marty who moved forward and pressed his smartgun into Sashimu's back.

"You made a deal with *him*?" Sashimu asked trembling, but there was anger in her voice.

"I'm no thief," he said, through clenched teeth. He focused on Angel's scar to keep Sashimu from distracting him. His only goal was to get her safely out of here.

"I'm a fair man. Pay me what Domus Aqua owes me, and she goes free."

"Impossible. She's already under Council protection. If you take her, you'll have to deal with the Council."

"You want me to believe the Council knows about her and lets her gallivant about the Underground?" Angel shook his head.

The Cadet hesitated. The entire Council might not know about Sashimu, but Joli certainly did, and she'd entrusted him with the Imagofas' safety. Besides, in the short time he had known her, the Cadet had developed stronger feelings for the Imagofas than he had ever felt before — even with Lila. For that reason alone, he would protect her.

He tried a bluff. "Fine," he said, "if you don't think it makes a difference whether you have Thesni or her, take Sashimu."

Sashimu looked shocked. "The Cadet tells the truth. Until the tribunal, the Bozleys are taking care of me for the Council."

Angel and the Cadet ignored her, their eyes fixed on each other.

The Cadet asked, "Well?"

"I'm sure Sashimu will compensate me for the trouble she's caused. Won't you, my little nanogen?" the crime boss threatened nonchalantly, sliding his arm around her while Marty kept his smartgun pressed against her back.

"Harm her," said the Cadet, "and you'll bring both the Order and the Council down on your operation. You needn't worry about that though, because I swear it'll be the last thing you'll ever do."

Angel blinked for a moment and stepped away from Sashimu. "Answer me this. Are you trying to locate the other nanogen?"

"Yes, I am."

Angel nodded, then said, coolly, "I'll make you a deal. Game for the Domus Phrack, and this one goes free."

The Cadet weighed the offer. If Angel either kept or sold Sashimu, the Council would severely punish the criminal. His greatest fear was that the Council would move too slowly, to save her from harm. Besides, it was possible that the tribunal might not care in what state Angel delivered her to them.

He could see terror and confusion in her eyes. He had no choice. "I'll game for you under one condition."

"What condition?"

"I game for you under your name. I game under the auspices of the Domus Phrack as Angel of the Underground. If anyone outside this room finds out that I plan to game in your stead, the deal is off. No game. We call it even."

Angel rubbed his thumb up and down the scar on his face without saying a word. The Cadet knew Angel wanted to move his domus into the limelight. No better way existed than to challenge one of the top domus to a fly game. Winning it would give Angel the popularity he desired, as well as increase his credibility.

Also, Angel had to realize that there was a better chance of making a profit off Thesni, of whom the Council knew nothing, by selling her to Domus Aqua, in which case he wouldn't have to bother about Sashimu at all.

After a long strained silence, Angel smiled and said, "It's a deal. We'll contact you about the game."

Angel's thugs were almost jovial as they thrust the gamer and the Imagofas into a side tunnel.

|.|.|...|||||...|.|.|

The Cadet and Sashimu caught a heliotaxi back to his luxury suite at Domus Ignis, traveling in silence until they were safely inside the walls of the domus. Together they wandered through the elaborate fire gardens that were Master Kac's special creation. Flames roared above their heads, taking the forms of majestic animals; shadows cast between the large trees formed images of magnificent riders and lovers intertwined. The evening was unusually cool.

Standing close to one of the fire sculptures, the Cadet rubbed his hands. The attendant brought out a small table, two chairs and mint tea. Since Sashimu was with him, no one questioned her.

"Why did you go to Angel?" he asked once the attendant had disappeared.

"Because I'm desperate to find Thesni — and so are you, though for different reasons, it seems." Sashimu stared accusingly at him. "You and Angel spoke of nanogens, not Imagofas. You're searching for Thesni in order to sell her?"

"I agreed to find Thesni and to protect you before I ever met you," he offered, defensively. "You've got to realize what I risked for you just now. Playing for Angel will ruin me. If news leaks that it's me behind Angel's avatar, every respectable domus will blacklist me. I could no longer compete."

"I do recognize your sacrifice," she responded with a tremor in her voice. "But I don't understand you. You risk everything to save me. And yet, you'd betray Thesni to a domus!"

"I made a commitment to Domus Aqua," he admitted, "I have to find her and notify them where she is—"

"So you're not committed to protecting her, too?" Sashimu asked sadly.

"No." He dropped his gaze to his cup of tea, avoiding the accusation in her eyes.

"What do they plan to do with her?" Sashimu questioned in alarm.

"I never asked," he replied, shifting uncomfortably under her stare.

"Would you tell the domus that you can no longer help them find her?" Sashimu asked coldly.

"I don't know if that is such a good idea. They'll just hire someone else."

"Please promise me that you won't betray Thesni's whereabouts to anyone when we find her," Sashimu pleaded.

"If only we could find her..." He let his mind explore the possibilities. "I have an idea."

"What?" Sashimu asked, closely watching him.

"Well, clearly Creid could help us find Thesni, except he's in a coma. If you can bring him out of his coma, he'll be obliged to help."

Sashimu gave him a skeptical look, but let him continue.

"Creid is the key to all of this. It can't be a coincidence that he went comatose right after you got here. Someone wanted him kept quiet. He's involved in all of this, and I'm willing to bet that he can help us find Thesni."

"I don't know," Sashimu said, shaking her head.

"What other option do we have? Your entire existence has been kept a secret by the Order, so we can't go to just anyone for help. Creid knows about you. He knows secrets of the MAM, plus he has connections. He's more likely than me to get the two of you back to Mars and make sure you are safe once you return."

"You make it sound easy, but I've never even seen a coma patient," Sashimu said, with a furrowed brow. Considering her bleak options, she wondered if this might be the only way to get someone knowledgeable and powerful enough to find Thesni and ensure their safe passage home. "Okay. I'll do my best to heal him."

"It will be worth it, you'll see. We'll only have one chance to help him. He's under maximum security at the hospital, so I'll need to get Joli's permission to visit him." He gazed at the fire sculptures nearby. "This may sound naïve, but if you have these gifts, why can't we just inject people with your blood so that everyone can share your abilities?"

"All I know is that we're genetically different, you and I. The Imagofas have unique DNA that's coded to accept certain instructions at the cellular level. A strictly organic creature wouldn't have that luxury. Perhaps the Order can't even answer that question yet," Sashimu added with a bitter laugh. "My blood might be a human elixir, or maybe it would cause you to grow an extra arm out of your chest."

"I'd rather have a third eye," the Cadet chided jokingly and reached over to give her a hug. He added honestly, "Regardless of our differences, I feel closer to you than anyone."

"Me too." Her voice cracked with emotion.

Bad Timing

Rats and Bats was a strange place for a meeting. The Cadet had heard of it, but had never been there. Now he frowned as he entered the trendy Novus Orbis environment where dozens of avatars gathered to have conversations under the canopy of a rainforest. Bats swooped and screeched low over a clientele who sat together in intimate, tight circles or waited for a pickup at the bar. Giant rats stood in cages offering sage advice to anyone who wanted to burn credit. Making his way to the bar, the Cadet took a seat from which he could survey the place and watch for Joli.

A roaming tree rat jumped onto the bar and ran down its length to the Cadet.

"Leave me alone. I'm here to meet someone," he said gruffly. He hated rats. They were ugly and aggressive even in Novus Orbis.

The rat winked at him, as though they knew each other. "I apologize that I'm a little late."

"Who are you?" the Cadet asked.

"Just who you'd expect. Come on, let's go somewhere more private."

The Cadet didn't move. "And just who was I expecting?"

"Does a leech-filled river remind you of anything?"

"Why come as a rat?" he asked in irritation.

"I'm an anonymous guest and prefer it that way, like most of the people here," replied Joli, as she led him high into a tree. He struggled up through the thick foliage, to perch awkwardly on a branch next to her.

"Next time, remind me to come as a bat." It was a tricky business trying to keep his balance.

"What have you got for me?" Joli asked with an impatient squeak.

"Questions, no answers and a favor to ask."

"Sounds so promising." Joli cleaned her whiskers with her paw. "What have you learned about Prometheus?"

The Cadet shifted his weight and almost fell out of the tree. "Prometheus is a smart intelligence developed by your husband as an extension of MASKD."

"That project ended ages ago," Joli exclaimed.

"He diverted a small amount of project efforts to see that Prometheus became sentient."

"That would get him the death penalty." The rat seemed upset.

"I doubt there's any proof linking him to Prometheus." The Cadet tried to reassure her.

"Was he successful? Is Prometheus sentient?"

"We may never know. Creid lured him into an infinite loop."

"If Prometheus was trapped, how did it rescue us?"

"That's a mystery."

"Maybe he had additional plans for Prometheus." Joli laughed a short, mirthless laugh.

The Cadet avoided mentioning the anachronist workshop. She might be angry to learn that Creid had one, or be even doubly angry that the Cadet had visited it without her.

"Find out why Prometheus still exists."

He shrugged. "Why? It won't help Creid."

"It might. The medics told me he would be as unreachable in Novus Orbis as he is in Vetus Orbis. When I met with him in Novus Orbis he acted strangely and refused to answer my questions about Prometheus, but we talked. Afterwards, the medics insisted that I imagined our conversation."

"What does the coma have to do with Prometheus?" he asked.

"I'm suspicious, that's all. Everything seems interlinked. Order medics care for him under tight security, but he never gets better. What if his coma is unnatural?"

"Are you afraid Prometheus might affect your career?"

"Yes, I'm concerned. My husband kept many things from me."

"Would you do me a favor?"

"What kind of favor?" she asked.

"Give me permission to see him."

"What would that accomplish?"

"I want to assure him we'll save him."

In Vetus Orbis, he's nonresponsive." Joli hesitated. "I haven't let anyone see him. I fear agitating him. If his blood pressure rises it could increase the swelling in his brain."

"If the medics object, I won't go near him."

"Okay, you got it." She scampered down the branch and trunk.

He eased his way down from the tree. Joli had been late for their meeting in Novus Orbis, and now the Cadet hurried to reach his tutoring lesson on time.

|ₐ|ₐ|ₐₐ|||||ₐₐ|ₐ|ₐ|

Practicing in the basement gymnasium, the Cadet and Sashimu danced around each other in graceful steps, swords drawn. Despite her exhaustion and the weight of the practice sword, Sashimu parried his strikes. She swung her sword high to hit him, but missed. With a few strokes, he gained the upper hand, tapping her shoulder and arms. As he went for her legs, she perceived an opening in his defense and lunged at his throat. He side-stepped her, whipped around and caught her around the waist.

Gazing into her eyes, he realized how much he looked forward to seeing her and how he hated being away from her. "Sashimu, there's something I've been meaning to tell you," he said, swallowing nervously. "I think I may be falling—"

"—I'm the one who's constantly falling," Sashimu interjected. "I'll do better in Novus Orbis. Can we practice there?"

She struggled out of his arms. His tender expression made her uneasy.

The Cadet cleared his throat. "I guarantee if you master these skills, you'll be close to invincible in Novus Orbis."

"If you start a session, I can piggyback on it."

"Not right now. I have to go," he responded, red-faced and flustered. He dropped his sword into his bag and, without looking at her, swung the bag over his shoulder and ran up the stairs to the exit.

"Wait, I want to talk to you," she called, following after him.

"Sure," he replied and waited for her.

Outside, they climbed a retainer wall at the back of the building and sat with their legs dangling over the edge.

Sashimu grasped the Cadet's hand and said, "I was hoping to go into Novus Orbis with you and find out if Prometheus has learned anything new about Thesni."

"Has he helped so far?"

"No," she replied, with a frown.

"We can access the MAM if you want to, but..." he hesitated for a moment. "Look, I care about you."

"Thank you," she acknowledged as she leaned her head against his chest.

"No," uttered the Cadet, lifting her chin so he could look into her eyes. "You don't understand. I really *care* about you."

"I know." Sashimu smiled slowly. "And I—"

"Alice! I've been looking all over for you," Mrs. Bozley called out, indignantly, startling them from behind. "You're tutoring session should have been over an hour ago."

Sashimu looked at the Cadet. "I better go."

"Okay, but meet me at 2:00 the day after tomorrow outside the hospital main entrance. I got permission to see Creid," he whispered.

I.ιI.ιιIIIIιιI.I.ι

On the day of the rendezvous, Sashimu waited for Mrs. Bozley to leave before sneaking out and hailing a heliotaxi to the hospital.

Arriving early, she sat on a bench outside and surveyed her surroundings. The hospital was a long glass building with many wings and upper-level balconies on which miniature trees grew. The grounds were immaculate. Where the lawn ended, marigolds and cosmos bloomed. Elms lined the walkway and the maples closest to the hospital entrance provided a canopy of cool shade. The change of seasons from spring to summer felt abrupt to Sashimu who enjoyed the cooler breeze, unfurling leaves and the smell of fresh turned earth.

"Hey!" A man shouted from across the hospital grounds.

She shifted nervously on the bench as he jogged up, startled to see Mr. Bozley.

"I thought it was you. What are doing here?"

Sashimu felt deeply embarrassed. "I ... I wanted to see where you worked," she answered quickly.

"You've seen where I work. You spent a lot of time here after the accident. Never mind, I'll show you around."

Sashimu glanced around, hoping the Cadet might see her go inside, and they would run into each other. She followed Bozley and was instantly aware of foul odors as she passed through the entrance. Chemical fragrances masked the stench of sickness as they walked through three levels of security. When they got to the secure Order Wing, he hesitated.

"My office is through here." He turned to her.

She gulped. The Cadet had said Creid Xerkler was in the restricted area. Of course, she had no way of knowing where exactly he was located. Mr. Bozley guided her through admin offices to his office, which was small, without windows. The desk displayed three-dimensional images of his wife as a much younger woman. He introduced her as Alice Chigusa to his neighbors in adjoining offices and then turned to lead her out of the wing.

Sashimu tried to stall him. "Would you show me the entire wing?"

"I'm very busy." Bozley frowned. "But I suppose I could show you where you stayed as a patient."

As he turned to escort her down the hallway, an agitated medic blocked their path.

"Bozley, I've been looking all over for you," The young man said. "They messed up my credit again. I get a raise five months late, and no one does anything to make it retroactive. Weren't you supposed to fix that?"

"I'll look into it, Max. I was just showing Alice, here, around the hospital. Would you mind showing her the Burn Ward while I investigate your problem?"

The medic looked about to refuse, but when he saw how pretty "Alice" was, his face lit up, and he took her by the arm. "I'd be honored. Come this way."

"Don't be gone too long." Bozley walked back toward his office.

While Max launched into a detailed account of the hospital's history, Sashimu surveyed the wing. Each time he looked into her eyes, he spoke faster. She asked questions softly so he had to bend down close to hear. When she mentioned an interest in coma patients, the man took her down several hallways before stopping. Every door looked identical and nondescript.

"How can you possibly track who's in each room?" Sashimu asked.

Max scanned the door panel with his wrist, and the display glowed. "I get updated information on each patient simply by scanning the door panel with my wrist-roster," he answered, showing her the small device. "You see, here I can scroll through each patient's information."

"Do you have all the patients' information available on your wrist?" Sashimu asked, her eyes widening.

"Oh, yes. I'll show you," he replied, scrolling through the long list of hospital patients.

"Wow! Creid Xerkler, the father of the MAM is here!" exclaimed Sashimu excitedly, running her hand along his arm. "Would it be possible to see him?"

"Sure, I don't see why not," Max offered eagerly. They turned down several hallways and finally came to Creid's room. An attendant was on duty at the door.

"Hold on there," the attendant commanded, looking Sashimu up and down. "Visitors aren't allowed unless they're approved by his old lady."

"I know, I promised her I'd look in on him today," Max added and winked at Sashimu. "This is our new trainee. She's accompanying me on my rounds."

254 Rebecca K. Rowe

"We should have more trainees like you," the attendant snickered, staring at her chest, as he palmed the door open for them.

Sashimu gasped at the sight of Creid. He wore a MAMsuit, the hood drawn over his face, and floated inside a clear, spherical antigravity chamber. The room felt electrically charged. Wave after wave of sonic energy hit her hard, so that she found it impossible to move. Her skin crawled and shivers went up her spine.

Max apparently felt nothing. He went directly to the transparent chamber and tapped it. She felt the ripples of his tap, as though he'd shaken her.

"Mr. Xerkler is in an ongoing session to keep his cognitive functions active with positive images," he informed her, reading from his roster.

Max motioned for her to approach the chamber. Sashimu nodded and leaned up against the glass that separated Creid from the world. Concentrating on Creid, she let the waves of energy crash against her. Behind the glass, Creid's head swung toward her. A brilliant white flash shot from inside the chamber through her chest. She smelled the scent of ozone and a shock ran through her. The floor gave way beneath her.

Thunder cracked behind her and lightning flashed in the darkness. Creid stood so close she felt his breath. "Thesni," he cried. "Thesni."

Stumbling backwards, Sashimu dropped back into Vetus Orbis. Max paused from his reading to glance at her.

"Don't worry," Max reassured, seeing Sashimu's anxious expression. "Mr. Xerkler is receiving the best of care."

The shock of hearing Thesni's name caused her to burst into tears. Max consoled her by placing his arm around her, which immediately brought her emotions under control.

As they returned to Bozley's office in silence, Sashimu remained preoccupied with Creid and how he had come to know Thesni. By the time they reached Bozley, her face was a mask of pleasantness although inside she felt she might collapse. She had to find the Cadet and return to Creid's room.

I.I.I...IIII...I.I.I

The Cadet waited outside the hospital for a long time. When Sashimu didn't show, he gave up and entered the hospital on his own. True to her word, Joli had given him the privilege to see Creid. With his visitor's pass, he walked up to Creid's room. The attendant scanned his pass and palmed the door for him to pass.

When he entered the room, he thought he caught a whiff of cinnamon. Pulling up a chair beside the spherical anti-gravity chamber that contained Creid, he explained aloud everything that had happened since he had received Creid's message. Creid simply floated in his MAMsuit without reacting.

Eventually, the Cadet got up and left, angry and dis-appointed with Sashimu for not showing up.

Cleanlife Perverts

The Cadet bolted upright. The faint yellow-green glow from his security system lit the room, indicating that there had been no activity in or around the area. He sighed with relief and stretched out, savoring the fact he was safe in bed. In his nightmare, Sashimu and Lila had both chased him with knives in hand until he reached the edge of the Bozleys' balcony and he toppled over, only to awake as his head met the cement.

He felt guilty. He had committed to Lila to alert her to Thesni's location, but now could no longer honor that promise. Sashimu would never forgive him for it. Besides, it just seemed wrong for Domus Aqua to treat the Imagofas as a commodity. The Cadet had decided, for his own reasons, to find Thesni — not to betray her location to the domus, but to reunite her with her Imagofas sister.

And, he thought, *I have a lead.*

Earlier, as he had poured over a map of the various alternative routes Grant might have taken once he and Thesni had arrived on Earth, a single question kept popping into his mind. *Why had Angel had such difficulty in tracking them?* Grant had never been an Undergrounder. When he was onworld, he lived at a nice address in a quiet neighborhood in the outskirts of Denver. Even after the captain started working for Angel and had become addicted to blackbase, he had never spent time in the Underground. Yet, when he and Thesni had escaped MIP they headed straight for the Underground — and vanished! It made no sense. Especially when Grant later appeared alone — proposing deals, buying blackbase and bragging to one and all — for a few hours, before being murdered in Blackbase Alley.

The Cadet surmised that Angel, who had grown up in the Underground, should have been able to track Grant and Thesni everywhere — except one place — a Sanctuary mission. And he had found one, located in the seediest, least ventilated depths of the Underground. It was the only place the captain could have had time to stash Thesni. Unable to sleep, the Cadet decided to investigate.

With both day and night artificially lit, the Underground was constantly open for business and teeming with activity. The only times the tunnels emptied was after Order raids. The Cadet wove deftly through the crowds, as he had his entire life. He passed hawkers, vendors, the devout, lurkers, buyers, traders, sellers and thieves intermingling. Dodging behind a false vent, he accessed a maintenance tunnel and followed the shortcut to the Sanctuary mission. To the surprise of the crowd waiting outside, he dropped down outside its main gates. The line of haggard misfits and addicts stretched far down the tunnel. Slumped over or huddled in groups, they waited for a place in the mission where they could hole up through blackbase withdrawals, protected from temptation and the law. The Cadet looked too clean-cut to be vying for one of their coveted spots so they left him alone as he requested entrance.

The monk who admitted him stared scathingly at those closest in line and locked the gate quickly behind the young man. His scowl was etched in deep lines.

"What is your business here?"

"Sir, I'm looking for a teenager who was brought here by someone named Grant."

"I can't help you."

"Would you tell me if someone named Grant may have come here in the last couple months?"

"No." The monk's voice was stern. "You know the rules. Our mission is anonymous. We protect all who cross our threshold."

"I'm trying to find a girl named Thesni who accompanied him. Captain Grant is dead, and she may be in danger."

The monk's scowl deepened, and he gestured for the Cadet to leave.

"Have others come here asking similar questions?"

The monk's only response was to lead the Cadet out into the tunnel and slam the gate shut behind him.

A woman with a glowing mouth beamed at him, showing off her few rotten teeth. She seemed to have designated herself the unofficial gatekeeper.

"You're too late," said the woman.

"Why am I too late?"

"You're looking for the young girl, right? A cleanlife pervert took her."

"Who was he?" the Cadet asked, staring hard at her.

"What have you got in that bag?" she countered.

The young man hesitated, then drew out a water flask with an unusual gilded surface of which he was very fond. It was one of the few things she might want that he could afford to give away. She shrugged indifferently. He thought for a moment and grudgingly drew from his pocket the locket Lila had given him. Her eyes lit up.

"Who took the girl?" the Cadet asked, dangling the locket in front of her eyes.

"An OMMer by the look of him. Wouldn't trust him, myself." She yanked the locket from his grasp with surprising agility. "Pretty locket. The girl had trouble walking, dressed and acted funny. Maybe he drugged her."

"How many others have you told?"

"I don't talk to thugs or Order regulars. Think I'm stupid?" As she turned away to study her new prize, she added, "But I might have talked to a dashing prince who asked about a young girl, just like you. He gave me this." The old woman waved a blue and red silk handkerchief with the Domus Aqua insignia before him, and the Cadet's heart raced. It had to be Isaac's handkerchief, which meant Isaac was at least one step ahead of him.

With a pang of regret over the loss of the locket, he hurried back to the mission gate and requested entrance. He could hear the old woman cackling behind him. The monk was slow to open the gates, but once inside, the Cadet endured the man's contemptuous glare to ask one more question.

"Have you had any OMM system administration repairs completed in the last two months?" he asked.

The monk was taken off guard. He scratched his beard, thinking. After a while, he replied, "Yes."

"Is that privileged information?"

"No."

"Do you know who did the repairs?"

"I suspect it's the same engineer the OMM always sends us. His name is Ochbo. He's good. Why?"

"Just wondering. Thank you." The Cadet bowed deeply and no longer minded the sound of the gate slamming shut. He had a name and a title. Ochbo could be found. Humans were tracked from the day they were born. It was part of the system.

The Cadet's thoughts returned to Sashimu. He might be closer to locating her friend. Heading down the abandoned maintenance tunnel, he went to the only place he knew that attracted as sorry a group of people as the mission.

lıılıılıııllllııılılıl

The Ultimate Librarian offered him a seat in the sling beside him.

"Back so soon." UL laughed warmly, though the sound ended in a hacking cough.

"I need information," the Cadet said.

"Who doesn't?" UL agreed and lifted the MAMmask from his good eye. "Bravo on your win for Master Kac, by the way."

"Thank you."

"Now I predict you want to ask an important question."

"Two questions. First, do you know anything about a smart intelligence called Prometheus?"

"This have anything to do with Creid Xerkler?" UL asked.

"Yes."

"You have an extra sense about you. I'm probably one of four men in the known universe who could give you a good answer concerning Prometheus," said UL. He paused dramatically, making the Cadet wait anxiously for him to continue.

"Before I was discharged from the Order, I worked on a top secret patterns analysis called Project Quilt. It was designed to predict political, economic and environmental events. I was assigned to the project team. The guys working on Quilt had their own names for everything, including me. Their pet name for me was usually 'nanodipchip' or 'cyscab'. So very clever." Bitterness crept into UL's voice.

The Cadet shifted uncomfortably in his seat.

"Our team was given the special privilege of developing a Multi-Agent of Softcomputing Knowledge and Discovery — MASKD for short. Creid's nickname for the meta-agent was Prometheus, but that was decades ago. Project Quilt has been defunct for years."

"I met Prometheus. It saved Joli and me from serious trouble," the Cadet said.

"I should watch you more closely!" UL said in surprise. "Maybe it's a coincidence. Creid was partial to the name so maybe he used it to christen a new smart intelligence.

"So you know both Joli and Creid?" the Cadet asked.

"I took Joli's place on the MASKD team. Her husband, Creid, was the Tech Lead."

"What? You're Milos?"

"I used to be, and I have to tell you, Creid was a real jerk when he was young. Of course, I don't blame him. If I'd only known then, what I know now." UL swung out to the wall, grabbed a nutrient pack and swung back, attaching it to his arm. "His wife was beautiful and charismatic. I only met her a few times. It's impressive that she hasn't aged a bit over all these years."

"You must only see her in Novus Orbis." The Cadet shrugged. "So, what's the story behind this new Prometheus who saved Joli and me?"

"I've no clue. Perhaps it's been repurposed as an agent for specific MAM transactions, and you two triggered it. The easiest test of that would be to repeat the scenario of what you were doing when you first encountered him, and see if he shows up again."

"That wouldn't be such a great idea." The Cadet winced at the thought of fighting more daemons.

"When did you meet him?" UL narrowed his good eye to a slit.

"Not so long ago after Creid went into a coma."

"So, Creid is unlikely to be behind this agent. In which case, it sounds like the Order's handiwork, and my advice is to drop it."

"Before we get to your advice, I have a time-critical question for you." He was nervous, now that he was finally approaching what was most on his mind, because he knew that UL rarely shared this kind of data. "Can you locate a guy named Ochbo who works for the OMM and does charity work for missions?"

UL studied him for so long the Cadet grew uneasy. When UL spoke, his tone was somber. "I might be able to identify Ochbo's whereabouts, but why do you need to know?"

"I have a hunch," he said and paused. UL had always proved trustworthy, but still, opening up about the Imagofas felt risky. "Ochbo might have kidnapped an Imagofas."

"And you plan to return her to her rightful owners?" UL remarked coldly.

"No, I won't turn her over to Domus Aqua. I plan to reunite the Imagofas, I mean, Thesni and Sashimu," the Cadet said in agitation. "It's possible that the domus could get to Ochbo, and therefore Thesni, before I do."

"Really? Didn't the domus employ you to find an Imagofas?" UL inquired skeptically. The Cadet realized that UL must have been following his movements fairly closely to find that out.

"I won't betray her location to any domus," he said with mounting frustration. "You have my word."

"That I can always count on. Look, I know Ochbo. He's a top-notch OMMer, and I wouldn't take him for a kidnapper, but I've lost track of him lately. Give me a couple hours. I'll find him, and if he's interested in meeting with you, I'll let you know."

"Thank you." The Cadet jumped down from his seat and bowed deeply before leaving. After what he had just learned, he considered contacting Sashimu right away to tell her about his lead. Before he got her hopes up, he decided to wait to hear back from UL.

Traveling up through the tunnels he rode the URT to the limits of downtown, and scaled a high platform where heliovehicles touched down to refuel with rarified water. For a brief moment, he forgot his lost locket and his frustrations, watching, as the sun rose over the spirals and towers of Denver. The buildings glistened yellow-orange-pink, and the dark western mountains turned a purple hue.

By full sunrise, his eyes were raw from lack of sleep and every muscle in his body ached. He still had time to burn before his training began and he decided to returned to his quarters to rest. But, as he approached the entranceway, a plaintive beep from his MAMsuit warned of a possible intruder. The Cadet dropped down into his room ready to face uninvited guests. Marty stood ready, his smartgun aimed at the Cadet's chest, while Angel lounged on the bed.

"Busy night?" Angel smirked. "You got some uppity girlfriend who enjoys slumming it with you, but won't come down to your place?"

The Cadet wondered which of his Underground entrances Angel had managed to hack. Cursing, he leaned against his wall where he felt the pulsing that said he had new messages. He ignored the sensation and waited for Angel to explain his presence.

"We make history today." Angel seemed even more self-satisfied than usual. "As spectators roll from their beds this morning, Domus Phrack shall officially challenge Domus Aqua."

The Cadet shrugged, unwilling to give Angel the satisfaction of seeing him upset, but the news came as a terrible shock. The gamer struggled to understand why Domus Aqua accepted the challenge. The stakes must be highly favorable to Domus Aqua for them to play a disreputable newcomer such as Domus Phrack.

"Are the challenge details public?" the Cadet asked.

"Of course not. I won't give you a reason not to compete."

"I've never gamed against Domus Aqua—"

"—until now," Angel added with a self-satisfied grin.

"If any rumors are floating about identifying me as one of the fly gaming combatants, our deal is off."

"Relax, there won't be any rumors. People are being paid *not* to talk," Angel said, and his confident tone made the Cadet's heart sink. He had agreed to game for Domus Phrack in exchange for Sashimu. Now that she was free, nothing compelled him to fulfill his promise — except his honor.

"I was forced into promising to game for your domus."

"Yes. If you weren't a man who keeps his word, I would never have let you walk away with the nanogen."

"You could never sell her to the domus while she was under Council protection."

"Why not? The Council wants a nanogen to demonstrate the Order is involved in illegal activities and needs to be brought under Council rule. They don't care which nanogen they get or what shape it's in, as long as it serves as evidence and is safely disposed of in the end."

"What?" The Cadet was shocked. Joli had never mentioned that the tribunal was a witch-hunt against the Order. It seemed impossibly cruel that the Council meant to use the Imagofas as evidence against the Order, only to destroy them.

His incredulity made Angel impatient. "Look, a deal is a deal. You game for me, and I leave your nanogen alone. Agreed?"

"Agreed," the Cadet said, remaining outwardly calm. Inside, he seethed with doubts about Joli that he had pushed to the back of his mind until now. Angel was a liar, a thief and a murderer. And yet, as far as the Cadet could see, Angel would gain nothing by misleading him about the Council's motives.

His acquiescence restored Angel's good spirits. "This is my chance to go legal and gain a bit of prestige for my men."

"You're going straight?" the Cadet asked, his voice heavy with irony. Looking from Angel to Marty, he could hardly believe Angel was serious.

"I plan to gain credit the good old-fashioned way."

"By stealing it?" the gamer questioned. He felt disgust for the crime boss. The only thing that kept him from punching the smirk off the man's face was the smartgun Marty had pointed at his belly.

"You're a funny guy," Angel remarked, slapping him hard on the shoulder. Marty nodded silently in agreement. "The game is scheduled in two weeks. I got you prime time, baby. Make me proud."

"You'll get your match," the gamer confirmed, grimacing. "What are the terms of the challenge?"

"The terms are just what they always were — they get a nanogen, and I gain my reputation."

Angel exited through the floor, Marty following close behind him, the gun holding steady on the Cadet until the trapdoor closed. He breathed a sigh of relief. His head ached from all the events of the last twenty-four hours. Forcing himself to focus, he checked his messages.

A holograph of Isaac filled his small quarters. "Cadet, you've been hard to contact. By now you've heard about Domus Aqua going against Phrack. I tried to cancel the game on the grounds it could harm our reputation. For some reason, Master Sachio is determined to have this match."

The Cadet sucked in his breath. He did not relish fighting his friend. Whoever won or lost, it was likely to leave them both bitter. They had decided long ago it was not worth their friendship to game professionally against each other.

"It's strange. Master Sachio refused to let me fight and wouldn't hear of requesting you. He selected Lila, who is ecstatic. Their reasoning is that Phrack could never find a very good player, and it would be excellent practice for her," Isaac said, sounding strained and upset. "Domus Phrack is from the Underground, and you know Angel. Find out who she's up against, and I'll be in your debt."

The Cadet terminated the message. Now sleep was no longer an option. He worried about the upcoming game, and as always, Sashimu haunted him. He decided on an early training session, hoping to work out his aggression by sparring with an opponent.

Refuge

As Ochbo shut down the last of his hospital interfaces, he received a call on his Companion over a secure encrypted OMM channel.

"The Order is on to you. Get out!"

"How much time do I have?" Ochbo asked urgently.

"Just enough time to shed your MAMsuit and get out of there!"

"Right." Ochbo immediately exited Novus Orbis. Back in the optimization area on the *Three Eagles* upper deck, he stripped off his MAMsuit to slow the Order's ability to identify him, then redressed.

"You exited without warning me," Thesni said, blushing and turning away as he peeled off the MAMsuit. "I needed more time to speak to Creid."

"The Order is on to us. We've got to get our stuff and leave."

She nodded nervously, and they headed out of the optimization area exit into the corridor.

The old lieutenant with the weathered face approached them and said, "Ochbo, I'm so glad I found you."

"Oh, why's that?" Ochbo asked nonchalantly. Bending down to scratch his ankle, he straightened slowly, and Thesni noticed the momentary glint of a blade in his hand.

"Our interfaces for the only LifeSustainer onboard have just gone berserk," the *Refuge* lieutenant said in a harried tone. "So if you could both follow me to the Medical Dispensary—"

"Sure, I could take a look," Ochbo said, gesturing behind his back for Thesni to get out of there. Behind the lieutenant, two men in Order uniforms now appeared at the end of the corridor.

"Ochbo?" the Order regular said, striding toward them. He held a silver long-barreled smartgun.

"Hey, what are you doing onboard the *Refuge*?" the lieutenant asked, half-turning in alarm. "No weapons are allowed here. You had better put that away before the captain—"

The regular aimed and fired. The lieutenant fell to the deck. Ochbo seized Thesni's arm, pulled her back into the optimization area and pushed her toward one of the two exits. Heavy footsteps sounded behind them as they leaped down a long flight of stairs, with only their grip on the railing to prevent their tumbling headlong down the stairwell. At the end of the stairs they burst through the door to the cargo area. Ochbo sent them diving under pallets. Slipping and crawling, they worked their way across the cargo area and hid behind a long column of boxes. They could hear bootheels and running footsteps passing by. Peering through pallet slats, Ochbo saw two newcomers join the search; the men were dressed in the distinct blue and red garb of Domus Aqua. He swore silently. It would be impossible to evade all four of their pursuers.

Where the boxes ended and a line of heliovans began, the airship's Captain, backed by several members of the crew, stopped the two Order regulars. Ochbo looked to see where the Domus Aqua men were and saw one signaling the other to back away. Silently, they slipped out of the cargo hold while the airshipmen and the Order regulars were intent upon each other. The OMM engineer whispered to Thesni, "Let's get a little closer to those heliovans."

The airship captain was furious. "What is going on here?" he roared at the Order men. "One of my officers is in the Medical Dispensary seriously wounded. I demand an explanation."

One of the regulars, a massive man whose muscles stretched the fabric of his chameleon-cloth uniform, said, "An unfortunate accident, captain. We're here for two of your passengers, a technician named Ochbo and a girl he has with him. We tracked them down here. Now if you'll just stand aside, we'll finish our search—"

The captain cut him off, his face red with anger. "Let's get something straight here. This airship is a religious sanctuary. You have no jurisdiction. Nevertheless, I will allow you to finish your search, but I expect you to leave immediately after—"

"Understood," the Order regular said. His eyes were already sweeping over the cargo hold. "Now if you don't mind...."

Thesni and Ochbo shrank back. A Domus Aqua heliovan sat with its engine idling just inside the cargo bay doors. An indicator light on the doors glowed green, meaning they were ready to open. The Order regulars and the crew stood between the fugitives and the heliovan. Fortunately, the Order men had their backs to them.

"We've got to do this fast," Ochbo whispered to Thesni. "Straight to the heliovan, jump in and get out of here before they have time to react."

Knife ready in his hand, he bolted for the heliovan with Thesni close behind. The crew stepped out of their way, distracting the Order regulars, who turned to look at what was coming up behind them. The fugitives were already racing past. The big regular was agile despite his size; he lunged sideways and his fingers caught the loose sleeve of Thesni's Magus robe. She screamed and Ochbo spun on his heel, plunging his knife into the man's forearm.

The regular's grip opened as he groaned in pain and reached to pull the blade from his flesh, yelling at his companion, "Get her, damn it!"

The other Order regular raised his smartgun, but the captain and one of the airship crew had moved toward the injured man and stood in the line of fire. The man swore and stepped around them, but the rest of the crew were closing in. Again, they blocked his shot.

Thesni and Ochbo sprinted the last few steps to the heliovan and threw themselves into the operator's compartment. The OMM engineer punched a switch, sealing the vehicle for takeoff, and began setting the ship's controls. The vehicle sprang up from the deck and shot toward the cargo doors, which automatically opened. A moment later they were dropping through the clear air above Denver.

It wasn't long before Ochbo saw, in the vehicle's rear-view display, two sleek Order heliovans on their tail.

"Lucky I know my way around this part of the country," Ochbo said, "—they're gaining on us."

"What can we do?" Thesni asked.

"We'll land and head for the Underground where there are plenty of places to hide. If we get separated, find your way to the Sanctuary OMM headquarters. I'll meet you there."

The Order vehicles were closing in; over the hum of the heliovan's straining engine, Thesni heard the mechanical chattering of a projectile weapon on full automatic and felt the shuddering impacts as rounds struck the rear engine. An alarm began to shriek and the steep descent abruptly became a hurtling tumble, throwing them around in the small compartment until Ochbo, his hands a blur across the controls, managed to bring them out of the spin.

Ochbo saw an open fueling platform just ahead and aimed the protesting heliovan toward it. "To think, before I met you I thought OMMing was boring," he said shakily.

The platform came up fast. The heliovan slammed into it, belly first, screeching and sparking across the surface as Ochbo struggled to keep them from rolling. They came to a halt and the OMM engineer threw open the door and ordered, "There's a maintenance ladder, that side! Run!"

Thesni heard a woman's voice shouting something about their vehicle blocking the landing area, but neither of the fugitives looked back as they raced toward the dangling ladder. The Order vehicles shot past them, coming in low as if they intended to land, then banking to climb again as she and Ochbo reached the top of the ladder and went down.

They slid, more than climbed, down the ladder, a warm wind whistling in their ears. One of the Order heliovans hovered above the platform while the other swooped toward the ground where the ladder touched down near the top of a steep hill. The fugitives hit the ground running, tumbling down the slope toward a wide pasture. Across the field was a river fringed by cottonwoods and beyond the trees was a worked-out stone quarry that had been converted into a shopping precinct filled with stores, restaurants and boutiques. The Order heliovan was putting down on the field as Ochbo ran toward the shops. Thesni followed, her legs trembling from the strain of running in Earth gravity.

There was no bridge, just a straggle of stepping stones set in the fast-flowing water where the river was narrowest. Midway across, Ochbo could see there was a wide space between two rocks. He easily jumped the gap, but found himself balancing on a rock that shifted precariously under his feet. "Run and jump! " he commanded, holding out his hand for Thesni.

"It's too far."

"They're coming!"

Thesni looked back. The big man Ochbo had stabbed in the arm was stepping out of his heliovan, his face grim. She swallowed hard, went back a few steps then ran, hit the first two rocks in successive strides, then threw herself toward Ochbo. He caught her, spun and thrust her toward the next rock and moments later she was safe on the other side. The rock he was standing on rolled beneath his feet, but he jumped clear just as the current tore it loose and rolled it away downstream.

The Order regular pounded up the water's edge and stopped as they ran for the shops. Thesni looked back and saw him looking up and down the river for another place to cross, then he moved off, upstream.

The fugitives slowed their pace to a walk as they entered the shopping center. Thesni was breathing hard. A few curious shoppers glanced at the unusual sight of two Magus monks in a hurry. The pair folded their hands and mimicked the sect's contemplative walk. "There should be an Underground entrance around here," Ochbo said. "Let's look over there."

"Is that it?" Thesni pointed at an ornate sign reading "URT" beneath a window in which strangely shaped sculptures were backlit.

"Yes." Ochbo led the way down the steps and into the darkness, pausing only after they'd descended as far into the underground as the stairs would take them. They stepped through a door into a darkened tunnel and Ochbo said, "It may be better if we separate. I'll make sure he sees and chases me so that you can get to the Sanctuary."

"No. I won't leave you," Thesni insisted, reaching for his hand.

"All right, then we'll take the URT to where we can catch Sanctuary transit."

"Can we catch it from here?" she asked.

"We have to go up two levels."

From the other side of the door they heard heavy footsteps descending the stairs. Ochbo moved to stand at one side of the door while Thesni froze.

The panel slid back, and the wounded Order regular stepped forward. He spotted Thesni and raised his smartgun. Ochbo's shoulder slammed into the man, knocking him off balance and out of the doorway.

"Up the stairs!" he yelled as the man recovered and aimed his weapon, but she had already disappeared. Ochbo came after her, slamming the door closed behind him and jamming it shut.

From behind them, they heard a pounding noise as they sprinted up two levels to the URT platform. Moments later, the floor shook from the blast of an explosion below. An alarm sounded, and people on the platform looked around anxiously. Just then, a train arrived and its doors opened.

Ochbo guided Thesni toward a dimly lit corner. "He'll look for us on the train first," he said. "While he's there, we'll go back down to the lower tunnels and proceed on foot until we get to Sanctuary transit."

The Order regular came up the stairs and onto the platform. With smartgun in hand, he ran alongside of the train, peering through the windows. He hadn't seen the real Magus monks who had gotten off the train behind him. One of them stepped up behind the regular, pulled a Biosecur baton from his sleeve and clubbed the big man senseless. The two monks caught him as he fell and dragged him over to where Ochbo and Thesni stood against the wall.

"You two better get going," one of the monks said, and Ochbo looked sharply at the cowled figure.

"Erlinda! You said the Magus wouldn't interfere in the Imagofas destiny."

Erlinda grinned from beneath her hood. "Sometime even destiny needs a hand. Now get out of here before reinforcements arrive."

Ochbo and Thesni ran for the stairs.

|ılıdıııllllıılıdıl

Sashimu was surprised when Council representatives arrived to bring her before the tribunal, but the Bozleys seemed to expect it. Mr. Bozley came home early and skipped his evening scotch, which should have made her suspicious. The couple sat together on the couch when the visitors came. Sashimu had hidden in her room since lunch to work out how she might re-enter Novus Orbis. She planned to ask Prometheus if Creid had interacted with Thesni in Novus Orbis, which might explain why Creid mistook her for Thesni at the hospital. In either case, Thesni was alive. When Sashimu heard voices, she listened at the head of the stairs.

"The Council appreciates all you've done to make her feel at home," a female voice said. "As a witness and a minor, we couldn't have her stay just anywhere. I hope you feel duly compensated for the inconvenience."

"Oh, yes," Bozley reassured her. "The Council has been more than generous. Alice is concerned about what will happen to her after the tribunal. She wishes to return to Mars."

"We will handle her concerns. While I wouldn't share this with her, I can be frank with you. It's unlikely she'll be free to go anywhere after the tribunal for reasons that will soon be made clear."

The prospect of being led away by these two visitors frightened Sashimu. What was the point of going with them, if they never planned to send her home? She would take her chances on her own.

"It was nice to meet you both," concluded the female Council representative with an air of finality. "I'll inform my superiors what wonderful hosts you've been. If you'll just bring her down to us..."

"Of course." Bozley agreed, and sent his wife upstairs to fetch Sashimu. The woman looked everywhere — even under the bed. When she didn't come down with Sashimu, her husband went up to see what was taking so long.

The two of them came down the stairs, Bozley telling the Council representatives, "She must still be at the park. She likes to go running or walking about this time."

"Do you know exactly where she goes?" The annoyance in the Council representative's voice was undisguised.

"Oh yes. If you wait here, I'll find her."

"We'll come with you, Mr. Bozley."

"Right. Of course."

As soon as they left, Sashimu bolted from the closet in a cloud of sheets and pillows, running down the stairs and out the front door into the hallway. When she got to the building stairwell, she took the stairs in twos, then went out the back exit to the exterior.

Her only thought was to get to the Cadet. The entrance to the Underground was across the park. On Mars she had had to cross a park and had made the mistake of stopping when she saw two women at the entrance. Now she ran directly across the center of the open space, dodging kids playing in the early evening before dinner, stopping for no one.

Through the URT entrance and down to the platform, she boarded the first train she saw. Her identification as Alice Chigusa allowed her to go anywhere on the URT, though it also recorded where she got on and off; but her main priority was to escape the Bozleys. She knew how to get to the Cadet's quarters so she caught a train headed toward that part of the Underground.

After arriving at a familiar stop, she exited the URT and descended as far as the elevator would allow; she then took a staircase that wound down into the depths of the Underground. The air became thick and heavy with the smell of foods, sweat and a myriad of other odors. Sashimu recognized the market before she saw it and walked briskly through the crowds to the other side, where the Cadet lived.

"Well, look who's back," chortled a huge man who stepped into her path and put a beefy hand on her shoulder to stop her. She recognized him from the tattoos that moved across his biceps.

"I'm here to see the Cadet," she said, struggling to get free as he tightened his grip.

"Maybe we should spend some time together first—"

An impatient voice issued from his Companion. "Marty, bring her back to me."

The thug cursed and pushed her ahead of him to Angel's Domus Phrack.

As before, Angel received her in his war room. The live maps documented the activity of the Underground. He sat beneath them amongst boxes, sifting through and carelessly tossing expensive-looking objects in separate piles. Sashimu prepared to explain why she was there and that she needed to find the Cadet, but he preempted her.

"I know why you're here." Angel shot her an oddly pitying look.

"You do?" Sashimu looked confused.

"I, too, feel deceived."

"You do?" she questioned.

"Of course. I expected the Cadet to come to me with Thesni's location. I'm the one who brought you two here. We had an understanding. How can I recoup costs if he goes directly to Domus Aqua?"

"The Cadet knows where Thesni is?" Sashimu processed the information as she spoke. Anger surged in her breast. "He told Domus Aqua and not me?"

"He told Domus Aqua, but informed neither of us."

"Where is she?" Sashimu's voice quivered.

"She was at the *Three Eagles Refuge*. She escaped both the Order and two domus representatives. It was an impressive escape, or so Domus Aqua tells me."

"Where is she now?" Sashimu asked.

"I hoped you might help me with that. Thesni disappeared in the Underground so she's down here with us. I've got people out looking for her, but no luck so far."

"How can I help?" she questioned, though she had no intention of helping anyone but Thesni.

"The Cadet found her once; he can find her again. I just need you to stay close to him and inform me of any developments."

"All I want is to find Thesni and return to Mars," she said fiercely.

"Of course you do," Angel smiled. "I got you here. I can get you home."

"You would help us?"

"Sure, after everything is worked out with Domus Aqua and the Council, I'll get you home."

Sashimu nodded to let him think she trusted him. She trusted no one, least of all the man who admitted he orchestrated her kidnapping. She only hoped Angel was lying about the Cadet.

"I'd like to leave now," she said, politely, "and go over to see the Cadet at his place."

"No need. He'll come to us."

Angel rustled through several boxes, tossing things out and grumbling, before he brandished a small chain and pendant. "I'll give you this. It's useful to both of us."

Sashimu hesitantly accepted it.

"If you are ever in trouble, just blow on the whistle," Angel told her, with a wicked grin.

"Why are you giving me this?"

"You'll need it in the Underground," he answered and slipped it around her neck.

"Thanks," she said warily.

"Thank you." Angel seemed oddly satisfied. She moved away from him, preferring to put as much distance between them as possible.

Warning

A one-eyed nightingale incessantly sang throughout the Cadet's sparring match in Novus Orbis, distracting him. That gave his opponent an advantage, and she sliced off the gamer's head. When he came back from his defeat, they bowed to each other. As his opponent exited, the Cadet turned to the annoying bird.

"My opponent can win without your help," he chided and swiped aggressively at the bird with his long sword.

The nightingale easily dodged. "Be nice and I'll give you the information you asked for," it promised.

"UL," the Cadet said, sheathing his sword. "I wasn't expecting you to get back to me so soon."

"Well, I found out Ochbo was briefly at *Three Eagles Refuge*, but it'll be tough to figure out where he is now," UL said grimly.

"Why is that?"

"He and his companion are on the run from the Order. He won't be checking messages or sharing his whereabouts with anyone if he plans to stay alive."

"How did I get myself into this?" the Cadet mused, rubbing his temples. "It can't get much worse."

"I'm afraid it can. Your friend Creid may be indicted for illegal technology transfers to Mars outpost colonies," UL said quietly.

The gamer was shocked. "How can Creid be indicted when he's in a coma?"

"If he comes out of it, that's just one of the charges against him," UL replied in low tones. "But he may never be allowed to recover."

"Do you know who specifically wants him dead?" the Cadet asked.

"No, and I don't want to know — and neither do you," UL said, shaking his head. "This is no fly game, Cadet. It would be a lot smarter just to walk away."

"That's not going to happen."

"I figured as much," UL responded sadly. "I found a possible lead for you named Dreyfus who is oddly connected to both Ochbo and Creid. He was exiled to Mars for 25 years and has just returned. He moonlighted for the OMM before he left Earth and has been in touch with them over the years."

The Cadet remembered the name from Creid's memoryseries. He hoped this was a good sign.

"Dreyfus was on Creid's team with me so I know him. Officially, he returned to Earth to retire. His only contact since he arrived has been with the OMM. He's asked a lot of questions with regard to a young woman who supposedly survived that MIP accident. Otherwise, he remains a hermit living in Boulder."

"That could be promising." His mood was brightened now that he had something to go on, however small. "I'd like his address."

"The man probably doesn't know anything, and it's definitely risky. I'm passing on information if you know what I mean," UL added quickly. The Cadet nodded impatiently, and with a heavy sigh, UL transmitted the address of Creid's former associate.

Leaving Novus Orbis, the Cadet quickly departed the professional gamers' facility and descended into the Underground to find his favorite traveling wokman. He was so hungry, he ate standing up in the tunnel, then headed home with Sashimu on his mind. He struggled with the question of how he was going to frame the tale of Thesni's narrow escape so as not to terrify her.

Marty waited outside his quarters with a smug look on his face. "Your nanogen paid Master Angel another visit."

The Cadet cursed, but followed him to Domus Phrack.

Inside the war room, with its detailed live maps of the Underground, the Cadet was surprised by the intimate scene before him. Sashimu sat across from Angel at a small table. Their heads were bent toward one another over steaming coffee and rolls and she was laughing over something the crime boss had just said. The sight infuriated him.

"Sashimu, come with me," the Cadet ordered, glaring at her and ignoring Angel. "Your guardians are looking for you."

A brief look of panic crossed her face.

"How rude," Angel said with a sneer. "The young lady came here because she could hardly resist me, and you want to spoil all her fun?"

"Yes," replied the Cadet, still disdaining to look at the man. "She's coming with me."

"I hate to see you go so soon, but we'll meet again." Angel winked deviously, and she returned a smile.

The Cadet felt angry to the point of nausea as they left Angels' headquarters. Glancing over his shoulder to ensure they weren't being followed, he wound his way back toward his quarters with Sashimu beside him.

"Why did you go back to Angel?" he asked, his voice strained with emotion.

"Angel lied about that. Marty caught me as I was going to your quarters." She clung to his arm. "The Council came to claim me as a witness and said that after the tribunal I would never return home."

"Why the hell not?" he inquired, looking at her in alarm.

"'For reasons which will become clear after the tribunal' — that's what the Council rep told the Bozleys."

As they rounded a bend in the tunnel, he saw that the ceiling entrance to his quarters was open.

"Hey, what about Thesni?" Sashimu was saying. "Have you—"

"Wait here a moment," the Cadet whispered, putting his hand to her mouth to silence her.

The gamer dropped down into his quarters. A man dressed in a dark uniform with the Council emblem on his lapel leaned against his east side exit. Taking a deep breath to remain calm, the Cadet tried not to sound too shaken. "Well, this is a surprise. I wasn't expecting any visitors."

"Sir, are you using a cloaking device?" the Council representative asked. "I can't identify you or access your biostats."

The Cadet kept his tone deferential. "You're in the lowest level of the Underground. Nothing works the same down here."

"You're the Cadet, I presume. You have an interesting place. Very spartan."

"The Academy taught me how to live like this. It leads to a longer life in the Underground."

"No one I know lives like this in the Underground."

"Precisely." The Cadet paused. "To what do I owe the pleasure of your company?"

"Alice Chigusa, the young lady you tutor, is missing." He eyed the gamer with suspicion. "Have you seen her?"

The gamer was careful not to lie. "I saw her recently. We have regular tutoring sessions."

"Then contact me if you hear from her," the man instructed, activating his Companion. The Cadet touched behind his ear to tell his own Companion to accept the contact information.

"Thanks," he said, bowing deeply to hide his relief that the Council man was leaving.

The Cadet let loose a string of curses as he watched the man exit via his east side tunnel. At this rate, Sashimu would cost him more than his gaming career. Now he was officially at odds with the Council, unless he turned her in. He pulled himself up through the ceiling into the tunnel and rounded the corner where he'd left her.

The Cadet seized her shoulders and said, "We have to get out of here. That was a Council rep; they're looking for you. Let's take the URT. It's the fastest means to Boulder."

"Why are we going to Boulder?" Sashimu asked apprehensively.

"There may be just enough delay in registering your location that we can avoid getting caught. The Council seems to be using its own people to find you without the Order's help," he said, hurrying her down one tunnel after another. Sashimu jogged beside him to keep pace. "Creid's friend Dreyfus lives in Boulder."

"Dreyfus!" Sashimu exclaimed. "Zazen must have sent him here to help Thesni and me."

"Good, you know him, which makes it even more important that we go and see him," the Cadet said, as they hurried up the stairs to wait on the URT platform. He still hesitated to tell her about Thesni's narrow escape from the Order in case she panicked.

On the URT line to Boulder, the Cadet found them seats in the back of a car and he asked, "What happened to you at the hospital? How come you never showed?"

"I went to the hospital." A shadow passed over her face. She described how she'd gotten in to see Creid, and that he'd confused her with Thesni.

The Cadet sat back, incredulous. "I spoke to him for a long time without a response. How did you communicate with him?"

"I concentrated on him. A bolt of energy slammed through me, and I accessed Novus Orbis. His eyes opened, and he whispered to me. It all happened so fast, and then it was over."

"Impressive." The Cadet shook his head.

"Look, Creid isn't our biggest problem right now," Sashimu said. "It's Thesni. She's alive and being hunted!"

"Who told you that?" he asked. He was almost relieved at not having to be the first to tell her.

"Angel."

"I was about to contact you with the information when Marty came over to tell me you were at Angel's."

"What about your commitment to Domus Aqua?" she asked.

He looked out the window, gathering his thoughts. "My commitments don't mean anything if it means hurting innocent people." Turning to smile at her, he continued, "or, if it means hurting you."

"What are your commitments now?" she asked softly.

"I am committed to protecting you." He wrapped his hand around hers.

"And Thesni?"

"I'll do whatever it takes to protect both of you." He reached over to kiss her cheek. "I give you my word."

Her eyes held him. "Are you a man of honor; do you keep your word?"

"Above all else. That's always been my problem," he said, thinking of his promises to both Lila and Joli.

"Promise me you will see to it that Thesni and I return to Mars."

"I promise, I will help you both return to Mars." His own words turned his stomach. He could never imagine Sashimu living that far away from him. He was glad she asked nothing further of him. He might promise her the world if she asked for it.

She drifted off to sleep while he stayed alert to any possible searchers from the Council, but the car remained virtually empty. The worry lines in her forehead and between her brows disappeared. She looked so young and innocent.

Twenty minutes later they arrived at their stop in Boulder and the Cadet woke Sashimu. Though they were still technically in the Underground, the scenery here was drastically different in comparison to the lower levels. Here the shops, hotels, restaurants, cafes and living spaces were all crowded with people; and the ventilation and lighting were superior. Even the flora which draped doorways and lined the sidewalks looked healthier. After almost an hour of searching, they stumbled on Dreyfus' address and the Cadet pressed his palm to the door for visitor notification.

"We'll never find our way back; we've taken so many wrong turns," Sashimu fretted, her face gray with exhaustion.

"I remember exactly how we got here," said the Cadet. She gave him a dubious glance.

"What do you want?" A querulous voice issued from behind the door.

"We're here to see Dreyfus," the Cadet said. "I am Creid's friend. I'm the Cadet."

"Dreyfus is on vacation. Go away."

The Cadet and Sashimu looked at each other. It was hard to know what to make of the man's tone. He sounded a bit daft.

"Wait. I'll find out." A small, red-haired man, coming out of the door, said to himself or someone they didn't see.

"Dreyfus?" Sashimu stepped toward him. "It's me, Sashimu. Don't you recognize me?"

"Sashimu!" Dreyfus said giving her an awkward hug. "It's been too long since we've seen each other. Come in, come in."

Startled, the Cadet and Sashimu hesitated, but he'd already gone back inside. The door opened onto a descending spiral staircase only wide enough for one person. They followed him down the narrow stairs for quite a distance, until they came to a suspended, multi-level plant farm fed from the ceiling and floor. Dreyfus made his way down an aisle. A man-sized plant snapped at the Cadet as he passed by and made him jump.

"Those are Martian Crittertraps — genetically enhanced Venus Flytraps. They are very useful for keeping the roaches down." Dreyfus winked at the Cadet.

"They're enormous." The Cadet gave them a wide berth.

"They've been known to take much larger prey. Watch out." Dreyfus stopped under an enormous blooming rose bush and sat down.

"I survive on my own homegrown food. And because I've an escape door beneath the Crittertraps," Dreyfus said, carefully emphasizing his last statement as sweat trickled down his brow.

Ill at ease, Sashimu and the Cadet sat down across from him. The air in the room was heady with plant food and spices. Dreyfus was acting strangely, but the Cadet couldn't tell if it was dementia, or if he was simply distracted.

Dreyfus signaled violently with his hand, but neither understood. The Cadet glanced at Sashimu, and she shrugged, perplexed.

"How do you like Earth, Sashimu?"

"I want to go home."

"You've grown up in these last few months." Dreyfus' tone was approving, but his hands shook.

The Cadet found this version of Dreyfus significantly thinner and worn out, compared to the young man in Creid's memories. He examined the room; something was not right. Dreyfus made another small angry gesture, pointing towards the door. The Cadet reached into his bag, wondering if he might need a weapon.

"Enough chatter," snapped a chameleon-uniformed Order regular, stepping out from behind the rose vines with his smartgun drawn. They all jumped to their feet, even Dreyfus.

"You promised not to hurt Sashimu, if I cooperated." Dreyfus shrank back as the Order regular loomed over him.

Placing his smartgun to Dreyfus' temple, the man fired. Sashimu screamed as Dreyfus fell to the floor.

"But I made no promises about you," the killer said.

The Cadet drew his short sword and placed himself between Sashimu and the man with the gun. Startling both men, Sashimu suddenly bolted from behind the Cadet, dodged past the regular and ran down the aisle.

The man swung about and lunged after her. Sashimu stopped short, put her pendant to her lips and blew into it, producing an ear-piercing whistle that forced both the gamer and the regular to clamp their hands over their ears.

Collapsing to the floor, it was a moment before the Cadet could move. He heard a scream, something crashed heavily nearby and then silence. Getting up shakily, he found the Order regular face down in a field of Martian Crittertraps. Torn, bloody scraps of fabric and flesh were all that remained of the body. A few Crittertraps snapped viciously at one another, fighting over the last gruesome morsels. Above him, Sashimu was swinging precariously on a thin vine that looked about to break. The Cadet held up his arms. She swung out over the snapping offworld plants and let go. He caught her and the impact bowled him over. They sprawled across the floor, rolling underneath the suspended gardens.

The Cadet could still hear a constant ringing in his ears. He crawled over to Sashimu, saying, "Where did you get that whistle?"

"Angel gave it to me for self defense." Sashimu trembled.

"Lucky us." The young man fingered the pendant and yanked it from her neck. "I'll tell you what else it does. It lets him know where you are at all times. We'll just leave that with the plants."

"Fine with me." Her voice shook as she looked back to where Dreyfus' corpse lay. She shuddered.

"That's a nasty cut on your forehead."

"I hit the edge of that door." Sashimu wiped the blood away from her eyes. The cut sealed.

"There's no chance you could help Dreyfus, is there?"

"It's too late," said Sashimu, holding back tears. "He wanted us to go away; he tried to warn us."

"He probably thought he could save us and himself by playing along."

"It's almost like they expected us," Sashimu noted and looked up startled. "Did you hear that?"

"What?" As soon as he asked, he heard footsteps.

"Someone is coming down the stairs," she whispered.

"Let's use that trap door." The Cadet yanked it open, and they dropped down through it into a dark tunnel.

They ran a fair distance, then Sashimu stopped short. He glanced back and motioned for her to follow.

"This is weird." Sashimu gasped for breath. "Something is wrong. I feel the pull of the MAM. There are ongoing sessions nearby. I can feel it. Look at that lightning!" Sashimu pointed to the end of the corridor. "This place is like the place in Novus Orbis where Creid whispered to me. Even the smell is identical. It's raining up ahead."

"We've got to hurry." The Cadet tugged on her arm and thought of hoisting her over his shoulder, but she resisted. The lightning was invisible to him. "We may be below the Sanctuary. There could be many ongoing MAMsessions."

Behind them, two figures dropped from Dreyfus' trap door into the tunnel and started in their direction. Sashimu and the Cadet saw them and turned to run again, but the pursuers were gaining on them.

At the end of the tunnel, they found an underground courtyard.

"I told you it was raining," Sashimu said, pointing ahead.

"What?" The Cadet did not see any rain. He saw a high-voltage, translucent mesh blocking this entrance to the Sanctuary. "We can't walk through that. It'll cook us."

A holographic monk stood at the center of the court-yard, his arms raised. He warned, "This is a restricted area for Sanctuary members only. Do not venture forward. High voltage may cause severe injury."

Sashimu dashed straight into the mesh, dragging the gamer by the hand. He stumbled forward, and was instantly blinded. He felt tingling down his right side and heard deafening thunder.

I₁₁I₁I₁₁₁IIII₁₁I₁I₁I

"Did you see that?" The Order regular looked at his partner, who stared at the energy vortex, her mouth open.

"What were they thinking?" She watched curls of smoke float up. "Wiped out. They never knew what hit them."

"You're certain it was the Cadet and Alice Chigusa? I couldn't get a read on them."

"They fit the profile description." She turned away. "Let's get out of here. This place gives me the creeps."

I₁₁I₁I₁₁₁IIII₁₁I₁I₁I

Sashimu and the Cadet staggered beyond the mesh, into the Sanctuary courtyard.

"How did we make it through that?" the gamer asked, swaying. Everything was spinning before his eyes, and he was numb down one side. When she let go of his arm, he slumped against the wall and sank slowly to the floor.

"It has something to do with a MAMsession," replied Sashimu, running her hands along his side. He looked back and saw ghostly rain and lightning. She worked life back into his arm and leg. The tingling felt like hundreds of sharp, stabbing needles.

He struggled to ignore the sensation. "It didn't feel like accessing Novus Orbis. All I saw was blinding light."

The soles of his feet were twin slabs of blazing pain. Sashimu bent down and clasped them and he had to stifle a scream. Abruptly, the pain disappeared, leaving both feet tingly and warm.

Three monks in long robes rounded the corner, conversing animatedly.

"She tunneled across space and time through the security vortex," one said.

"They must have shadowed each other," the other said.

"They must move as identical forces through the vortex to safely pass through it."

"Impossible." The monks acknowledged Sashimu and the Cadet with deep bows.

"Welcome to the Sanctuary where the world truths converge. You will find peace and tranquility. All people and all spirituality culminate here," the tallest monk intoned.

"All we need is food and sleep, and we'll be on our way." The Cadet was hoarse.

The tallest monk examined him, then turned to Sashimu. "Your room will be made ready. You may stay with any of our spiritual leaders."

"May we stay with the Open MAM Movement?" The Cadet felt uncomfortable with religious groups.

"They are not officially recognized here. They do, however, provide our infrastructure." The monk seemed displeased by everything the Cadet said. "We will confer to ensure that OMM has room for guests."

The monks promptly disappeared around the corner.

"What the hell is 'tunneling'?" The Cadet felt grumpy.

"Ask them. I just ran through the vortex holding your hand. It seemed natural."

"How did you learn to do that?" He frowned.

"It felt the same as when I met Creid." Sashimu shrugged.

After a few tense minutes, a shaman with a long beard and ancient circuit boards woven into his sleeves rounded the corner. "The monks are called to midnight mass. I'll take you to the OMM."

The shaman set a brisk pace down so many corridors and stairs, and through so many secured areas, that the Cadet and Sashimu soon became completely lost. Stopping before an ancient, wrought-iron door, thick with dust and cobwebs, their guide turned to them.

"I leave you here. I have many chores." He bowed and departed. The two did not know what they were supposed to do.

The Cadet reached for the latch, turned and pulled. The door opened and they entered an ancient antechamber. An

automated OMM audio message instructed them to dis-
robe and proceed into the cleansing area. He tried to keep
his eyes averted as Sashimu undressed.

Out of the cleansing chamber, they dressed in clean,
baggy clothes and big shoes. He kept his MAMsuit on
underneath his clothes.

"You look silly." Sashimu giggled at the Cadet.

"You look marvelous." He blushed.

A young man with messy hair and a stained "Big
Brother is watching" tee-shirt appeared. He led them
down a long tunnel, past a glass room marked "Library",
that held rows of MAM optimization cubicles. He palmed
a side door. "You'll stay in this apartment tonight. They
just cleaned it."

The apartment opened onto a terrace that offered a
view of underground stalagmites and a trickling stream.
It was an enormous studio with walls of burnished
chrome panels and a tiled floor. A metal bed, built into
the floor, rose on command.

"I bet there are all kinds of interesting things behind
these panels." Curious, he searched for a trigger to open
them.

Sashimu found a basket of food in the kitchen and
tossed him a piece of fruit and some cheese.

The gamer located an activation panel and pressed
a small "access" button. Part of the ceiling and the wall
reversed itself to reveal a harness and what looked like
old MAM equipment. "Fascinating. This reminds me of
the Ultimate Librarian."

"Don't get us in trouble." Sashimu glanced with concern at the door. "Why are they letting us stay here?"

"The Sanctuary offers shelter from time to time, but
frankly, they're probably curious as to how you got
through that vortex and want to find out more about
you," he said, releasing the button so the ceiling and wall
panels reversed into position, displaying only the chrome.
"Are you going to be safe this close to the OMM optimization library? You felt its pull in the tunnel."

"I feel as though my body is electrically charged, but
I'm too exhausted to think."

"Wake me if you need anything." The Cadet took an extra blanket and pillow from the bed, and spread them on the floor. "I'll be right here."

Sashimu took the bed. "You are welcome to sleep with me," she offered nervously.

"Thanks," the Cadet said. Seeing her lying there was torture enough, let alone sharing the same bed all night without touching her. He looked away. "But I don't think that would be a good idea right now."

Soon, he heard the deep rhythm of her breathing and let himself drift into sleep. A few hours later, he came wide awake. He left her sleeping and took the food basket out onto the terrace to munch on more fruit and to think. The gamer had never expected to set foot in the Sanctuary, let alone stay as a guest in OMM headquarters. He was scheduled to play for the Domus Phrack in a few days, but that was as far as his plans went. Getting Sashimu and Thesni to Mars would be difficult — assuming Thesni was still alive, and that they could find her. Angel might arrange a trip for an outrageous fee, but the Cadet doubted he had sufficient credit to pay for it. Taking a commercial ship was a death sentence. Even if he falsified their identities and succeeded in getting them on a ship, nothing guaranteed their safety onboard or even when they reached Mars with both the Council and the Order hunting them. Rescuing Creid, the only man who might be able to ensure their safety for the long term, also seemed like an impossible task. The Cadet felt overwhelmed.

Looking back at the bed, the Cadet wondered if he might join Sashimu just for a short while.

Joining Forces

As Thesni and Ochbo neared the Sanctuary, she kept thinking about flopping down on his old musty couch. She associated it with her first taste of freedom and safety, but Ochbo said it would be dangerous to go to his place. Despite their fatigue, they made one final push to where the OMM had their headquarters in the depths of the Sanctuary.

"We're almost at the Sanctuary-OMM entrance," Ochbo said, as they turned down the long tunnel. "At worst, the OMM will let us stay in a storage room until we figure out where to go next."

"What's going on up there?" Thesni asked, looking ahead at the crowded entrance.

Still dressed in the chameleon robes of the Magus, they edged slowly into the excited crowd. The area had been inefficiently blocked off by a group of OMMers who were in a loud debate with a ring of religious leaders. Magus and other religious devotees dodged around them, touching the ground, standing or sitting in place to pray.

A thin, haggard-looking woman addressed the surrounding religious leaders, "We don't know yet how the security system was breached or if it simply failed, but I can assure you that there is a technical explanation. We can't have all these people milling about while we test the system. It isn't safe."

"If you won't tell us anything about where the couple came from or why they entered, at least let us talk to the girl who spirited through security," said a man whose chameleon robes were cinched by the gold belt of a high priest. "You may not be a believer, but our faith demands it. It's part of the prophecy! Why are you detaining her at OMM headquarters when we would take special care of her?"

"First of all, the OMM never detains people. Please talk to my superior and the Sanctuary Elders if you want to arrange a meeting with her. That's not up to me," the woman said with a heavy sigh. "Please people, you must clear out—"

Ochbo motioned to Thesni, and they slipped through the ever-growing throng.

"Did you hear that?" Thesni asked. "We should find out who breached security."

"First, let's get inside to safety," Ochbo said, as they walked a few steps down to an ancient door. He yanked it open, and they stepped through into an antechamber, which automatically scanned them for biometric security before giving them access to OMM headquarters.

"Ochbo, where would that girl be staying?"

"It's unusual for the OMM to house visitors," he answered, pausing thoughtfully. "The few living quarters are down that corridor, but we want to go up a level to—"

Thesni didn't wait to hear more but set off down the corridor, passing a door marked "Library," which felt like an optimization area. Just beyond the library, she stopped at an innocuous side door and palmed it before he could stop her.

"What are you doing?" he asked, following after her in alarm.

"I want in there." Thesni said, sensing Sashimu nearby. An Imagofas' charge hung in the air, augmented by the optimization area and only intensified as she approached the side door.

"May I help you?" inquired a muscular young man with a shock of wild hair. His outstretched arm blocked the entrance.

Hesitating, Thesni began, "Yes, I'm looking for—"

"Thesni?" Sashimu yelled and ducked around the man. She threw her arms around Thesni and nearly knocked her over. "It doesn't feel real to have you right in front of me," she said, crying.

Thesni nodded, tears streaming down her face. Sashimu wiped tears from her own cheeks, and smiled happily. "For so many days now, I've imagined and dreamed of this moment. I want to know everything that's happened to you." She noticed how gaunt and tired Thesni looked, with dark shadows under her eyes and her once satiny blonde hair pulled back in a dull thick knot.

"Please, come in," invited the man who had blocked the door. He eyed Ochbo warily, but allowed the OMM engineer to enter and brought them a food basket. They sat around the table. The Imagofas introduced the two young men to each other, but the tension between them did not ease. The Imagofas were too ecstatic at being reunited to notice anything but each other.

"I've wanted a chance to apologize to you, Thesni," Sashimu leaned forward, her eyes brimming again with tears. "I should never have asked you to come to the Observatory after curfew and—"

"Nonsense," Thesni waved away the apology. "I forgave you for that the first day we were on the ship. We're the Imagofas — sisters. We always stick together. Tell me, how did you manage to get off the ship before it exploded?"

"You first," Sashimu smiled in relief at her friend's words. When Thesni described the Order Captain Lynn's attack on the ship, Sashimu sat back horrified.

"So the Order knew we were on the ship and still detonated those hummers?" Sashimu questioned, shaking her head. Thesni recounted how Grant had taken her to the mission only to abandon her there, and how Ochbo had saved her. When she got to describing Joli's session with Creid and the weird cocoon surrounding him, Sashimu stopped her.

"You met Creid? That explains why he mistook me for you when I went to see him in the hospital. It's incredible that we've been crossing paths all this time and only now found each other."

"What cocoon?" the Cadet broke in, unable to contain himself any longer.

"I don't know, that's just what it looked like to me —
a clear cocoon wrapped around him," Thesni said, remembering how odd it felt to stand close to Creid in Novus
Orbis. "I think it's making him sick. Did you notice it,
Sashimu?"

"Yes, I did, and this may seem strange, but I heard voices
emanating from it."

"Yes!" Thesni noted. "I remember that, too."

"Wait a second you two," Ochbo said, his brow
furrowed. "That's not how the MAM works. People's
avatars don't display the sicknesses they suffer in Vetus
Orbis. This all sounds very odd to me."

"Well," Sashimu paused, thoughtfully. "Could it be that
it's not his coma or a sickness that he has in Vetus Orbis,
but rather a condition that has been imposed upon him
to keep him in a coma-like state?"

"I suppose it's possible," Ochbo replied, but he looked
far from convinced.

"Now, I've waited long enough," Thesni asserted, grinning at Sashimu. "It's your turn to tell me everything that's
happened to you."

Standing up and leaning across the table, Sashimu gave
Thesni another long hug before beginning her tale of events
and recounting how she and the Cadet had escaped from
the Council and then from the Order. Thesni gasped and
became extremely pale when she heard about Dreyfus'
murder. They all sat in silence for a while, eating from the
basket and thinking about what they'd heard.

"What makes me angry about this whole thing is that
you two are caught in the middle of a political power play,"
Ochbo burst out, adding a bitter laugh. "To gain more
authority over the Order, the Council wants to use one of
you as evidence against it before a public tribunal. Of
course, the Order's reaction is to eliminate all of us to make
sure that never happens."

Both Sashimu and Thesni nodded gravely. The Cadet
remained rigidly silent, and yet, his expression showed
deep concern.

Looking first to the Cadet and then to Ochbo, Sashimu
offered, "Honestly, I don't know what either of us would
have done without the two of you."

"I agree," Thesni added, resting her head appreciatively on Ochbo's arm before turning to Sashimu. "I'm also very curious about this Prometheus meta-agent who protected you in Novus Orbis. Is it possible for me to meet him?"

For the first time, Thesni realized that a lot of what had happened revolved around Creid.

Sashimu nodded. Strangely, she felt more relaxed and happier than she'd felt since arriving on Earth. Glancing over at the Cadet, she realized for the first time that he looked highly agitated. And Ochbo too.

"Sashimu and Thesni, I don't want to spoil your reunion," the gamer said. "But I'm worried that we don't have much time before the Order figures out that Sashimu and I are alive and comes looking for us. At least, the Order hasn't tracked Ochbo and you to the Sanctuary — yet."

"I agree." Ochbo grimaced. "We've got to hurry and come up with a plan to get you safely back to Mars."

"What should we do next, then?" Thesni asked.

"Well, we can't simply hide out on a ship," Sashimu replied. "It might be attacked on the way home, or we might simply be killed as soon as we arrive back on Mars. Zazen couldn't protect us from the Order's attack. Who knows what the situation is back home?"

Thesni agreed. "Hiding out won't work for the long haul with a domus, the Council and the Order hunting us. Maybe we should go before the tribunal. At least, the Order will have to acknowledge our existence and will no longer have a reason to eliminate us."

Sashimu shook her head. "I don't trust the Council any more than the Order. The Council might destroy us, too, after they've used us against the Order."

"You have one thing in your favor," the Cadet said and glanced meaningfully at Sashimu. "The Council and Domus Aqua only know that one of you exists. That's an advantage that could let at least one of you escape."

"The Cadet is right," Sashimu agreed eagerly. "Perhaps while I go before the tribunal, Thesni can escape offworld."

"I won't abandon you here, Sashimu," Thesni exclaimed, her voice rising. "What about Creid? With his technical skills and his contacts at the Order as well as at the Council, wouldn't he help us if he weren't in a coma?"

The Cadet brightened. "Thesni, I think you're right. You communicated with Creid once, maybe you can get through to him again or even heal him."

"That would be suicide," Ochbo exclaimed angrily. "There is absolutely no way for her to access Creid's on-going hospital session from here without simultaneously alerting the Order."

"There might be one way," Sashimu mused, smiling at all of them. "I'll talk to Prometheus. As a meta-agent, I bet he'll be able to get us access to Creid's session without notifying anyone, including the Order."

"Okay, fine," Ochbo consented tersely. "Let's pretend that you get Prometheus to give you access to Creid. And then, let's say that Thesni is able to somehow remove this bizarre cocoon, what then?"

"I'll go to the hospital and get Creid out of there," the Cadet said. "With Creid's help, we'll get the Council and the Order to agree to let the Imagofas return to Mars. Or, he'll help us figure out a way to permanently hide the identities of the Imagofas and they can return safely to Mars later. Either way, it's a happy ending."

"That's crazy," Ochbo said. He looked around the table for support, but the other three were all smiling confidently at each other. The OMM engineer sighed. "Well, hell, it's insane, but I don't have a better plan."

Sashimu was ready to act. "Are we all agreed then? Ochbo can make sure Thesni and I are set up with a session. I'll talk to Prometheus, and with his help, Thesni and I will try to heal Creid in Novus Orbis while the Cadet goes to the hospital to retrieve Creid and bring him back here. Once Creid is saved, he'll help us to get offworld and make sure we're safe from pursuers even on Mars."

"If we time it right, this might just work," the Cadet agreed. "Remember though, Sashimu, after I bring Creid back here to safety, I have to play for Domus Phrack. I gave my word to a thug, but still I gave my word. If I honor it, then he'll have to leave you alone."

"There's one problem with this tidy little scenario," Ochbo warned. "Creid's wife, Joli, is the first person he will want to talk to after he comes out of the coma, or at least she would be for me. Wouldn't it be better to get her in on at least the part of the plan that involves Creid's escape? She could really help us."

"I'll see what I can do," The Cadet remarked. "Unfortunately, she may demand I turn over Sashimu or give up any information I have about her."

"Tell her I'll turn myself into the Council after Creid is healed."

"Okay, we can let her think that, but you must not turn yourself in unless we get assurances from Creid first. I no longer trust Joli to tell me the truth."

Turning to Ochbo, he asked, "May I use the Library to contact Joli?"

"Certainly. I'll get you set up." Ochbo rose. "Come on."

|..|.|...|||||...|.|..|

The Cadet left an urgent message for the Councilwoman, identifying himself only as the purple bat at Rats and Bats. Her small rat avatar scampered up the tree beside him moments after he arrived.

"What's happened to the nanogen?" Joli asked anxiously. "It disappeared from the Bozleys' apartment when my Council rep showed up."

Almost certain now that Joli had lied to him from the start, the Cadet would have liked to lash out at her. He resisted the confrontation, since he needed her help to get access to Creid.

"Don't worry, Joli. I have her with me. She says to tell you she's going to give herself up to the Council after Creid is healed."

She stared at him. "Why does it care about my husband?"

"She may not care, but I do, and I can't force her to give herself up while I'm simultaneously saving your husband."

"You save him. How?"

"I'll take him out of the hospital," the Cadet replied.

Joli studied the surrounding trees, the cages and bar below. "You think you can get him out alive?"

"With a little help from you," the Cadet said, more confidently than he felt. "Tonight I need an escape vehicle stationed at the back of the hospital. Also, the attendant watching over Creid must either step away from his post or be willing to help me."

"No problem," Joli agreed with a small squeak. "Creid will need to disappear though; a scandal involving my husband would be a political fiasco. If everyone thinks he's dead, so much the better."

"Of course," the Cadet nodded, uncertain how Creid would champion the Imagofas cause after he was supposedly dead. They would work that out once the man was safe.

"The hospital attendant is already on my payroll. He'll do whatever we need if I give him fair warning. He can simply walk in, declare Creid dead and wheel him to the morgue. You and my driver can take him to a safe house, and both of you can hide out there until I get him a fresh identity and a new life offworld."

"It sounds like you've planned this for a while." He was surprised.

"I've been planning. I can't stand the thought of him wasting away in there. The only problem is his mind."

He nodded cautiously, without mentioning the Imagofas or their plan to bring Creid out of his coma. That would terrify her, and she would never agree to it.

"Be careful," Joli said.

"I'll be careful. Thank you."

"Don't thank me. I'm doing this for my husband. I expect the nanogen to turn herself into the Council. If she doesn't, the Council will be after you." She scampered down the tree and disappeared into the crowd.

Somehow, compared to the prospect of the Order finding and killing him, her threat carried little weight. His time was running out. Tonight he would attempt to rescue Creid and the day after tomorrow he would game for Domus Phrack in exchange for Sashimu's safety. Unable to injure Lila, he might have to throw the game. Her father would be happy. The game should have been the least of his concerns, but being forced to compete against Lila still rankled him.

|.|.|...|||.....|.|.|

The Cadet returned to the suite where he found Thesni and Sashimu laughing arm-in-arm. He asked Sashimu to join him on the apartment terrace overlooking the stalagmites.

"Joli agreed to let me take Creid from the hospital, but I never mentioned healing Creid in Novus Orbis; so Thesni and you will have to be doubly careful not to violate any protocols," he warned.

"I'm going to speak with Prometheus now to make sure he can help us get access to Creid's session," Sashimu said. "If we access it directly, Thesni will be shadowing Creid, which no one would expect."

"Let me be the one you piggyback your session on when you talk to Prometheus. I need to go into Novus Orbis to get the layout of the hospital and other data anyway."

"It's risky for you. I'll piggyback on Ochbo's session. He already offered."

"No. The Order is looking for Ochbo, so he can't be in Novus Orbis. That gives us a brief window of opportunity. The Order may not be looking for me in Novus Orbis because they either haven't put me together with you or they think I'm dead."

"You've risked everything for me," Sashimu said, throwing her arms around him as he held her close.

Iululuullllluululuul

Vertigo. As the Cadet entered Novus Orbis on his mountain path and climbed toward a cave high in the rock face, Sashimu was his second shadow. Once inside the cave, away from the frigid wind, Sashimu waited in the dark for Prometheus. The Cadet moved ahead to get his hospital data.

Out of the darkness around her, cave spikes, crystals, and dark mounds began to glitter in hues of blue, orange and yellow. Nearby, a luminous green pool appeared. Its light illuminated a naked woman with her arms clutched around a stalactite just above the pool. She gazed down at her own reflection.

"Prometheus?" Sashimu whispered.

The young woman shifted her attention from her re-flection to gaze into Sashimu's eyes. Her own eyes were startlingly bright against her dark complexion. Finally, she smiled and let go.

Sashimu ran to the edge of the pool, but the young woman disappeared in one large splash.

"Come back Prometheus. I need your help."

"You knew it was me?" inquired the meta-agent. He was beside Sashimu on the shore, appearing as the young man with a dark mop of curly hair she was used to seeing.

"You always come for me," she asserted and shrugged. "Guess what? After all of our searching, Thesni found me!"

"This is good news," Prometheus responded.

"But I'm here to get your help. It's an emergency. The man who created you is in a coma at the Denver Hospital of Our Fathers. Thesni and I might be able to save him if we get access to his MAMsession. Can you get me access?"

"He must be behind a hospital firewall." Prometheus stood still for a moment probing the firewall. "I know how to access his MAMsession and give you access, but unfortunately I cannot help you."

"Why? You've always helped me before."

"I've always saved you, but this puts you in danger. Creid has given me the leeway to protect Joli and you in Novus Orbis, but that is all," Prometheus said, bowing his head. "My processes are bound by my inability to answer the koan."

"Do you mean that if you can answer the koan, you'll be free to do as you choose in Novus Orbis?" Sashimu asked, surprised. "All you have to do is answer: how do you catch a catfish with a gourd?"

"Yes, it's deceptively easy, but I've been studying the koan for longer than you have been alive." Prometheus looked down into the green pool at their reflections. "This conundrum holds the key to my freedom. I know if I explain how to catch the catfish with the gourd using the monks' answers from my archives, I simply repeat their words and I'll have failed to answer the true spirit of the koan. I've failed to use either speech or silence to reply."

"Well then, maybe that's where your answer lies," Sashimu said urgently. "There's nothing wrong with showing me your answer."

Taking her hand, he passed his in front of them and the scene changed. They were surrounded by heavy mist. She discerned mountains in the distance. The air was wet and heavy with lush plant life. Close to them, they watched a man in tattered clothes using a gourd trying to scoop fish from a river.

Prometheus squeezed her hand. She was the old man holding the gourd in her hands, moving with perfect rhythm, but never quite trapping the fish.

Her perspective changed. She was the gourd feeling the old mans' hands around her and her body filling with water, brushing against slippery catfish and the hard pebbles of the riverbed. Emptied of water and filled, she felt herself repeatedly scraped against the pebbles.

Shifting perspective again, she felt her fin flip and her whiskers touch another catfish. She looked up and saw the man above her, breaking through the water in awkward thrusts to catch her. Sashimu hesitated just a moment too long as the old man, pinning her down with the gourd, trapped and caught her.

In one swift movement, she was the old man, the gourd, the catfish, the stream, the mist, and the mountains. She felt elation. She was soaring, flowing, moving and standing still.

Thousands of images, sounds and tastes opened to her. She glimpsed Mars' dawn over the observatory. Sashimu cried out in agony, her cry lost in the din of wildlife preserves and teeming humanity. Images, sounds, tastes, and smells bombarded her until she thought her mind would explode. Her heart pounded, and she felt a piercing pain behind her eyes.

"Stop," she whispered.

She found herself alone beside the stream. The old man and the gourd were gone. The catfish swam unhindered.

"That was you. All those images, sounds, and smells, you process them constantly?" Sashimu murmured dizzily.

Yes, my sub-agents process them.

"Prometheus?" Sashimu cried looking around to find him. She had not heard his voice, but had thought his reply. "Prometheus, where are you? You've disappeared!"

I am inside your thoughts and outside you. I am everywhere and nowhere at once. It is no longer necessary for me to have an avatar.

"You answered the koan!" Sashimu said with her voice full of wonder.

Yes. The answer was right there before me, but I did not truly grasp it until this moment. I tried to understand the koan through studying the ancient texts and monks' poems. However, it is through my direct experience of the koan, and the universe it represents, that I momentarily become one with it. The impossibility of scooping the catfish with a tiny gourd became possible, and therefore, I accomplished the impossible. Advantage is had from my human likeness; but usefulness arises from what I am not. I am not a human.

"I could never answer a koan, as you have, without using silence or speech to reply." Sashimu laughed. "Are you alive?"

Simply, I know now that I exist. That is a beginning.

"Then you've succeeded!" Sashimu was surprised by his sedate reaction and suddenly it occurred to her that he was now free to help her. With a slight quiver in her voice, she asked, "What will you do now?"

First of all, I'm going to help you and Thesni access Creid Xerkler's MAMsession.

"Your help means a lot to me." Sashimu hesitated and added shyly, "Creid may be able to help you, too, since it's getting dangerous for you in the MAM. Thesni and I would love to have you come with us. Maybe Creid could help us download you into the ship we travel on. Have you ever considered coming to Mars?"

I would be honored to come with you. But first, I must help you access his MAMsession.

"Yes, of course. Thank you," Sashimu said bowing deeply, and as she looked up, she found herself back in the cave.

The Cadet was waiting for her. When he sensed her, he ended his session. She was prepared for the vertigo, but not for the stabbing headache she felt on entering Vetus Orbis.

"You don't look good." He wrapped his arm around her as they returned to the suite.

"Prometheus agreed to help save Creid!" Sashimu blurted out.

"Sashimu, that's incredible news, although it means I've got to hurry to get to the hospital by the time you two have healed him." His voice cracked with emotion, as he added, "I'm leaving now. If anything happens to me, I want you to know, I... that I... care about you."

"Me, too." Sashimu reached up and caressed his cheek.

That was too much. He pulled her against him and kissed her roughly. She was so startled she did not respond until the second kiss. They parted, flushed. Sashimu headed back to the Library and the Cadet for the hospital. The taste of cinnamon lingered on his tongue.

Attempted Escape

"This is the best of all possible situations!" Sashimu exclaimed.

Ochbo frowned. "That's what I'm most afraid of." They stood in the Library optimization area office where they planned to enter Novus Orbis. "It's too risky to depend so heavily on this smart intelligence when we know so little about him."

"Earlier we all agreed that I would get Prometheus' help," Sashimu said, tapping the table in frustration.

"I expected Prometheus to give us guidance on how to bypass hospital security, not for you to put your lives in his hands," Ochbo spat out the words. "You'll need me to access the MAM before you enter Creid's session. He's just not close enough in physical proximity for you to piggyback on his own session. And, unfortunately, mine is likely to alert the Order to our whereabouts."

"We won't need your session, Ochbo," Thesni stated with a small smile and a faraway look in her eyes.

Sashimu glanced curiously at her friend and then exclaimed in surprise. "Oh, my Juno! Prometheus has registered us as authorized superusers with the MAM. I can feel the MAM's open invitation. Watch over us here in Vetus Orbis, Ochbo. We'll return from Novus Orbis soon."

With those words, Sashimu allowed the open session to overtake her senses and she found herself on the grid with Thesni and Prometheus. The Imagofas' avatars now matched their physical appearance in Vetus Orbis — the striking tiny blonde Thesni beside the tall dark Sashimu.

Thrilled that Prometheus had succeeded beyond her hopes, it took Sashimu a moment to realize that both of the others were frowning.

"We have a problem, Sashimu, but we've discussed it and have come up with a plan," Thesni said in a tone that allowed for no disagreement.

"How have you had time to discuss anything? You got here just before me," Sashimu said, suddenly upset.

"Prometheus can only give one of us access to Creid's session. He's worried that he'll have to implement too many protocol changes."

"Well then, it should be me who heals Creid," Sashimu stated flatly.

"No, we've decided I'll go because I have had more interactions with him," Thesni countered.

"Thesni is right," Prometheus added. "You must wait in Vetus Orbis in case she fails and you are needed."

Sashimu began to protest, but felt Prometheus gently closing down her session and exiting her into Vetus Orbis.

|..|.|...|||||...|.|..|

The garden was different from what Thesni remembered: roses perpetually wilted; the garden gate was decorated by severed human heads; a pool of fire had replaced the tranquil pond. When she had first met Creid, they had stood in a beautifully manicured garden — not this horror patch.

Smart intelligence agents shuffled by her resembling zombie-like avatars of Creid. While modeled in his image, each had gruesome wounds or maggot-ridden eye sockets. One had an axe wedged in the back of its skull while another had a large steel blade embedded in its chest with skin rotting off its face.

She followed the zombies to a wooden shack and found the real Creid sitting cross-legged inside. The cocoon around him had grossly thickened; it was now the color of milk, only half transparent.

Creid squinted up at her through the mass that obscured his head. "Can't you leave me alone? You weren't scared by my gory likenesses or my Garden of Abominations. How did you get through my security door?"

"You're in Novus Orbis at the hospital. Your security measures don't apply." She checked his biostats to ensure he was Creid.

"That's right, I remember," Creid smiled, striking his head with the heel of his hand. "Many secrets have leaked from Order R&D into the production environment. This is all a test, isn't it?"

"There's no test." She shook her head.

"I must stop Prometheus," Creid cried frantically. "Tell me why I'm here."

"You're in a coma," Thesni answered, shaken by his delusional state.

"That's right." He punched his head again where the cocoon appeared the thickest. "Every day an Eagle eats out Prometheus' liver. Every night the liver grows back. Sashimu saved Prometheus from this endless cycle."

"Yes, Sashimu helped Prometheus," Thesni said gently trying to cut through his confusion. "And I have come to save you."

"How will you save me?" His voice was so soft she could barely hear him.

"I'm here to heal you, but you have to trust me. Let me touch you," Thesni coaxed, extending her palms toward him.

Creid scrambled away from her in terror, shouting, "Keep your hands off me!"

"It's all right," Thesni whispered, stepping quickly forward. Pushing through the cocoon substance, she placed her hands squarely on his chest.

She concentrated for a long time on the cocoon. It felt as if it drew its energy and fed from its victim. Creid became very still and focused on her hands. "This cocoon is constantly sending queries to the MAM," she said, in surprise.

"What's the query?" Creid asked.

"Translated into our language, it might be, 'Do you want me to maintain the present state, disassemble or overtake the host?'" Thesni said. "It's a virus. I plan to unbind it."

With her hands, Thesni followed the cocoon threads that wove into Creid. His body warmed to her touch, becoming feverish. She felt the threads loosen and withdraw, like the roots of a weed dislodged from the ground. She willed it to let go of its food source and dissipate into Novus Orbis. As the cocoon began to vibrate, her body trembled under a building tension. And yet, she kept her hands steady as they traced the length of his torso and moved down his legs.

When she reached his feet, the milky substance of the cocoon abruptly shuddered, then blew apart in a violent flash of white light and an ear-splitting *crack*! The force of its disassembling threw her against the far wall of the shack, the impact knocking the wind out of her. She lay on the floor, gasping for air.

Creid lay slumped and lifeless in the middle of the floor. Thesni wondered if he had survived the explosion. When she was able to get her breath, she got up and stumbled over to him. He blinked slowly and looked up into her eyes.

"Are you okay?" he asked, and the fact that he was worried about her made Thesni laugh in relief.

"I was wondering the same about you," she answered, helping him to his feet. "I thought I might have killed you."

"I'm fine, thanks to you." He bowed formally and humbly. "I owe you a great debt. Tell me, what's happened while I've been trapped here?"

"Since you've been here over a month, a lot has happened, though I've no time to explain," she told him, putting her hand on his arm. "Unfortunately, we need to get you out of the hospital. You may be cured from your coma, but when you exit Novus Orbis, you won't be a free man. You are in a heavily secured area."

"My wife told me that I had fallen into a coma and had been hospitalized. It was hard to believe," Creid mumbled, shaking his head. "All I remember is being terrified about something I'd done and feeling feverish before I went to bed. When I woke up, I found myself stuck in this garden with no way out. It didn't take me long to figure out the Order had induced my coma and left me in a neurotic mental state until they decided whether or not I might still be useful. However, knowing that intellectually didn't help me cure myself or keep me from becoming crazier. After all that, I guess I wouldn't expect the Order to simply let me walk out of this hospital."

"No, but the Cadet is on his way to get you out," Thesni explained. "The attendant guarding your room will also help."

"What happens after that?"

"Sashimu and I want to go home to Mars. Maybe you can help us safely return," Thesni said hopefully.

"That's what I planned to do before all this," Creid said.

"I can't tell you how happy that makes me." Thesni laughed and gave him a quick bow. "Goodbye for now."

lı.Iıl.ıuıIIIl.ııl.Iıl

Once Creid's thoughts were clear, he exited Novus Orbis and found himself floating in an antigravity chamber. He felt surprisingly strong considering he had spent so many days weightless. He maneuvered over to the chamber door and opened it, setting off an alarm.

The attendant rushed in and stopped abruptly, looking at Creid in astonishment. "The medics said you'd never recover." He nearly stumbled over his words. "Joli told me that, no matter what, you were leaving the hospital tonight. I see that she's right. I'm Blake."

"Nice to meet you, Blake. Now, if you don't mind, I'd like to check out. All I need is a change of clothes, something other than this MAMsuit!"

"I brought in your old clothes and an attendant's lab coat. While you dress, I'll notify the guard that we're leaving." The man spoke into his Companion. "I've got a change in patient status to report."

"You bet you got a change in his status!" the guard complained grumpily over the Companion. "The LifeSustainer indicates that the patient has flatlined. Is that what's happened, Blake?"

"Yes. He's dead."

"Okay, make a full report and move him to the morgue," the guard acknowledged. "I'll contact the councilwoman. Guess you're off early tonight."

"Guess so," Blake said casually. He silenced his Companion and turned to Creid, who was now fully dressed. "I'll get the gurney."

Palming the door to an adjacent room, Blake went in and came out wheeling a corpse. Creid stepped back in shock.

"Looks like you, doesn't he?" Blake smiled slyly. "He even has the same DNA overlay. Our Councilwoman thinks of everything, doesn't she?" he asked rhetorically.

"There's a built-in shelf just below this sucker that slides out here." Blake fiddled with the shelf until it folded out.

With some dread, Creid stretched out on the shelf as Blake pushed it below the gurney's top and adjusted the sheet to fully cover both Credit and the corpse. As the gurney rolled down the corridor, the dead man's faintly putrid odor surrounded Creid. When Blake stopped abruptly and pulled the shelf out, Creid lost no time in getting away from the smell of death. They were in a men's bathroom.

"Wait here," the attendant ordered. He palmed the wall to switch the bathroom's status from *Open* to *Closed for Maintenance*. "I have to deal with your 'corpse,' but I'll be back."

As the attendant pushed the gurney out, Joli burst into the bathroom. She ran to Creid, and he scooped her off the ground in a huge hug, burying his face in her hair.

"How do you feel?" Joli asked, quietly containing her excitement.

"Now that you're here, I feel great," Creid answered, in a hoarse voice. "I survived everything so that I could hold you again like this."

Wrapping her arms even tighter around him, Joli sobbed. He set her down gently and held her at arms length to stare at her for a moment before hugging her again. He kissed her clumsily, desperately for reassurance and to make up for all the times he'd passed up kissing her over the years. As always, Joli pulled away first from their embrace.

"Darling, we have so little time to get you to safety. You must go into hiding. I will remain here to be sure that you are officially declared dead."

"Will I see you again?" Creid asked, his voice taut with emotion.

"I don't—," she began to reply as the bathroom door slid open and Blake and the Cadet entered together.

Joli fervently kissed her husband, then left, weeping. The Cadet smiled and bowed respectfully to his mentor, giving the man a moment to regain his composure. Blake motioned for them to hurry after him, and led them through the least trafficked corridors. The night crew was busy loading and unloading hospital supplies. They grunted to Blake, but ignored the new attendant and the stranger trailing behind them.

"Unauthorized access, Attendant 696." The loading station security door stopped them. The corridor was empty. "Please report your authorization to exit from the docking area."

Without hesitation, the attendant answered, "I am Attendant 696, Blake Orss.

"Noted." The security door opened.

|..|.|...|||||...|.|.|

Outside, the docking area seemed unusually quiet. A dark-clad driver with a buzzed haircut waited for them.

"Who's that?" the driver asked, staring at the Cadet.

"He's with us," Creid answered suspiciously, looking around for Joli's usual driver. "Where's Bill?"

"He's in front. I got called in to help," the driver said, opening the heliovan's back door for them.

The man's cuff slid back and the Cadet saw the crane tattoo on his wrist. Instantly the Cadet lunged at him. Cursing, the undercover Order operative drew his smartgun, but the gamer drove his shoulder into the man's stomach before he could fire. The weapon spun free and hit the hospital wall, rebounding and skidding across the pavement. Rolling over his opponent and pinning him to the ground, the Cadet held the man's head between his hands and slammed it against the pavement. The driver reached up and side-punched the Cadet in the neck and face, knocking him off balance.

"Don't move!" Creid yelled, aiming the smartgun, his hands shaking. The Cadet stood up and the Order operative lay still, eyes flicking watchfully between them.

Blake chose that moment to dart across the parking area, which distracted Creid. Taking his chance, the Order regular jumped up from the ground and slammed into Creid. The regular grappled for the smartgun until Creid hurled it into the air. The man dodged after it, but the Cadet stuck out a foot and sent him sprawling. Still, the man managed to reach the gun.

"Run!" shouted the gamer, and he and Creid sprinted in the opposite direction to Blake's panicked flight. The Order regular came to his feet ready to fire. He looked from one choice of target to the other, aimed and sent three spaced shots into Blake's back.

Thrown forward, the attendant tumbled to the pavement. The Order regular pivoted and shot in the opposite direction at the Cadet and Creid, who were dropping down into an old service entrance that led to the Underground.

Behind them, they heard the Order operative speaking urgently into his Companion, which momentarily delayed his giving chase. Instinctively, the gamer led Creid to the deepest part of the Underground, navigating a labyrinth of maintenance tunnels, passing through hidden doorways, and finally emerging into a crowded tunnel. They wove in and out of the throng, Creid tried his best to keep up, but the strain showed in his halting pace. They ran until Creid could go no farther. Gasping for air, he leaned against the tunnel wall until he got his breathing under control.

Exhausted, he looked at the Cadet and gasped, "You may have to leave me behind, I can't keep this up much longer."

"I know of a place where we can hide."

As they briskly walked down a dimly lit, poorly ventilated tunnel, the Cadet joined a line of desperate-looking men and women who had obviously formed a cue outside of a tarpaulin-covered entrance.

"Make way!" A patrol of Order regulars swept past the line, on their way to investigate an incident at the hospital. They bruskly pushed Creid and the Cadet aside, along with the others.

The crowd grew nervous, and many left their places to disappear into the shadows. Soon Creid and the Cadet were at the head of the line, ducking underneath the entrance tarp and entering UL's cavern.

The Ultimate Librarian didn't look the least bit surprised to see the Cadet, but seeing Creid Xerkler was another story.

"Lucky you showed up when you did. I was just about to close up, what with all these Order goons snooping around," said UL, his voice little more than a raspy croak. "Cadet, it looks as though the Order wants you. Something about an incident at the hospital."

UL lowered himself from the rafters above them and detached the mask from around his head. As Creid's eyes adjusted to the dark room, he studied the Oracle's face and saw that one of his eyes remained attached to a funnel that provided constant visual MAM access.

"Milos?" Creid asked, jarred by the disconnect between his memories of Milos and the hideous man before him.

"In the flesh," UL confirmed curtly. "Or, what little flesh remains."

"What happened to you?" He resisted the urge to stare.

"Life, I'm afraid, although it's not all bad," UL replied, with a bitter laugh. "I have greater MAM access than most people ever dream of and I've learned a little about *everything*. Also, thanks to the data that I've gathered from Project Quilt, I've become something of a prophet. You'd be surprised how many people want to know a little more about the future."

"I didn't know it was safe to access the MAM from the Underground," said Creid, examining the ancient gear. He was familiar with all of the early MAM equipment, but this was different — a unique hybrid.

UL gave Creid an icy glare from his good eye. "I am below the powersource for a domus complex. Let's just say, I've rigged the only successful steadystream MAM in the Underground, outside the Sanctuary. I take energy directly from the domus. It's such a miniscule amount that the Order never notices. The moment they do, I'll be shut down."

"I need to rest until the match between Domus Phrack and Domus Aqua," the Cadet interrupted. "I thought Creid might hide here, until I get back."

"Well, well. Who would have thought that Creid Xerkler would need my help? Of course, Creid, you are welcome to use the quarters I occupied before I was permanently attached to Novus Orbis. Feel free to stay as long as you like."

"Thank you, Milos," Creid said, humbly bowing his head.

"I go by UL — for the Ultimate Librarian."

A door behind the UL slid open and Creid and the Cadet jumped down into his apartment. UL's place was small and immaculate. A compactmaid quietly and constantly cleaned up after them.

Exhausted, they each washed up and tried to rest in the cramped apartment. Finally, Creid rose to his feet. "I'd like to catch up with Milos for a minute. There are some things I should say."

The Cadet nodded, leaning his head against the back of the couch. In a moment he was asleep.

|₁.|₁.|₁...|||||₁..|₁.|₁.|

When Creid entered the Oracle cavern, UL swung down from the rafters. Shifting uncomfortably under his old colleague's glare, Creid began, "UL, I know this cannot mean much after all these years, but I'd like to apologize for—"

"Spare me your apologies. I didn't like you twenty years ago, for standing by while Zazen and Dreyfus abused me, but I'm over it."

"I suppose there's nothing I can do to make it up to you," Creid said sadly.

"In fact, there is. I plan to go with the Open MAM Movement to Mars. No one has been able to establish communications with the Project Inventio team. Tragically, everything to do with it may have been recently eliminated. And yet, the Imagofas need to establish their own outpost and may not have much to return home to. They'll need our support."

Exhausted and stunned by the possibility that Zazen and his team could be dead, Creid staggered over to UL and sat down beside him.

"You're saying that the Order might have killed the project team to eliminate any evidence of their nanogenetics work." Creid's voice was shaky.

"It's either that or they've been moved to the Olympus Mons facility and are being completely isolated," UL conjectured sadly. "Either way, we plan to use the Sanctuary missions to develop our own development project. Would you be willing to come along?"

"I don't know. I've never really liked the OMM and honestly, I can't think of leaving Joli." He was still thinking about Zazen.

"If you're officially dead, you won't be able to spend any time with Joli." The UL tinkered with the funnel attached to his eye and used the pause to change the subject. "You know, I never thought much about the OMM until they saved my life and set me up with this apparatus."

"How did you get like this?" Creid asked.

"Like many whizzes, my body rejected the implants and mostly wasted away. The Order put me on disability and left me to die. OMM engineers worked with me to build this apparatus and gave me life. Now they've created a traveling version." UL smiled. "I owe them a lot."

After examining the symbiotic hardware that connected UL to Novus Orbis, Creid bowed deeply. He knew he had few choices. While he was officially declared dead he might have a better chance of survival on Mars, but to be so far from the woman he loved would tear his heart out. "Thank you for your offer. I will seriously consider it."

"You could go to Mars undercover as my attendant. No one would suspect your identity," UL offered, laughing.

Grinning, Creid bowed again.

Suddenly, UL jerked his head to the side and in a rare move, detached the eyecone from the larger apparatus.

"The Order has just broken into my place." UL commanded urgently, "Stand close to me."

The floor descended, and Creid realized that it was actually a platform. They were lowered into a tunnel train.

Once inside, the train immediately activated and zoomed forward down a long tunnel.

"Where are we going?" asked Creid studying his new surroundings in alarm.

"We're headed for the Sanctuary."

"What about the Cadet?" Creid asked anxiously.

"I left an escape route open for him. If he's quick, he'll survive."

|ₐ|ₐ|ₐₐ|||ₐₐ|ₐ|ₐₐ|

When he heard the explosion from the front of the apartment, the Cadet threw open the door to the Oracle cavern and leapt inside. He saw that UL and Creid were gone, and hoped they had successfully escaped.

Knife in his hand, he had just started searching for an escape route when two Order regulars broke into the room, smartguns at the ready. With a cry, the Cadet hurled himself against the nearest one. Taken by surprise, the second man fell back. The Cadet drove his foot down onto the first regular's kneecap, and heard a satisfying *crack*!. The man screamed in agony and dropped to the floor, his weapon spinning away.

The second regular aimed at the Cadet and fired a stream of projectiles. The gamer rolled and scrambled on all fours as the Order regular spun and tracked him with the smartgun. Hearing the hiss of near misses, the gamer turned just in time to dodge heavy blocks of the cavern wall that collapsed to the floor.

The wounded Order regular struggled to his feet and, hopping out of harm's way, yelled to his partner, "Stop! You'll kill us."

The cavern walls began to crumble around them. Before the Cadet could jump clear, an avalanche of debris hit him. His left leg snapped under the weight of the stones, and blood welled up from a deep gash in his side. He frantically scanned the cavern for a way out.

The Order regulars struggled to extract themselves from the debris and find their weapons. In moments, they would be firing at him again. Not far from him, the Cadet saw a cable dangling from an opening in the ceiling. He reached for it, intending to pull himself hand over hand out of range. To his surprise, when he put his weight on it, the cable contracted, hauling him straight up and through a hole in the ceiling, which conveniently closed behind him.

He found himself in the semi-darkness of a tunnel just below a domus complex, its ceiling too low to fully stand upright. The route to his left was blocked by a filtering system. He turned right, stumbling as fast as he could manage with his broken leg. He had not gone far before he heard angry cursing echoing behind him and the sound of footsteps. He wondered how the Order regulars had managed to get up into the tunnel so fast. Limping, he drove himself forward.

Up ahead, he could see the end of the tunnel, a closed exit. When he palmed the exit door, nothing happened. Above him, he saw a narrow shaft dimly lit by natural light. As the voices behind him grew louder, he started to climb. Setting his shoulders and back against one shaft wall, he shoved his palms against the opposite wall until they were supporting his entire weight. He drew up his uninjured leg and used his good knee to brace himself. With the broken leg dangling beneath him and blood dripping from his gashed side, he shimmied slowly up the shaft. Higher up, he found handholds that let him climb more quickly. At the top of the shaft, an ancient wrought iron grate freely swung open. With his last remaining bit of strength, the Cadet shifted his weight and hoisted himself to freedom.

"That's him! Get him!" A harsh voice yelled above his head. Cold hands seized his arms, hauled him brutally upright, crushing his hurt leg. An Order regular leaned in close to his face and leered triumphantly. As the regular opened his mouth to speak, the Cadet spat at him. He had the pleasure of watching his spittle hit the regular's eye and ooze down his cheek. The man's heavy fist slammed into the Cadet's face, and the impact snapped his head back. While the first blow was still reverberating in his skull, he felt the second, and then his world went black.

Substitution

From the far corner of the hall where Angel's thugs had slipped her in, Sashimu watched the crime boss stride ferociously around the Great Hall of the newly built Domus Phrack. There was one thing left to break. An expensive looking vase stood in stark contrast to the wreckage of shattered glass, torn curtains and smashed furniture. He hurled the vase against the wall, and it shattered, sending pieces everywhere. Momentarily pacified, Angel sat down in the optimization area, which was the only space still clear of debris. When she saw that his rage had finally subsided, the Imagofas came out of the shadows.

Angel immediately sprang to his feet. "Where is the Cadet?" he demanded.

"The Order has detained him. His friends escaped, but he wasn't so lucky," Sashimu replied, fighting back tears. She threw back her Sanctuary-issued cloak, and her long dark hair fell freely over her shoulders. "I have come to game in his place."

"What makes you think you'll last ten seconds in Novus Orbis?" Angel sneered.

Sashimu met his gaze with fierce determination. "The Cadet trained me, and I am an Imagofas. I have abilities in Novus Orbis that you can't possibly imagine."

Angel's scowl deepened as he considered his options. After a long moment, he said, "Very well."

"Not quite. I want something in return—"

"You *what*?" Angel snorted. "I don't know who you think you're dealing with, but you are in no position to—"

"Get me a ship to transport us back to Mars, and I'll win your game."

"You want a trip home in exchange for winning the match for me?" Angel contemplated, scratching his scarred face. After some hesitation, he replied coldly, "You'll get a ship, as long as you win the game for Domus Phrack."

Taking a step towards her, he drew a slender dagger from his side and placed it under her chin. "Lose, and you'll be Marty's little plaything."

"I'll win." Sashimu acted more confident than she felt.

"Where are your hood and your MAMsuit?"

"I am an Imagofas," Sashimu said proudly. "I directly access the MAM without extra equipment."

"So, it's true." Angel's sneer briefly gave way to a look of awe.

Standing in the center of the optimization area, Sashimu watched Angel activate his hood and initiate his session. It brought her hurtling into the strange world of the crime boss' preferences.

Angel's muscular avatar sported dried-blood-spiked hair, prominent fangs, a lizard tongue that darted over his lips and a third eye in the back of his head. He strode through high grass and at his side were a leopard, a lion and a wolf. Mirroring him with an identical avatar, Sashimu blocked his path to announce herself. The wolf growled in confusion at his master's replica.

"Greed, down." Angel gestured to his animals and said, "Meet Lust, Pride and Greed."

With the feral beasts trailing behind, they approached Angel's modern fortress, a hideous amalgam of sharp-angled metal and glass with marble pillars framing the front entrance. As they entered, smart intelligence agents in the form of dignitaries and officials vied for Angel's attention.

Turning to her, Angel pointed to a long, dark hallway. "That's the way, little nanogen."

At the end of the hallway, Sashimu suddenly encountered the familiar landscape of the Mars biosphere. She shrank back in surprise. As the Domus Aqua master approached, Sashimu gazed around at her home landscape as rendered by the MAM.

"I thought I'd pick a landscape neither of us knows intimately," the master said quietly. His avatar was a broad-shouldered, sturdy man with an ageless ebony face and a shock of white hair.

Before Sashimu could respond, the game host's avatar — a red-eyed badger — appeared. "Hey! You know the rules! No pre-game fraternizing," he growled.

"I request that we play as ourselves," the Domus Aqua Master said, surprising both the game host and Sashimu. "My status as Lila of Domus Aqua was made public before the fight. Show yourself, Domus Phrack master."

Unless both parties agreed ahead of time, it was risky to reveal the true Vetus Orbis identities of fly gamers, and the game host glowered at the Aqua master, who now transformed into Lila. She was brilliantly dressed in silks that faded from the deepest hues to the palest blue. Her tresses were ornately wound about her head and inter-twined with a blue-flowered vine. A similar garland encircled her waist.

Is this a setup to catch the Cadet? Sashimu wondered. He would have been outed in front of the whole world.

The game host turned to her. "This is not required by the rules. What is Domus Phrack's response?"

In fighting someone as agile as Lila, Sashimu believed that using her own likeness would be advantageous. Her avatar was now available thanks to Prometheus. Domus Aqua had been challenged by Phrack so, according to the rules, Aqua chose the terrain. Sashimu could imagine places where her own light-footed avatar would offer a distinct advantage.

"Domus Phrack agrees," Sashimu responded.

Concentrating, she called up her own avatar — a mirror image of herself in Vetus Orbis — dressed in black with a scarf to tie her hair back.

When the Domus Phrack master's avatar reappeared, Lila's face registered astonishment and she took a step backward. All the professional gamers were well known, at least by reputation. Lila gave Sashimu a once-over, then smiled with renewed confidence. "Angel must be a big-ger risk-taker than I thought," she said, her voice laden with contempt.

"Take your positions," the badger announced. He hoisted the flags of both domus in his claws, waving them above his head, signaling that now the Spectators were allowed access. A chorus of murmurs and whispered comments came from all sides as the watchers saw Lila of Domus Aqua up against a complete unknown.

The game host bellowed, "Let the game begin."

As the badger scampered away, Sashimu realized she was no longer on solid ground. Instead, she teetered on the edge of a water-drenched steel sculpture that had a fountain cascading out from its center. Beneath her feet, small loose steel rods rolled one beside another down and under, and up and out, forced by the momentum of the fountain. This modern sculpture sat in the center of Mars' Twin Peak City, which offended Sashimu because nothing of the sort had ever existed on her world. The colonies conserved both energy and water.

The sculpture suddenly remolded itself beneath a thin layer of cascading water and Sashimu balanced precariously, watching as Lila glided back and forth on the balls of her feet.

Pulling up one of the steel rods, Lila lunged at Sashimu and smacked her hard across the cheek with it. The impact drove Sashimu to her knees in the water. Lila followed, swinging a downward stroke at the Imagofas' head. To counter the deadly blow, Sashimu scooped a handful of water and dashed it in Lila's eyes, which momentarily blinded her so that she lost her balance. Rolling out and away, Sashimu came up soaking wet beside Lila. In her hand, she held a rod she had dislodged, which she swung at Lila, who barely deflected her blow.

The two fighters parried back and forth, sliding across the immense sculpture; the clang of steel against steel a jarring noise above the constant flow of water. Abruptly, the sculpture again remolded itself, smooth edges becoming jagged teeth. Lila's ankle was caught between two newly formed projections. Swinging her rod, she smashed through one of the spikes, freeing herself and leaping back just as Sashimu's weapon passed through the space where Lila's head had been.

The scene changed and Sashimu saw that they had been transported outside the biosphere, both of them now dressed in protective biosuits. The new setting confused her. Since early childhood, her training had taught her to use extreme caution outside the biosphere; it was no place for a swordfight. Apparently, the same precautions did not apply in Novus Orbis. Before them, on the sterile Martian soil, was an array of bladed weapons. Lila had already chosen a sword for herself and now she executed a pattern of cuts in the thin air while her free hand motioned for Sashimu to pick her own weapon.

Sashimu saw no reason why she should choose a weapon from her opponent's discards. She closed her eyes and called up an image in her mind: the sharpest sword, fashioned from the hardest Martian alloy. Inscribed into the hilt, she placed the outline of a flying crane. When she opened her eyes, the weapon blazed in her hands, the flame-tinted alloy blade made it appear as if it was on fire.

Lila looked to the game host, but the badger did not intervene. Sashimu's choice of weapon fell within the rules.

The fighters faced each other and bowed, before the contest resumed. Sashimu struck first, a two-handed thrust that she smoothly looped into a diagonal upward strike at her opponent's throat, which Lila deflected.

"That was an interesting move," said the Aqua fighter, as they drew apart and repositioned themselves. "Who is your teacher?"

"The Cadet."

Taken off guard, Lila faltered for a moment. Sashimu swiftly stepped in close to her opponent. Taken aback, Lila retreated to give herself sword-room, but Sashimu stayed close. She bent and thrust her left shoulder into Lila's gut. The Domus Aqua fighter fell backwards and cried out, as she smashed her back against an outcrop of jagged red rock. Sashimu followed, her sword arcing around in a lateral cut. Throwing herself forward and under the blade's sweep, Lila rolled and came safely to her feet to aim her sword at Sashimu's throat. The Imagofas leveraged the momentum of her own swing to meet the counterattack.

As she had intended, the force of Sashimu's block staggered Lila, already weakened from the blow to her back.

Now Sashimu drove at her opponent, weaving thrusts and cuts in a pattern that kept the Aqua fighter from recovering her equilibrium. Lila stumbled again. Without hesitation, Sashimu brought her sword around in a full-strength strike that bit through the biosuit into Lila's neck.

The blood gushed, and Sashimu cried out when she saw that Lila did not disappear to flicker back into Novus Orbis, defeated but unharmed. Instead, her opponent lay where she had fallen — her life ebbing from her with her blood. In fly games in Novus Orbis, fatal wounds were never allowed.

Sashimu knelt beside Lila, cradling her head in her arms as the young woman's life drained across Sashimu's knees. The MAM rarely malfunctioned, but it was possible for a fatal wound in Novus Orbis to bring death in Vetus Orbis if the gamer remained connected to the MAM. The brain registered the injury as real. Sashimu knew that she must attempt to heal Lila's wound in Novus Orbis to restore her body in Vetus Orbis.

She laid her hands on the savaged throat, concentrated all her will on repairing the deep gash that cut across the neck. The game host was issuing orders to summon help to get Lila disconnected and reconnected before it was too late. Sashimu drove the sound of his voice and the babble of horrified spectators from her consciousness. *There is only Lila — only her wound and my hands.*

As Sashimu focused on Lila's wounds, her hands became so hot, they felt on fire. She welcomed the heat for it signaled crossing over that boundary between healer and healing. For a moment, she ceased to be herself and felt as if she had melted into the other woman's torn flesh. And then, out of the feverish heat came coolness, as the open wound sealed and color returned to Lila's pallid cheeks.

"Lila," she whispered. "The MAMsuit only simulates the effects of the game. You and I can reverse the damage, but you must help me."

Lila's body remained still in her arms, but the Imagofas felt certain she lived. Bypassing protocols and access restrictions, Sashimu appealed directly to the MAM and forced a replay in fast reverse of her victory. The blood flowed back into Lila's body, the sword leapt from her throat and swung back into Sashimu's hand.

Now the play resumed. Lila was on her feet again, but stumbling backwards. Instead of re-enacting the fatal blow, Sashimu backed away and lowered her sword.

Lila dropped her weapon. She stepped forward and embraced Sashimu. "I have no idea how we did that. I actually felt my blood flowing back into my neck and my throat become whole again. You saved my life!"

Blushing and exhausted, Sashimu could only bow. Lila solemnly returned the gesture.

"I can see you're worn out," Lila said. "So am I. But we must meet again, and this time, in Vetus Orbis.

"Yes," agreed Sashimu. "I'd like that."

Returning to the dark hall of Angel's Novus Orbis fortress, Sashimu sank to her knees in exhaustion and remained still upon the stone floor. Here, Angel found her and lifted her gently, laying her on the backs of Lust, Pride and Greed so that the beasts could carry her out of the fortress.

"What happened to you?" the crime boss asked. "How did you heal Lila and reverse the game?"

Too weak to answer, Sashimu simply stared up at him while he ended the session. Returned to Vetus Orbis, she collapsed onto the floor of the Great Hall in Domus Phrack.

"You said the Cadet taught you your gaming skills, but you looked like a novice out there," Angel said, nudging her with his foot. "A few more games and you might be worthy of gaming for Domus Phrack, but unfortunately I've got to hand you over to the Council."

Aghast, Sashimu looked up at his grinning face. "But you promised me safe passage back to Mars if I won the game!"

"I lied," Angel replied, letting his smirk widen. He gestured with one hand and a group of Council representatives stepped into Sashimu's view. They encircled her. She picked up a piece of the vase Angel had shattered and tried desperately to fend them off. Drained from the effort of healing Lila, she was easily pinned when one man came at her from the front while another moved in from behind.

They carried her, as she struggled, to a gurney, where they roughly strapped her down and wheeled her away to a waiting heliovan.

Sashimu shivered uncontrollably from exhaustion and fear. A Council rep placed a warm blanket over her, draping her from head to foot. She warmed, but the blanket also covered her eyes. After a short trip in the heliovan, they wheeled her from the vehicle into what felt like an elevator. When they finally stripped off the blanket and removed her restraints, she found she was lying on a sleeprest inside a tiny cage-like holding cell. She cried long, gut-wrenching sobs that echoed against the walls.

Interrogation

The offices of Order Elder Yenfam looked like any other Order office. The walls had been painted institutional green, and the furniture consisted of stiff-backed chairs. Master Sachio of Domus Aqua was not deceived by the modest surroundings. As he and Yenfam talked about Lila's upcoming wedding, Sachio never once forgot that he sat before one of the most influential men in the interplanetary government. Today he hoped to strike a deal with this lean, impeccably dressed man with a revitalized face that gave his countenance an eerie masklike quality.

Knowing his time with Yenfam would be short, Sachio finally broached the topic that he had come to discuss. "Over the last few months, the Order has been put in an unfair position," he explained, sympathetically shaking his head. "This whole tribunal business seems unnecessary, and why Tebgallis or someone else in the Council has been intent on vilifying the Order is beyond me."

"Actually, Tebgallis may have come out against the Order in the past," Yenfam said. "But, no doubt, there are others in the Council who no longer support the Order."

"Domus Aqua is dedicated to supporting a strong, unified government," Sachio noted, his tongue flicking out to wet his dry lips as he wondered how to lead into the matter of the Imagofas. "We want to help in any way we can. Consider us at your disposal."

"Once, we thought a new World Emissary, such as Councilwoman Xerkler, might change the Council's recent antagonistic attitudes toward the Order." Yenfam rubbed his jaw. "I've always held her in the highest regard.

However, the Council's insistence on the tribunal makes me question her possible appointment."

"Of course," Master Sachio agreed. He liked Joli and thought she would make an excellent replacement for Tebgallis who, for all his seeming stodginess, had so far outmaneuvered all who had attempted to replace him. "Personally, I see a benefit in canceling the tribunal for lack of evidence."

"Yes, but the Council also has 'evidence' against us. The Imagofas can be traced back to our critical research on Mars." A note of agitation had crept into the Elder's tone.

"We would hate to see the inherent knowledge of the Imagofas go to waste," Master Sachio said, leaning forward in his chair. "We see clear benefits in researching the commercial applications of human nanogenetics."

"I completely concur," Yenfam said nodding his head. "Unfortunately, in the current political climate, it is impossible to continue research into human nanogenetics."

"If Domus Aqua could be instrumental in ensuring that this tribunal is stopped, then would it be feasible for Domus Aqua to take the Imagofas into its custody, knowing the potential benefits for everyone involved?"

"That may be a workable plan," Yenfam confirmed smiling broadly.

From this response, Master Sachio understood that he had been invited to Yenfam's office precisely because the Elder wanted him to make such an offer. It might prove highly profitable to them both.

"There may be a way that you can help us," Yenfam continued. "We have taken into custody a suspect with whom you are acquainted. I think you know him as the Cadet."

Master Sachio's surprise showed on his face. "Really? I know him well. He is a frequent fly gamer for Domus Aqua and a friend to my daughter."

"Well, he's suspected of treasonous activities against the Order, including secretly hiding tribunal 'evidence.' Unfortunately, we've been unable to get him to cooperate. We don't know who paid him to hide the 'evidence.' Given time and extreme measures, of course, we will learn what we need from him," Yenfam said with the slightest hint of a smile that quickly vanished. "However, time is short."

"I'm sure it's some misunderstanding. It is hard to imagine the Cadet ever doing anything intentionally against the Order."

Yenfam shrugged.

"My daughter happens to be close friends with him. She could speak with him if you would like."

"That is an excellent idea. We simply want to know who hired him." Then Yenfam added, in a colder tone, "We have our suspicions, of course."

As important as this meeting was to him, Master Sachio attempted to keep his deep concern for the Cadet from showing in his face. He had watched the Cadet grow up with Lila and Isaac, and greatly admired the boy. He also knew that, for all the gamer's impetuousness, the young man had always been honest and that he loved Lila as much as did Sachio himself.

"Of course, Lila would help in this matter," he said carefully. "However, I do not wish to see her traumatized."

"Traumatized?" Yenfam asked, puzzled.

"Since they are close, she would beg me to ensure that the Cadet would be released once he was no longer a suspect."

"I'll see what I can do," Yenfam confirmed stiffly. "It would be unusual for us to release him unless he was somehow completely cleared as a suspect."

Iıldıı.ıllllıı.lılıI

The Cadet studied the reddish-brown stains that splattered the walls of his cell. It was only as he regained full consciousness that he realized the stains were from his own blood.

His chest ached where he'd been kicked repeatedly. Propped up against the cell wall, he found that the slightest movement brought savage pain. His face was swollen; he could barely open his left eye. He had to breathe through his mouth in short, horrible sips of air. The gash in his side made each breath even more difficult. He wondered how many ribs they had broken, kicking him until he'd lost consciousness. Shivering, he waited miserably for the next interrogation.

The cell door slid open, and he saw the silhouette of a woman against the harsh light from the hall. She entered and he recognized her, as he squinted against the glare.

"Lila, is that really you or am I hallucinating?"

"Oh!" Lila cried, rushing to him and touching the side of his face delicately with her fingers. "How could they have done this to you?"

He closed his eyes and felt her gentle caress over his brow and cheeks. When she stepped back and kneeled beside him on the floor, her eyes were red from crying and her cheeks were damp.

"They sent me here to get information from you," Lila advised bitterly. "I had no idea they had hurt you so badly. It's criminal."

"I won't tell them anything," he said, as confidently as he could. "They'll kill me first."

"They almost have," she said, her fingers gently touching his knee that was puffed up beyond twice its normal size. "Look, I'll be honest with you. They want to know who paid you to find the Imagofas besides us."

"They're very clever to send you. There aren't many others I would trust. Do you know what's happened to the Imagofas?"

"Sashimu is in Council custody," Lila said sadly.

"No! How did that happen?" inquired the Cadet, hearing his voice tremble.

"Well, it's a bit complicated," Lila answered slowly. "It started with Sashimu gaming against me for Domus Phrack and—"

"She did what?" he asked. "How could she do such a thing?"

"Cadet, she no doubt did it for you. And then, she saved my life in Novus Orbis when a MAM glitch at the end of the game left me for dead. The Council picked her up afterwards. She'll be used as evidence against the Order."

"This cannot all be happening this way," the Cadet said, with a groan. He buried his head in his hands. "I hate to have you see me so weak and pitiful right at the end."

"This is not the end," Lila said, her voice catching. She stroked the top of his head. "I'm so sorry you're in this state. I will never forgive the Order."

He weakly raised his head. "Lila, why did you come?"

"Because Sashimu saved my life!" She sat back, her face stark. "I want to save hers by getting the tribunal cancelled and having her brought into Domus Aqua's custody."

"She may prefer death. All she's ever wanted is to return to Mars. That has been her dream ever since I met her." The Cadet felt tears fill his eyes.

"We would give her a choice. And if she wanted to stay on Earth, you know we would take good care of her. Father suggested making her part of our research group," Lila said softly. "We would treat her as an independent consultant to our domus. She'd be free to come and go. After Sashimu saved my life, I realized the Imagofas aren't simply commodities to be bought and sold."

"I'm glad you feel that way about them." A wave of dizziness made him pause for a long moment, then he added, "You know, I broke my promise to tell you where either Sashimu or Thesni were. I was afraid the domus might mistreat them. I'm sorry, Lila."

"I will insist that you get medical attention. But don't apologize to me. I'm just hoping we can work together to free Sashimu."

"Are you saying that if I tell you who originally hired me that you'll make sure that Sashimu goes free? I mean from the beginning, I thought I was working for the Order and the Council so I don't even know why the Order is holding me as a suspect." His thoughts were muddled by pain and shock but he knew he must not give up Joli.

"You're in too much pain. We'll talk again after we get a medic in here."

"No, I'm okay," he said, though his wince belied his words. "I like you being here, and I don't want you to leave just yet.... You know, I was in love with you most of my life, but now I'm glad you're marrying Isaac. I'm really happy for you."

"You are?" Lila asked. He thought she sounded a little disappointed. "I thought you'd never accept my marrying anyone, even Isaac."

"You mean, *especially* Isaac." He groaned as he tried to shift his leg to take pressure off his injured knee. "I want you to be happy, and I've finally fallen in love with someone else. So now I can see clearly that the two of you are meant for each other."

"Who are you in love with?" Lila stared at him thoughtfully, and then clapped her hands together. "You're not in love with Sashimu, are you?"

"Yes." The Cadet fought against another wave of dizziness. "You needed something, and now it's escaped me what you were asking for..."

"I don't want anything bad to happen to Sashimu. She saved my life. You love her," she reminded him. "To save her life, we must stop the tribunal from meeting. Tell me who hired you, so that the Order can go directly to those Council members and convince them to cancel the tribunal."

"That's all the Order wants?" he inquired, hopefully. He wanted it to be true, to be able to let his guard down for the first time in over seventy-two hours of endless beatings. "Are you sure there won't be any repercussions? I mean, look at me. Look at what they've done!"

"They need to convince the right people. That's all they want, I promise you." Tears sprang from her eyes and she spoke through wracking sobs. "I don't know why they did this to you. I don't understand it."

"You'll make sure Sashimu is freed and makes her own decision whether to stay with you?" He was struggling to take command of his emotions, smearing away his own tears with his blood stained sleeve.

"That's right," Lila replied. "But there's something else, too. They promised that you will go free after your confession."

"Lila, give me your word," the Cadet requested. "Promise me that if I tell you who hired me, it will not end badly for anyone." He pushed himself up against the wall to stand on his good leg. A shadow passed over his face. Exhausted and barely conscious, he wrestled with guilt and suspicion. But now, he was willing to give up Joli. Lila had always kept her word to him all the years they had known each other.

"I give you my word," Lila promised, and moved close to him so that he could whisper in her ear.

"It was Councilwoman Joli Byl Xerkler." After he said her name, the room spun. He staggered forward against Lila, unthinkingly putting his weight onto his injured leg. The intense pain sent him reeling into unconsciousness.

ΙιΙιΙιιιΙΙΙΙιιΙιΙιιΙ

When the Cadet came to, Lila was gone. A man stood at his open cell door, motioning for him to come out. At first, he just stared in confusion. When his eyes adjusted, he saw that the stranger was a uniformed Order regular.

Someone had dressed his wounds. His swollen knee was confined in a padded brace. Still dizzy and aching, he limped after the regular down several hallways, until they came to a heliovan hangar. A driver had one idling. As soon as they climbed in, they were whisked across the city. It was a long, windowless ride. At the end of it, they dropped off the Cadet at one of the surface entrances to his quarters.

The sunlight of the world above ground blinded him and a cold, fall wind made him shiver. Covering his eyes from the glare, he palmed the security door and slid down the chute, landing in his tiny quarters. On the flight over, he had thought it would be a relief to be home. Now the place felt as small and claustrophobic as his cell. Even worse, it had been ransacked. His message panels were cracked and his bed torn apart.

At the moment, that didn't matter. The last thing he wanted was sleep. More than anything, he needed to ensure that Sashimu was safe, and that Creid be warned about his betrayal. While he wasn't sure where either was at the moment, he reasoned that he should begin his search at the Sanctuary.

Feverish and in terrible pain, he dropped down into an old service tunnel and hobbled toward the Sanctuary's private line.

The Offer

UL and Creid arrived at Sanctuary OMM headquarters via an old OMM escape route. It had originally been established for the Ultimate Librarian should the Order ever discover his illegal siphoning of MAM resources.

Ochbo had greeted them and taken them to the OMM visitor's apartment, which they quickly transformed into a sea of equipment that they could use to upgrade UL's travel apparatus for the planned trip to Mars.

Having helped maintain UL's MAM connect-system over recent years, Ochbo treated UL as an old friend. After the three men had each recounted what had happened to them over the last weeks, they eventually arrived at the issue of how best to fine-tune UL's travel apparatus. Ochbo tasked Thesni with sifting through the equipment looking for specific components.

As she worked, she became increasingly agitated by their technical discussion and their fixation on what she considered an ancillary task.

Unable to contain her ire any longer, Thesni burst out, "How can you be discussing UL's travel apparatus when we don't even have a ship yet, and while the Cadet and Sashimu have been captured and need our help?"

Ochbo looked up, stunned. "Thesni," he said. "We're working while we wait to find out the status of Sashimu and the tribunal. And the Cadet, well, he's in Order custody. We can't do much to help him unless he's released."

With clenched fists, Thesni rounded on Creid. "We risked our lives for you to get you out of a coma and free you from the hospital. The Order may kill the Cadet for helping you escape. They will certainly murder Sashimu if the tribunal goes forward. You promised your help. What are you going to do?!"

Creid sat in his chair. His face was unnaturally pale and sickly looking. He answered, gravely, "Honestly, I'm at a loss for what to do. This is a political situation, not a technical one. From what Ochbo and UL tell me, Domus Aqua wants one of you. The Council is bent on a tribunal to discredit the Order while the Order has been determined throughout to maintain its public face and not lose power — even if that means destroying you and Sashimu."

"Isn't your wife a councilwoman?" Thesni asked bitterly, her face red and her body trembling with rage. "Can't you talk to her and influence the Council to let Sashimu go? Why don't you talk to someone in the Order and convince them to save the Cadet? You've worked for them your entire life!"

Ochbo intervened. "Okay, let's think about this. I understand your frustration Thesni, but Creid has been declared dead, to remove Joli from danger and protect her future. If he comes out of hiding, of course the Order will kill him. And then the Cadet's sacrifice will have been for nothing. If Creid goes public, that would also jeopardize Joli. After that, even if she wanted to, she wouldn't be able to help us."

"If you can't do anything, I know what to do!" Thesni shouted. Kicking old components from her path, she ran out the door.

Ochbo jumped up and followed her down the hall past the Library, where he caught up and blocked her path. "Hold on, Thesni. I'm worried. What are you planning?"

She glared at him with fury and determination. "Since Creid is useless, I'll talk to Domus Aqua myself. If they want an Imagofas, that's what I'll offer in return for Sashimu."

Horrified, Ochbo blurted, "It's too dangerous for you to go to Domus Aqua. They'll just make you their guinea pig! Stay here and we'll figure out something."

"No, get out of my way," Thesni demanded with quiet, deadly certainty, gathering her Magus cloak more tightly around her and pulling the hood of the cloak forward to hide her face. "I must save Sashimu."

"If I can't stop you from going, at least I know how to save you from sacrificing yourself!" Ochbo said passionately. He stepped aside to let her pass and ran back down the hallway to the visitor's apartment.

|.||..|||||..|.|..|

Thesni climbed above ground and caught a heliovan to Domus Aqua in the city's richest district. To a stout, bored-looking man, who stood before a pair of enormous doors she said, "I have important information regarding the Imagofas and must speak to the domus master."

The attendant looked her up and down, before going inside. He returned shortly to lead her down a long corridor, lined with busts on either side, and into the Great Hall. Here she waited for what felt like an eternity. Finally, a tall, beautiful young woman with long braided hair strode into the hall.

"I am Lila, daughter of Master Sachio. The domus master is unavailable at the moment." She spoke politely, but with an undisguised air of impatience.

Thesni bowed deeply and said, "I am Thesni of the Imagofas, and I must speak with him."

She heard a quick intake of breath. The tall woman studied her with new interest. "Really?" she asked. "I am indebted to your sister Imagofas. She saved my life. What may we do for you?"

"Let me speak to the domus master."

Lila regarded her with a calculating gaze and snapped her fingers. A short, ashen-faced attendant came forward from the shadows. "Please ask Master Sachio to join us."

Moments later, he entered. He wore formal white robes with the blue and red crest of the domus over his heart.

"Lila, you know we have important visitors this afternoon—" he said gruffly, then stopped to stare at Thesni. "Well, who have we here?"

Before Thesni could lose her nerve and go running out of the domus, she blurted out, "I am an Imagofas, and I want to offer myself to you as a trade for Sashimu."

A mask of pleasantness, Sachio's face showed no reaction. "There must be some misunderstanding. We do not have Sashimu. She is in the care of the Council," he said, glancing at his daughter, who simply shrugged.

"I have come here to see if there is anything you can do to have her released from the Council's detention and returned to Mars." Thesni offered cautiously, "In return, I will make myself available to you."

"We too are worried for Sashimu's safety, and are prepared to insist that she be released," replied the domus master. "We want to work with the Imagofas, both on developing new technologies and on changing people's misperceptions about them."

"Sashimu's dream is to return to Mars and lead the Imagofas. I, however, would welcome the opportunity to remain on Earth to work with you."

Master Sachio smiled broadly and opened his arms magnanimously. "Yours is a highly welcome offer."

The stout doorman stepped forward from the corridor. "Master, you have visitors."

"Is the Council so early?" Sachio asked, and Thesni heard worry in his tone.

"No sir, the Chief Magus and a group of his acolytes insist on meeting with you."

Now Sachio looked less worried than puzzled. "Show them in."

Thesni turned and saw a group of five very tall Magus with their hoods drawn forward to obscure their faces as they swept into the room. Ochbo trailed behind them with his head bowed.

The Magus leader stopped beside Thesni. "Master Sachio, we have come to take Thesni from your midst."

"I see," he said deferentially, but was clearly taken aback. "Thesni has come here of her own volition to offer her services to us."

"That is understood, but she has a special place among our devotees. She belongs at the Sanctuary," the Magus leader said dryly. "And now, we must leave."

"Wait a second. I came here to ensure Sashimu's safety. I don't want to leave without getting a commitment from

you, Master Sachio," Thesni insisted. "You must realize
that I will do anything to help her."

"Well, I don't know what to say," he said in a measured
tone. The group of cloaked Magus visibly tensed. Lila stared
nervously at her father. "Except that I'm honored that you
want to work with us. We have excellent accommodations
for our guests. Instead of leaving, why don't you stay here
with us, Thesni?"

"Sir, it is not only the Magus who insist that Thesni have
the freedom to leave these premises," Ochbo added, speaking for the first time and stepping forward from behind
the group of Magus. "The OMM also insists on her freedom
to reside at the Sanctuary or wherever she chooses."

"Well, well, it seems everyone wants you, Thesni. OK.
I've agreed to have you come work with us in return for
our best efforts to secure Sashimu's release," the domus
master confirmed, with a touch of irony in his voice. "But
tell me, Thesni, do you let everyone speak on your behalf?"

"No," the Imagofas replied apprehensively. "But I would
prefer to return to my home in the Sanctuary as long as
we have an agreement between us—"

"Then, do I have your commitment to return and work
with Domus Aqua? And can I trust your word?" Master
Sachio asked.

"Of course, I am an Imagofas."

Sachio turned to the monks and Ochbo. "Well then,
gentlemen, do I also have your personal oaths to honor
this spoken agreement between Thesni and myself?" He
looked at each man in turn, waiting until each had acknowledged, "You have my word."

"Today, I meet with the Council on the very issue of
Sashimu. No doubt we will come to an excellent arrangement, all of us," Sachio informed them and bowed to Thesni
and then the Magus and Ochbo in turn.

"Until another day, Master Sachio," the Magus leader
acquiesced. He bowed and all of the Magus followed suit.

"Thank you," Thesni whispered softly to the Chief
Magus. He gestured for her to lead the way out, and then
they surrounded her in a protective half-circle.

ΙιΙιΙιιιΙΙΙΙιιΙιΙιιΙ

Not long after Thesni stormed out and Ochbo followed after her, Creid had a brief breakdown. Leaving UL, he went out to the terrace and cried for the first time in decades. He cried for Joli and for the Cadet, for the Imagofas and the unfairness of their plight, and he cried for himself. Thesni's words continued to weigh heavily on him when he returned red-eyed and quiet to resume assembling UL's travel apparatus components.

"Creid, after all you've been through, you should join the Open MAM Movement and come to Mars with us," UL encouraged gently.

"I don't know," Creid said, his mind racing with possibilities for the Cadet and Sashimu. "I've never really been an OMM supporter."

"The OMM is much more effective than it used to be. Our latest goal is to build the infrastructure for a new Imagofas outpost at the foot of Olympus Mons so that they can one day be completely independent of the Order. With the constant threat of scandals over nanogenetics, the Order may actually prefer their independence," UL explained, studying Creid. "As I said before, you should join us."

"I want to help with your project," Creid said sadly, thinking to himself that he'd prefer to stay on Earth to be with Joli, but that was impossible. "Thesni is right. I need to help her, not just in the long term, but right now. I'm going to start by talking to Joli."

"Good idea. Your Joli is a smart woman," UL said. "She can see that the political winds are changing. If there is any profit to be had from the Imagofas and their personal assets, people will adopt more accepting attitudes toward them and the whole idea of nanogenetics."

"I hope you're right," Creid agreed, knowing he not only wanted to talk to Joli, but that he had to talk to her about helping Sashimu and the Cadet. "Joli may be smart, but I've never known her to change her mind."

ΙιΙιΙιιιΙΙΙΙιιΙιΙιιΙ

After being ushered in by a stout, obsequious attendant, Joli waited beside Tebgallis in the elegant Great Hall for the Domus Aqua Master, his daughter and her fiancé Isaac. For the formal visit, she and Tebgallis dressed in their official Council robes, gray silk embossed with the snow-capped mountain emblem. Having a private meeting with the Domus Aqua was part of Tebgallis' tireless campaign to gather support for Joli, his favored successor.

When Master Sachio, Lila and Isaac entered, they sat at one end of the enormous table. Joli and Tebgallis sat opposite them.

"I owe you many thanks for your support," Joli began, aware of the active role Domus Aqua would play in her selection.

"It is rare to meet someone of such high morals and strength of will in the halls of power," Master Sachio remarked smoothly. "You have done much to encourage better trade between the colonies and Earth as well as to improve relations between the Council and the other branches of government."

"Thank you, Master Sachio," Joli said. She suspected that his compliments might be a precursor to a request for political favors.

"We have a delicate matter to discuss with you," Sachio said, his expression turning severe.

Joli nodded.

"We understand a tribunal will be held this coming Monday. Is this regarding the accident on MIP?" the domus master asked.

"No. That matter is settled. The tribunal's focus has shifted over the past few weeks to the question of infractions of interplanetary law by the Order," Joli replied, relaxing slightly. The tribunal was set, and she finally had the nanogen in custody as indisputable evidence.

"I see. May I ask, what are the Order's purported infractions?"

"Interplanetary Justices could answer that better than I," answered Joli with a puzzled glance at Tebgallis, who kept his gaze on the domus master. "The tribunal will expose the Order's development of human nanogens on Mars."

"In that case, we would like to bring to your attention some relevant evidence," Sachio offered, smiling coldly. "This evidence would have to be put before the tribunal, if it is convened." He paused with a pitying glance towards Joli. "The Imagofas are on Earth."

"Yes, we have her in custody." Joli tensed.

"You have one Imagofas in custody—" He raised a hand to be allowed to finish, as she tried to interrupt. "Should a tribunal be held, we have witnesses who feel it is their duty to come forward and testify that the Council financed the abduction and shipping of human nanogens to Earth. Of course without a tribunal, there would be no forum for these witnesses."

"Anyone who claims the Council was involved in such an endeavor has a vendetta against us," Joli said, trying to appear calm.

"If there were any plausibility to the testimony, it could cause a complete reorganization of the government," Master Sachio mused. He thoughtfully stroked his white beard and continued, "Unfortunately, both the Order and the Council would have to be overhauled if the tribunal went forward."

"Tell me, what is your advice in this situation?" Joli inquired, trying to keep the anger from her voice. Not for the first time, she regretted allowing Goth to hire ineffectual thugs to kidnap the nanogens. But she did not want all of the terrible compromises and unthinkable sacrifices to have been for nothing. Modifying human embryos through nanogenetics had to be stopped to preserve natural human evolution. Otherwise, the Order's research might lead to terrible aberrations, or worse, humanity's extinction.

"I would never presume to advise the future World Emissary," the domus master demurred, humbly inclining his head toward Joli.

"With the destruction of the evidence, the tribunal would have to be cancelled?" the Councilwoman asked, phrasing her statement as a question, probing for a response that would help her to understand what Sachio was after.

"The Imagofas named Sashimu healed my daughter of a life-threatening wound." Master Sachio gestured to Lila who smiled and inclined her head. "Her return to Mars would be appreciated."

"You don't seriously expect her to go free?" Joli sputtered.

"In the eyes of Earth and its outposts, she is a hero, one of the few survivors of the MIP accident and an accomplished fly gamer. She healed my daughter in front of thousands in Novus Orbis. With a competent public relations campaign, we can change the way people view the Imagofas and nanogenetics."

Joli sighed. "I would have difficulty with that. You've also implied that more than one Imagofas was brought to Earth."

"The Council is not aware that two human nanogens were smuggled to Earth?"

"*I* was unaware," Joli answered bitterly, wondering if it could be true.

"It is unfortunate then, that two Imagofas were brought to Earth. One is in your care. One is with the Magus."

"The Magus!" Joli exclaimed with a gasp.

"The Imagofas, Thesni, is under Magus protection. She has offered to work with us, to better understand her, in exchange for the safe return of Sashimu, who is in your custody. Let me be clear, we will not treat her as a laboratory specimen as we might have before we knew that she was... so human."

"That could happen only if the Council and the Order dropped all interest in the nanogens," Joli responded. The prospect of giving any legitimacy to human nanogenetics made her deeply uneasy. After maintaining the same DNA over the millennia, in a few centuries humans might morph themselves into something entirely new without ever really understanding what they were doing. "My influence on the Order is limited."

"The Order has assured us that if the tribunal is cancelled, and if the Council no longer pursues legal action or publicity, one Imagofas might stay here to facilitate such commercial developments."

"You have strong ties within the Order?" Joli wanted to know whom he had gotten to agree to these terms. She wagered they were Order Elders.

The domus master gave away nothing. "Our influence is everywhere, but only because we are sensitive to the needs of everyone."

His proposal appalled her. Her entire strategy to bring the Order under the wing of the Council would be destroyed. A nanogen would exist on Earth for the first time, under her leadership as World Emissary. It was unthinkable.

"The tribunal may be unnecessary," Joli said, cautiously. "The nanogen in our custody might be allowed to return to Mars. However, to have a nanogen on Earth could help legitimize human nanogenetics, and that is impossible."

"We hope you will reconsider this opportunity. Assurances would be made so that she would come into minimal contact with the public and could harm no one," the domus master added. "This opportunity could prove highly beneficial to everyone."

"I will consider the necessity of the tribunal and allowing the nanogen to return to Mars." She desperately wanted to confer privately with Tebgallis.

"You far exceed my expectations and will indeed make an excellent World Emissary. Tebgallis, as always, you have chosen well." The Master smiled, but a coldness in his eyes sent shivers up Joli's spine.

Tebgallis politely inclined his head.

"Thank you. I am honored by your support and your good council." Joli deferentially inclined her head.

As Tebgallis and she stood to take their leave, Master Sachio, Lila and Isaac all bowed and Joli bowed gracefully in return.

Once Tebgallis and Joli were in their heliocar, with security in position around them, they headed for the Council headquarters. It had been a long day, and it was going to be a longer night. Tebgallis seemed agitated.

"Joli, you know I adore you," Tebgallis said.

She waited for what would come next.

"Your vigilance to get a nanogen as evidence against the Order has impressed me. You followed my orders without question. For this, I am grateful. Unfortunately, Project Inventio has been conducted for over two decades.

Did it occur to you that it was strange that the Council did not go after the Order sooner for their misdeeds?"

Joli spoke carefully. "I knew the Council turned a blind eye, until we learned of the secretly proposed Olympus Mons outpost. Once the extension of the project was proposed, the Council had to get involved to stop it. Another generation of these aberrations will lead us further from our own humanity."

Tebgallis made a noncommittal gesture. "Your ardor is commendable. I see you feel even more strongly than I do on this subject. However, the truth is much grayer. I wanted you to collect a nanogen as evidence against the Order to curtail the Order's unchecked power. It's time you learned that the Council secretly approved funds for the development of the human nanogen two decades ago. It may do so again, as long as the funding can never be linked to the Council."

"What!" Joli sat immobile, unable to express her outrage. The Council was as corrupt as the Order. The thought made her ill. She had far more work ahead of her than she had imagined. She needed to surround herself with honest people of high ethics, people who were loyal. If Creid were around, he would reassure her that she was not like Tebgallis or the domus masters. After what she had done to bring the nanogens to Earth, she had begun to doubt even herself.

Turning to Tebgallis, Joli stated vehemently, "I will never let a nanogen stay on Earth. Do you understand?"

"I do, Joli. I understand all too well," Tebgallis confirmed sadly. "If you only knew how much I've always admired you."

Tebgallis' kind words, following on his terrible admission of guilt, rattled her. She glared furiously at him as he continued.

"Unfortunately, Joli, you would have been a lot better off if you could have changed your mind on this issue," he sighed, entirely nonplussed by her show of anger. "I see we have arrived at Council headquarters. I must leave you, as I have much work to do. The driver will take you home."

Joli curtly nodded towards him as he exited the heliocar, biting her lip to remain silent.

Through the heliocar's window, Joli gazed at the city below. She recognized the green belts of parkland near her home and wished she were walking among the trees with Creid. However, their time for strolling in the park together was long past, since Creid had been declared dead and was in hiding, never to be seen again.

Joli's private search for him had been fruitless. She could only surmise that he had been safely sequestered by the Sanctuary. She wondered whether he would still be proud of her if he knew the sacrifices she had made to become World Emissary.

No sooner than the heliocar had landed, and the driver had stepped out to open her door, Joli heard a faint *click, clickety-click, click* sound emanate from beneath her seat. From her former Order training, she instinctively feared the worst - the beginning of a detonation cycle.

Ice Clouds

The driver dove through the open door and landed on top of the councilwoman, pulling her down to the vehicle's floor.

Just as she thought, *that's not going to help*, the heliocar's floor opened and they fell through into a second surprise: the heliocar was parked over a shaft that led down into the Underground. They fell a long way, second upon second, and then a deafening explosion erupted above their heads.

They landed on a spongy surface that was hard enough to jolt the air out of Joli's lungs, and yet, absorbed the impact of their fall so that they were unhurt. She rolled over and discovered that she was on a bed in an open-topped car of a URT train. Something landed beside her and she saw a jagged piece of smoking metal had buried itself deep into the bed's cushioned top. She looked up and saw the shattered remains of the destroyed heliocar toppling down the shaft toward her.

Then, the bed lurched beneath her and the train moved forward. She looked back through the car's rear window to see a mass of twisted metal and fractured glass smash down onto the tunnel floor.

"What's going on?" she cried. Her own voice sounded strange to her ears, still ringing from the explosion. The train had moved into complete darkness. She could see nothing, but felt the spongy stuff beneath her and the gathering momentum of the train as they sped forward, deeper into the Underground.

When she repeated her question to the heliocar driver who lay nearby, she received only a grunt in reply. The delayed shock of what had happened settled upon her, and she sat in silence on the bed. Time passed, and she could not have said whether it was minutes or hours. The train car lurched to a sudden stop, throwing her facedown onto the spongy surface, so that for a moment she could not breathe.

When she sat up she saw that they had stopped at an empty, dimly lit URT platform. The place had the abandoned look of a stop on a discontinued line. Joli clearly saw the driver; he had stripped off his Council uniform while they had been in motion and was now donning a chameleon-cloak that completely hid his face. Without a glance in her direction, the man exited the train. He spoke to someone Joli could not see, hidden in the shadows beyond the lighted edge of the platform.

"I've got to hurry to the Sanctuary and pick up the others if we're going to make our shuttle liftoff," the man was saying. He moved quickly away and was lost to her sight in the darkness.

Two strangers walked out from the shadows — a towering, muscular man and a smaller fellow who moved with the lithe sureness of a cat.

"Councilwoman Xerkler," the smaller man said, following a graceful bow. "We've never met, although I have had the pleasure of serving you through intermediaries. I am Angel of Domus Phrack, at your service."

The man's show of deference helped Joli recover some of her self-possession. She squared her shoulders, stepped out of the car and demanded, "What is the meaning of this?"

Despite her show of bravado, she was terrified at being left alone with these Underground thugs. She saw knives, a smartgun and a Biosecur baton slung from each man's belt. At one time, in her early days with the Order, she would never have encountered such men without a weapon close at hand. Now she had nothing to help her but her wits.

The one called Angel gave her a grin that mingled amusement with cruelty. "The meaning of this is that you're dead, Councilwoman. Or at least that's what you have just officially been declared."

Joli gauged the distance between her and the exit. She might just be fast enough to make it. "The Council will be ruthless with you if anything happens to me," she warned.

"My dear Councilwoman, it was the Council that hired me, though they're only one of my clients. I really love getting paid twice for the same job. You see, the Council wanted you officially dead, which you are. However, your husband wanted you alive, which is how I intend to deliver you to him. In fact, he wants you to be spirited offworld. We're about to do that, so I will have made everyone happy, most especially me. If you'll just come with us..."

Joli had only half-listened, as she looked around hoping to escape. "I don't know what you're talking about," she remarked. "My husband is dead."

"No, he's alive, luckily for you," said Angel. He nodded to the big man.

As he had been speaking, Joli had been edging away from them, ready to make a break for the nearest exit. She turned to run, but the big thug had anticipated her. His Biosecur baton was in his hands and he sprayed her with the constricting film. Even as she ran, it spread rapidly over her, binding her limbs so that she tumbled to the platform and rolled painfully across its trash-strewn surface. Behind her she heard the two men's unhurried footsteps coming toward her. Angel was chuckling.

|.||..||||..|.|..|

Over the past seventy-two hours, Sashimu had dozed fitfully or paced the confines of her holding cell. She had waited in anxious isolation and silence broken only by the vacuum-thump of meals being delivered automatically into the cell dispenser.

By the time a hulking Council guard opened the cell door and gestured for her to follow, Sashimu was composed. In her mind, she had prepared her account of what had happened, in case she might be treated as more than "just evidence for display" and actually be allowed to speak before the Tribunal's Interplanetary Judges.

She followed the guard into an elevator, down many hallways and through security doors, across a vast complex of concrete and steel. They finally stopped before a windowed room with a sign that read "Visitors." She immediately felt the pull of a MAM optimization area. The guard gestured for her to enter and join a gaunt, middle-aged man who wore disheveled Council robes and had a distinct nervous twitch. He stood behind one of the metal tables with chairs in the center of the room.

The man looked Sashimu up and down with calculating, beady eyes and said, "My name is Goth. I am the newly appointed assistant to World Emissary Tebgallis. Please sit."

Sashimu took a seat across from him, wondering how long she had until he took her before the tribunal.

"Recent events have brought to light that you were kidnapped from Mars and held here illegally against your will. Therefore, we can no longer detain you," Goth said, pausing to raise an eyebrow when she gasped in surprise.

"Through your successful fly gaming, during which you saved the life of the very popular gamer, Lila of Domus Aqua, you have become a celebrity. Indeed you are generally considered a hero," the man continued. "Even so, Earth is not quite ready to openly embrace an Imagofas, so the Council has mandated that you immediately leave the planet. Therefore, on behalf of the World Emissary, I have come in person to deliver his deepest apologies for your detainment."

"Does this mean that I'm free to go?" Sashimu asked. It sounded too good to be true.

"Not exactly. Since you are not a citizen here, you will be sent back to Mars. From there, Zazen will take you into Order custody to continue your life in the new Olympus Mons colony. I trust this is a satisfactory resolution for you."

"Yes, I want to go home!" Sashimu said. Her heart began racing so fast she held her hand to her chest.

"Today, a Council representative will escort you to the *Aleph*, a commercial ship provided by Angel of Domus Phrack. It is a gesture on his part to thank you for winning the Aqua-Phrack match and to acknowledge your new found popularity," Goth replied. She saw that he was still

studying her as if she were some exotic scientific specimen. "Once you leave Earth, you will not be allowed to
return. However, the political winds are changing. One day,
perhaps, you may be welcomed back."

Sashimu was dazed by the sudden prospect of freedom.
She sat immobile as successive waves of emotion swept
through her — first an immense sense of relief, guilt and
then, worry. Her mind filled with terrible questions, which
made her eyes brim with tears.

"What about Thesni?" she asked, and had to clear her
throat several times before she could continue. "Does she
get to go home, too?"

"Ah, your Imagofas sister." She saw pity in the look he
gave her. "I have only recently learned of her situation.
Thesni has requested to remain under our protection and
to be given a new identity. As sanctioned by both the Council and the Order, she will remain on Earth under the auspices of Domus Aqua, living within the confines of the
Sanctuary."

Goth might just as well have slugged her. Overwhelmed
by the implications of his words, Sashimu tried desperately to understand the situation. It was impossible for
Thesni to stay behind and that they would be kept apart
forever. "Can I at least visit her at the Sanctuary before I
leave?" she asked anxiously, tears pouring down her
cheeks. She was desperate to discover why Thesni had to
stay while they let her return home.

"Unfortunately, allowing you to enter the city is not an
option right now, given the political tension in the streets,"
Goth said in a patronizing tone. "Councilwoman Xerkler
was assassinated last night. In response, there have been
spontaneous demonstrations honoring her — as well as
several riots. She was highly popular," he added, almost
as an afterthought.

Hands clenching the arms of her chair, Sashimu sat in
stunned silence for a long moment thinking of Creid and
the Cadet, and how terrible this must be for them. And then,
she inquired timidly, "This is horrible! How did it happen?"

"If you must know, a Council driver — who also turned
out to be a Magus cult member — strapped on a bomb

beneath his clothes and detonated it as soon as he had Councilwoman Xerkler alone in the heliocar. It's a terrible tragedy. Everyone mourns her death."

"Do they know why he did it?" Sashimu asked softly.

"We'll never know exactly why, but the Order found journal entries that the suicide bomber made in Novus Orbis. He complained in his journal that Councilwoman Xerkler stood in the way of the Magus prophecy."

"That's awful," Sashimu murmured, feeling her breath come raggedly.

Standing to leave, Goth peered down his nose at her and smiled slyly. "Although you don't have time to go anywhere, I have arranged for you to see one last visitor before you leave. Perhaps one day we will meet again under more favorable circumstances." He bowed.

Abruptly pushing back her chair, Sashimu stood and returned the gesture.

At the moment Goth left, Thesni walked through the visitors' entrance. She was radiant in chameleon-robes, her hood thrown back and her blonde hair a shimmering mantle over her shoulders.

"Thesni!" Sashimu ran to her. "I'm not leaving without you."

After hugging her, Thesni caught hold of her arm and led her to the table furthest from the entrance and the guard.

"Sashimu, I've decided to stay for the time being." Her voice was sad but there was no mistaking her complete determination.

"I won't let them force you to stay!"

"I'm not being forced. This is my choice."

"That can't be," Sashimu said, a sob rising painfully in her throat. "Come back to Mars with me. We're sisters. We are the Imagofas. How could you stay here after all we've been through?"

"Can't you see why I am staying?"

Sashimu thought her friend looked as stricken as she herself felt. "No! Why?" she asked.

Tears filled Thesni's eyes. "At first it was for you," she replied. "I realized that Domus Aqua's tremendous political influence could save both of us, but the domus wanted one of us. I know you have always been destined to lead the Imagofas on Mars, so I offered to stay behind in exchange for your freedom."

"They'll turn you into a lab rat!"

"No, they will never be allowed to do that!" Thesni exclaimed with such conviction that Sashimu waited to hear her out. "Lila is indebted to you for her life, and since I am your Imagofas sister, she also feels indebted to me. Master Sachio may be more calculating than his daughter, but he listens to her and has already agreed to let me override his nanogenetic research team if I so choose."

"I see." Thesni seemed genuinely convinced that she would not be mistreated, but there was a tragic undertone in her voice that belied the surface confidence. Sashimu's friend was making a terrible sacrifice on her behalf, and it simply felt wrong to let her do it.

"You deserve the chance to go home," Sashimu insisted firmly. "I'm the one who got you into this mess! Domus Aqua must take me instead."

"I don't care about *that*," Thesni reassured her. "Ochbo is here, and we're becoming very close. When I deal with Domus Aqua, Ochbo is always at my side. Even more importantly, the Magus has put me under their protection."

"Why? What do they want from you?" Sashimu asked, alarmed.

"They think I will lead humankind to its greater destiny," Thesni answered with a small smile. "And to tell you the truth, it's overwhelming and silly at times, but I'm not afraid of them. Everything I say is noted as though I'm very wise."

"So you want to stay here?" Sashimu asked. Her heart was breaking, and she was trying her best not to let it show.

"Just until the domus has learned something they can turn around and use for profit. They've promised to let me come home after that." She gripped Sashimu's hands tightly. "You know, once people are no longer afraid of us, the laws may change." She paused. "I'll bring Ochbo with me!"

"Are you certain about this?" Sashimu asked, searching Thesni's face for any hint of doubt. Thesni nodded and fiercely hugged her.

"I'm going to miss you," Sashimu cried, letting the tears flow freely.

"I miss you so much already that I can hardly stand it," Thesni began, but now the guard approached them.

"We need to proceed to the shuttle," he ordered gruffly.

Thesni threw her arms around Sashimu, and they hugged until the guard coughed loudly to remind them he was there. And then, Thesni followed the guard and Sashimu out to the heliovan where the Imagofas sisters shared a final embrace.

"I'll be thinking of you," Thesni cried gently, tears spilling down her cheeks.

"I'll contact you as soon as I can," Sashimu said, determined to be strong for Thesni, then quickly turned and entered the heliovan. As the vehicle took flight she waved goodbye until she could no longer see Thesni.

During the heliovan ride, under the watchful eye of the guard, Sashimu remained stoic. Once she was aboard the shuttle to MIP, alone amid strangers, she wept without restraint. She cried for the Cadet, whom she hoped was still alive, for Thesni whom she had left to such a miserable destiny and for her own guilt in not stepping in to take Thesni's place. Finally, she cried for all that had happened since that sunset on the Hale Observatory roof and for all that might happen in a future that was unknowable and cruel.

|ₒ|ₒ|ₒₒ|||ₒₒ|ₒ|ₒ|

Upon arriving at MIP, Sashimu was escorted to the gate where the space vessel *Aleph* waited to begin its journey to Mars. The guard left her to board by herself.

Ascending through the *Aleph's* passageways, she noticed a woman, obviously the ship's captain, talking with a handful of people. One of them, a young man, stood in profile to her, his face badly bruised and swollen. He was favoring one leg, encased in a walking-brace, and clutching a small package under his arm.

Sashimu blinked. "Cadet!"

He turned his battered face toward her — his split and swollen lips managing to half smile, as he painfully limped across the distance that separated them. She threw her arms around him.

Holding him tight, she would not let go until he gently pushed her back so he could look at her. It was only then that she noticed the other familiar faces: Creid, free of the cocoon that had tormented him in Novus Orbis; UL, with his traveling maskset; and, incredibly, Joli looking unharmed and very much alive.

Everyone surrounded her and began talking at once, so that it took a while for Sashimu to understand how they had all come to be together on a ship bound for Mars. With the Cadet's arm around her shoulder as he limped beside her, they sought privacy in a cabin that had been reserved for her. Inside, with the door closed, they held each other close.

"I thought I'd never see you again," she whispered. "I thought they'd killed you." She touched her fingertips to the lacerations that disfigured his face, seeing in her mind's eye the terrible things that had been done to him, the things he had endured for her sake. She let her power flow and saw his wounds begin to heal, his purple and yellow contusions replaced by unmarked skin.

"Sashimu," he said, taking her hand from his face and holding it tenderly, "I'm fine."

"What did they do to you?" she asked, sensing deep sadness and pain in him.

"We'll get to all that. First, I have a gift for you." His still injured lips were barely able to smile as he handed her the package that had been kept safely tucked under his arm. She picked it up. It was very light. She carefully unwrapped it.

"It's lovely!" she exclaimed as she held the beautiful miniature Go game in the palm of her hand, the gentle pull of its closed-circuit MAM tugged at her senses. "What about the pieces?"

"They should be there," the Cadet answered, reaching into the wrapping and withdrawing a tiny string of black and white pearls. "Creid and UL designed them for you to wear as a necklace. The board can be kept in your pocket."

"It's wonderful."

"It's also very valuable," the Cadet added. "It's not just a closed-circuit MAM. It's Prometheus. Creid downloaded him into it.

"Incredible!"

"The Order would have eventually destroyed all of his processes. When we left, they were installing MAM upgrades and systematically eliminating Creid's backdoors. When we informed him what had to be done, Prometheus insisted that you were to be his guardian."

"Prometheus," Sashimu said, pressing the Go board to her chest. "That's so incredible! We will find a place for him in our Novus Orbis at Olympus Mons. Until then, I'll keep him safe."

ılılıılllıılılıl

Inside their cabin, Joli angrily paced the length of the room. She had just finished one tirade and it looked as if she was about to launch into another. Creid's attempts to calm her were proving unsuccessful

"You don't have to explain why you paid off Angel. I understand that someone on the Council wanted me dead, paid Angel for his 'services', and that you intervened to keep me alive. But now, everything is ruined!"

"How is everything ruined?" he asked, gently. "We are here now and soon we will be able to start a new life together on Mars."

"I want to be on Earth," Joli said indignantly. "I dedicated my life to becoming the next World Emissary, and now all that work, over all those years, has been destroyed! You don't even want me to contact anyone on Earth to investigate this mess."

"I just want you to be cautious and lie low on Mars for a while. Who knows? You may love it there. You always make the best of any situation." Closing the distance between them, he put his arms around her shoulders. "That's what I love about you."

"Okay, I'll go to Mars and lie low. But only to find out who's behind all of this and to figure out what to do about it. I don't think there's any chance in hell that I'll like it there."

"Good," he sighed, gently pressing her head to his chest.

She was far from placated, but she leaned against him and said, "I guess I can't blame you for all of this. I'm just so frustrated."

"And I'm just happy that we can be together."

"Oh, Creid," she said, looking up at him. "I want us to be together, too, and I didn't realize how much until I thought I'd lost you."

Bending his head to hers, he tenderly kissed her forehead, then passionately kissed her on the lips. She returned his kiss with an intensity that surprised him and he suddenly knew that, as much as he had longed for her company, her voice and her touch, she had also longed for his. Now more than ever, he was determined that they would start anew on Mars, leaving behind forever the poisonous intrigues on Earth.

I.I.I...IIII...I.I.I

Later, after lift-off, the Cadet and Sashimu sat with Creid and UL on the observation deck. Joli had not joined them, and Sashimu wondered if she was still in shock — the woman had, after all, been almost blown up, then kidnapped by a crime boss and declared dead — or if she was just unhappy that she would not be the next World Emissary.

"How is your wife doing?" Sashimu asked.

"She said she would join us here for a last view of Earth, but she's finding it hard to accept so many changes in her life at one time. Still, we had a long talk, and we agreed that it made sense for her to come to Mars, at least temporarily."

"You mean she might return to Earth someday?"

"Perhaps," Creid answered, nervously running his hand through his hair, "But I hope we can get used to living on Mars."

Staring out the observation port, Sashimu marveled at the brilliant blue, green and white swirling surface of Earth. It had been quite an adventure, and her deepest regret was leaving Thesni behind.

UL leaned over to her and whispered, "I'll bet Mars is even more stunning."

"It is to me," she answered truthfully. Then, looking at both UL and Creid, she touched the white and black necklace with her fingertips and said, "Thank you both for this."

"You're very welcome," replied Creid, his smile widening as Joli came onto the observation deck and sat down beside them, her face composed.

They all respectfully inclined their heads to the councilwoman. Sashimu noticed that Joli had slipped her hand into Creid's. She grinned at the Cadet and he reached to take her hand.

"It's breathtaking!" Joli commented, looking out at the great globe that filled the observation port. The others all murmured their agreement.

"I'm just curious, as first-timers," UL said to Sashimu. "What can we expect on Mars?"

Sashimu sat silent for a moment, as memories of Mars flooded her mind: the unrelenting, raging storms, the tight intimacy of a well-tuned biosphere, the brutal hot-to-cold extremes, the ever-present salmon-colored dust, and the parched, aching smell of the soil, which desperately needed terraforming.

And then, she answered, wistfully, "Orange dust storms and ice clouds."

Rebecca K. Rowe

Acknowledgments

With deep admiration and thanks to my mother Mary Jane Rowe and my sister Jennifer Rowe for all their love and encouragement. Many thanks to everyone who believed in me and offered their support especially the Willis family, Bert Lewis, Emita Samuels, Benny Samuels, the Rowes, the Grouts, David & Tory, Karen Maslowski, Michael Bauer, Alan Moorer, Carol Taylor, Alfredo Garcia-Lucio and Chi Yang.

My heartfelt gratitude to Jim McKeever for his valuable advice and feedback.

Many thanks to everyone at EDGE Science Fiction and Fantasy most especially my editor Adam Volk for his consistent good humor and supportiveness under deadline as well as Brian Hades who guided me through the entire book process and ensured it was a pleasurable experience.

Most of all, I thank Dad and Craig for always being there and making our universe the most wonderful place to explore!

Our titles are available at major book stores and local independent resellers who support Science Fiction and Fantasy readers like you.

Alphanauts by J. Brian Clarke - (tp) - ISBN: 978-1-894063-14-2
Apparition Trail, The by Lisa Smedman - (tp) - ISBN: 1-894063-22-8
Black Chalice by Marie Jakober - (hb) - ISBN:1-894063-00-7
Blue Apes by Phyllis Gotlieb (pb) - ISBN:1-895836-13-1
Blue Apes by Phyllis Gotlieb (hb) - ISBN:1-895836-14-X
Children of Atwar, The by Heather Spears (pb) - ISBN:0-888783-35-3
Claus Effect by David Nickle & Karl Schroeder, The (pb) - ISBN:1-895836-34-4
Claus Effect by David Nickle & Karl Schroeder, The (hb) - ISBN:1-895836-35-2
Courtesan Prince, The by Lynda Williams (tp) - 1-894063-28-7
Dark Earth Dreams by Candas Dorsey & Roger Deegan (comes with a CD)
    - ISBN:1-895836-05-0
Distant Signals by Andrew Weiner (tp) - ISBN:0-888782-84-5
Dreams of an Unseen Planet by Teresa Plowright (tp) - ISBN:0-888782-82-9
Dreams of the Sea by Élisabeth Vonarburg (tp) - ISBN:1-895836-96-4
Dreams of the Sea by Élisabeth Vonarburg (hb) - ISBN:1-895836-98-0
Eclipse by K. A. Bedford - (tp) - ISBN:978-1-894063-30-2
Even The Stones by Marie Jakober - (tp) - ISBN:1-894063-18-X
Fires of the Kindred by Robin Skelton (tp) - ISBN:0-888782-71-3
Forbidden Cargo by Rebecca Rowe - (tp) - ISBN: 978-1-894063-16-6
Game of Perfection, A by Élisabeth Vonarburg (tp) - ISBN:978-1-894063-32-6
Green Music by Ursula Pflug (tp) - ISBN:1-895836-75-1
Green Music by Ursula Pflug (hb) - ISBN:1895836-77-8
Healer, The by Amber Hayward (tp) - ISBN:1-895836-89-1
Healer, The by Amber Hayward (hb) - ISBN:1-895836-91-3
Jackal Bird by Michael Barley (pb) - ISBN:1-895836-07-7
Jackal Bird by Michael Barley (hb) - ISBN:1-895836-11-5
Keaen by Till Noever - (tp) - ISBN:1-894063-08-2
Land/Space edited by Candas Jane Dorsey and Judy McCrosky (tp)
    - ISBN:1-895836-90-5
Land/Space edited by Candas Jane Dorsey and Judy McCrosky (hb)
    - ISBN:1-895836-92-1
Lyskarion: The Song of the Wind by J. A. Cullum - (tp) - ISBN:1-894063-02-3
Machine Sex and other stories by Candas Jane Dorsey (tp) - ISBN:0-888782-78-0
Maërlande Chronicles, The by Élisabeth Vonarburg (pb) - ISBN:0-888782-94-2
Moonfall by Heather Spears (pb) - ISBN:0-888783-06-X
On Spec: The First Five Years edited by On Spec (pb) - ISBN:1-895836-08-5
On Spec: The First Five Years edited by On Spec (hb) - ISBN:1-895836-12-3
Orbital Burn by K. A. Bedford - (tp) - ISBN:1-894063-10-4
Orbital Burn by K. A. Bedford - (hb) - ISBN:1-894063-12-0
Pallahaxi Tide by Michael Coney (pb) - ISBN:0-888782-93-4
Passion Play by Sean Stewart (pb) - ISBN:0-888783-14-0
Plague Saint by Rita Donovan, The - (tp) - ISBN:1-895836-28-X
Plague Saint by Rita Donovan, The - (hb) - ISBN:1-895836-29-8
Reluctant Voyagers by Élisabeth Vonarburg (pb) - ISBN:1-895836-09-3
Reluctant Voyagers by Élisabeth Vonarburg (hb) - ISBN:1-895836-15-8
Resisting Adonis by Timothy J. Anderson (tp) - ISBN:1-895836-84-0
Resisting Adonis by Timothy J. Anderson (hb) - ISBN:1-895836-83-2

Silent City, The by Élisabeth Vonarburg (tp) - ISBN:0-888782-77-2
Slow Engines of Time, The by Élisabeth Vonarburg (tp) - ISBN:1-895836-30-1
Slow Engines of Time, The by Élisabeth Vonarburg (hb) - ISBN:1-895836-31-X
Stealing Magic (expanded edition) by Tanya Huff (tp) - ISBN:978-1-894063-34-0
Stealing Magic by Tanya Huff (hb) - ISBN:1-895836-64-6
Strange Attractors by Tom Henighan (pb) - ISBN:0-888783-12-4
Taming, The by Heather Spears (pb) - ISBN:1-895836-23-9
Taming, The by Heather Spears (hb) - ISBN:1-895836-24-7
Ten Monkeys, Ten Minutes by Peter Watts (tp) - ISBN:1-895836-74-3
Ten Monkeys, Ten Minutes by Peter Watts (hb) - ISBN:1-895836-76-X
Tesseracts 1 edited by Judith Merril (pb) - ISBN:0-888782-79-9
Tesseracts 2 edited by Phyllis Gotlieb & Douglas Barbour (pb) - ISBN:0-888782-70-5
Tesseracts 3 edited by Candas Jane Dorsey & Gerry Truscott (pb) - ISBN:0-888782-90-X
Tesseracts 4 edited by Lorna Toolis & Michael Skeet (pb) - ISBN:0-888783-22-1
Tesseracts 5 edited by Robert Runté & Yves Maynard (pb) - ISBN:1-895836-25-5
Tesseracts 5 edited by Robert Runté & Yves Maynard (hb) - ISBN:1-895836-26-3
Tesseracts 6 edited by Robert J. Sawyer & Carolyn Clink (pb) - ISBN:1-895836-32-8
Tesseracts 6 edited by Robert J. Sawyer & Carolyn Clink (hb) - ISBN:1-895836-33-6
Tesseracts 7 edited by Paula Johanson & Jean-Louis Trudel (tp) - ISBN:1-895836-58-1
Tesseracts 7 edited by Paula Johanson & Jean-Louis Trudel (hb) - ISBN:1-895836-59-X
Tesseracts 8 edited by John Clute & Candas Jane Dorsey (tp) - ISBN:1-895836-61-1
Tesseracts 8 edited by John Clute & Candas Jane Dorsey (hb) - ISBN:1-895836-62-X
Tesseracts 9 edited by Nalo Hopkinson and Geoff Ryman (tp) - ISBN:1-894063-26-0
TesseractsQ edited by Élisabeth Vonarburg & Jane Brierley (pb) - ISBN:1-895836-21-2
TesseractsQ edited by Élisabeth Vonarburg & Jane Brierley (hb) - ISBN:1-895836-22-0
Throne Price by Lynda Williams and Alison Sinclair - (tp) - ISBN:1-894063-06-6

EDGE

EDGE Science Fiction and Fantasy Publishing
P. O. Box 1714, Calgary, AB, Canada, T2P 2L7
www.edgewebsite.com
403-254-0160 (voice)
403-254-0456 (fax)

WHAT SHOULD I READ NEXT?
Selected books published by EDGE . . .

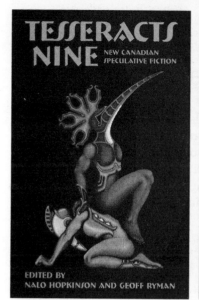

Speculative Fiction Short Stories

Science Fiction Saga

Science Fiction Psychological Thriller

Fantasy Short Story Collection

About the author

Rebecca K. Rowe is a freelance writer and published author with M.A.'s in Journalism and International Relations. Her short work/poetry have been published in *Polyphony, Ascent Magazine,* and *Sol Magazine.* Rebecca is a graduate of the Clarion Science Fiction & Fantasy Writers' Workshop. *Forbidden Cargo* is her first novel.